PENGUIN BOOKS

ME BEFORE YOU

Jojo Moyes is the #1 *New York Times* bestselling author of *After You*, *One Plus One*, *The Girl You Left Behind*, *Me Before You*, *The Last Letter from Your Lover*, *Silver Bay*, and *The Ship of Brides*. She lives with her husband and three children in Essex, England.

Me Before You

Jojo Moyes

PENGUIN BOOKS

PENGUIN BOOKS

An imprint of Penguin Random House LLC

375 Hudson Street

New York, New York 10014

First published in Great Britain by Michael Joseph,
an imprint of Penguin Books Ltd, 2012
First published in the United States of America by Viking Penguin,
a member of Penguin Group (USA) Inc., 2012
Published in Penguin Books 2013
This edition published 2016

A Pamela Dorman / Penguin Book

THE LIBRARY OF CONGRESS HAS CATALOGED THE HARDCOVER
EDITION AS FOLLOWS:

Moyes, Jojo, date.

Me before you : a novel / Jojo Moyes
p.   cm.

ISBN 978-0-670-02660-9 (hc.)

ISBN 978-0-14-310946-4 (pbk. movie tie-in)

ISBN 978-0-14-313015-4 (premium mass market movie tie-in)

1. Young women—Fiction.   1. Title.

PR6113.094M4 2012

823'.92—dc23   2012029301

Printed in the United States of America

3   5   7   9   10   8   6   4   2

TO CHARLES, WITH LOVE

ACKNOWLEDGMENTS

Thank you to my agent, Sheila Crowley at Curtis Brown, and to my editor at Penguin UK, Mari Evans, both of whom immediately saw this book for what it was—a love story.

Special thanks to Maddy Wickham, who encouraged me at a point when I was not sure whether I could, or should, actually write it.

At Penguin USA, I would like to thank my fantastic editors Pamela Dorman and Julie Miesionczek, as well as Clare Ferraro, president of Viking, who has been such a strong supporter of this book. At Penguin UK, I would also particularly like to thank Louise Moore, Clare Ledingham, and Shân Morley Jones.

Thanks to the wonderful team at Curtis Brown, especially Jonny Geller, Tally Garner, Katie McGowan, Alice Lutyens, and Sarah Lewis, for enthusiasm and fine agenting.

Huge gratitude to all on the Writersblock board—my own private Fight Club. Minus the Fighty bit.

Similarly to India Knight, Sam Baker, Emma Beddington, Trish Deseine, Alex Heminsley, Jess Ruston, Sali Hughes, Tara Manning, and Fanny Blake.

Thanks to Lizzie and Brian Sanders, and to Jim, Bea, and Clemmie Moyes. But most of all, as ever, to Charles, Saskia, Harry, and Lockie.

Me Before You

Prologue

2007

When he emerges from the bathroom she is awake, propped up against the pillows and flicking through the travel brochures that were beside his bed. She is wearing one of his T-shirts, and her long hair is tousled in a way that prompts reflexive thoughts of the previous night. He stands there, enjoying the brief flashback, rubbing the water from his hair with a towel.

She looks up from a brochure and pouts. She is probably slightly too old to pout, but they've been going out a short enough time for it still to be cute.

"Do we really *have* to do something that involves trekking up mountains, or hanging over ravines? It's our first proper holiday together, and there is literally not one single trip in these that doesn't involve either throwing yourself off something or"—she pretends to shudder—"wearing *fleece*."

She throws the brochures down on the bed, stretches her caramel-colored arms above her head. Her voice is husky, testament to their missed hours of sleep. "How about a luxury spa in Bali? We could lie around on the sand . . . spend hours being pampered . . . long, relaxing nights . . ."

"I can't do those sorts of holidays. I need to be doing something."

"Like throwing yourself out of airplanes."

"Don't knock it till you've tried it."

She pulls a face. "If it's all the same to you, I think I'll stick with knocking it."

His shirt is faintly damp against his skin. He runs a comb through his hair and switches on his mobile phone, wincing at the list of messages that immediately pushes its way through onto the little screen.

"Right," he says. "Got to go. Help yourself to breakfast." He leans over the bed to kiss her. She smells warm and perfumed and deeply sexy. He inhales the scent from the back of her hair, and briefly loses his train of thought as she wraps her arms around his neck, pulling him down toward the bed.

"Are we still going away this weekend?"

He extricates himself reluctantly. "Depends what happens on this deal. It's all a bit up in the air at the moment. There's still a possibility I might have to be in New York. Nice dinner somewhere Thursday, either way? Your choice of restaurant." His motorbike leathers are on the back of the door, and he reaches for them.

She narrows her eyes. "Dinner. With or without Mr. BlackBerry?"

"What?"

"Mr. BlackBerry makes me feel like Miss Gooseberry." The pout again. "I feel like there's always a third person vying for your attention."

"I'll turn it on to silent."

"Will Traynor!" she scolds. "You must have some time when you can switch it off."

"I turned it off last night, didn't I?"

"Only under extreme duress."

He grins. "Is that what we're calling it now?" He pulls on his leathers. And Lissa's hold on his imagination is finally broken. He throws his motorbike jacket over his arm, and blows her a kiss as he leaves.

There are twenty-two messages on his BlackBerry, the first of which came in from New York at 3:42 A.M. Some legal problem. He takes the lift down to the underground car park, trying to update himself with the night's events.

"Morning, Mr. Traynor."

The security guard steps out of his cubicle. It's weather-proof, even though down here there is no weather to be protected from. Will sometimes wonders what he does down here in the small hours, staring at the closed-circuit television and the glossy bumpers of £60,000 cars that never get dirty.

He shoulders his way into his leather jacket. "What's it like out there, Mick?"

"Terrible. Raining cats and dogs."

Will stops. "Really? Not weather for the bike?"

Mick shakes his head. "No, sir. Not unless you've got an inflatable attachment. Or a death wish."

Will stares at his bike, then peels himself out of his leathers. No matter what Lissa thinks, he is not a man who believes in taking unnecessary risks. He unlocks the top box of his bike and places the leathers inside, locking it and throwing the keys at Mick, who catches them neatly with one hand. "Stick those through my door, will you?"

"No problem. You want me to call a taxi for you?"

"No. No point both of us getting wet."

Mick presses the button to open the automatic barrier and Will steps out, lifting a hand in thanks. The early morning is dark and thunderous around him, the Central London traffic already dense and slow despite the fact that it is barely half past seven. He pulls his collar up around his neck and strides down the street toward the junction, from where he is most likely to hail a taxi. The roads are slick with water, the gray light shining on the mirrored pavement.

He curses inwardly as he spies the other suited people standing on the edge of the curb. Since when did the whole of London begin getting up so early? Everyone has had the same idea.

He is wondering where best to position himself when his phone rings. It is Rupert.

"I'm on my way in. Just trying to get a cab." He catches sight of a taxi with an orange light approaching on the other side of the road, and begins to stride toward it, hoping nobody else has seen. A bus roars past, followed by a lorry whose brakes squeal, deafening him to Rupert's words. "Can't hear you, Rupe," he yells against the noise of the traffic. "You'll have to say that again." Briefly marooned on the island, the traffic flowing past him like a current, he can see the orange light glowing, holds up his free hand, hoping that the driver can see him through the heavy rain.

"You need to call Jeff in New York. He's still up, waiting for you. We were trying to get you last night."

"What's the problem?"

"Legal hitch. Two clauses they're stalling on under section . . . signature . . . papers . . ." His voice is drowned out by a passing car, its tires hissing in the wet.

"I didn't catch that."

The taxi has seen him. It is slowing, sending a fine spray of water as it slows on the opposite side of the road. He spies the man farther along whose brief sprint slows in disappointment as he sees Will will get there before him. He feels a sneaking sense of triumph. "Look, get Cally to have the paperwork on my desk," he yells. "I'll be there in ten minutes."

He glances both ways, then ducks his head as he runs the last few steps across the road toward the cab, the word "Blackfriars" already on his lips. The rain is seeping down the gap between his collar and his shirt. He will be soaked by the time he reaches the office, even walking this short distance. He may have to send his secretary out for another shirt.

"And we need to get this due diligence thing worked out before Martin gets in—"

He glances up at the screeching sound, the rude blare of a horn. He sees the side of the glossy black taxi in front of him, the driver already winding down his window, and at the edge of his field of vision something he can't quite make out, something coming toward him at an impossible speed.

He turns toward it, and in that split second he realizes that he is in its path, that there is no way he is going to be able to get out of its way. His hand opens in surprise, letting the BlackBerry fall to the ground. He hears a shout, which may be his own. The last thing he sees is a leather glove, a face under a helmet, the shock in the man's eyes mirroring his own. There is an explosion as everything fragments.

And then there is nothing.

1

2009

There are 158 footsteps between the bus stop and home, but it can stretch to 180 if you aren't in a hurry, like maybe if you're wearing platform shoes. I turned the corner onto our street (68 steps), and could just see the house—a four-bedroom semi in a row of other three- and four-bedroom semis. Dad's car was outside, which meant he had not yet left for work.

Behind me, the sun was setting behind Stortfold Castle, its dark shadow sliding down the hill like melting wax to overtake me. On a different sort of day, I could have told you all the things that had happened to me on this route: where Dad taught me to ride a bike without stabilizers; where Mrs. Doherty with the lopsided wig used to make us Welsh cakes; the hedge where Treena knocked a wasp's nest and we ran screaming all the way back to the castle.

Thomas's tricycle was upturned on the path and, closing the gate behind me, I dragged it under the porch and opened the door. The warmth hit me with the force of an air bag; Mum is a martyr to the cold and keeps the heating on all year round. Dad is always opening windows, complaining that she'd bankrupt the lot of us. He says our heating bills are larger than the GDP of a small African country.

"That you, love?"

"Yup." I hung my jacket on the peg, where it fought for space among the others.

"Which you? Lou? Treena?"

"Lou."

I peered around the living-room door. Dad was face-down on the sofa, his arm thrust deep between the cushions, as if they had swallowed his limb whole. Thomas, my five-year-old nephew, was on his haunches, watching him intently.

"Lego." Dad turned his face toward me, puce from exertion. "Why they have to make the damned pieces so small I don't know."

"Where's Mum?"

"Upstairs. How about that? A two-pound piece!"

I looked up, just able to hear the familiar creak of the ironing board. Josie Clark, my mother, never sat down. It was a point of honor. She had been known to stand on an outside ladder painting the windows, occasionally pausing to wave, while the rest of us ate a roast dinner.

"Will you have a go at finding this bloody arm for me? He's had me looking for half an hour and I've got to get ready for work."

"Are you on nights?"

"Yeah. It's half past five."

I glanced at the clock. "Actually, it's half past four."

He extracted his arm from the cushions and squinted at his watch. "Then what are you doing home so early?"

I shook my head vaguely, as if I might have misunderstood the question, and walked into the kitchen.

Granddad was sitting in his chair by the kitchen window, studying a Sudoku. The health visitor had told us it would be good for his concentration, help his focus after the strokes. I suspected I was the only one to notice he simply filled out all the boxes with whatever number came to mind.

"Hey, Granddad."

He looked up and smiled.

"You want a cup of tea?"

He shook his head, and partially opened his mouth.

"Cold drink?"

He nodded.

I opened the fridge door. "There's no apple juice." Apple juice, I remembered now, was too expensive. "Water?"

He nodded, murmured something that could have been a thank-you as I handed him the glass.

My mother walked into the room, bearing a huge basket of neatly folded laundry. "Are these yours?" She brandished a pair of socks.

"Treena's, I think."

"I thought so. Odd color. I think they must have got in with Daddy's plum pajamas. You're back early. Are you going somewhere?"

"No." I filled a glass with tap water and drank it.

"Is Patrick coming around later? He rang here earlier. Did you have your mobile off?"

"Mm."

"He said he's after booking your holiday. Your father says he saw something on the television about it. Where is it you liked? Ipsos? Kalypsos?"

"Skiathos."

"That's the one. You want to check your hotel very carefully. Do it on the Internet. He and Daddy watched something on the news at lunchtime. Apparently they're building sites, half of those budget deals, and you wouldn't know until you got there. Daddy, would you like a cup of tea? Did Lou not offer you one?" She put the kettle on, then glanced up at me. It's possible she had finally noticed I wasn't saying anything. "Are you all right, love? You look awfully pale."

She reached out a hand and felt my forehead, as if I were much younger than twenty-six.

"I don't think we're going on holiday."

My mother's hand stilled. Her gaze had that X-ray thing that it had held since I was a kid. "Are you and Pat having some problems?"

"Mum, I—"

"I'm not trying to interfere. It's just, you've been

together an awful long time. It's only natural if things get a bit sticky every now and then. I mean, me and your father, we—"

"I lost my job."

My voice cut into the silence. The words hung there, searing themselves on the little room long after the sound had died away.

"You what?"

"Frank's shutting down the café. From tomorrow." I held out a hand with the slightly damp envelope I had gripped in shock the entire journey home. All 180 steps from the bus stop. "He's given me my three months' money."

———

The day had started like any other day. Everyone I knew hated Monday mornings, but I never minded them. I liked arriving early at the Buttered Bun, firing up the huge tea urn in the corner, bringing in the crates of milk and bread from the backyard, and chatting to Frank as we prepared to open.

I liked the fuggy bacon-scented warmth of the café, the little bursts of cool air as the door opened and closed, the low murmur of conversation, and, when quiet, Frank's radio singing tinnily to itself in the corner. It wasn't a fashionable place—its walls were covered in scenes from the castle up on the hill, the tables still sported Formica tops, and the menu hadn't altered since I started, apart from the addition of chocolate brownies to the iced-bun tray.

But most of all I liked the customers. I liked Kev and Angelo, the plumbers, who came in most mornings and teased Frank about where his meat might have come from. I liked the Dandelion Lady, nicknamed for her shock of white hair, who ate one egg and chips from Monday to Thursday and sat reading the complimentary newspapers and drinking her way through two cups of tea. I always made an effort to chat with her. I suspected it might be the only conversation the old woman got all day.

I liked the tourists, who stopped on their walk up to and down from the castle, the shrieking schoolchildren, who stopped by after school, the regulars from the offices across the road, and Nina and Cherie, the hairdressers, who knew the calorie count of every single item the Buttered Bun had to offer. Even the annoying customers, like the red-haired woman who ran the toy shop and disputed her change at least once a week, didn't trouble me.

I watched relationships begin and end across those tables, children transferred between ex-spouses, the guilty relief of those parents who couldn't face cooking, and the secret pleasure of pensioners at a fried breakfast. All human life came through, and most of them shared a few words with me, trading jokes or comments over the mugs of steaming tea. Dad always said he never knew what was going to come out of my mouth next, but in the café it didn't matter.

Frank liked me. He was quiet by nature, and said having me there kept the place lively. It was a bit like being a barmaid, but without the hassle of drunks.

And then that afternoon, after the lunchtime rush had ended, and with the place briefly empty, Frank, wiping his hands on his apron, had come out from behind the hot plate and turned the little CLOSED sign to face the street.

He was twisting a tea towel between his two hands and looked more uncomfortable than I had ever seen him. I wondered, briefly, whether someone had complained about me. And then he motioned to me to sit down.

"Sorry, Louisa," he said, after he had told me. "But I'm going back to Australia. My dad's not too good, and it looks like the castle is definitely going to start doing its own refreshments. The writing's on the wall."

I think I sat there with my mouth actually hanging open. And then Frank handed me the envelope, and answered my next question before it left my lips. "I know we never had, you know, a formal contract or anything, but I wanted to look after you. There's three months' money in there. We close tomorrow."

———

"Three months!" Dad exploded, as my mother thrust a cup of sweet tea into my hands. "Well, that's big of him, given she's worked like a ruddy Trojan in that place for the last six years."

"Bernard." Mum shot him a warning look, nodding toward Thomas. My parents minded him after school every day until Treena finished work.

"What the hell is she supposed to do now? He could have given her more than a day's bloody notice."

"Well . . . she'll just have to get another job."

"There are no bloody jobs, Josie. You know that as well as I do. We're in the middle of a bloody recession."

Mum shut her eyes for a moment, as if composing herself before she spoke. "She's a bright girl. She'll find herself something. She's got a solid employment record, hasn't she? Frank will give her a good reference."

"Oh, fecking marvelous . . . 'Louisa Clark is very good at buttering toast, and a dab hand with the old teapot.'"

"Thanks for the vote of confidence, Dad."

"I'm just saying."

I knew the real reason for Dad's anxiety. They relied on my wages. Treena earned next to nothing at the flower shop. Mum couldn't work, as she had to look after Granddad, and Granddad's pension amounted to almost nothing. Dad lived in a constant state of anxiety about his job at the furniture factory. His boss had been muttering about possible redundancies for months. There were murmurings at home about debts and the juggling of credit cards. Dad had had his car written off by an uninsured driver two years previously, and somehow this had been enough for the whole teetering edifice that was my parents' finances to finally collapse. My modest wages had been a little bedrock of housekeeping money, enough to help see the family through from week to week.

"Let's not get ahead of ourselves. She can head down to the Job Center tomorrow and see what's on offer. She's got enough to get by for now." They spoke as if I weren't there. "And she's smart. You're smart, aren't you, love? Perhaps she could do a typing course. Go into office work."

I sat there as my parents discussed what other jobs my limited qualifications might entitle me to. Factory work, machinist, roll butterer. For the first time that afternoon I wanted to cry. Thomas watched me with big, round eyes, and silently handed me half a soggy biscuit.

"Thanks, Tommo," I mouthed silently, and ate it.

———

He was down at the athletics club, as I had known he would be. Mondays to Thursdays, regular as a station timetable, Patrick was there in the gym or running in circles around the floodlit track.

"Run with me," he puffed, as he got closer. His breath came in pale clouds. "I've got four laps to go."

I hesitated just a moment, and then began to run alongside him. It was the only way I was going to get any kind of conversation out of him. I was wearing my pink trainers with the turquoise laces, the only shoes I could possibly run in.

I had spent the day at home, trying to be useful. I'm guessing it was about an hour before I started to get under my mother's feet. Mum and Granddad had their routines, and having me there interrupted them. Dad was asleep, as he was on nights this month, and not to be disturbed. I tidied my room, then sat and watched television with the sound down, and when I remembered, periodically, why I was at home in the middle of the day, I felt an actual brief pain in my chest.

"I wasn't expecting you."

"I got fed up at home. I thought maybe we could do something."

He looked sideways at me. There was a fine film of sweat on his face. "The sooner you get another job, babe, the better."

"It's all of twenty-four hours since I lost the last one. Am I allowed to just be a bit miserable and floppy? You know, just for today?"

"But you've got to look at the positive side. You knew you couldn't stay at that place forever. You want to move upward, onward." Patrick had been named Stortfold Young Entrepreneur of the Year two years previously, and had not yet quite recovered from the honor. He had since acquired a business partner, Ginger Pete, offering personal training to clients over a forty-mile area, and two liveried vans on credit. "Being made redundant can change people's lives, Lou." He glanced at his watch, checking his lap time. "What do you want to do? You could retrain. I'm sure they do a grant for people like you."

"People like me?"

"People looking for a new opportunity. What do you want to be? You could be a beautician. You're pretty enough." He nudged me as we ran, as if I should be grateful for the compliment.

"You know my beauty routine. Soap, water, the odd paper bag."

Patrick was beginning to look exasperated.

I was starting to lag behind. I hate running. I hated him for not slowing down.

"Look . . . shop assistant. Secretary. Estate agent. I don't know . . . there must be something you want to do."

But there wasn't. I had liked it in the café. I liked knowing everything there was to know about the Buttered Bun, and hearing about the lives of the people who came through it. I had felt comfortable there.

"You can't mope around, babe. Got to get over it. All the best entrepreneurs fight their way back from rock bottom. Jeffrey Archer did it. So did Richard Branson." He tapped my arm, trying to get me to keep up.

"I doubt if Jeffrey Archer ever got made redundant from toasting teacakes." I was out of breath. And I was wearing the wrong bra. I slowed, dropped my hands down onto my knees.

He turned, running backward, his voice carrying on the still, cold air. "I'm just saying. Sleep on it, put on a smart suit, and head down to the Job Center. Or I'll train you to work with me, if you like. You know there's money in it. And don't worry about the holiday. I'll pay."

I smiled at him.

He blew a kiss and his voice echoed across the empty stadium. "You can pay me back when you're back on your feet."

———

I made my first claim for Jobseeker's Allowance. I attended a forty-five-minute interview, and a group interview, where I sat with a group of twenty or so mismatched men and women, half of whom wore the same slightly stunned expression I suspected I did, and the other half the blank, uninterested faces of people who had been here too many times before. I wore what my dad deemed my "civilian" clothes.

As a result of these efforts, I endured a brief stint filling in on a night shift at a chicken processing factory (it gave me nightmares for weeks), and two days at a training session as a "home energy adviser." I realized pretty quickly that I was essentially being instructed to befuddle old people into switching energy suppliers, and told Syed, my personal "adviser," that I couldn't do it. He insisted that I continue, so I listed some of the practices that they had asked me to employ, at which point he went a bit quiet and suggested we (it was always "we" even though it was pretty obvious that one of us *had* a job) try something else.

I did two weeks at a fast-food chain. The hours were okay, I could cope with the fact that the uniform made my hair static, but I found it impossible to stick to the "appropriate responses" script, with its "How can I help you today?" and its "Would you like large fries with that?" I was let go after one of the doughnut girls caught me debating the varying merits of the free toys with a four-year-old. What can I say? She was a smart four-year-old. I also thought the Sleeping Beautys were sappy.

Now I sat at my fourth interview as Syed scanned through the touch screen for further employment "opportunities." Even Syed, who wore the grimly cheerful demeanor of someone who had shoehorned the most unlikely candidates into a job, was starting to sound a little weary.

"Um . . . Have you ever considered joining the entertainment industry?"

"What, as in mime artist? Opera singer?"

"Actually, no. But there is an opening for a pole dancer. Several, in fact."

I raised an eyebrow. "Please tell me you are kidding."

"It's thirty hours a week on a self-employed basis. I believe the tips are good. You said you were good with people. And you seem to like . . . theatrical . . . clothing." He glanced at my tights, which were green and glittery. I had thought they would cheer me up. Thomas had hummed the theme tune from *The Little Mermaid* at me for almost the whole of breakfast.

Syed tapped something into his keyboard. "How about 'adult chat line supervisor'?"

I stared at him.

He shrugged. "You said you liked talking to people."

"No. And no to seminude bar staff. Or masseuse. Or webcam operator. Come on, Syed. There must be something I can do that wouldn't actually give my dad a heart attack."

This appeared to stump him. "There's not much left outside flexi-hour retail opportunities."

"Nighttime shelf stacking?" I had been here enough times now to speak their language.

"There's a waiting list. Parents tend to go for it, because it suits the school hours," he said apologetically. He studied the screen again. "So we're really left with care assistant."

"Wiping old people's bottoms."

"I'm afraid, Louisa, you're not qualified for much else. If you wanted to retrain, I'd be happy to point you in the right direction. There are plenty of courses at the adult education center."

"But we've been through this, Syed. If I do that, I lose my Jobseeker money, right?"

"If you're not available for work, yes."

We sat there in silence for a moment. I gazed at the doors, where two burly security men stood. I wondered if they had got the job through the Job Center.

"I'm not good with old people, Syed. My granddad lives at home since he had his strokes, and I can't cope with him."

"Ah. So you have some experience of caregiving."

"Not really. My mum does everything for him."

"Would your mum like a job?"

"Funny."

"I'm not being funny."

"And leave me looking after my granddad? No, thanks. That's from him, as well as me, by the way. Haven't you got anything in any cafés?"

"I don't think there are enough cafés left to guarantee you employment, Louisa. We could try Kentucky Fried Chicken. You might get on better there."

"Because I'd get so much more out of offering a Bargain Bucket than Chicken McNuggets? I don't think so."

"Well, then perhaps we'll have to look farther afield."

"There are only four buses to and from our town. You know that. And I know you said I should look into the tourist bus, but I rang the station and it stops running at 5 P.M. Plus it's twice as expensive as the normal bus."

Syed sat back in his seat. "At this point in the proceedings, Louisa, I really need to make the point that as a fit and able person, in order to continue qualifying for your allowance, you need—"

"—to show that I'm trying to get a job. I know."

How could I explain to this man how much I wanted to work? Did he have the slightest idea how much I missed my old job? Unemployment had been a concept, something droningly referred to on the news in relation to shipyards or car factories. I had never considered that you might miss a job like you missed a limb—a constant, reflexive thing. I hadn't thought that as well as the obvious fears about money, and your future, losing your job would make you feel inadequate, and a bit useless. That it would be harder to get up in the morning than when you were rudely shocked into consciousness by the alarm. That you might miss the people you worked with, no matter how little you had in common with them. Or even that you might find yourself searching for familiar faces as you walked the high street. The first time I had seen the Dandelion Lady wandering past the shops, looking as aimless as I felt, I had fought the urge to go and give her a hug.

Syed's voice broke into my reverie. "Aha. Now this might work."

I tried to peer around at the screen.

"Just came in. This very minute. Care assistant position."

"I told you I was no good with—"

"It's not old people. It's a . . . a private position. To help in someone's house, and the address is less than two miles from your home. 'Care and companionship for a disabled man.' Can you drive?"

"Yes. But would I have to wipe his—"

"No bottom wiping required, as far as I can tell." He scanned the screen. "He's a . . . a quadriplegic. He needs someone in the daylight hours to help feed and assist. Often in these jobs it's a case of being there when they want to go out somewhere, helping with basic stuff that they can't do themselves. Oh. It's good money. Quite a lot more than the minimum wage."

"That's probably because it involves bottom wiping."

"I'll ring them to confirm the absence of bottom wiping. But if that's the case, you'll go along for the interview?"

He said it like it was a question.

But we both knew the answer.

I sighed, and gathered up my bag, ready for the trip home.

———

"Jesus Christ," said my father. "Can you imagine? If it wasn't punishment enough ending up in a ruddy wheelchair, then you get our Lou turning up to keep you company."

"Bernard!" my mother scolded.

Behind me, Granddad was laughing into his mug of tea.

2

I am not thick. I'd just like to get that out of the way at this point. But it's quite hard not to feel a bit deficient in the Department of Brain Cells, growing up next to a younger sister who was moved up not just a year into my class, but then to the year above.

Everything that is sensible, or smart, Katrina did first, despite being eighteen months younger than me. Every book I ever read she had read first, every fact I mentioned at the dinner table she already knew. She is the only person I know who actually likes exams. Sometimes I think I dress the way I do because the one thing Treena can't do is put clothes together. She's a pullover-and-jeans kind of girl. Her idea of smart is ironing the jeans first.

My father calls me a "character," because I tend to say the first thing that pops into my head. My mother calls me "individual," which is her polite way of not quite understanding the way I dress.

But apart from a brief period in my teens, I never wanted to look like Treena, or any of the girls at school; I preferred boys' clothes till I was about fourteen, and now tend to please myself—depending on what mood I am in on the day. There's no point in me trying to look conventional. I am small, dark-haired, and, according to my dad, have the face of an elf. That's not as in "elfin beauty." I am not plain, but I don't think anyone is ever going to call me beautiful. I don't have that graceful thing going on. Patrick calls me gorgeous when he wants to get his leg over, but he's fairly transparent like that. We've known each other for coming up to seven years.

I was twenty-six years old and I wasn't really sure what I was. Up until I lost my job I hadn't even given it any thought. I supposed I would probably marry Patrick, knock out a few 'kids, live a few streets away from where I had always lived. Apart from an exotic taste in clothes, and the fact that I'm a bit short, there's not a lot separating me from anyone you might pass in the street. You probably wouldn't look at me twice. An ordinary girl, leading an ordinary life. It actually suited me fine.

———————

"You must wear a suit to an interview," Mum had insisted. "Everyone's far too casual these days."

"Because wearing pinstripes will be vital if I'm spoon-feeding a geriatric."

"Don't be smart."

"I can't afford to buy a suit. What if I don't get the job?"

"You can wear mine, and I'll iron you a nice blouse, and just for once don't wear your hair up in those"—she gestured to my hair, which was normally twisted into two dark knots on each side of my head—"Princess Leia things. Just try to look like a normal person."

I knew better than to argue with my mother. And I could tell Dad had been instructed not to comment on my outfit as I walked out of the house, my gait awkward in the too-tight skirt.

"Bye, love," he said, the corners of his mouth twitching. "Good luck now. You look very . . . businesslike."

The embarrassing thing was not that I was wearing my mother's suit, or that it was in a cut last fashionable in the late 1980s, but that it was actually a tiny bit small for me. I felt the waistband cutting into my midriff, and pulled the double-breasted jacket across. As Dad says of Mum, there's more fat on a hairpin.

I sat through the short bus journey feeling faintly sick. I had never had a proper job interview. I had joined the

Buttered Bun after Treena bet me that I couldn't get a job in a day. I had walked in and simply asked Frank if he needed a spare pair of hands. It had been his first day open, and he had looked almost blinded by gratitude.

Now, looking back, I couldn't even remember having a discussion with him about money. He suggested a weekly wage, I agreed, and once a year he told me he'd upped it a bit, usually by a little more than what I would have asked for.

What did people ask in interviews anyway? Syed had said there was a male caregiver who covered his "intimate needs" (I shuddered at the phrase). The secondary caregiver's job was, he said, "a little unclear at this point." I pictured myself wiping drool from the old man's mouth, maybe asking loudly, "DO YOU WANT A CUP OF TEA?"

When Granddad had first begun his recovery from his strokes he hadn't been able to do anything for himself. Mum had done it all. "Your mother is a saint," Dad said, which I took to mean that she wiped his bum without running screaming from the house. I was pretty sure nobody had ever described me as such. I cut Granddad's food up for him and made him cups of tea but as for anything else, I wasn't sure I was made of the right ingredients.

Granta House was on the other side of Stortfold Castle, close to the medieval walls, on the long unpavemented stretch that comprised only four houses and the National Trust shop, bang in the middle of the tourist area. I had passed this house a million times in my life without ever actually properly seeing it. Now, walking past the car park and the miniature railway, both of which were empty and as bleak as only a summer attraction can look in February, I saw it was bigger than I had imagined, redbrick with a double front, the kind of house you saw in old copies of *Country Life* while waiting at the doctor's.

I walked up the long drive, trying not to think about whether anybody was watching out the window. Walking up a long drive puts you at a disadvantage; it automatically makes you feel inferior. I was just contemplating whether to actually tug at my forelock when the door opened, and I jumped.

A woman, not much older than me, stepped out onto the porch. She was wearing white slacks and a medical-looking tunic and carried a coat and a folder under her arm. As she passed me she gave a polite smile.

"And thank you so much for coming," a voice said, from inside. "We'll be in touch. Ah." A woman's face appeared, middle-aged but beautiful, under expensive precision-cut hair. She was wearing a trouser suit that I guessed cost more than my dad earned in a month.

"You must be Miss Clark."

"Louisa." I shot out a hand, as my mother had impressed upon me to do. The young people never offered up a hand these days, my parents had agreed. In the old days you wouldn't have dreamed of a "hiya" or, worse, an air kiss. This woman did not look like she would have welcomed an air kiss.

"Right. Yes. Do come in." She withdrew her hand from mine as soon as humanly possible, but I felt her eyes linger upon me, as if she were already assessing me.

"Would you like to come through? We'll talk in the drawing room. My name is Camilla Traynor." She seemed weary, as if she had uttered the same words many times that day already.

I followed her through to a huge room with floor-to-ceiling French windows. Heavy curtains draped elegantly from fat mahogany curtain poles, and the floors were carpeted with intricately decorated Persian rugs. It smelled of beeswax and antique furniture. There were little elegant side tables everywhere, their burnished surfaces covered with ornamental boxes. I wondered briefly where on earth the Traynors put their cups of tea.

"So you have come via the Job Center advertisement, is that right? Do sit down."

While she flicked through her folder of papers, I gazed surreptitiously around the room. I had thought the house might be a bit like a nursing home, all hoists and wipe-clean surfaces. But this was like one of those scarily expensive hotels, steeped in old money, with well-loved things that looked valuable in their own right. There were silver-framed photographs on a sideboard, but they were too far away for me to make out the faces. As she scanned her pages, I shifted in my seat, to try to get a better look.

And it was then that I heard it—the unmistakable sound of stitches ripping. I glanced down to see that the two pieces of material that joined at the side of my right leg had torn apart, sending frayed pieces of silk thread shooting upward in an ungainly fringe. I felt my face flood with color.

"So . . . Miss Clark . . . do you have any experience with quadriplegia?"

I turned to face Mrs. Traynor, wriggling so that my jacket covered as much of the skirt as possible.

"No."

"Have you been a caregiver for long?"

"Um . . . I've never actually done it," I said, adding, as if I could hear Syed's voice in my ear, "but I'm sure I could learn."

"Do you know what a quadriplegic is?"

I faltered. "When . . . you're stuck in a wheelchair?"

"I suppose that's one way of putting it. There are varying degrees, but in this case we are talking about complete loss of use of the legs, and very limited use of the hands and arms. Would that bother you?"

"Well, not as much as it would bother him, obviously." I raised a smile, but Mrs. Traynor's face was expressionless. "Sorry—I didn't mean—"

"Can you drive, Miss Clark?"

"Yes."

"Clean license?"

I nodded.

Camilla Traynor ticked something on her list.

The rip was growing. I could see it creeping inexorably up my thigh. At this rate, by the time I stood up I would look like a Vegas showgirl.

"Are you all right?" Mrs. Traynor was gazing at me.

"I'm just a little warm. Do you mind if I take my jacket off?" Before she could say anything, I wrenched the jacket off in one fluid motion and tied it around my waist, obscuring the split in the skirt. "So hot," I said, smiling at her, "coming in from outside. You know."

There was the faintest pause, and then Mrs. Traynor looked back at her folder. "How old are you?"

"I'm twenty-six."

"And you were in your previous job for six years."

"Yes. You should have a copy of my reference."

"Mm . . ." Mrs. Traynor held it up and squinted. "Your previous employer says you are a 'warm, chatty, and life-enhancing presence.'"

"Yes, I paid him."

That poker face again.

Oh hell, I thought.

It was as if I were being studied. Not necessarily in a good way. My mother's shirt felt suddenly cheap, the synthetic threads shining in the thin light. I should just have worn my plainest trousers and a shirt. Anything but this suit.

"So why are you leaving this job, where you are clearly so well regarded?"

"Frank—the owner—sold the café. It's the one at the bottom of the castle. The Buttered Bun. Was," I corrected myself. "I would have been happy to stay."

Mrs. Traynor nodded, either because she didn't feel the need to say anything further about it, or because she too would have been happy for me to stay there.

"And what exactly do you want to do with your life?"

"I'm sorry?"

"Do you have aspirations for a career? Would this be a

stepping-stone to something else? Do you have a professional dream that you wish to pursue?"

I looked at her blankly.

Was this some kind of trick question?

"I . . . I haven't really thought that far. Since I lost my job. I just—" I swallowed. "I just want to work again."

It sounded feeble. What kind of person came to an interview without even knowing what she wanted to do? Mrs. Traynor's expression suggested she thought the same thing.

She put down her pen. "So, Miss Clark, why should I employ you instead of, say, the previous candidate, who has several years' experience with quadriplegics?"

I looked at her. "Um . . . honestly? I don't know." This met with silence, so I added, "I guess that would be your call."

"You can't give me a *single reason* why I should employ you?"

My mother's face suddenly swam into view. The thought of going home with a ruined suit and another interview failure was beyond me. And this job paid more than nine pounds an hour.

I sat up a bit. "Well . . . I'm a fast learner, I'm never ill, I only live on the other side of the castle, and I'm stronger than I look . . . probably strong enough to help move your husband around—"

"My husband? It's not my husband you'd be working with. It's my son."

"Your son?" I blinked. "Um . . . I'm not afraid of hard work. I'm good at dealing with all sorts of people and . . . and I make a mean cup of tea." I began to blather into the silence. The thought of it being her son had thrown me. "I mean, my dad seems to think that's not the greatest reference. But in my experience there's not much that can't be fixed by a decent cup of tea . . ."

There was something a bit strange about the way Mrs. Traynor was looking at me.

"Sorry," I spluttered, as I realized what I had said. "I'm not suggesting the thing . . . the paraplegia . . . quadriplegia . . . with . . . your son . . . could be solved by a cup of tea."

"I should tell you, Miss Clark, that this is not a permanent contract. It would be for a maximum of six months. That is why the salary is . . . commensurate. We wanted to attract the right person."

"Believe me, when you've done shifts at a chicken processing factory, working in Guantánamo Bay for six months looks attractive." *Oh, shut up, Louisa.* I bit my lip.

But Mrs. Traynor seemed oblivious. She closed her file. "My son—Will—was injured in a road accident almost two years ago. He requires twenty-four-hour care, the majority of which is provided by a trained nurse. I have recently returned to work, and the caregiver would be required to be here throughout the day to keep him company, help him with food and drink, generally provide an extra pair of hands, and make sure that he comes to no harm." Camilla Traynor looked down at her lap. "It is of the utmost importance that Will has someone here who understands that responsibility."

Everything she said, even the way she emphasized her words, seemed to hint at some stupidity on my part.

"I can see that." I began to gather up my bag.

"So would you like the job?"

It was so unexpected that at first I thought I had heard her wrong. "Sorry?"

"We would need you to start as soon as possible. Payment will be weekly."

I was briefly lost for words. "You'd rather have me instead of—" I began.

"The hours are quite lengthy—eight A.M. till five P.M., sometimes later. There is no lunch break as such, although when Nathan, his daily nurse, comes in at lunchtime to attend to him, there should be a free half an hour."

"You wouldn't need anything . . . medical?"

"Will has all the medical care we can offer him. What we want for him is somebody robust . . . and upbeat. His life is . . . complicated, and it is important that he is encouraged to—" She broke off, her gaze fixed on something outside the French windows. Finally, she turned back to me. "Well, let's just say that his mental welfare is as important to us as his physical welfare. Do you understand?"

"I think so. Would I . . . wear a uniform?"

"No. Definitely no uniform." She glanced at my legs. "Although you might want to wear . . . something a bit less revealing."

I glanced down to where my jacket had shifted, revealing a generous expanse of bare thigh. "It . . . I'm sorry. It ripped. It's not actually mine."

But Mrs. Traynor no longer appeared to be listening. "I'll explain what needs doing when you start. Will is not the easiest person to be around at the moment, Miss Clark. This job is going to be about mental attitude as much as any . . . professional skills you might have. So. We will see you tomorrow?"

"Tomorrow? You don't want . . . you don't want me to meet him?"

"Will is not having a good day. I think it's best that we start afresh then."

I stood up, realizing Mrs. Traynor was already waiting to see me out.

"Yes," I said, tugging Mum's jacket across me. "Um. Thank you. I'll see you at eight o'clock tomorrow."

———

Mum was spooning potatoes onto Dad's plate. She put two on, he parried, lifting a third and fourth from the serving dish. She blocked him, steering them back onto the serving dish, finally rapping him on the knuckles with the serving spoon when he made for them again. Around the little table sat my parents, my sister and Thomas, my granddad, and Patrick—who always came for dinner on Wednesdays.

"Daddy," Mum said to Granddad. "Would you like someone to cut your meat? Treena, will you cut Daddy's meat?"

Treena leaned across and began slicing at Granddad's plate with deft strokes. On the other side she had already done the same for Thomas.

"So how messed up is this man, Lou?"

"Can't be up to much if they're willing to let our daughter loose on him," Dad remarked. Behind me, the television was on so that Dad and Patrick could watch the football. Every now and then they would stop, peering around me, their mouths stopping midchew as they watched some pass or near miss.

"I think it's a great opportunity. She'll be working in one of the big houses. For a good family. Are they posh, love?"

In our street "posh" could mean anyone who didn't have a family member in possession of an antisocial behavior order.

"I suppose so."

"Hope you've practiced your curtsy." Dad grinned.

"Did you actually meet him?" Treena leaned across to stop Thomas from elbowing his juice onto the floor. "The crippled man? What was he like?"

"I meet him tomorrow."

"Weird, though. You'll be spending all day every day with him. Nine hours. You'll see him more than you see Patrick."

"That's not hard," I said.

Patrick, across the table, pretended he couldn't hear me.

"Still, you won't have to worry about the old sexual harassment, eh?" Dad said.

"Bernard!" said my mother, sharply.

"I'm only saying what everyone's thinking. Probably the best boss you could find for your girlfriend, eh, Patrick?"

Across the table, Patrick smiled. He was busy refusing

potatoes, despite Mum's best efforts. He was having a noncarb month, in preparation for a marathon in early March.

"You know, I was thinking, will you have to learn sign language? I mean, if he can't communicate, how will you know what he wants?"

"She didn't say he couldn't talk, Mum." I couldn't actually remember *what* Mrs. Traynor had said. I was still vaguely in shock at actually having been given a job.

"Maybe he talks through one of those devices. Like that scientist bloke. The one on *The Simpsons*."

"Bugger," said Thomas.

"Nope," said Dad.

"Stephen Hawking," said Patrick.

"That's you, that is," Mum said, looking accusingly from Thomas to Dad. She could cut steak with that look. "Teaching him bad language."

"It is not. I don't know where he's getting it from."

"Bugger," said Thomas, looking directly at his grand-father.

Treena made a face. "I think it would freak me out, if he talked through one of those voice boxes. Can you imagine? 'Get-me-a-drink-of-water,'" she mimicked.

Bright—but not bright enough not to get herself knocked up, as Dad occasionally muttered. She had been the first member of our family to go to university, until Thomas's arrival had caused her to drop out during her final year. Mum and Dad still held out hopes that one day she would bring the family a fortune. Or possibly work in a place with a reception desk that didn't have a security screen around it. Either would do.

"Why would being in a wheelchair mean he had to speak like a robot?" I said.

"But you're going to have to get up close and personal with him. At the very least you'll have to wipe his mouth and give him drinks and stuff."

"So? It's hardly rocket science."

"Says the woman who used to put Thomas's nappy on inside out."

"That was once."

"Twice. And you only changed him three times."

I helped myself to green beans, trying to look more sanguine than I felt.

But even as I had ridden the bus home, the same thoughts had already started buzzing around my head. What would we talk about? What if he just stared at me, head lolling, all day? Would I be freaked out? What if I couldn't understand what it was he wanted? I was legendarily bad at caring for things; we no longer had houseplants at home, or pets, after the disasters that were the hamster, the stick insects, and Randolph the goldfish. And how often was that stiff mother of his going to be around? I didn't like the thought of being watched all the time. Mrs. Traynor seemed like the kind of woman whose gaze turned capable hands into fingers and thumbs.

"Patrick, what do you think of it all, then?"

Patrick took a long slug of water, and shrugged.

Outside, the rain beat on the windowpanes, just audible over the clatter of plates and cutlery.

"It's good money, Bernard. Better than working nights at the chicken factory, anyway."

There was a general murmur of agreement around the table.

"Well, it comes to something when the best you can all say about my new career is that it's better than hauling chicken carcasses around the inside of an aircraft hangar," I said.

"Well, you could always get fit in the meantime and go and do some of your personal training stuff with Patrick here."

"Get fit. Thanks, Dad." I had been about to reach for another potato, and now changed my mind.

"Well, why not?" Mum looked as if she might actually sit down—everyone paused briefly, but no, she was up again, helping Granddad to some gravy. "It might be worth bearing in mind for the future. You've certainly got the gift of the gab."

"She has the gift of the flab," Dad snorted.

"I've just *got* myself a job," I said. "Paying more than the last one too, if you don't mind."

"But it is only temporary," Patrick interjected. "Your dad's right. You might want to start getting in shape while you do it. You could be a good personal trainer, if you put in a bit of effort."

"I don't *want* to be a personal trainer. I don't fancy . . . all that . . . bouncing." I mouthed an insult at Patrick, who grinned.

"What Lou wants is a job where she can put her feet up and watch daytime telly while feeding old Ironside there through a straw," said Treena.

"Yes. Because rearranging limp dahlias into buckets of water requires so much physical and mental effort, doesn't it, Treen?"

"We're teasing you, love." Dad raised his mug of tea. "It's great that you've got a job. We're proud of you already. And I wouldn't worry about it only being for six months. I bet you, once you slide those feet of yours under the table at the big house those buggers won't want to let you go."

"Bugger," said Thomas.

"Not me," said Dad, chewing, before Mum could say a thing.

3

"This is the annex. It used to be stables, but we realized it would suit Will rather better than the house as it's all on one floor. This is the spare room so that Nathan can stay over if necessary. We needed someone quite often in the early days."

Mrs. Traynor walked briskly down the corridor, gesturing from one doorway to another, without looking back, her high heels clacking on the flagstones. There seemed to be an expectation that I would keep up.

"The keys to the car are here. I've put you on our insurance. I'm trusting the details you gave me were correct. Nathan should be able to show you how the ramp works. All you have to do is help Will position properly and the vehicle will do the rest. Although . . . he's not desperately keen to go anywhere at the moment."

"It is a bit chilly out," I said.

Mrs. Traynor didn't seem to hear me.

"You can make yourself tea and coffee in the kitchen. I keep the cupboards stocked. The bathroom is through here—"

She opened the door and I stared at the white metal and plastic hoist that crouched over the bath. There was an open wet area under the shower, with a folded wheelchair beside it. In the corner a glass-fronted cabinet revealed neat stacks of shrink-wrapped bales. I couldn't see what they were from here, but it all gave off a faint scent of disinfectant.

Mrs. Traynor closed the door, and turned briefly to face me. "I should reiterate, it is very important that Will has someone with him all the time. A previous caregiver disappeared for several hours once to get her car fixed, and Will . . . injured himself in her absence." She swallowed, as if still traumatized by the memory.

"I won't go anywhere."

"Of course you will need . . . comfort breaks. I just want to make it clear that he can't be left for periods longer than, say, ten or fifteen minutes. If something unavoidable comes up either ring the intercom, as my husband, Steven, may be home, or call my mobile number. If you do need to take any time off, I would appreciate as much notice as possible. It is not always easy finding cover."

"No."

Mrs. Traynor opened the hall cupboard. She spoke like someone reciting a well-rehearsed speech.

I wondered briefly how many caregivers there had been before me.

"If Will is occupied, then it would be helpful if you could do some basic housekeeping. Wash bedding, run a vacuum cleaner around, that sort of thing. The cleaning equipment is under the sink. He may not want you around him all the time. You and he will have to work out your level of interaction for yourselves."

Mrs. Traynor looked at my clothes, as if for the first time. I was wearing the very shaggy waistcoat thing that Dad says makes me look like an emu. I tried to smile. It seemed like an effort.

"Obviously I would hope that you could . . . get on with each other. It would be nice if he could think of you as a friend rather than a paid professional."

"Right. What does he . . . um . . . like to do?"

"He watches films. Sometimes he listens to the radio, or to music. He has one of those digital things. If you position it near his hand, he can usually manipulate it himself. He has some movement in his fingers, although he finds it hard to grip."

I felt myself brightening. If he liked music and films, surely we could find some common ground? I had a sudden picture of myself and this man laughing at some Hollywood comedy, me running the Hoover around the bedroom while he listened to his music. Perhaps this was going to be okay. Perhaps we might end up as friends.

"Do you have any questions?"

"No."

"Then let's go and introduce you." She glanced at her watch. "Nathan should have finished dressing him by now."

We hesitated outside the door and Mrs. Traynor knocked. "Are you in there? I have Miss Clark to meet you, Will."

There was no answer.

"Will? Nathan?"

A broad New Zealand accent. "He's decent, Mrs. T."

She pushed open the door. The annex's living room was deceptively large, and one wall consisted entirely of glass doors that looked out over open countryside. A wood burner glowed quietly in the corner, and a low beige sofa faced a huge flat-screen television, its seats covered by a wool throw. The mood of the room was tasteful, and peaceful—a Scandinavian bachelor pad.

In the center of the room stood a black wheelchair, its seat and back cushioned by sheepskin. A solidly built man in white collarless scrubs was crouching down, adjusting a man's feet on the footrests of the wheelchair. As we stepped into the room, the man in the wheelchair looked up from under shaggy, unkempt hair. His eyes met mine, and after a pause, he let out a bloodcurdling groan. Then his mouth twisted, and he let out another unearthly cry.

I felt his mother stiffen.

"Will, stop it!"

He didn't even glance toward her. Another prehistoric sound emerged from somewhere near his chest. It was a terrible, agonizing noise. I tried not to flinch. The man was grimacing, his head tilted and sunk into his shoulders as he stared at me through contorted features. He looked grotesque, and vaguely angry. I realized that where I held my bag, my knuckles had turned white.

"Will! Please." There was a faint note of hysteria in his mother's voice. "Please, don't do this."

Oh God, I thought. *I'm not up to this*. I swallowed, hard. The man was still staring at me. He seemed to be waiting for me to do something.

"I—I'm Lou." My voice, uncharacteristically tremulous, broke into the silence. I wondered, briefly, whether to hold out a hand and then, remembering that he wouldn't be able to take it, gave a feeble wave instead. "Short for Louisa."

Then to my astonishment his features cleared, and his head straightened on his shoulders.

Will Traynor gazed at me steadily, the faintest of smiles flickering across his face. "Good morning, Miss Clark," he said. "I hear you're my latest minder."

Nathan had finished adjusting the footrests. He shook his head as he stood up. "You are a bad man, Mr. T. Very bad." He grinned, and held out a broad hand, which I shook limply. Nathan exuded an air of unflappability. "I'm afraid you just got Will's best Christy Brown impression. You'll get used to him. His bark is worse than his bite."

Mrs. Traynor was holding the cross at her neck with slim white fingers. She moved it back and forth along its thin gold chain, a nervous habit. Her face was rigid. "I'll leave you all to get on. You can call through using the intercom if you need any help. Nathan will talk you through Will's routines, and his equipment."

"I'm here, Mother. You don't have to talk across me. My brain isn't paralyzed. Yet."

"Yes, well, if you're going to be foul, Will, I think it's best if Miss Clark does talk directly to Nathan." His mother wouldn't look at him as she spoke, I noticed. She kept her gaze about ten feet away on the floor. "I'm working from home today. So I'll pop in at lunchtime, Miss Clark."

"Okay." My voice emerged as a squawk.

Mrs. Traynor disappeared. We were silent while we listened to her clipped footsteps disappearing down the hall toward the main house.

Then Nathan broke the silence. "You mind if I go and talk Miss Clark through your meds, Will? You want the television? Some music?"

"Radio Four please, Nathan."

"Sure thing."

We walked through to the kitchen.

"You've not had much experience with quadriplegics, Mrs. T says?"

"No."

"Okay. I'll keep it fairly simple for today. There's a folder here that tells you pretty much everything you need to know about Will's routines, and all his emergency numbers. I'd advise you to read it, if you get a spare moment. I'm guessing you'll have a few."

Nathan took a key from his belt and opened a locked cabinet, which was packed full of boxes and small plastic canisters of medication. "Right. This lot is mostly my bag, but you do need to know where everything is in case of emergencies. There's a timetable there on the wall so you can see what he has when on a daily basis. Any extras you give him you mark in there"—he pointed—"but you're best to clear anything through Mrs. T, at least at this stage."

"I didn't realize I was going to have to handle drugs."

"It's not hard. He mostly knows what he needs. But he might need a little help getting them down. We tend to use this beaker here. Or you can crush them with this pestle and mortar and put them in a drink."

I picked up one of the labels. I wasn't sure I had ever seen so many drugs outside a pharmacy.

"Okay. So he has two meds for blood pressure, this to lower it at bedtime, this one to raise it when he gets out of bed. These he needs fairly often to control his muscular spasms—you will need to give him one mid-morning, and again at midafternoon. He doesn't find those too hard to swallow, because they're the little coated ones. These are for bladder spasms, and these here are for acid reflux. He sometimes needs these after eating if he gets uncomfortable. This is his antihistamine for the morning, and these are his nasal sprays, but I mostly do those last thing before I leave, so you shouldn't have to worry. He can have paracetamol if he's in pain, and he does have the odd sleeping pill, but these tend to make him more irritable in the daytime, so we try to restrict them.

"These"—he held up another bottle—"are the antibiotics he has every two weeks for his catheter change. I do those unless I'm away, in which case I'll leave clear instructions. They're pretty strong. There are the boxes of rubber gloves, if you need to clean him up at all. There's also cream there if he gets sore, but he's been pretty good since we got the air mattress."

As I stood there, he reached into his pocket and handed another key to me. "This is the spare," he said. "Not to be given to anyone else. Not even Will, okay? Guard it with your life."

"It's a lot to remember." I swallowed.

"It's all written down. All you need to remember for today are his antispasm meds. Those ones. There's my mobile number if you need to call me. I'm studying when I'm not here, so I'd rather not be called too often but feel free till you feel confident."

I stared at the folder in front of me. It felt like I was about to sit an exam I hadn't prepared for. "What if he needs . . . to go to the loo?" I thought of the hoist. "I'm not sure I could, you know, lift him." I tried not to let my face betray my panic.

Nathan shook his head. "You don't need to do any of that. His catheter takes care of that. I'll be in at lunchtime to change it all. You're not here for the physical stuff."

"What am I here for?"

Nathan studied the floor before he looked at me. "Try to cheer him up a little? He's . . . he's a little cranky. Understandable, given . . . the circumstances. But you're going to have to have a fairly thick skin. That little skit this morning is his way of getting you off balance."

"Is this why the pay is so good?"

"Oh yes. No such thing as a free lunch, eh?" Nathan clapped me on the shoulder. I felt my body reverberate with it. "Ah, he's all right. You don't have to pussyfoot around him." He hesitated. "I like him."

He said it like he might be the only person who did.

I followed him back into the living room. Will Traynor's chair had moved to the window, and he had his back to us and was staring out, listening to something on the radio.

"That's me done, Will. You want anything before I go?"

"No. Thank you, Nathan."

"I'll leave you in Miss Clark's capable hands, then. See you lunchtime, mate."

With a rising sense of panic, I watched the affable helper putting on his jacket.

"Have fun, you guys." Nathan winked at me, and then he was gone.

I stood in the middle of the room, hands thrust in my pockets, unsure what to do. Will Traynor continued to stare out the window as if I weren't there.

"Would you like me to make you a cup of tea?" I said, finally, when the silence became unbearable.

"Ah. Yes. The girl who makes tea for a living. I wondered how long it would be before you wanted to show off your skills. No. No, thank you."

"Coffee, then?"

"No hot beverages for me just now, Miss Clark."

"You can call me Lou."

"Will it help?"

I blinked, my mouth opening briefly. I closed it. Dad always said it made me look more stupid than I actually was. "Well . . . can I get you anything?"

He turned to look at me. His jaw was covered in several weeks of stubble, and his eyes were unreadable. He turned away.

"I'll—" I cast around the room. "I'll see if there's any washing, then."

I walked out of the room, my heart thumping. From the safety of the kitchen I pulled out my mobile phone and thumped out a message to my sister.

> *This is awful. He hates me.*

The reply came back within seconds.

> *You have only been there an hour,*
> *you wuss! M & D really*
> *worried about money. Just get a grip*
> *& think of hourly rate. X*

I snapped my mobile phone shut, and blew out my cheeks. I went through the laundry basket in the bathroom, managing to raise a paltry quarter load of washing, and spent some minutes checking the instructions to the machine. I didn't want to misprogram it or do anything that might prompt Will or Mrs. Traynor to again look at me like I was stupid. I started the washing machine and stood there, trying to work out what else I could legitimately do. I pulled the vacuum cleaner from the hall cupboard and ran it up and down the corridor and into the two bedrooms, thinking all the while that if my parents could see me they would have insisted on taking a commemorative photograph. The spare bedroom was almost empty, like a hotel room. I suspected Nathan did not stay over often. I thought I probably couldn't blame him.

I hesitated outside Will Traynor's bedroom, then reasoned that it needed vacuuming just like anywhere else. There was a built-in shelf unit along one side, upon which sat around twenty framed photographs.

As I vacuumed around the bed, I allowed myself a quick peek at them. There was a man bungee jumping from a cliff, his arms outstretched like a statue of Christ. There was a man who might have been Will in what looked like a jungle, and him again in the midst of a group of drunken friends. The men wore bow ties and dinner jackets and had their arms around one another's shoulders.

There he was on a ski slope, beside a girl with dark glasses and long blond hair. I picked up the frame, to get a better view of him in his ski goggles. He was clean-shaven in the photograph, and even in the bright light his face had that expensive sheen to it that moneyed people get through going on holiday three times a year. He had broad, muscular shoulders visible even through his ski jacket. I put the photograph carefully back on the shelf and continued to vacuum around the back of the bed. Finally, I turned the vacuum cleaner off, and began to wind the cord up. As I reached down to unplug it, I caught a movement in the corner of my eye and jumped, letting out a small shriek. Will Traynor was in the doorway, watching me.

"Courchevel. Two and a half years ago."

I blushed. "I'm sorry. I was just—"

"You were just looking at my photographs. Wondering how awful it must be to live like that and then turn into a cripple."

"No." I blushed even more furiously.

"The rest of my photographs are in the bottom drawer if you find yourself overcome with curiosity again," he said.

And then with a low hum the wheelchair turned to the right, and he disappeared.

The morning sagged and decided to last for several years. I couldn't remember the last time minutes and hours stretched so interminably. I tried to find as many jobs to occupy myself as I could—dusting shelves and the like— and went into the living room as seldom as possible, knowing I was being cowardly, but not really caring.

At twelve thirty, Nathan arrived, bringing with him the cold air of outside, and a raised eyebrow. "All okay?" he said.

I had rarely been so happy to see someone in my life. "Fine."

"Great. You can take a half hour now. Me and Mr. T have a few things we attend to at this point in the day."

I almost ran for my coat. I hadn't planned on going out for lunch, but I was almost faint with relief at getting out of that house. I pulled up my collar, slung my handbag over my shoulder, and set off at a brisk pace down the drive, as if I had somewhere I actually wanted to go. In fact, I just walked around the surrounding streets for half an hour, expelling hot clouds of breath into my tightly wrapped scarf.

There were no cafés at this end of town, now that the Buttered Bun was closed. The castle was deserted. The nearest eating place was a gastropub, the kind of place where I doubted I could afford a drink, let alone a quick lunch. All the cars in the car park were huge and expensive with recent number plates.

I stood in the castle car park, making sure I was out of view of Granta House, and dialed my sister's number. "Hey."

"You know I can't talk at work. You haven't walked out, have you?"

"No. I just needed to hear a friendly voice."

"Is he that bad?"

"Treen, he *hates* me. He looks at me like I'm something the cat dragged in. And he doesn't even drink tea. I'm hiding from him."

"I can't believe I'm hearing this."

"What?"

"Just talk to him, for crying out loud. Of course he's miserable. He's stuck in a bloody wheelchair. And you're probably being useless. Just talk to him. Get to know him. What's the worst that can happen?"

"I don't know . . . I don't know if I can stick it out."

"I'm not telling Mum you're giving up your job after half a day. They won't give you any benefits, Lou. You can't do this. We can't afford for you to do this."

She was right. I realized I hated my sister.

There was a brief silence. Treena's voice turned uncharacteristically conciliatory. This was really worrying. It meant she knew I did actually have the worst job in the world. "Look," she said, "it's just six months. Just do the six months, have something useful on your CV, and you can get a job you actually like. And hey—look at it this way: at least it's not working nights at the chicken factory, right?"

"Nights at the chicken factory would feel like a holiday compared with—"

"I'm going now, Lou. I'll see you later."

———

"So would you like to go somewhere this afternoon? We could drive somewhere if you like."

Nathan had been gone for almost half an hour. I had

spun out the washing of the tea mugs as long as humanly possible, and I thought that if I spent one more hour in this silent house my head might explode.

He turned his head toward me. "Where did you have in mind?"

"I don't know. Just a drive in the country?" I was doing this thing I sometimes do of pretending I'm Treena. She is one of those people who are completely calm and competent, and as a result no one ever messes with her. I sounded, to my own ears, professional and upbeat.

"The country," he said, as if considering it. "And what would we see. Some trees? Some sky?"

"I don't know. What do you normally do?"

"I don't *do* anything, Miss Clark. I can't do anything anymore. I sit. I just about exist."

"Well," I said, "I was told that you have a car that's adapted for wheelchair use."

"And you're worried that it will stop working if it doesn't get used every day?"

"No, but I—"

"Are you telling me I should go out?"

"I just thought—"

"You thought a little drive would be good for me? A breath of fresh air?"

"I'm just trying to—"

"Miss Clark, my life is not going to be significantly improved by a drive around Stortfold's country lanes." He turned away.

His head had sunk into his shoulders, and I wondered whether he was comfortable. It didn't seem to be the time to ask him. We sat in silence.

"Do you want me to bring you your computer?"

"Why, have you thought of a good quadriplegic support group I could join? Quads R Us? The Tin Wheel Club?"

I took a deep breath, trying to make my voice sound

confident. "Okay . . . well . . . seeing as we're going to spend all this time in each other's company, perhaps we could get to know something about each other—"

There was something about his face then that made me falter. He was staring straight ahead at the wall, a tic moving in his jaw.

"It's just . . . it's quite a long time to spend with someone. All day," I continued. "Perhaps if you could tell me a little of what you want to do, what you like, then I can . . . make sure things are as you like them?"

This time the silence was painful. I heard my voice slowly swallowed by it, and couldn't work out what to do with my hands. Treena and her competent manner had evaporated.

Finally, the wheelchair hummed and he turned slowly to face me.

"Here's what I know about you, Miss Clark. My mother says you're chatty." He said it like it was an affliction. "Can we strike a deal? Whereby you are very *un*-chatty around me?"

I swallowed, feeling my face flame.

"Fine," I said, when I could speak again. "I'll be in the kitchen. If you want anything just call me."

———

"You can't give up already."

I was lying sideways on my bed with my legs stretched up the wall, like I did when I was a teenager. I had been up here since supper, which was unusual for me. Since Thomas was born, he and Treena had moved into the bigger room, and I was in the box room, which was small enough to make you feel claustrophobic should you sit in it for more than half an hour at a time.

But I didn't want to sit downstairs with Mum and Granddad because Mum kept looking at me anxiously and saying things like "It will get better, love" and "No job is great on the first day"—as if she'd had a ruddy job in the last twenty years. It was making me feel guilty. And I hadn't even done anything.

"I didn't say I was giving up. Oh God, Treen. It's worse than I thought. He is so miserable."

"He can't move. Of course he's miserable."

"No, but he's sarcastic and mean with it. Every time I say something or suggest something he looks at me like I'm stupid, or says something that makes me feel about two years old."

"You probably did say something stupid. You just need to get used to each other."

"I really didn't. I was so careful. I hardly said anything except 'Would you like to go out for a drive?' or 'Would you like a cup of tea?'"

"Well, maybe he's like that with everyone at the start, until he knows whether you're going to stick around. I bet they go through loads of helpers."

"He didn't even want me in the same room as him. I don't think I can stick it out, Katrina. I really don't. Honest—if you'd been there you would understand."

Treena said nothing then, just looked at me for a while. She got up and glanced out the door, as if checking whether there was anybody on the landing.

"I'm thinking of going back to college," she said, finally.

It took my brain a few seconds to register this change of tack.

"Oh my God," I said. "But—"

"I'm going to take a loan to pay for the fees. But I can get some special grant too, because of having Thomas, and the university is offering me reduced rates because they . . ." She shrugged, a little embarrassed. "They say they think I could excel. Someone's dropped out of the business studies course, so they can take me for the beginning of the next term."

"What about Thomas?"

"There's a nursery on campus. We can stay there in a

subsidized flat in halls during the week, and come back here most weekends."

"Oh."

I could feel her watching me. I didn't know what to do with my face.

"I'm really desperate to use my brain again. Doing the flowers is doing my head in. I want to learn. I want to improve myself. And I'm sick of my hands always being freezing cold from the water."

We both stared at her hands, which were pink tinged, even in the tropical warmth of our house.

"But—"

"Yup. I won't be working, Lou. I won't be able to give Mum anything. I might . . . I might even need a bit of help from them." This time she looked quite uncomfortable. Her expression, when she glanced up at me, was almost apologetic.

Downstairs Mum was laughing at something on the television. We could hear her exclaiming to Granddad. She often explained the plot of the show to him, even though we told her all the time she didn't need to.

I couldn't speak. The significance of my sister's words sank in slowly but inexorably. I felt the way a Mafia victim must feel, watching the concrete setting slowly around his ankles.

"I really need to do this, Lou. I want more for Thomas, more for both of us. The only way I'll get anywhere is by going back to college. I haven't got a Patrick. I'm not sure I'll ever have a Patrick, given that nobody's been remotely interested since I had Thomas. I need to do the best I can by myself."

When I didn't say anything, she added, "For me and Thomas."

I nodded.

"Lou? Please?"

I had never seen my sister look like that before. It made me feel really uncomfortable. I lifted my head, and raised a smile. My voice, when it emerged, didn't even sound like my own.

"Well, like you say, it's just a matter of getting used to him. It's bound to be difficult in the first few days, isn't it?"

4

Two weeks passed and with them emerged a routine of sorts. Every morning I would arrive at Granta House at eight, call out that I was there, and then, after Nathan had finished helping Will dress, listen carefully while he told me what I needed to know about Will's meds—or, more important, his mood.

After Nathan had left I would program the radio or television for Will, dispense his pills, sometimes crushing them with the little marble pestle and mortar. Usually, after ten minutes or so he would make it clear that he was weary of my presence. At this point I would eke out the little annex's domestic tasks, washing tea towels that weren't dirty, or using random vacuum attachments to clean tiny bits of skirting or windowsill, religiously popping my head around the door every fifteen minutes as Mrs. Traynor had instructed. When I did, he would be sitting in his chair looking out into the bleak garden.

Later I might take him a drink of water, or one of the calorie-filled drinks that were supposed to keep his weight up and looked like pastel-colored wallpaper paste, or give him his food. He could move his hands a little, but not his arm, so he had to be fed forkful by forkful. This was the worst part of the day; it seemed wrong, somehow, spoon-feeding a grown man, and my embarrassment made me clumsy and awkward. Will hated it so much he wouldn't even meet my eye while I was doing it.

And then shortly before one, Nathan would arrive and I would grab my coat and disappear to walk the streets, sometimes eating my lunch in the bus shelter outside the castle. It was cold, and I probably looked pathetic perched there eating my sandwiches, but I didn't care. I couldn't spend a whole day in that house.

In the afternoon I would put a film on—Will had a membership in a DVD club and new films arrived by post every day—but he never invited me to watch with him, so I'd usually go and sit in the kitchen or in the spare room. I started bringing in a book or magazine, but I felt oddly guilty not actually working, and I could never quite concentrate on the words. Occasionally, at the end of the day, Mrs. Traynor would pop in—although she never said much to me, other than "Everything all right?" to which the only acceptable answer seemed to be "Yes."

She would ask Will if he wanted anything, occasionally suggest something he might like to do the next day—some outing, or visit some friend who had asked after him—and he would almost always answer dismissively, if not with downright rudeness. She would look pained, run her fingers up and down that little gold chain, and disappear again.

His father, a well-padded, gentle-looking man, usually came in as I was leaving. He was the kind of man you might see watching cricket in a Panama hat, and he had apparently overseen the management of the castle since retiring from his well-paid job in the city. I suspected this was like a benign landowner planting the odd potato just "to keep his hand in." He finished every day at 5 P.M. promptly and would sit and watch television with Will. Sometimes I heard him making some remark about whatever was on the news as I left.

I got to study Will Traynor up close, in those first couple of weeks. I saw that he seemed determined not to look anything like the man he had been; he had let his light-brown hair grow into a shapeless mess, his stubble crawl across his jaw. His gray eyes were lined with exhaustion, or the effect of constant discomfort (Nathan said he was rarely comfortable). They bore the hollow look of someone who was always a few steps removed from the world around him. Sometimes I wondered if it was a defense mechanism, whether the only way to cope with his life was to pretend it wasn't him it was happening to.

I wanted to feel sorry for him. I really did. I thought he was the saddest person I had ever met, in those moments when I glimpsed him staring out the window. And as the days went by and I realized that his condition was not just a matter of being stuck in that chair, of the loss of physical freedom, but a never-ending litany of indignities and health problems, of risks and discomforts, I decided that if I were Will, I would probably be pretty miserable too.

But, oh Lord, he was vile to me. Everything I said, he had a sharp answer for. If I asked him if he was warm enough, he would retort that he was quite capable of letting me know if he needed another blanket. If I asked if the vacuum cleaner was too noisy for him—I hadn't wanted to interrupt his film—he asked me, Why, had I worked out a way to make it run silently? When I fed him, he complained that the food was too hot or too cold, or that I had brought the next forkful up to his mouth before he had finished the last. He had the ability to twist almost anything I said or did so that I seemed stupid.

During those first two weeks, I got quite good at keeping my face completely blank, and I would turn away and disappear into the other room and just say as little to him as I possibly could. I started to hate him, and I'm sure he knew it.

I hadn't realized it was possible to miss my old job more than I already did. I missed Frank, and the way he actually looked pleased to see me when I arrived in the morning. I missed the customers, their company, and the easy chatter that swelled and dipped gently like a benign sea around me. This house, beautiful and expensive as it was, was as still and silent as a morgue. *Six months,* I repeated under my breath, when it felt unbearable. *Six months*.

And then on Thursday, just as I was mixing Will's mid-morning, high-calorie drink, I heard Mrs. Traynor's voice in the hall. Except this time there were other voices too. I waited, the spoon stilled in my hand. I could just make out a woman's voice, young, well-spoken, and a man's.

Mrs. Traynor appeared in the kitchen doorway, and I tried to look busy, whisking briskly at the beaker.

"Is that made up with sixty-forty water and milk?" she asked, peering at the drink.

"Yes. It's the strawberry one."

"Will's friends have come to see him. It would probably be best if you—"

"I've got lots of things I should be doing in here," I said. I was actually quite relieved that I would be spared his company for an hour or so. I screwed the lid onto the beaker. "Would your guests like some tea or coffee?"

She looked almost surprised. "Yes. That would be very kind. Coffee. I think I'll . . ."

She seemed even more tense than usual, her eyes darting toward the corridor, from where we could hear the low murmur of voices. I guessed that Will didn't get many visitors.

"I think . . . I'll leave them all to it." She gazed out into the corridor, her thoughts apparently far away. "Rupert. It's Rupert, his old friend from work," she said, suddenly turning toward me.

I got the feeling that this was in some way momentous, and that she needed to share it with someone, even if it was just me.

"And Alicia. They were . . . very close . . . for a bit. Coffee would be lovely. Thank you, Miss Clark."

———

I hesitated a moment before I opened the door, leaning against it with my hip so that I could balance the tray in my hands.

"Mrs. Traynor said you might like some coffee," I said as I entered, placing the tray on the low table. As I put Will's beaker in the holder of his chair, turning the straw so that he needed to adjust only his head position to reach it, I sneaked a look at his visitors.

It was the woman I noticed first. Long-legged and blond, with pale caramel skin, she was the kind of woman who makes me wonder if all humans really are the same species. She looked like a human racehorse. I had seen these women occasionally; they were usually bouncing up the hill to the castle, clutching small Boden-clad children, and when they came into the café their voices would carry, crystal clear and unself-conscious, as they asked, "Harry, darling, would you like a coffee? Shall I see if they can do you a macchiato?" This was definitely a macchiato woman. Everything about her smelled of money, of entitlement, and a life lived as if through the pages of a glossy magazine.

Then I looked at her more closely and realized with a jolt that (a) she was the woman in Will's skiing photograph, and (b) she looked really, really uncomfortable.

She had kissed Will on the cheek and was now stepping backward, smiling awkwardly. She was wearing a brown shearling gilet, the kind of thing that would have made me look like a yeti, and a pale-gray cashmere scarf around her neck, which she began to fiddle with, as if she couldn't decide whether to unwrap herself or not.

"You look well," she said to him. "Really. You've . . . grown your hair a bit."

Will didn't say a thing. He was just looking at her, his expression as unreadable as ever. I felt a fleeting gratitude that it wasn't just me he looked at like that.

"New chair, eh?" The man tapped the back of Will's chair, chin compressed, nodding in approval as if he were admiring a top-of-the-line sports car. "Looks . . . pretty smart. Very . . . high-tech."

I didn't know what to do. I stood there for a moment,

shifting from one foot to the other, until Will's voice broke into the silence.

"Louisa, would you mind putting some more logs on the fire? I think it needs building up a bit."

It was the first time he had used my Christian name.

"Sure," I said.

I busied myself by the log burner, stoking the fire and sorting through the basket for logs of the right size.

"Gosh, it's cold outside," the woman said. "Nice to have a proper fire."

I opened the door of the wood burner, prodding at the glowing logs with the poker.

"It's a good few degrees colder here than London."

"Yes, definitely," the man agreed.

"I was thinking of getting a wood burner at home. Apparently they're much more efficient than an open fire." Alicia stooped a little to inspect this one, as if she'd never actually seen one before.

"Yes, I've heard that," said the man.

"I must look into it. One of those things you mean to do and then . . . " After a pause she added, "Lovely coffee."

"So—what have you been up to, Will?" The man's voice held a kind of forced joviality to it.

"Not very much, funnily enough."

"But the physio and stuff. Is it all coming on? Any . . . improvement?"

"I don't think I'll be skiing anytime soon, Rupert," Will said, his voice dripping with sarcasm.

I almost smiled to myself. This was the Will I knew. I began brushing ash from the hearth. I had the feeling that they were all watching me. The silence felt loaded. I wondered briefly whether the label was sticking out of my sweater and fought the urge to check.

"So . . . ," Will said finally. "To what do I owe this pleasure? It's been . . . eight months?"

"Oh, I know. I'm sorry. It's been . . . I've been awfully busy. I have a new job over in Chelsea. Managing Sasha Goldstein's boutique. Do you remember Sasha? I've been doing a lot of weekend work too. It gets terribly busy on Saturdays. Very hard to get time off." Alicia's voice had become brittle. "I did ring a couple of times. Did your mother tell you?"

"Things have been pretty manic at Lewins. You . . . you know what it's like, Will. We've got a new partner. Chap from New York. Bains. Dan Bains. You come up against him at all?"

"No."

"Bloody man seems to work twenty-four hours a day and expects everyone else to do the same." You could hear the man's palpable relief at having found a topic he was comfortable with. "You know the old Yank work ethic—no more long lunches, no smutty jokes— Will, I tell you. The whole atmosphere of the place has changed."

"Really."

"Oh God, yes. Presenteeism writ large. Sometimes I feel like I daren't leave my chair."

All the air seemed to disappear from the room in a vacuumed rush. Someone coughed.

I stood up, and wiped my hands on my jeans. "I'll . . . I'm just going to fetch some more logs," I muttered, in Will's general direction.

And I picked up the basket and fled.

It was freezing outside, but I lingered out there, killing time while I selected pieces of wood. I was trying to calculate whether it was preferable to lose the odd finger to frostbite rather than put myself back into that room. But it was just too cold and my index finger, which I use for sewing stuff, went blue first and finally I had to admit defeat. As I approached the living room I heard the woman's voice, weaving its way through the slightly open door.

"Actually, Will, there is another reason for us coming here," she was saying. "We . . . have some news."

I hesitated by the door, the log basket braced between my hands.

"I thought—well, *we* thought—that it would only be right to let you know . . . but, well, here's the thing. Rupert and I are getting married."

I stood very still, calculating whether I could turn around without being heard.

The woman continued, lamely. "Look, I know this is probably a bit of a shock to you. Actually, it was rather a shock to me. We—it—well, it only really started a long time after . . ."

My arms had begun to ache. I glanced down at the basket, trying to work out what to do.

"Well, you know you and I . . . we . . ."

Another weighty silence.

"Will, please say something."

"Congratulations," he said finally.

"I know what you're thinking. But neither of us meant for this to happen. Really. For an awfully long time we were just friends. Friends who were concerned about you. It's just that Rupert was the most terrific support to me after your accident—"

"Big of him."

"Please don't be like this. This is so awful. I have absolutely dreaded telling you. We both have."

"Evidently," Will said flatly.

Rupert's voice broke in. "Look, we're only telling you because we both care about you. We didn't want you to hear it from someone else. But, you know, life goes on. You must know that. It's been two years, after all."

There was silence. I realized I did not want to listen to any more, and started to move softly away from the door, grunting slightly with the effort. But Rupert's voice, when it came again, had grown in volume so that I could still hear him.

"Come on, man. I know it must be terribly hard . . . all this. But if you care for Lissa at all, you must want her to have a good life."

"Say something, Will. Please."

I could picture his face. I could see that look of his that managed both to be unreadable and to convey a kind of distant contempt.

"Congratulations," he said again. "I'm sure you'll both be very happy."

Alicia started to protest then—something indistinct— but was interrupted by Rupert. "Come on, Lissa. I think we should leave. Will, it's not like we came here expecting your blessing. It was a courtesy. Lissa thought—well, we both just thought—you should know. Sorry, old chap. I . . . I do hope things improve for you and I hope you do want to stay in touch when things . . . you know . . . when things settle down a bit."

I heard footsteps, and stooped over the basket of logs, as if I had only just come in. I heard them in the corridor, and then Alicia appeared in front of me. Her eyes were red-rimmed, as if she were about to cry.

"Can I use the bathroom?" she said, her voice thick and choked.

I slowly lifted a finger and pointed mutely in its direction.

She looked at me hard then, and I realized that what I felt probably showed on my face. I have never been much good at hiding my feelings.

"I know what you're thinking," she said, after a pause. "But I did try. I really tried. For months. And he just pushed me away." Her jaw was rigid, her expression oddly furious. "He actually didn't want me here. He made that very clear."

She seemed to be waiting for me to say something.

"It's really none of my business," I said, eventually.

We both stood facing each other.

"You know, you can only actually help someone who wants to be helped," she said.

And then she was gone.

I waited a few minutes, listening for the sound of their car disappearing down the drive, and then I went into the kitchen. I stood there and boiled the kettle even though I didn't want a cup of tea. I flicked through a magazine that I had already read. Finally, I went back into the corridor and, with a grunt, picked up the log basket and hauled it into the living room, bumping it slightly on the door before I entered so that Will would know I was coming.

"I was wondering if you wanted me to—" I began.

But there was nobody there.

The room was empty.

It was then that I heard the crash. I ran out into the corridor just in time to hear another, followed by the sound of shattering glass. It was coming from Will's bedroom. *Oh God, please don't let him have hurt himself.* I panicked—Mrs. Traynor's warning drilled through my head. I had left him for more than fifteen minutes.

I ran down the corridor, slid to a halt in the doorway, and stood, both hands gripping the door frame. Will was in the middle of the room, upright in his chair, a walking stick balanced across the armrests, so that it jutted eighteen inches to his left—a jousting stick. There was not a single photograph left on the long shelves; the expensive frames lay in pieces all over the floor, the carpet studded with glittering shards of glass. His lap was dusted with bits of glass and splintered wood frames. I took in the scene of destruction, feeling my heart rate slowly subside as I grasped that he was unhurt. Will was breathing hard, as if whatever he had done had cost him some effort.

His chair turned, crunching slightly on the glass. His eyes met mine. They were infinitely weary. They dared me to offer him sympathy.

I looked down at his lap, and then at the floor around him. I could just make out the picture of him and Alicia, her face now obscured by a bent silver frame, among the other casualties.

I swallowed, staring at it, and slowly lifted my eyes to his. Those few seconds were the longest I could remember.

"Can that thing get a puncture?" I said, finally, nodding at his wheelchair. "Because I have no idea where I would put the jack."

His eyes widened. Just for a moment, I thought I had really blown it. But the faintest flicker of a smile passed across his face.

"Look, don't move," I said. "I'll get the vacuum cleaner."

I heard the walking stick drop to the floor. As I left the room, I thought I might have heard him say sorry.

———

The Kings Head was always busy on a Thursday evening, and in the corner of the rear bar area it was even busier. I sat squashed between Patrick and a man whose name appeared to be the Rutter, staring periodically at the horse brasses pinned to the oak beams above my head and the photographs of the castle that punctuated the joists, and tried to look even vaguely interested in the talk around me, which seemed to revolve chiefly around body-fat ratios and carb loading.

I had always thought the fortnightly meetings of the Hailsbury Triathlon Terrors must be a publican's worst nightmare. I was the only one drinking alcohol, and my solitary packet of crisps sat crumpled and empty on the table. Everyone else sipped at mineral water, or checked the sweetener ratios on their Diet Cokes. When, finally, they ordered food, there wouldn't be a salad that was allowed to brush a leaf against a full-fat dressing, or a piece of chicken that still sported its skin. I often ordered chips, just so that I could watch them all pretend they didn't want one.

I couldn't say I enjoyed the Triathlon Terrors' gatherings, but what with my increased hours and Patrick's training timetable it was one of the few times I could be guaranteed to see him. He sat beside me, muscular thighs clad in shorts despite the extreme cold outside. It was a badge of honor among the members of the club to wear as few clothes as possible. The men were wiry, brandishing obscure and expensive sports layers that boasted extra "wicking" properties, or lighter-than-air body weights. They were called Scud or Trig, and flexed bits of body at one another, displaying injuries or alleged muscle growth. The girls wore no makeup, and had the ruddy complexions of those who thought nothing of jogging for miles through icy conditions. They looked at me with faint distaste—or perhaps even incomprehension—no doubt weighing up my fat-to-muscle ratio and finding it wanting.

"It was awful," I told Patrick, wondering whether I could order cheesecake without them all giving me the Death Stare. "His girlfriend and his best friend."

"You can't blame her," he said. "Are you really telling me you'd stick around if I was paralyzed from the neck down?"

"Of course I would."

"No, you wouldn't. And I wouldn't expect you to."

"Well, I would."

"But I wouldn't want you there. I wouldn't want someone staying with me out of pity."

"Who says it would be pity? You'd still be the same person underneath."

"No, I wouldn't. I wouldn't be anything like the same person." He wrinkled his nose. "I wouldn't want to live. Relying on other people for every little thing. Having strangers wipe your arse—Jesus. Think of all the things you couldn't do . . ." He shook his head. "No more running, no more cycling." He looked at me as if it had just occurred to him. "No more *sex*."

"Of course you could have sex. It's just that the woman would have to get on top."

"We'd be doomed, then."

"Funny."

"Besides, if you're paralyzed from the neck down I'm

guessing the . . . um . . . equipment doesn't work as it should."

I thought of Alicia. *I did try*, she said. *I really tried. For months.*

"I'm sure it does with some people. Anyway, there must be a way around these things if you . . . think imaginatively."

"Hah." Patrick took a sip of his water. "You'll have to ask him tomorrow. Look, you said he's horrible. Perhaps he was horrible before his accident. Perhaps that's the real reason she dumped him. Have you thought of that?"

"I don't know . . ." I thought of the photograph. "They looked like they were really happy together." Then again, what did a photograph prove? I had a framed photograph at home where I was beaming at Patrick like he had just pulled me from a burning building, yet in reality I had just called him an "utter dick" and he had responded with a hearty "Oh, piss off!"

Patrick had lost interest. "Hey, Jim . . . Jim, did you take a look at that new lightweight bike? Any good?"

I let him change the subject, thinking about what Alicia had said. I could well imagine Will pushing her away. But surely if you loved someone it was your job to stick with him? To help him through the depression? In sickness and in health, and all that?

I had started to feel a little guilty about the way we were discussing my employer. Especially when I realized that he probably endured it all the time. It was almost impossible not to speculate about the more intimate aspects of his life. Patrick nudged me.

"I'm thinking about doing the big one."

"The big what?"

"Triathlon. The Xtreme Viking. Sixty miles on a bike, thirty miles on foot, and a nice long swim in subzero Nordic seas."

The Viking was spoken about with reverence, those who had competed bearing their injuries like veterans of some distant and particularly brutal war. He was almost smacking his lips with anticipation. I looked at my boyfriend and wondered if he was actually an alien. I thought briefly that I had preferred him when he worked in telesales and couldn't pass a petrol station without stocking up on Mars bars.

"You're going to do it?"

"Why not? I've never been fitter."

I thought of all that extra training—the endless conversations about weight and distance, fitness and endurance. It was hard enough getting Patrick's attention these days at the best of times.

"You could do it with me," he said, although we both knew he didn't believe it.

"I'll leave you to it," I said. "Sure. Go for it."

And I ordered the cheesecake.

If I had thought the events of the previous day would create a thaw back at Granta House, I was wrong.

I greeted Will with a broad smile and a cheery hello, and he didn't even bother to look around from the window.

"Not a good day," Nathan murmured, as he shouldered his way into his coat.

It was a filthy, low-cloud sort of a morning, where the rain spat meanly against the windows and it was hard to imagine the sun coming out ever again. Even I felt glum on a day like this. It wasn't really a surprise that Will should be worse. I began to work my way through the morning's chores, telling myself all the while that it didn't matter. You didn't have to like your employer anyway, did you? Lots of people didn't. The photographs were stacked carefully in the bottom drawer, where I had placed them the previous day, and now, crouched on the floor, I began laying them out and sorting through them, assessing which frames I might be able to fix. I am quite good at fixing things. Besides, I thought it might be a useful way of killing time.

I had been doing this for about ten minutes when the discreet hum of the motorized wheelchair alerted me to Will's arrival.

He sat there in the doorway, looking at me. There were dark shadows under his eyes. Sometimes, Nathan told me, he barely slept at all. I didn't want to think how it would feel, to lie trapped in a bed you couldn't get out of with only dark thoughts to keep you company through the small hours.

"I thought I'd see if I could fix any of these frames," I said, holding one up. It was the picture of him bungee jumping. I tried to look cheerful. *He needs someone upbeat, someone positive.*

"Why?"

I blinked. "Well . . . I think some of these can be saved. I brought some wood glue with me, if you're happy for me to have a go at them. Or if you want to replace them I can pop into town during my lunch break and see if I can find some more. Or we could both go, if you fancied a trip out . . ."

"Who told you to start fixing them?"

His stare was unflinching.

Uh-oh, I thought. "I . . . I was just trying to help."

"You wanted to fix what I did yesterday."

"I—"

"Do you know what, Louisa? It would be nice—just for once—if someone paid attention to what I wanted. Me smashing those photographs was not an accident. It was not an attempt at radical interior design. It was because I actually don't want to look at them."

I got to my feet. "I'm sorry. I didn't think that—"

"You thought you knew best. Everyone thinks they know what I need. *Let's put the bloody photos back together. Give the poor invalid something to look at.* I don't want to have those bloody pictures staring at me every time I'm stuck in my bed until someone comes and bloody well gets me out again. Okay? Do you think you can get your head around that?"

I swallowed. "I wasn't going to fix the one of Alicia— I'm not that stupid . . . I just thought that in a while you might feel—"

"Oh Christ . . ." He turned away from me, his voice scathing. "Spare me the psychological therapy. Just go and read your bloody gossip magazines or whatever it is you do when you're not making tea."

My cheeks were aflame. I watched him maneuver in the narrow hallway, and my voice emerged even before I knew what I was doing.

"You don't have to behave like an arse."

The words rang out in the still air.

The wheelchair stopped. There was a long pause, and then he reversed and turned slowly, so that he was facing me, his hand on the little joystick.

"What?"

I faced him, my heart thumping. "Your friends got the shitty treatment. Fine. They probably deserved it. But I'm just here day after day trying to do the best job I can. So I would really appreciate it if you didn't make my life as unpleasant as you do everyone else's."

Will's eyes widened a little. There was a beat before he spoke again. "And what if I told you I didn't want you here?"

"I'm not employed by you. I'm employed by your mother. And unless she tells me she doesn't want me here anymore, I'm staying. Not because I particularly care about you, or like this stupid job, or want to change your life one way or another, but because I need the money. Okay? I really need the money."

Will Traynor's expression hadn't outwardly changed much but I thought I saw astonishment in there, as if he were unused to anyone disagreeing with him.

Oh hell, I thought, as the reality of what I had just done began to sink in. *I've really blown it this time.*

But Will just stared at me for a bit and, when I didn't look away, let out a small breath, as if about to say something unpleasant.

"Fair enough," he said, and he turned the wheelchair around. "Just put the photographs in the bottom drawer, will you? All of them."

And with a low hum, he was gone.

5

The thing about being catapulted into a whole new life—
or at least, shoved up so hard against someone else's life
that you might as well have your face pressed against
their window—is that it forces you to rethink your idea
of who you are. Or how you might seem to other people.

To my parents, I had in four short weeks become just
a few degrees more interesting. I was now the conduit to
a different world. My mother, in particular, asked me
daily questions about Granta House and its domestic
habits in the manner of a zoologist forensically examin-
ing some strange new creature and its habitat. "Does
Mrs. Traynor use linen napkins at every meal?" she
would ask, or "Do you think they vacuum every day, like
we do?" or "What do they do with their potatoes?"

She sent me off in the mornings with strict instructions
to find out what brand of loo roll they used, or whether
the sheets were a poly-cotton mix. It was a source of
great disappointment to her that most of the time I
couldn't actually remember. My mother was secretly
convinced that posh people lived like pigs—ever since I
had told her, at age six, of a well-spoken school friend
whose mother wouldn't let us play in their front room
"because we'd disturb the dust."

When I came home to report that, yes, the dog was
definitely allowed to eat in the kitchen, or that, no, the
Traynors didn't scrub their front step every day as my
mother did, she would purse her lips, glance sideways at

my father, and nod with quiet satisfaction, as if I had just confirmed everything she'd suspected about the slovenly ways of the upper classes.

Their dependence on my income, or perhaps the fact that they knew I didn't really like my job, meant that I also received a little more respect within the house. This didn't actually translate into much—in my dad's case, it meant that he had stopped calling me "lardarse," and, in my mother's, that there was usually a mug of tea waiting for me when I came home.

To Patrick, and to my sister, I was no different—still the butt of jokes, the recipient of hugs or kisses or sulks. I felt no different. I still looked the same, still dressed, according to Treena, like I had had a wrestling match in a charity shop.

I had no idea what most of the inhabitants of Granta House thought of me. Will was unreadable. To Nathan, I was, I suspected, just the latest in a long line of hired caregivers. He was friendly enough but a bit detached. I got the feeling he wasn't convinced I was going to be there for long. Mr. Traynor nodded at me politely when we passed in the hall, occasionally asking me how the traffic was, or whether I had settled in all right. I'm not sure he would have recognized me if he'd been introduced to me in another setting.

But to Mrs. Traynor—oh Lord—to Mrs. Traynor I was apparently the stupidest and most irresponsible person on the planet.

It had started with the photo frames. Nothing in that house escaped Mrs. Traynor's notice, and I should have known that the smashing of the frames would qualify as a seismic event. She quizzed me as to exactly how long I had left Will alone, what had prompted it, how swiftly I had cleared up the mess. She didn't actually criticize me—she was too genteel even to raise her voice—but the way she blinked slowly at my responses, her little "hmm-hmm" as I spoke, told me everything I needed to know. It came as no surprise when Nathan told me she was a magistrate.

She thought it might be a good idea if I didn't leave Will for so long next time, no matter how awkward the situation, *hmm*? She thought perhaps the next time I dusted I could make sure things weren't so close to the edge that they might accidentally get knocked to the floor, *hmm*? (She seemed to prefer to believe that it had been an accident.) She made me feel like a first-class idiot, and consequently I became a first-class idiot around her. She always arrived just when I had dropped something on the floor, or was struggling with the cooker dial, or she would be standing in the hallway looking mildly irritated as I stepped back in from collecting logs outside, as if I had been gone much longer than I actually had.

Weirdly, her attitude got to me more than Will's rudeness. A couple of times I had even been tempted to ask her outright whether there was something wrong. *You said that you were hiring me for my attitude rather than my professional skills*, I wanted to say. *Well, here I am, being cheery every ruddy day. Being robust, just as you wanted. So what's your problem?*

But Camilla Traynor was not the kind of woman you could have said that to. And besides, I got the feeling nobody in that house ever said anything direct to anyone else.

"Lily, our last girl, had rather a clever habit of using that pan for two vegetables at once" meant *You're making too much mess*.

"Perhaps you'd like a cup of tea, Will" actually meant *I have no idea what to say to you*.

"I think I've got some paperwork that needs sorting out" meant *You're being rude, and I'm going to leave the room*.

All pronounced with that slightly pained expression, and the slender fingers running up and down the chain with the crucifix. She was so held in, so restrained. She made my own mother look like Ozzy Osbourne. I smiled politely, pretended I hadn't noticed, and did the job I was paid to do.

Or, at least I tried.

"Why the hell are you trying to sneak carrots onto my fork?"

I glanced down at the plate. I had been watching the female television presenter and wondering what my hair would look like dyed the same color.

"Uh? I didn't."

"You did. You mashed them up and tried to hide them in the gravy. I saw you."

I blushed. He was right. I was sitting feeding Will, while both of us vaguely watched the lunchtime news. The meal was roast beef with mashed potato. His mother had told me to put three sorts of vegetables on the plate, even though he had said quite clearly that he didn't want vegetables that day. I don't think there was a meal that I was instructed to prepare that wasn't nutritionally balanced to within an inch of its life.

"Why are you trying to sneak carrots into me?"

"I'm not."

"So there are no carrots in that?"

I gazed at the tiny pieces of orange. "Well . . . okay . . ."

He was waiting, eyebrows raised.

"Um . . . I suppose I thought vegetables would be good for you?"

It was part deference to Mrs. Traynor, part force of habit. I was so used to feeding Thomas, whose vegetables had to be mashed to a paste and hidden under mounds of potato, or secreted in bits of pasta. Every fragment we got past him felt like a little victory.

"Let me get this straight. You think a teaspoon of carrot would improve my quality of life?"

It *was* pretty stupid when he put it like that. But I had learned it was important not to look cowed by anything Will said or did.

"I take your point," I said evenly. "I won't do it again."

And then, out of nowhere, Will Traynor laughed. It exploded out of him in a gasp, as if it were entirely unexpected.

"For Christ's sake." He shook his head.

I stared at him.

"What the hell else have you been sneaking into my food? You'll be telling me to open the tunnel so that Mr. Train can deliver some mushy Brussels sprouts to the red bloody station next."

I considered this for a minute. "No," I said, straight-faced. "I deal only with Mr. Fork. Mr. Fork does not look like a train."

Thomas had told me so, very firmly, some months previously.

"Did my mother put you up to this?"

"No. Look, Will, I'm sorry. I just . . . wasn't thinking."

"Like that's unusual."

"All right, all right. I'll take the bloody carrots off, if they really upset you so much."

"It's not the bloody carrots that upset me. It's having them sneaked into my food by a madwoman who addresses the cutlery as Mr. and Mrs. Fork."

"It was a joke. Look, let me take the carrots and—"

He turned away from me. "I don't want anything else. Just do me a cup of tea." He called out after me as I left the room, "And don't try and sneak a bloody zucchini into it."

Nathan walked in as I was finishing the dishes. "He's in a good mood," he said, as I handed him a mug.

"Is he?" I was eating my sandwiches in the kitchen. It was bitterly cold outside, and somehow the house hadn't felt quite as unfriendly lately.

"He says you're trying to poison him. But he said it— you know—in a good way."

I felt weirdly pleased by this information.

"Yes . . . well . . . ," I said, trying to hide it. "Give me time."

"He's talking a bit more too. We've had weeks where he would hardly say a thing, but he's definitely up for a bit of a chat the last few days."

I thought of Will telling me if I didn't stop bloody whistling he'd be forced to run me over. "I think your definition of chatty and mine are a bit different."

"Well, we had a bit of a chat about the cricket. And I gotta tell you"—Nathan dropped his voice—"Mrs. T asked me a week or so back if I thought you were doing okay. I said I thought you were very professional, but I knew that wasn't what she meant. Then yesterday she came in and told me she'd heard you guys laughing."

I thought back to the previous evening. "He was laughing *at* me," I said. Will had found it hilarious that I didn't know what pesto was. I had told him supper was "the pasta in the green gravy."

"Ah, she doesn't care about that. It's just been a long time since he laughed at anything."

It was true. Will and I seemed to have found an easier way of being around each other. It involved mainly him being rude to me, and me occasionally being rude back. He told me I did something badly, and I told him if it really mattered to him then he could ask me nicely. He swore at me, or called me a pain in the backside, and I told him he should try being without this particular pain in the backside and see how far it got him. It was a bit forced but it seemed to work for both of us. Sometimes it even seemed like a relief to him that there was someone prepared to be rude to him, to contradict him or tell him he was being horrible. I got the feeling that everyone had tiptoed around him since his accident—apart from perhaps Nathan, who Will seemed to treat with an automatic respect, and who was probably impervious to any of his sharper comments anyway. Nathan was like an armored vehicle in human form.

"You just make sure you're the butt of more of his jokes, okay?"

I put my mug in the sink. "I don't think that's going to be a problem."

The other big change, apart from atmospheric conditions inside the house, was that Will didn't ask me to leave him alone quite as often, and a couple of afternoons had even asked me if I wanted to stay and watch a film with him. I hadn't minded too much when it was *The Terminator*—even though I have seen all the *Terminator* films—but when he showed me the French film with subtitles, I took a quick look at the cover and said I thought I'd probably give it a miss.

"Why?"

I shrugged. "I don't like films with subtitles."

"That's like saying you don't like films with actors in them. Don't be ridiculous. What is it you don't like? The fact that you're required to read something as well as watch something?"

"I just don't really like foreign films."

"Everything after *Local* bloody *Hero* has been a foreign film. D'you think Hollywood is a suburb of Birmingham?"

"Funny."

He couldn't believe it when I admitted I'd never actually watched a film with subtitles. But my parents tended to stake ownership of the remote control in the evenings, and Patrick would be about as likely to watch a foreign film as he would be to suggest we take night classes in crochet. The multiplex in our nearest town showed only the latest shoot-'em-ups or romantic comedies and was so infested with catcalling kids in hoodies that most people around the town rarely bothered.

"You have to watch this film, Louisa. In fact, I order you to watch this film." Will moved his chair back, and nodded toward the armchair. "There. You sit there. Don't move until it's over. Never watched a foreign film. For Christ's sake," he muttered.

It was an old film, about a hunchback who inherits a house in the French countryside, and Will said it was based on a famous book, but I can't say I'd ever heard of it. I spent the first twenty minutes feeling a bit fidgety, irritated by the subtitles and wondering if Will was going to get grouchy if I told him I needed the loo.

And then something happened. I stopped thinking about how hard it was listening and reading at the same time, forgot Will's pill timetable, and whether Mrs. Traynor would think I was slacking, and I started to get anxious about the poor man and his family, who were being tricked by unscrupulous neighbors. By the time Hunchback Man died, I was sobbing silently, snot running into my sleeve.

"So," Will said, appearing at my side. He glanced at me slyly. "You didn't enjoy that at all."

I looked up and found to my surprise that it was dark outside. "You're going to gloat now, aren't you?" I muttered, reaching for the box of tissues.

"A bit. I'm just amazed that you can have reached the ripe old age of—what was it?"

"Twenty-six."

"Twenty-six, and never have watched a film with subtitles." He watched me mop my eyes.

I glanced down at the tissue and realized I had no mascara left. "I hadn't realized it was compulsory," I grumbled.

"Okay. So what do you do with yourself, Louisa Clark, if you don't watch films?"

I balled my tissue in my fist. "You want to know what I do when I'm not here?"

"You were the one who wanted us to get to know each other. So come on, tell me about yourself."

He had this way of talking where you could never quite be sure that he wasn't mocking you. I was waiting for the payoff. "Why?" I said. "Why do you want to know all of a sudden?"

"Oh, for Christ's sake. It's hardly a state secret, your social life, is it?" He had begun to look irritated.

"I don't know . . . ," I said. "I go for a drink at the pub.

I watch a bit of telly. I go and watch my boyfriend when he does his running. Nothing unusual."

"You watch your boyfriend running."

"Yes."

"But you don't run yourself."

"No. I'm not really"—I glanced down at my chest—"built for it."

That made him smile.

"And what else?"

"What do you mean, what else?"

"Hobbies? Traveling? Places you like to go?"

He was beginning to sound like my old careers teacher.

I tried to think. "I don't really have any hobbies. I read a bit. I like clothes."

"Handy," he said, drily.

"You asked. I'm not really a hobby person." My voice had become strangely defensive. "I don't do much, okay? I work and then I go home."

"Where do you live?"

"On the other side of the castle. Renfrew Road."

He looked blank. Of course he did. There was little human traffic between the two sides of the castle. "It's off the dual carriageway. Near the McDonald's."

He nodded, although I wasn't sure he really knew where I was talking about.

"Holidays?"

"I've been to Spain, with Patrick. My boyfriend," I added. "When I was a kid we only really went to Dorset. Or Tenby. My aunt lives in Tenby."

"And what do you want?"

"What do I want what?"

"From your life?"

I blinked. "That's a bit deep, isn't it?"

"Only generally. I'm not asking you to psychoanalyze yourself. I'm just asking, what do you want? Get married? Pop out some ankle biters? Dream career? Travel the world?"

There was a long pause.

I think I knew my answer would disappoint him even before I said the words aloud. "I don't know. I've never really thought about it."

———

On Friday we went to the hospital. I'm glad I hadn't known about Will's appointment before I arrived that morning, as I would have lain awake all night fretting about having to drive him there. I can drive, yes. But I say I can drive in the same way that I say I can speak French. Yes, I took the relevant exam and passed. But I haven't used that particular skill more than once a year since I did so. The thought of loading Will and his chair into the adapted minivan and carting him safely to and from the next town filled me with utter terror.

For weeks I had wished that my working day involved some escape from that house. Now I would have done anything just to stay indoors. I located his hospital card among the folders of stuff to do with his health—great fat binders divided into "transport," "insurance," "living with disability," and "appointments." I grabbed the card and checked that it had today's date. A little bit of me was hoping that Will had been wrong.

"Is your mother coming?"

"No. She doesn't come to my appointments."

I couldn't hide my surprise. I had thought she would want to oversee every aspect of his treatment.

"She used to," Will said. "Now we have an agreement."

"Is Nathan coming?"

I was kneeling in front of him. I had been so nervous that I had dropped some of his lunch down his lap and was now trying in vain to mop it up, so that a good patch of his trousers was sopping wet. Will hadn't said anything, except to tell me to please stop apologizing, but it hadn't helped my general sense of jitteriness.

"Why?"

"No reason." I didn't want him to know how fearful I felt. I had spent much of that morning—time I usually spent cleaning—reading and rereading the instruction manual for the chairlift but I was still dreading the moment when I was solely responsible for lifting him two feet into the air.

"Come on, Clark. What's the problem?"

"Okay. I just . . . I just thought it would be easier the first time if there was someone else there who knew the ropes."

"As opposed to me," he said.

"That's not what I meant."

"Because I can't possibly be expected to know anything about my own care?"

"Do you operate the chairlift?" I said, baldly. "You can tell me exactly what to do, can you?"

He watched me, his gaze level. If he had been spoiling for a fight, he appeared to change his mind. "Fair point. Yes, he's coming. He's a useful extra pair of hands. Plus I thought you'd work yourself into less of a state if you had him there."

"I'm not in a state," I protested.

"Evidently." He glanced down at his lap, which I was still mopping with a cloth. I had got the pasta sauce off, but he was soaked. "So, am I going as an incontinent?"

"I'm not finished." I plugged in the hair dryer and directed the nozzle toward his crotch.

As the hot air blasted onto his trousers he raised his eyebrows.

"Yes, well," I said. "It's not exactly what I expected to be doing on a Friday afternoon either."

"You really are tense, aren't you?"

I could feel him studying me.

"Oh, lighten up, Clark. I'm the one having scalding hot air directed at my genitals."

I didn't respond. I heard his voice over the roar of the hair dryer.

"Come on, what's the worst that could happen—I end up in a wheelchair?"

It may sound stupid, but I couldn't help but laugh. It was the closest Will had come to actually trying to make me feel better.

———

The car looked like a normal people carrier from the outside, but when the rear passenger door was unlocked a ramp descended from the side and lowered to the ground. With Nathan looking on, I guided Will's outside chair (he had a separate one for traveling) squarely onto the ramp, checked the electrical lock-down brake, and programmed it to slowly lift him up into the car. Nathan slid into the other passenger seat, belted him, and secured the wheels. Trying to stop my hands from trembling, I got into the driver's seat, released the hand brake, and drove slowly down the drive toward the hospital.

Away from home, Will appeared to shrink a little. It was chilly outside, and Nathan and I had bundled him up into his scarf and thick coat, but still he grew quieter, his jaw set, somehow diminished by the greater space of his surroundings. Every time I looked into my rearview mirror (which was often—I was terrified even with Nathan there that somehow the chair would break loose from its moorings) he was gazing out the window, his expression impenetrable. Even when I stalled or braked too hard, which I did several times, he just winced a little and waited while I sorted myself out.

By the time we reached the hospital I had actually broken out in a fine sweat. I drove around the hospital car park three times, too afraid to reverse into any but the largest of spaces, until I could sense that the two men were beginning to lose patience. Then, finally, I lowered the ramp and Nathan helped roll Will's chair out onto the tarmac.

"Good job," Nathan said, clapping me on the back as he let himself out, but I found it hard to believe it had been.

There are things you don't notice until you accompany someone with a wheelchair. One is how rubbish most pavements are, pockmarked with badly patched holes, or just plain uneven. Walking slowly next to Will as he wheeled himself along, I saw how every uneven slab caused him to jolt painfully, or how often he had to steer carefully around some potential obstacle. Nathan pretended not to notice, but I saw him watching too. Will just looked grim-faced and resolute.

The other thing is how inconsiderate most drivers are. They park up against the sloped cutouts on the sidewalks, or so close together that there is no way for a wheelchair to actually cross the road. I was shocked, and a couple of times even tempted to leave some rude note tucked into a windscreen wiper, but Nathan and Will seemed used to it. Nathan pointed out a suitable crossing place and, each of us flanking Will, we finally crossed.

Will had not said a single word since leaving the house.

The hospital itself was a gleaming low-rise building, the immaculate reception area more like that of some modernistic hotel, perhaps testament to private insurance. I held back as Will told the receptionist his name, and then followed him and Nathan down a long corridor. Nathan was carrying a huge backpack that contained anything that Will might be likely to need during his short visit, from beakers to spare clothes. He had packed it in front of me that morning, detailing every possible eventuality. "I guess it's a good thing we don't have to do this too often," he had said, catching my appalled expression.

I didn't follow Will into the appointment. Nathan and I sat on the comfortable chairs outside the consultant's room. There was no hospital smell, and there were fresh flowers in a vase on the windowsill. Not just any old flowers, either. Huge exotic things that I didn't know the names of, artfully arranged in minimalist clumps.

"What are they doing in there?" I said after we had been there half an hour.

Nathan looked up from his book. "It's just his six-month checkup."

"What, to see if he's getting any better?"

Nathan put his book down. "He's not getting any better. It's a spinal cord injury."

"But you do physio and stuff with him."

"That's to try and keep his physical condition up—to stop him atrophying and his bones demineralizing, his legs pooling, that kind of thing."

When he spoke again, his voice was gentle, as if he thought he might disappoint me. "He's not going to walk again, Louisa. That only happens in Hollywood movies. All we're doing is trying to keep him out of pain, and keep up whatever range of movement he has."

"Does he do this stuff for you? The physio stuff? He doesn't seem to want to do anything that I suggest."

Nathan wrinkled his nose. "He does it, but I don't think his heart's in it. When I first came, he was determined. He'd come pretty far in rehab, but after a year with no improvement I think he found it tough to keep believing it was worth it."

"Do you think he should keep trying?"

Nathan stared at the floor. "Honestly? He's a C5-6 quadriplegic. That means nothing works below about here . . ." He placed a hand on the upper part of his chest. "They haven't worked out how to fix a spinal cord yet."

I stared at the door, thinking about Will's face as we drove along in the winter sunshine, the beaming face of the man on the skiing holiday. "There are all sorts of medical advances taking place, though, right? I mean . . . somewhere like this . . . they must be working on stuff all the time."

"It's a pretty good hospital," he said evenly.

"Where there's life, and all that?"

Nathan looked at me, then back at his book. "Sure," he said.

———

I went to get a coffee at a quarter to three, on Nathan's say-so. He said these appointments could go on for some time, and that he would hold the fort until I got back. I dawdled a little in the reception area, flicking through the magazines in the newsagent's, lingering over chocolate bars.

Perhaps predictably, I got lost trying to find my way back to the corridor and had to ask several nurses where I should go, two of whom didn't even know. When I got there, the coffee cooling in my hand, the corridor was empty. As I drew closer, I could see that the consultant's door was ajar. I hesitated outside, but I could hear Mrs. Traynor's voice in my ears all the time now, criticizing me for leaving him. I had done it again.

"So we'll see you in three months' time, Mr. Traynor," a voice was saying. "I've adjusted those antispasm meds and I'll make sure someone calls you with the results of the tests. Probably Monday."

I heard Will's voice. "Can I get these from the pharmacy downstairs?"

"Yes. Here. They should be able to give you some more of those too."

A woman's voice. "Shall I take that folder?"

I realized they must have been about to leave. I knocked, and someone called for me to come in. Two sets of eyes swiveled toward me.

"I'm sorry," said the consultant, rising from his chair. "I thought you were the physio."

"I'm Will's . . . helper," I said, hanging on to the door. Will was braced forward in his chair as Nathan pulled down his shirt. "Sorry—I thought you were done."

"Just give us a minute, will you, Louisa?" Will's voice cut into the room.

Muttering my apologies, I backed out, my face burning.

It wasn't the sight of Will's uncovered body that had shocked me, slim and scarred as it was. It wasn't the vaguely irritated look of the consultant, the same sort of look that Mrs. Traynor gave me day after day—a look that made me realize I was still the same blundering idiot, even if I did earn a higher hourly rate.

No, it was the livid red lines scoring Will's wrists, the long, jagged scars that couldn't be disguised, no matter how swiftly Nathan pulled down Will's sleeves.

6

The snow came so suddenly that I left home under a bright blue sky and not half an hour later I was headed past a castle that looked like a cake decoration, surrounded by a layer of thick white icing.

I trudged up the drive, my footsteps muffled and my toes already numb, shivering under my too-thin Chinese silk coat. A whirl of thick white flakes emerged from an iron-gray infinity, almost obscuring Granta House, blotting out sound, and slowing the world to an unnatural pace. Beyond the neatly trimmed hedge, cars drove past with a newfound caution, pedestrians slipped and squealed on the sidewalks. I pulled my scarf up over my nose and wished I had worn something more suitable than ballet pumps and a velvet minidress.

To my surprise, it wasn't Nathan who opened the door but Will's father.

"He's in bed," he said, glancing up at the sky from the doorway. "He's not too good. I was just wondering whether to call the doctor."

"Where's Nathan?"

"Morning off. Of course, it would be today. Bloody agency nurse came and went in six seconds flat. If this snow keeps on I'm not sure what we'll do later." He shrugged, as if these things couldn't be helped, and disappeared back down the corridor, apparently relieved that he no longer had to be responsible. "You know what he needs, yes?" he called over his shoulder.

I took off my coat and shoes and, as I knew Mrs.

Traynor was in court (she marked her dates on a diary in Will's kitchen), put my wet socks over a radiator to dry. A pair of Will's were in the clean-washing basket, so I put them on. They looked comically large on me but it was heaven to have warm, dry feet. Will didn't respond when I called out, so after a while I made him a drink, knocked quietly, and poked my head around the door. In the dim light I could just make out the shape under the duvet. He was fast asleep.

I took a step backward, closed the door behind me, and began working my way through the morning's tasks.

My mother seemed to glean an almost physical satisfaction from a well-ordered house. I had been vacuuming and cleaning daily for a month now, and I still couldn't see the attraction. I suspected there would never be a point in my life when I wouldn't prefer somebody else to do it.

But on a day like today, when Will was confined to bed, and the world seemed to have stilled outside, I could also see there was a kind of meditative pleasure in working my way from one end of the annex to the other. While I dusted and polished, I took the radio from room to room with me, keeping the volume low so that I didn't disturb Will. Periodically I poked my head around the door, just to see that he was breathing, and it was only when it got to one o'clock and he still hadn't woken up that I started to feel a little anxious.

I filled the log basket, noting that several inches of snow had now settled. I made Will a fresh drink, and then knocked. When I knocked again, I did so loudly.

"Yes?" His voice was hoarse, as if I had woken him.

"It's me." When he didn't respond, I said, "Louisa. Am I okay to come in?"

"I'm hardly doing the Dance of the Seven Veils."

The room was shadowed, the curtains still drawn. I walked in, letting my eyes adjust to the light. Will was on one side, one arm bent in front of him as if to prop himself up, as he had been before when I looked in. Sometimes it was easy to forget he would not be able to turn over by himself. His hair stuck up on one side, and a duvet was tucked neatly around him. The smell of warm, unwashed male filled the room—not unpleasant, but still a little startling as part of a working day.

"What can I do? Do you want your drink?"

"I need to change position."

I put the drink down on a chest of drawers, and walked over to the bed. "What . . . what do you want me to do?"

He swallowed carefully, as if it were painful. "Lift and turn me, then raise the back of the bed. Here . . ." He nodded for me to come closer. "Put your arms under mine, link your hands behind my back, and then pull back. Keep your backside on the bed and that way you shouldn't strain your lower back."

I couldn't pretend this wasn't a bit weird. I reached around him, the scent of him filling my nostrils, his skin warm against mine. I could not have been in any closer unless I had begun nibbling on his ear. The thought made me mildly hysterical, and I struggled to keep myself together.

"What?"

"Nothing." I took a breath, linked my hands, and adjusted my position until I felt I had him securely. He was broader than I had expected, somehow heavier. And then, on a count of three, I pulled back.

"Jesus," he exclaimed, into my shoulder.

"What?" I nearly dropped him.

"Your hands are bloody freezing."

"Yes. Well, if you bothered to get out of bed, you'd know that it's actually snowing outside."

I was half joking, but now I realized his skin was hot under his T-shirt—an intense heat that seemed to come from deep within him. He groaned slightly as I adjusted him against the pillow, and I tried to make my movements as slow and gentle as possible. He pointed out the remote control device that would bring his head and shoulders up. "Not too much, though," he murmured. "A bit dizzy."

I turned on the bedside light, ignoring his vague protest, so that I could see his face. "Will—are you okay?" I had to say it twice before he answered me.

"Not my best day."

"Do you need painkillers?"

"Yes . . . strong ones."

"Maybe some paracetamol?"

He lay back against the cool pillow with a sigh.

I gave him the beaker, watched him swallow.

"Thank you," he said afterward, and I felt suddenly uneasy.

Will never thanked me for anything.

He closed his eyes, and for a while I just stood in the doorway and watched him, his chest rising and falling under his T-shirt, his mouth slightly open. His breathing was shallow, and perhaps a little more labored than on other days. But I had never seen him out of his chair, and I wasn't sure whether it was something to do with the pressure of lying down.

"Go," he muttered.

I left.

———

Mum sent me a text message at 12:30 P.M., telling me that my father couldn't get the car down the road. "Don't set out for home without ringing us first," she instructed. I wasn't sure what she thought she was going to do—send Dad out with a sledge and a St. Bernard?

I listened to the local news on the radio—the motorway snarl-ups, train stoppages, and temporary school closures that the unexpected blizzard had brought with it. I went back into Will's room and looked at him again. I didn't like his color. He was pale, high points of something bright on each cheek.

"Will?" I said softly.

He didn't stir.

"Will?"

I began to feel the faint stirrings of panic. I said his name twice more, loudly. There was no response. Finally, I leaned over him. There was no obvious movement in his face, nothing I could see in his chest. His breath—I should be able to feel his breath. I put my face down close to his, trying to detect an out breath. When I couldn't, I reached out and touched his face gently.

He flinched, his eyes snapping open, just inches from my own.

"I'm sorry," I said, jumping back.

He blinked, glancing around the room, as if he had been somewhere far from home.

"It's Lou," I said, when I wasn't sure if he had recognized me.

His expression was one of mild exasperation. "I know."

"Do you want some soup?"

"No. Thank you." He closed his eyes.

"More painkillers?"

There was a faint sheen of sweat on his cheekbone. His duvet felt vaguely hot and sweaty. It made me nervous.

"Is there something I should be doing? I mean, if Nathan can't get here?"

"No . . . I'm fine," he murmured, and closed his eyes again.

I went through the folder, trying to work out if I was missing something. I opened the medical cabinet, the boxes of rubber gloves, and gauze dressings, and realized I had no idea at all what I should do with any of it. I rang the intercom to speak to Will's father, but the ringing sound disappeared into an empty house. I could hear it echoing beyond the annex door.

I was about to ring Mrs. Traynor when the back door opened, and Nathan stepped in, wrapped in layers of bulky clothing, a woolen scarf and hat almost obscuring his head. He brought with him a whoosh of cold air and a light flurry of snow.

It felt like the house had suddenly woken from a dreamlike state.

"Oh, thank God you're here," I said. "He's not well. He's been asleep most of the morning and he's hardly drunk anything. I didn't know what to do."

Nathan shrugged off his coat. "Had to walk all the way here. The buses have stopped running."

I set about making him some tea as he went to check on Will.

He reappeared before the kettle had even finished boiling. "He's burning up," he said. "How long has he been like this?"

"All morning. I did think he was hot, but he said he just wanted to sleep."

"Jesus. All morning? Didn't you know he can't regulate his own temperature?" He pushed past me and began rummaging around in the medicine cabinet. "Antibiotics. The strong ones." He held up a jar and emptied one into the pestle and mortar, grinding it furiously.

I hovered behind him. "I gave him a paracetamol."

"Might as well have given him an M&M."

"I didn't know. Nobody said. I've been wrapping him up."

"It's in the bloody folder. Look, Will doesn't sweat like we do. In fact he doesn't sweat at all from the point of his injury downward. It means if he gets a slight chill his temperature gauge goes haywire. Go find the fan. We'll move that in there until he cools down. And a damp towel, to put around the back of his neck. We won't be able to get him to a doctor until the snow stops. Bloody agency nurse. They should have picked this up in the morning."

Nathan was crosser than I'd ever seen him. He was no longer really even talking to me.

I ran for the fan.

It took almost forty minutes for Will's temperature to return to an acceptable level. While we waited for the extra-strong fever medication to take effect, I placed a towel over his forehead and another around his neck, as Nathan instructed. We stripped him down, covered his chest with a fine cotton sheet, and set the fan to play over it. Without sleeves, the scars on his arms were clearly exposed. We all pretended I couldn't see them.

Will endured all this attention in near silence, answering Nathan's questions with a yes or no, so indistinct sometimes that I wasn't sure if he knew what he was saying. I realized, now that I could see him in the light, that he looked really, properly ill, and I felt terrible for having failed to grasp it. I said I was sorry until Nathan told me it had become irritating.

"Right," he said. "You need to watch what I'm doing. It's possible you may need to do this alone later."

I didn't feel I could protest. But I found it hard not to feel squeamish as Nathan peeled down the waist of Will's pajama bottoms, revealing a pale strip of bare stomach, and carefully removed the gauze dressing around the little tube in his abdomen, cleaning it gently and replacing the dressing. He showed me how to change the bag on the bed, explained why it must always be lower than Will's body, and I was surprised at how matter-of-fact I was about walking out of the room with the pouch of warm fluid. I was glad that Will wasn't really watching me—not just because he would have made some sharp comment, but because I felt that me witnessing some part of this intimate routine would in some way have embarrassed him too.

"And that's it," Nathan said. Finally, an hour later, Will lay dozing, lying on fresh cotton sheets and looking, if not exactly well, then not scarily ill.

"Let him sleep. But wake him after a couple of hours

and make sure you get the best part of a beaker of fluids into him. More fever meds at five, okay? His temperature will probably shoot up again in the last hour, but nothing more before five."

I scribbled everything down on a notepad. I was afraid of getting anything wrong.

"Now, you're going to need to repeat what we just did this evening. You're okay with that?" Nathan wrapped himself up like an Inuit and headed out into the snow. "Just read the folder. And don't panic. Any problems, you just call me. I'll talk you through it all. I'll get back here again if I really have to."

I stayed in Will's room after Nathan left. I was too afraid not to. In the corner was an old leather armchair with a reading light, perhaps dating from Will's previous life, and I curled up on it with a book of short stories that I had pulled from the bookcase.

It was strangely peaceful in that room. Through the crack in the curtains I could see the outside world, blanketed in white, still and beautiful. Inside it was warm and silent, only the odd tick and hiss of the central heating to interrupt my thoughts. I read, and occasionally I glanced up and checked Will sleeping peacefully, and I realized that there had never been a point in my life before when I had just sat in silence and done nothing. You don't grow up used to silence in a house like mine, with its never-ending vacuuming, television blaring, and shrieking. During the rare moments that the television was off, Dad would put on his old Elvis records and play them at full blast. A café too is a constant buzz of noise and clatter.

Here, I could hear my thoughts. I could almost hear my heartbeat. I realized, to my surprise, that I quite liked it.

At five, my mobile phone signaled a text message. Will stirred, and I leaped out of the chair, anxious to get it before it disturbed him.

> *No trains. Is there any chance you could stay over*
> *tonight?*
> *Nathan cannot do it. Camilla Traynor.*

I didn't really think about it before I typed back.

> *No problem.*

I rang my parents and told them that I would stay over. My mother sounded relieved. When I told her I was going to get paid for sleeping over, she sounded overjoyed.

"Did you hear that, Bernard?" she said, her hand half over the phone. "They're paying her to sleep now."

I could hear my father's exclamation. "Praise the Lord. She's found her dream career."

I sent a text message to Patrick, telling him that I had been asked to stay at work and I would ring him later. The message came back within seconds.

> *Going cross-country snow running tonight.*
> *Good practice for Norway! X P.*

I wondered how it was possible for someone to get so excited at the thought of jogging through subzero temperatures in a vest and pants.

Will slept. I cooked myself some food, and defrosted some soup in case he wanted some later. I got the log fire going in case he felt well enough to go into the living room. I read another of the short stories and wondered how long it had been since I had bought myself a book. I had loved reading as a child, but I couldn't remember reading anything except magazines since. Treena was the reader. It was almost as if by picking up a book I felt like I was invading her patch. I thought about her and Thomas disappearing to the university and realized I still didn't know whether it made me feel happy or sad—or something a bit complicated in between.

Nathan rang at seven. He seemed relieved that I was staying over.

"I couldn't reach Mr. Traynor," I told him. "I even rang their landline number, but it went straight through to answerphone."

"Yeah. Well. He'll be gone."

"Gone?"

I felt a sudden instinctive panic at the idea that it would be just Will and me in the house all night. I was afraid of getting something fundamental wrong again, of jeopardizing Will's health. "Should I call Mrs. Traynor, then?"

There was a short silence on the other end of the phone. "No. Best not."

"But—"

"Look, Lou, he often . . . he often goes somewhere else when Mrs. T stays over in town."

It took me a minute or two to grasp what he was saying.

"Oh."

"It's just good that you're there, that's all. If you're sure Will's looking better, I'll be back first thing in the morning."

———

There are normal hours, and then there are invalid hours, when time stalls and slips, when life—real life—seems to exist at one remove. I watched some television, ate, and cleared up the kitchen, drifting around the annex in silence. Finally, I let myself back into Will's room.

He stirred as I closed the door, half lifting his head. "What time is it, Clark?" His voice was slightly muffled by the pillow.

"Quarter past eight."

He let his head drop, and digested this. "Can I have a drink?"

There was no sharpness to him now, no edge. It was as if being ill had finally made him vulnerable. I gave him a drink and turned on the bedside light. I perched on the side of his bed and felt his forehead, as my mother might have done when I was a child. He was still a little warm, but nothing like he had been.

"Cool hands."

"You complained about them earlier."

"Did I?" He sounded genuinely surprised.

"Would you like some soup?"

"No."

"Are you comfortable?"

I never knew how much discomfort he was in, but I suspected it was more than he let on.

"The other side would be good. Just roll me. I don't need to sit up."

I climbed across the bed and moved him over, as gently as I could. He no longer radiated a sinister heat, just the ordinary warmth of a body that had spent time under a duvet.

"Can I do anything else?"

"Shouldn't you be heading home?"

"It's okay," I said. "I'm staying over."

Outside, the last of the light had long been extinguished. The snow was still falling. Where it caught the porch glow through the window it was bathed in a pale-gold, melancholy light. We sat there in peaceful silence, watching its hypnotic descent.

"Can I ask you something?" I said, finally. I could see his hands on top of the sheet. It seemed so strange that they should look so ordinary, so strong, and yet be so useless.

"I suspect you're going to."

"What happened?" I kept wondering about the marks on his wrists. It was the one question I couldn't ask directly.

He opened one eye. "How did I get like this?"

When I nodded, he closed his eyes again. "Motorbike accident. Not mine. I was an innocent pedestrian."

"I thought it would be skiing or bungee jumping or something."

"Everyone does. God's little joke. I was crossing the road outside my home. Not this place," he said. "My London home."

I stared at the books in his bookshelf. Among the novels, the well-thumbed Penguin paperbacks, were business titles: *Corporate Law*, *TakeOver*, directories of names I did not recognize.

"And there was no way you could carry on with your job?"

"No. Nor the apartment, the holidays, the life . . . I believe you met my ex-girlfriend." The break in his voice couldn't disguise the bitterness. "But I should apparently be grateful, as for some time they didn't think I was going to live at all."

"Do you hate it? Living here, I mean?"

"Yes."

"Is there any way you might be able to live in London again?"

"Not like this, no."

"But you might improve. I mean, there are loads of advances in this kind of injury."

Will closed his eyes again.

I waited, and then I adjusted the pillow behind his head and the duvet around his chest. "Sorry," I said, sitting upright. "If I ask too many questions. Do you want me to leave?"

"No. Stay for a bit. Talk to me." He swallowed. His eyes opened again and his gaze slid up to mine. He looked unbearably tired. "Tell me something good."

I hesitated a moment, then I leaned back against the pillows beside him. We sat there in the near dark, watching the briefly illuminated flakes of snow disappear into the black night.

"You know . . . I used to say that to my dad," I said, finally. "But if I told you what he used to say back, you'd think I was insane."

"More than I do?"

"When I had a nightmare or was sad or frightened about something, he used to sing . . ." I started to laugh. "Oh . . . I can't."

"Go on."

"He used to sing me the 'Molahonkey Song.'"

"The what?"

"The 'Molahonkey Song.' I used to think everyone knew it."

"Trust me, Clark," he murmured, "I am a Molahonkey virgin."

I took a deep breath, closed my eyes, and began to sing.

> I wi-li-lished I li-li-lived in Molahonkey la-la-
>   land
> The la-la-land where I-li-li was bo-lo-lo-lo-lo-lo-
>   lorn
> So I-li-li could play-la-lay my o-lo-lold banjo-
>   lo-lo
> My o-lo-lold ban-jo-lo-lo won't go-lo-lo-lo-lo-
>   lo-lo.

"Jesus Christ."

I took another breath.

> I too-lo-look it to-lo-lo the me-le-lender's sho-
>   lo-lop to
> See-lee-lee what they-le-ley could do-lo-lo-lo-
>   lo-lo-lo
> They sai-lai-laid to me-le-le your stri-li-lings are
>   sho-lo-lot
> They're no-lo-lo more u-lu-luse to you-lo-lo-lo-
>   lo-lo-loo.

There was a short silence.

"You are insane. Your whole family is insane."

"But it worked."

"And you are a God-awful singer. I hope your dad was better."

"I think what you meant to say was, 'Thank you, Miss Clark, for attempting to entertain me.'"

"I suppose it makes about as much sense as most of the psychotherapeutic help I've received. Okay, Clark," he said, "tell me something else. Something that doesn't involve singing."

I thought for a bit.

"Um . . . okay, well . . . you were looking at my shoes the other day."

"Hard not to."

"Well, my mum can date my unusual shoe thing back to when I was three. She bought me a pair of bright turquoise glittery wellies; they were quite unusual back then—kids used to just have those green ones, or maybe red if you were lucky. And she said from the day she brought them home I refused to take them off. I wore them to bed, in the bath, to nursery school, all through the summer. My favorite outfit was those glitter boots and my bumblebee tights."

"Bumblebee tights?"

"Black and yellow stripes."

"Gorgeous."

"That's a bit harsh."

"Well, it's true. They sound revolting."

"They might sound revolting to you, but astonishingly, Will Traynor, not all girls get dressed just to please men."

"Bullshit."

"No, it's not."

"Everything women do is with men in mind. Everything anyone does is with sex in mind. Haven't you read *The Red Queen*?"

"I have no idea what you're talking about. But I can assure you I'm not sitting on your bed singing the 'Mola-honkey Song' because I'm trying to get my leg over. And when I was three, I just really, really liked having stripy legs."

I realized that the anxiety that had held me in its grip all day was slowly ebbing away with every one of Will's comments. I was no longer in sole charge of a poorly quadriplegic. It was just me, sitting next to a particularly sarcastic bloke, having a chat.

"So come on, then, what happened to these gorgeous glittery wellies?"

"She had to throw them away. I got terrible athlete's foot."

"Delightful."

"And she threw the tights away too."

"Why?"

"I never found out. But it broke my heart. I have never found a pair of tights I loved like that again. They don't do them anymore. Or if they do, they don't make them for grown women."

"Strange, that."

"Oh, you can mock. Didn't you ever love anything that much?"

I could barely see him now, the room shrouded in the near dark. I could have turned on the overhead light, but something stopped me. And almost as soon as I realized what I had said, I wished I hadn't.

"Yes," he said, quietly. "Yes, I did."

We talked a bit longer, and then Will nodded off. I lay there, watching him breathe, and occasionally wondering what he would say if he woke up and found me staring at him, at his too-long hair and tired eyes and scraggly beginnings of a beard. But I couldn't move. The hours had become surreal, an island out of time. I was the only other person in the house, and I was still afraid to leave him.

Shortly after eleven, I saw he had begun to sweat again, his breathing becoming shallower, and I woke him and made him take some fever medication. He didn't talk, except to murmur his thanks. I changed his top sheet and his pillowcase, and then, when he finally slept again, I lay down a foot away from him and, a long time later, I slept too.

———

I woke to the sound of my name. I was in a classroom, asleep on my desk, and the teacher was rapping a blackboard, repeating my name again and again. I knew I should be paying attention, knew that the teacher would see this slumber as an act of subversion, but I could not raise my head from the desk.

"Louisa."

"Mmmhghh."

"Louisa."

The desk was awfully soft. I opened my eyes. The words were being spoken over my head, hissed, but with great emphasis. *Louisa.*

I was in bed. I blinked, letting my eyes focus, then looked up to find Camilla Traynor standing over me. She wore a heavy wool coat and her handbag was slung over her shoulder.

"Louisa."

I pushed myself upright with a start. Beside me, Will was asleep under the covers, his mouth slightly open, his elbow bent at a right angle in front of him. Light seeped in through the window, telling of a cold, bright morning.

"Uh."

"What are you doing?"

I felt as if I had been caught doing something awful. I rubbed at my face, trying to gather my thoughts. Why was I in here? What could I tell her?

"What are you doing in Will's bed?"

"Will . . . ," I said, quietly. "Will wasn't well . . . I just thought I should keep an eye—"

"What do you mean, he wasn't well? Look, come out into the hall." She strode out of the room, evidently waiting for me to catch up.

I followed, trying to straighten my clothes. I had a horrible feeling my makeup was smeared all over my face.

She closed Will's bedroom door behind me.

I stood in front of her, trying to smooth my hair as I gathered my thoughts. "Will had a temperature. Nathan got it down when he came, but I didn't know about this regulating thing and I wanted to keep an eye on him . . . he said I should keep an eye on him . . ." My voice sounded thick, unformed. I wasn't entirely sure I was making coherent sentences.

"Why didn't you call me? If he was ill you should have called me immediately. Or Mr. Traynor."

It was as if my synapses had suddenly snapped together. *Mr. Traynor. Oh Lord.* I glanced up at the clock. It was a quarter to eight.

"I didn't . . . Nathan seemed to . . ."

"Look, Louisa. It's really not rocket science. If Will was ill enough for you to sleep in his room then that is something you should have contacted me about."

"Yes."

I blinked, staring at the ground.

"I don't understand why you didn't call. Did you attempt to call Mr. Traynor?"

Nathan said not to say anything.

"I—"

At that moment the door to the annex opened, and Mr. Traynor stood there, a newspaper folded under his arm. "You made it back!" he said to his wife, brushing snowflakes from his shoulders. "I've just fought my way up the road to get a newspaper and some milk. Roads are absolutely treacherous. I had to go the long way to Hansford Corner, to avoid the ice patches."

She looked at him, and I wondered for a moment

whether she was registering the fact that he was wearing the same shirt and sweater he'd worn the previous day.

"Did you know Will had been ill in the night?"

He looked straight at me. I dropped my gaze to my feet. I wasn't sure I had ever felt more uncomfortable.

"Did you try to call me, Louisa? I'm sorry—I didn't hear a thing. I suspect that intercom's on the blink. There have been a few occasions lately where I've missed it. And I wasn't feeling too good myself last night. Out like a light."

I was still wearing Will's socks. I stared at them, wondering if Mrs. Traynor was going to judge me for that too.

But she seemed distracted. "It's been a long journey home, I think . . . I'll leave you to it. But if anything like this happens again, you call me immediately. Do you understand?"

I didn't want to look at Mr. Traynor. "Yes," I said, and disappeared into the kitchen.

7

Spring arrived overnight, as if winter, like some unwanted guest, had abruptly shrugged its way into its coat and vanished, without saying good-bye. Everything became greener, the roads bathed in watery sunshine, the air suddenly balmy. There were hints of something floral and welcoming in the air, birdsong the gentle backdrop to the day.

I didn't notice any of it. I had stayed at Patrick's house the evening before. It was the first time I had seen him for almost a week due to his enhanced training schedule, but having spent forty minutes in the bath with half a pack of bath salts, he was so exhausted he could barely talk to me. I had begun stroking his back, in a rare attempt at seduction, and he had murmured that he was really too tired, his hand flicking as if he were swatting me away. I was still awake and staring at his ceiling discontentedly four hours later.

Patrick and I had met while I was doing the only other job I had ever held, that of trainee at the Cutting Edge, Hailsbury's only unisex hairdresser. He walked in while Samantha, the proprietor, was busy, asking for a number four. I gave him what he described afterward as not only the worst haircut that he had ever had, but the worst haircut in the history of mankind. Three months later, realizing that a love of fiddling with my own hair did not necessarily mean that I was cut out to do anyone else's, I left and got the job at the café with Frank.

When we started going out, Patrick had been working in sales and his favorite things could have been listed as beer, candy bars from the gas station, talking about sports, and sex (doing, not talking about), in that order. A good night out for us would probably comprise all four. He was ordinary-looking rather than handsome, and his bum was podgier than mine, but I liked it. I liked the solidity of him, the way he felt when I wrapped myself around him. His dad was dead and I liked the way he acted toward his mother, protective and solicitous. And his four brothers and sisters were like the Waltons. They actually seemed to like one another. The first time we went out on a date, a little voice in my head said: *This man will never hurt you*, and nothing he had done in the seven years since had led me to doubt it.

And then he turned into Marathon Man.

Patrick's stomach no longer gave when I nestled into him; it was a hard, unforgiving thing, like a sideboard, and he was prone to pulling up his shirt and hitting it with things, to prove quite how hard it was. His face was planed, and weathered from his time spent constantly outdoors. His thighs were solid muscle. That would have been sexy in itself, had he actually wanted to have sex. But we were down to about twice a month, and I wasn't the kind to ask.

It was as if the fitter he got, the more obsessed by his own shape he became and the less interested he was in mine. I asked him a couple of times if he didn't fancy me anymore, but he seemed pretty definite. "You're gorgeous," he would say. "I'm just shattered. Anyway, I don't want you to lose weight. The girls at the club—you couldn't make one decent boob out of all of theirs put together." I wanted to ask how exactly he had come to work out this complex equation, but it was basically a nice thing to say so I let it go.

I wanted to be interested in what he did, I really did. I went to the triathlon club nights, I tried to chat with the other girls. But I soon realized I was an anomaly—there were no girlfriends like me; everyone else in the club was single, or involved with someone equally physically impressive. The couples pushed each other in workouts, planned weekends in spandex shorts, and carried pictures of each other in their wallets completing triathlons hand in hand, or smugly comparing joint medals. It was unspeakable.

It's not that I was some kind of sex maniac—we'd been together a long time, after all. It's just that some perverse bit of me had begun to question my own attractiveness.

Patrick had never minded the fact that I dressed "inventively," as he put it. But what if he hadn't been entirely truthful? Patrick's job, his whole social life, now revolved around the control of flesh—taming it, reducing it, honing it. What if, faced with those tight little track-suited bottoms, my own suddenly seemed wanting? What if my curves, which I had always thought of as pleasantly voluptuous, now seemed doughy to his exacting eyes?

These were the thoughts that were still humming messily around my head as Mrs. Traynor came in and pretty much ordered Will and me to go outside. "I've asked the cleaners to come and do a special spring clean, so I thought perhaps you could enjoy the nice weather while they're all in there."

Will's eyes met mine with the faintest lift of his eyebrows. "It's not really a request, is it, Mother?"

"I just think it would be good if you took some air," she said. "The ramp is in place. Perhaps, Louisa, you might take some tea out there with you?"

It wasn't an entirely unreasonable suggestion. The garden was beautiful. It was as if with the slight lifting of temperatures everything had suddenly decided to look a little bit greener. Daffodils had emerged as if from nowhere, their yellowing bulbs hinting at the flowers to come. Buds burst from brown branches, perennials forcing their way tentatively through the dark, claggy soil. I opened the doors and we went outside, Will keeping his chair on the York stone path. He gestured toward a cast-iron bench with a cushion on it, and I sat there for some time, our faces lifted to the weak sunshine, listening to the sparrows squabbling in the hedgerow.

"What's up with you?"

"What do you mean?"

"You're quiet."

"You said you wanted me to be quiet."

"Not this quiet. It alarms me."

"I'm all right," I said. And then, "It's just boyfriend stuff, if you really want to know."

"Ah," he said. "Running Man."

I opened my eyes, just to see if he was mocking me.

"What's the matter?" he said. "Come on, tell Uncle Will."

"No."

"My mother is going to have the cleaners running around like lunatics in there for at least another hour. You're going to have to talk about something."

I pushed myself upright, and turned to face him. His house chair had a control button that elevated his seat so that he could address people at head height. He didn't often use it, as it frequently made him dizzy, but it was working now. I actually had to look up at him.

I pulled my coat around me, and squinted at him. "Go on, then, what do you want to know?"

"How long have you two been together?" he said.

"Bit over six years."

He looked surprised. "That's a long time."

"Yes," I said. "Well."

I leaned over and adjusted a rug across him. It was deceptive, the sunshine—it promised more than it could actually deliver.

"What does he do?"

"He's a personal trainer."

"Hence the running."

"Hence the running."

"What's he like? In three words, if it makes you uncomfortable."

I thought about it. "Positive. Loyal. Obsessed with body-fat ratios."

"That's seven words."

"Then you got four for free. So what was she like?"

"Who?"

"Alicia?" I looked at him the way he had looked at me, directly. He took a deep breath and gazed upward to a large plane tree. His hair fell down into his eyes and I fought the urge to push it to one side for him.

"Gorgeous. Sexy. High maintenance. Surprisingly insecure."

"What does she have to be insecure about?" The words left my mouth before I could help myself.

He looked almost amused. "You'd be surprised," he said. "Girls like Lissa trade on their looks for so long they don't think they have anything else. Actually, I'm being unfair. She's good with stuff. Things—clothes, interiors. She can make things look beautiful."

I fought the urge to say anyone could make things look beautiful if they had a wallet as deep as a diamond mine.

"She could move a few things around in a room, and it would look completely different. I never could work out how she did it." He nodded toward the house. "She did this annex, when I first moved in."

I found myself reviewing the perfectly designed living room. I realized my admiration of it was suddenly slightly less uncomplicated than it had been.

"How long were you with her?"

"Eight, nine months."

"Not that long."

"Long for me."

"How did you meet?"

"Dinner party. A really awful dinner party. You?"

"Hairdresser's. I was one. He was my client."

"Hah. You were his something extra for the weekend."

I must have looked blank because he shook his head and said softly, "Never mind."

Inside, we could hear the dull drone of the vacuum cleaner. There were four women in the cleaning company, all wearing matching housecoats. I had wondered what they would find to do for two hours in the little annex.

"Do you miss her?"

Will seemed to be watching something in the distance. "I used to." He turned to me, his voice matter-of-fact. "But I've been thinking about it, and I've decided that she and Rupert are a good match."

I nodded. "They'll have a ridiculous wedding, pop out an ankle biter or two, as you put it, buy a place in the country, and he'll be shagging his secretary within five years," I said.

"You're probably right."

I was warming to my theme now. "And she will be a little bit cross with him all the time without really knowing why and bitch about him at really awful dinner parties to the embarrassment of their friends, and he won't want to leave because he'll be scared of all the alimony."

Will turned to look at me.

"And they will have sex once every six weeks and he will adore his children while doing absolutely nothing to actually help look after them. And she will have perfect hair but get this kind of pinched face"—I narrowed my mouth—"through never saying what she actually means, and start an insane Pilates habit or maybe buy a dog or a horse and develop a crush on her riding instructor. And he will take up jogging when he hits forty, and maybe buy a Harley-Davidson, which she will despise, and every day he will go to work and look at all the young men in his office and listen in bars to who they pulled on the weekend or where they went on a jolly and feel like somehow—and he will never be quite sure how—he got suckered."

I turned.

Will was staring at me.

"Sorry," I said, after a moment. "I don't really know where that came from."

"I'm starting to feel just the tiniest bit sorry for Running Man."

"Oh, it's not him," I said. "It's working at a café for years. You see and hear everything. Patterns, in people's behavior. You'd be amazed at what goes on."

"Is that why you've never gotten married?"

I blinked. "I suppose so."

I didn't want to say I had never actually been asked.

———

It may sound as though we didn't do much. But, in truth, the days with Will were subtly different—depending on his mood and, more important, how much pain he was in. Some days I would arrive and I could see from the set of his jaw that he didn't want to talk to me—or to anyone—and, noting this, I would busy myself around the annex, trying to anticipate his needs so that I didn't have to bother him by asking.

There were all sorts of things that caused him pain. There were the general aches that came with loss of muscle—there was so much less holding him up, despite Nathan's best attempts at physio. There was stomach pain from digestive problems, shoulder pain, pain from bladder infections—an inevitability, apparently, despite everyone's best efforts. He had a stomach ulcer from taking too many painkillers early on in his recovery, when he apparently popped them like Tic Tacs.

Occasionally, there were pressure sores, from being seated in the same position for too long. A couple of times Will was confined to bed just to let them heal, but he hated being prone. He would lie there listening to the radio, his eyes glittering with barely suppressed rage. Will also got headaches—a side effect, I thought, of his anger and frustration. He had so much mental energy, and nothing to take it out on. It had to build up somewhere.

But the most debilitating was a burning sensation in his hands and feet; relentless, pulsing, it would leave him unable to focus on anything else. I would prepare a bowl of cold water and soak them, or wrap cold flannels around them, hoping to ease his discomfort. A stringy muscle would flicker in his jaw and occasionally he would just seem to disappear, as if the only way he could cope with the sensation was to absent himself from his own body. I had become surprisingly used to the physical requirements of Will's life. It seemed unfair that despite the fact that he could not use them, or feel them, his extremities should cause him so much discomfort.

Despite all this, Will did not complain. This was why it had taken me weeks to notice that he suffered at all. Now I could decipher the strained look around his eyes, the silences, the way he seemed to retreat inside his own skin. He would ask, simply, "Could you get the cold water, Louisa?" or "I think it might be time for some pain-killers." Sometimes he was in so much pain that his face actually leached color, turning to pale putty. Those were the worst days.

But on other days we tolerated each other quite well. He didn't seem mortally offended when I talked to him, as he had at the start. Today appeared to be a pain-free day. When Mrs. Traynor came out to tell us that the cleaners would be another twenty minutes, I made us both another drink and we took a slow stroll around the garden, Will sticking to the path and me watching my satin pumps darken in the damp grass.

"Interesting choice of footwear," Will said.

They were emerald green. I had found them in a thrift shop. Patrick said they made me look like a leprechaun drag queen.

"You know, you don't dress like someone from around here. I quite look forward to seeing what insane combination you're going to turn up in next."

"So how should 'someone from around here' dress?"

He steered a little to the left to avoid a bit of branch on the path. "Fleece. Or, if you're my mother's set, something from Jaeger or Whistles." He looked at me. "So where did you pick up your exotic tastes? Where else have you lived?"

"I haven't."

"What, you've only ever lived here?"

"Only here." I turned and looked at him, crossing my arms over my chest defensively. "So? What's so weird about that?"

"It's such a small town. So limiting. And it's all about the castle." We paused on the path and stared at it, rising up in the distance on its weird, domelike hill, as perfect as if it had been drawn by a child. "I always think this is the kind of place that people come back to. When they've become tired of everything else. Or when they don't have enough imagination to go anywhere else."

"Thanks."

"There's nothing *wrong* with it per se. But . . . Christ. It's not exactly dynamic, is it? Not exactly full of ideas or interesting people or opportunities. Around here they think it's subversive if the tourist shop starts selling place mats with a different view of the miniature railway."

I couldn't help but laugh. There had been an article in the local newspaper the previous week on exactly that topic.

"You're twenty-six years old, Clark. You should be out there, claiming the world as your own, getting in trouble in bars, showing off your strange wardrobe to dodgy men . . ."

"I'm happy here," I said.

"Well, you shouldn't be."

"You like telling people what they should be doing, don't you?"

"Only when I know I'm right," he said. "Can you adjust my drink? I can't quite reach it."

I twisted his straw around so that he could reach it more easily and waited while he took a drink. The faint cold had turned the tips of his ears pink.

He grimaced. "Jesus, for a girl who made tea for a living you make a terrible cup."

"You're just used to lesbian tea," I said. "All that lapsang souchong herbal stuff."

"Lesbian tea!" He almost choked. "Well, it's better than this stair varnish. Christ. You could stand a spoon up in that."

"So even my tea is wrong." I sat down on the bench in front of him. "So how is it okay for you to offer an opinion on every single thing I say or do, and yet nobody else gets to say anything at all?"

"Go on, then, Louisa Clark. Give me your opinions."

"On you?"

He gave a theatrical sigh. "Do I have a choice?"

"You could cut your hair. It makes you look like some kind of vagrant."

"Now you sound like my mother."

"Well, you do look bloody awful. You could shave, at least. Isn't all that facial hair starting to get itchy?"

He gave me a sideways look.

"It is, isn't it? I knew it. Okay—this afternoon I am going to take it all off."

"Oh no."

"Yes. You asked me for my opinion. This is my answer. You don't have to do anything."

"What if I say no?"

"I might do it anyway. If it gets any longer I'll be picking bits of food out of it. And, frankly, if that happens I'll have to sue you for undue distress in the workplace."

He smiled then, as if I had amused him. It might sound a bit sad, but Will's smiles were so rare that prompting one made me feel light-headed with pride.

"Here, Clark," he said. "Do me a favor?"

"What?"

"Scratch my ear for me, will you? It's driving me nuts."

"If I do you'll let me cut your hair? Just a bit of a trim?"

"Don't push your luck."

"Shush. Don't make me nervous. I'm not great with scissors."

———

I found the razors and some shaving foam in the bathroom cabinet, tucked well back behind the packets of wipes and cotton wool, as if they hadn't been used in some time. I made him come into the bathroom, filled a sink with warm water, got him to tilt his headrest back a little, and then placed a hot flannel over his chin.

"What is this? You're going to be a barbershop? What's the flannel for?"

"I don't know," I confessed. "It's what they do in the films. It's like the hot water and towels when someone has a baby."

I couldn't see his mouth, but his eyes creased with faint mirth. I wanted to keep them like that. I wanted him to be happy—for his face to lose that haunted, watchful look. I gabbled. I told jokes. I started to hum. Anything to prolong the moment before he looked grim again.

I rolled up my sleeves and began to lather the shaving foam over his chin, all the way up to his ears. Then I hesitated, the blade over his chin. "Is this the moment to tell you I've only ever done legs before?"

He closed his eyes, and settled back. I began to scrape gently at his skin with the blade, the silence broken only by the splash as I rinsed the razor in the basinful of water. I worked in silence, studying Will Traynor's face as I went, the lines that ran to the corners of his mouth, lines that seemed prematurely deep for his age. I smoothed his hair from the side of his face and saw the telltale tracks of stitches, perhaps from his accident. I saw the mauve shadows that told of nights and nights of lost sleep, the furrow between his brows that spoke of silent pain. A warm sweetness rose from his skin, the scent of the shaving cream, and something that was peculiar to Will himself, discreet and expensive. His face began to emerge and I could see how easy it must have been for him to attract someone like Alicia.

I worked slowly and carefully, encouraged by the fact that he seemed briefly at peace. The thought flashed by that the only time anyone ever touched Will was for some medical or therapeutic procedure, and so I let my fingers rest lightly upon his skin, trying as much as possible to make the movements as far from the dehumanized briskness that characterized Nathan's and the doctor's interactions with him.

It was a curiously intimate thing, this shaving of Will. I realized as I continued that I had assumed his wheelchair would be a barrier; that his disability would prevent any kind of sensual aspect from creeping in. Weirdly, it wasn't working like that. It was impossible to be this close to someone, to feel their skin tauten under your fingertips, to breathe in the air that they breathed out, to have their face only inches from yours, without feeling a little unbalanced. By the time I reached his other ear I had begun to feel awkward, as if I had overstepped an invisible mark.

Perhaps Will was able to read the subtle changes in my pressure on his skin; perhaps he was just more attuned to the moods of the people around him. But he opened his eyes, and I found them looking into mine.

There was a short pause, and then he said, straight-faced, "Please don't tell me you've shaved off my eyebrows."

"Only the one," I said. I rinsed the blade, hoping that

the color would have drained from my cheeks by the time I turned around. "Right," I said, finally. "Have you had enough? Won't Nathan be here in a bit?"

"What about my hair?" he said.

"You really want me to cut it?"

"You might as well."

"I thought you didn't trust me."

He shrugged, as far as he could. It was the smallest movement of his shoulders. "If it will stop you moaning at me for a couple of weeks I figure it's a small price to pay."

"Oh my God, your mum is going to be so delighted," I said, wiping a stray dab of shaving cream.

"Yes, well, we won't let that put us off."

———

We cut his hair in the living room. I lit the fire, we put on a film—an American thriller—and I placed a towel around his shoulders. I had warned Will that I was a bit rusty, but added that it couldn't look worse than it did already.

"Thanks for that," he said.

I set to work, letting his hair slide through my fingers, trying to remember the few basics I had learned. Will, watching the film, seemed relaxed and almost content. Occasionally he told me something about the film—what else the lead actor had starred in, where he had first seen it—and I made a vaguely interested noise (like I do with Thomas when he presents me with his toys), even though all my attention was actually focused on not mucking up his hair. Finally, I had the worst of it off, and whipped around in front of him to see how he looked.

"Well?" Will paused the DVD.

I straightened up. "I'm not sure I like seeing this much of your face. It's a bit unnerving."

"Feels cold," he observed, moving his head from left to right, as if testing the feel of it.

"Hold on," I said. "I'll get two mirrors. Then you can

see it properly. But don't move. There's still a bit of tidying up to be done. Possibly an ear to slice."

I was in the bedroom, going through his drawers in search of a small mirror, when I heard the door. Two sets of brisk footsteps, Mrs. Traynor's voice, lifted, anxious.

"Georgina, please don't."

The door to the living room was wrenched open. I grabbed the mirror and ran out of the room. I had no intention of being found absent again. Mrs. Traynor was standing in the living-room doorway, both hands raised to her mouth, apparently witnessing some unseen confrontation.

"You are the most selfish man I ever met!" a young woman was shouting. "I can't believe this, Will. You were selfish then and you're worse now."

"Georgina." Mrs. Traynor's gaze flicked toward me as I approached. "Please, stop."

I walked into the room behind her. Will, the towel around his shoulders, soft brown fronds of hair at the wheels of his chair, was facing a young woman. She had long dark hair pinned into a messy knot at the back of her head. Her skin was tanned, and she was wearing expensively distressed jeans and suede boots. Like Alicia, her features were beautiful and regular, her teeth the astonishing white of a toothpaste commercial. I knew they were because, her face puce with anger, she was still hissing at him. "I can't believe it. I can't believe you would even think of it. What do you—"

"*Please*. Georgina." Mrs. Traynor's voice lifted sharply. "This is not the time."

Will, his face impassive, was staring straight ahead of him at some unseen point.

"Um . . . Will? Do you need any help?" I said, quietly.

"Who are you?" the young woman said, whipping around. It was then that I saw her eyes were filled with tears.

"Georgina," Will said. "Meet Louisa Clark, my paid companion and shockingly inventive hairdresser. Louisa, meet my sister, Georgina. She appears to have flown all the way from Australia to shriek at me."

"Don't be facile," Georgina said. "Mummy told me. She's told me *everything*."

Nobody moved.

"Shall I give you a minute?" I said.

"That would be a good idea." Mrs. Traynor's knuckles were white on the arm of the sofa.

I slid out of the room.

"In fact, Louisa, perhaps now would be a good time to take your lunch break."

It was going to be a bus shelter kind of a day. I grabbed my sandwiches from the kitchen, climbed into my coat, and set off down the back path.

As I left, I could hear Georgina Traynor's voice lifting inside the house. "Has it ever occurred to you, Will, that, believe it or not, this might not be *just* about you?"

———

When I returned, exactly half an hour later, the house was silent. Nathan was washing a mug in the kitchen sink.

He turned as he saw me. "How you doing?"

"Has she gone?"

"Who?"

"The sister?"

He glanced behind him. "Ah. That who it was? Yeah, she's gone. Just skidding off in her car when I got here. Some sort of family row, was it?"

"I don't know," I said. "I was in the middle of cutting Will's hair and this woman came in and just started having a go at him. I assumed it was another girlfriend."

Nathan shrugged.

I realized he would not be interested in the personal minutiae of Will's life, even if he knew.

"He's a bit quiet, though. Nice work with the shave,

by the way. Good to get him out from behind all that shrubbery."

I walked back into the living room. Will was sitting staring at the television, which was still paused at the exact moment I had left it.

"Do you want me to turn this back on?" I said.

He didn't seem to hear me for a minute. His head was sunk in his shoulders, the earlier relaxed expression replaced by a veil. Will was closed off again, locked behind something I couldn't penetrate.

He blinked, as if he had only just noticed me there. "Sure," he said.

———

I was carrying a basket of washing down the hall when I heard them. The annex door was slightly ajar and the voices of Mrs. Traynor and her daughter carried down the long corridor, the sound coming in muted waves. Will's sister was sobbing quietly, all fury gone from her voice now. She sounded almost childlike.

"There must be something they can do. Some medical advance. Can't you take him to America? Things are always improving in America."

"Your father keeps a very close eye on all the developments. But no, darling, there is nothing . . . concrete."

"He's so . . . different now. It's like he's determined not to see the good in anything."

"He's been like that since the start, George. I think it's just that you didn't see him apart from when you flew home. Back then, I think he was still . . . determined. Back then, he was sure that something would change."

I felt a little uncomfortable listening in on such a private conversation. But the odd tenor drew me closer. I found myself walking softly toward the door, my socked feet making no sound on the floor.

"Look, Daddy and I didn't tell you. We didn't want to upset you. But he tried . . ." She struggled over the words. "Will tried to . . . he tried to kill himself."

"What?"

"Daddy found him. Back in January. It was . . . it was terrible."

Even though this really only confirmed what I had guessed, I felt all the blood drain from me. I heard a muffled cry, a whispered reassurance. There was another long silence. And then Georgina, her voice thick with grief, spoke again.

"The girl . . . ?"

"Yes. Louisa is here to make sure nothing like that happens again."

I stopped. At the other end of the corridor, from the bathroom, I could hear Nathan and Will talking in a low murmur, comfortably oblivious to the conversation that was going on just a few feet away. I took a step closer to the door. I suppose I had known it since I caught sight of the scars on his wrists. It made sense of everything, after all—Mrs. Traynor's anxiety that I shouldn't leave Will alone for very long, his antipathy to having me there, the fact that for large stretches of time I didn't feel like I was doing anything useful at all. I had been babysitting. I hadn't known it, but Will had, and he had hated me for it.

I reached for the handle of the door, preparing to close it gently. I wondered what Nathan knew. I wondered whether Will was happier now. I realized I felt, selfishly, a faint relief that it hadn't been me Will objected to, just the fact that I—that anyone—had been employed to watch over him.

"You can't let him do this, Mum. You have to stop him."

"It's not our choice, darling."

"But it is. It is—if he's asking you to be part of it," Georgina protested.

The handle stilled in my hand.

"I can't believe you're even agreeing to it. What about your religion? What about everything you've done? What was the point in you even bloody saving him the last time?"

Mrs. Traynor's voice was deliberately calm. "That's not fair."

"But you've said you'll take him. What does—"

"Do you think for a moment that if I said I refuse, he wouldn't ask someone else?"

"But Dignitas? It's just wrong. I know it's hard for him, but it will destroy you and Daddy. I know it. Think of how you would feel! Think of the publicity! Your job! Both your reputations! *He* must know it. It's a selfish thing to even ask. How can he? How can he do this? How can *you* do this?" She began to sob again.

"George . . ."

"Don't look at me like that. I do care about him, Mummy. I do. He's my brother and I love him. But I can't bear it. I can't bear even the thought of it. He's wrong to ask, and you're wrong to consider it. And it's not just his own life he will destroy if you go ahead with this."

I took a step back from the window. The blood thumped so loudly in my ears that I almost didn't hear Mrs. Traynor's response.

"Six months, George. He promised to give me six months. Now, I don't want you to mention this again, and certainly not in front of anyone else. And we must . . ." She took a deep breath. "We must just pray very hard that something happens in that time to change his mind."

8

CAMILLA

I never set out to help kill my son.

Even reading the words seems odd—like something you might see in a tabloid newspaper.

I was not the kind of person this happened to. Or at least, I thought I wasn't. My life was a fairly structured one—an ordinary one, by modern standards. I had been married for almost thirty-seven years, I raised two children, I kept my career, helped out at the school, the PTA, and joined the bench once the children didn't need me anymore.

I had been a magistrate for almost eleven years. I watched the whole of human life come through my court: the hopeless waifs who couldn't get themselves together sufficiently even to make a court appointment on time; the repeat offenders; the angry, hard-faced young men and exhausted, debt-ridden mothers. It's quite hard to stay calm and understanding when you see the same faces, the same mistakes made again and again. I could sometimes hear the impatience in my tone. It could be oddly dispiriting, the blank refusal of humankind to even attempt to function responsibly.

And our little town, despite the beauty of the castle, our many Grade II listed buildings, our picturesque country lanes, was far from immune to it. Our Regency Squares held cider-drinking teenagers; our thatched cottages muffled the sounds of husbands beating their wives and children. Sometimes I felt like King Canute, making vain pronouncements in the face of a tide of chaos and creeping devastation. But I loved my job. I did it because I believe in order, in a moral code. I believe that there is a right and a wrong, unfashionable as that view might be.

I got through the tougher days because of my garden. As the children grew it had become a bit of an obsession of mine. I could give you the Latin name of almost any plant you cared to point at. The funny thing was, I didn't even do Latin at school—mine was a rather minor public school for girls where the focus was on cooking and embroidery, things that would help us become good wives—but the thing about those plant names is that they do stick in your head. I only ever needed to hear one once to remember it forever: *Helleborus niger, Eremurus stenophyllus, Athyrium niponicum.* I can repeat those with a fluency I never had at school.

They say you only really appreciate a garden once you reach a certain age, and I suppose there is a truth in that. It's probably something to do with the great circle of life. There seems to be something miraculous about seeing the relentless optimism of new growth after the bleakness of winter, a kind of joy in the difference every year, the way nature chooses to show off different parts of the garden to its full advantage. There have been times—the times when my marriage proved to be somewhat more populated than I had anticipated—when it has been a refuge, times when it has been a joy.

There have even been times when it was, frankly, a pain. There is nothing more disappointing than creating a new border only to see it fail to flourish, or to watch a row of beautiful alliums destroyed overnight by some slimy culprit. But even when I complained about the time, the effort involved in caring for it, the way my joints protested an afternoon spent weeding, or my fingernails never looking quite clean, I loved it. I loved the sensual pleasures of being outside, the smell of it, the

feel of the earth under my fingers, the satisfaction of seeing things living, glowing, captivated by their own temporary beauty.

After Will's accident I didn't garden for a year. It
wasn't just the time, although the endless hours spent at
the hospital, the time spent to-ing and fro-ing in the car,
the meetings—oh God, the meetings—took up so much
of it. I took six months' compassionate leave from work
and there was still not enough of it.

It was that I could suddenly see no point. I paid a gardener to come and keep the garden tidy, and I don't
think I gave it anything but the most cursory of looks for
the best part of a year.

It was only when we brought Will back home, once
the annex was adapted and ready, that I could see a
point in making it beautiful again. I needed to give my
son something to look at. I needed to tell him, silently,
that things might change, grow, or fail, but that life did
go on. That we were all part of some great cycle, some
pattern that it was only God's purpose to understand. I
couldn't say that to him, of course—Will and I have
never been able to say much to each other—but I
wanted to show him. A silent promise, if you like, that
there was a bigger picture, a brighter future.

———

Steven was poking at the log fire. He maneuvered the
remaining half-burned logs expertly with a poker, sending glowing sparks up the chimney, then dropped a new
log onto the middle. He stood back, as he always did,
watching with quiet satisfaction as the flames took hold,
and dusted his hands on his corduroy trousers. He turned
as I entered the room. I held out a glass.

"Thank you. Is George coming down?"

"Apparently not."

"What's she doing?

"Watching television upstairs. She doesn't want company. I did ask."

"She'll come around. She's probably jet-lagged."

"I hope so, Steven. She's not very happy with us at the moment."

We stood in silence, watching the fire. Around us the room was dark and still, the windowpanes rattling gently as they were buffeted by the wind and rain.

"Filthy night."

"Yes."

The dog padded into the room and, with a sigh, flopped down in front of the fire, gazing up adoringly at us both from her prone position.

"So what do you think?" he said. "This haircut business."

"I don't know. I'd like to think it's a good sign."

"This Louisa's a bit of a character, isn't she?"

I saw the way my husband smiled to himself. *Not her too*, I found myself thinking, and then squashed the thought.

"Yes. Yes, I suppose she is."

"Do you think she's the right one?"

I took a sip of my drink before answering. Two fingers of gin, a slice of lemon, and a lot of tonic. "Who knows?" I said. "I don't think I have the faintest idea what is right and wrong anymore."

"He likes her. I'm sure he likes her. We were talking while watching the news the other night, and he mentioned her twice. He hasn't done that before."

"Yes. Well. I wouldn't get your hopes up."

"Do you have to?"

Steven turned from the fire. I could see him studying me, perhaps conscious of the new lines around my eyes, the way my mouth seemed set these days into a thin line of anxiety. He looked at the little gold cross, now ever present around my neck. I didn't like it when he looked at me like that. I could never escape the feeling that I was being compared to someone else.

"I'm just being realistic."

"You sound . . . you sound like you're already expecting it to happen."

"I know my son."

"Our son."

"Yes. Our son." More my son, I found myself thinking. *You were never really there for him. Not emotionally. You
were just the absence he was always striving to impress.*

"He'll change his mind," Steven said. "There's still a
long way to go."

We stood there. I took a long sip of my drink, the ice
cold against the warmth given out by the fire.

"I keep thinking . . . ," I said, staring into the hearth.
"I still keep thinking that I'm missing something."

My husband was still watching me. I could feel his
gaze on me, but I couldn't meet it. Perhaps he might
have reached out to me then. But I think we had probably gone too far for that.

He took a sip of his drink. "You can only do what you
can do, darling."

"I'm well aware of that. But it's not really enough,
is it?"

He turned back to the fire, poking unnecessarily at a
log until I turned and quietly left the room.

As he had known I would.

———

When Will first told me what he wanted, he had to tell
me twice, as I was quite sure I could not have heard him
correctly the first time. I stayed quite calm when I realized what it was he was proposing, and then I told him
he was being ridiculous and I walked straight out of the
room. It's an unfair advantage, being able to walk away
from a man in a wheelchair. There are two steps between the annex and the main house, and without Nathan's help he could not traverse them. I shut the door of
the annex and I stood in my own hallway with the
calmly spoken words of my son still ringing in my ears.

I'm not sure I moved for half an hour.

He refused to let it go. Being Will, he always had to have the last word. He repeated his request every time I went in to see him until I almost had to persuade myself to go in each day. *I don't want to live like this, Mother. This is not the life I chose. There is no prospect of my recovery, hence it is a perfectly reasonable request to ask to end it in a manner I see fit.* I heard him and could well imagine what he had been like in those business meetings, the career that had made him rich and arrogant. He was a man who was used to being heard, after all. He couldn't bear it that in some way I had the power to dictate his future, that I had somehow become *Mother* again.

It took his attempt to make me agree. It's not that my religion forbade it—although the prospect of Will being consigned to hell through his own desperation was a terrible one. (I chose to believe that God, a benign God, would understand our sufferings and forgive us our trespasses.)

It's just that the thing you never understand about being a mother, until you are one, is that it is not the grown man—the galumphing, unshaven, stinking, opinionated offspring—you see before you, with his parking tickets and unpolished shoes and complicated love life. You see all the people he has ever been all rolled up into one.

I looked at Will and I saw the baby I held in my arms, dewily besotted, unable to believe that I had created another human being. I saw the toddler, reaching for my hand, the schoolboy weeping tears of fury after being bullied by some other child. I saw the vulnerabilities, the love, the history. That's what he was asking me to extinguish—the small child as well as the man—all that love, all that history.

And then on January 22, a day when I was stuck in court with a relentless roll call of shoplifters and uninsured drivers, of weeping, angry ex-partners, Steven walked into the annex and found our son almost unconscious, his head lolling by his armrest, a sea of dark, sticky blood pooling around his wheels. He had located a rusty nail, barely half an inch emerging from some hurriedly finished woodwork in the back lobby, and, pressing his wrist against it, had moved his wheelchair backward and forward until his flesh was sliced to ribbons. I cannot to this day imagine the determination that kept him going, even though he must have been half delirious from the pain. The doctors said he was less than twenty minutes from death.

It was not, they observed with exquisite understatement, *a cry for help*.

When they told me at the hospital that Will would live, I walked outside into my garden and I raged. I raged at God, at nature, at whatever fate had brought our family to such depths. Now I look back and I must have seemed quite mad. I stood in my garden that cold evening and I hurled my large brandy twenty feet into the *Euonymus compactus* and I screamed, so that my voice broke the air, bouncing off the castle walls and echoing into the distance. I was so furious, you see, that all around me were things that could move and bend and grow and reproduce, and my son—my vital, charismatic, beautiful boy— was just this *thing*. Immobile, wilted, bloodied, suffering. Their beauty seemed like an obscenity. I screamed and I screamed and I swore—words I didn't know I knew— until Steven came out and stood, his hand resting on my shoulder, waiting until he could be sure that I would be silent again.

He didn't understand, you see. He hadn't worked it out yet. That Will would try again. That our lives would have to be spent in a state of constant vigilance, waiting for the next time, waiting to see what horror he would inflict upon himself. We would have to see the world through his eyes—the potential poisons, the sharp objects, the inventiveness with which he could finish the job that damned motorcyclist had started. Our lives had to shrink to fit around the potential for that one act. And he had the advantage—he had nothing else to think about, you see.

Two weeks later, I told Will, "Yes."

Of course I did.

What else could I have done?

9

I didn't sleep that night. I lay awake in the little box room, gazing up at the ceiling and carefully reconstructing the last two months based on what I now knew. It was as if everything had shifted, fragmented and settled in some other place, into a pattern I barely recognized.

I felt duped, the dim-witted accessory who hadn't known what was going on. I felt they must have laughed privately at my attempts to feed Will vegetables, or cut his hair—little things to make him feel better. What had been the point?

I ran over and over the conversation I had heard, trying to interpret it in some alternative way, trying to convince myself that I had misunderstood what they had said. But Dignitas wasn't exactly somewhere you went for a minibreak. I couldn't believe Camilla Traynor could contemplate doing that to her son. Yes, I had thought her cold and, yes, awkward around him. It was hard to imagine her cuddling him as my mother had cuddled us—fiercely, joyously—until we wriggled away, begging to be let go. If I'm honest, I just thought it was how the upper classes were with their children. I had just read Will's copy of *Love in a Cold Climate*, after all. But to actively, to voluntarily, play a part in her own son's death?

With hindsight her behavior seemed even colder, her actions imbued with some sinister intent. I was angry with her and angry with Will. Angry with them for letting me engage in a façade. I was angry for all the times I had sat and thought about how to make things better for him, how to make him comfortable, or happy. When I was not angry, I was sad. I would recall the slight break in her voice as she tried to comfort Georgina, and feel a great sadness for her. She was, I knew, in an impossible position.

But mostly I felt filled with horror. I was haunted by what I now knew. How could you live each day knowing that you were simply whiling away the days until your own death? How could this man whose skin I had felt that morning under my fingers—warm, and alive—choose to just extinguish himself? How could it be that, with everyone's consent, in four months' time that same skin would be decaying under the ground?

I couldn't tell anyone. That was almost the worst bit. I was now complicit in the Traynors' secret.

I refused supper. I lay in bed until my thoughts darkened and solidified to the point where I couldn't bear the weight of them, and at eight thirty I came back downstairs and sat silently watching television, perched on the other side of Granddad, who was the only person in our family guaranteed not to ask me a question. He sat in his favorite armchair and stared at the screen with glassy-eyed intensity. I was never sure whether he was watching, or whether his mind was somewhere else entirely.

"Are you sure I can't get you something, love?" Mum appeared at my side with a cup of tea. There was nothing in our family that couldn't be improved by a cup of tea, allegedly.

"No. Not hungry, thanks."

I saw the way she glanced at Dad. I knew that later on there would be private mutterings that the Traynors were working me too hard, that the strain of looking after such an invalid was proving too much. I knew they would blame themselves for encouraging me to take the job.

I would have to let them think they were right.

———

Paradoxically, the following day Will was in good form—unusually talkative, opinionated, belligerent. He talked, possibly more than he had talked on any previous day. It was as if he wanted to spar with me, and was disappointed when I wouldn't play.

"So when are you going to finish this hatchet job, then?"

I had been tidying the living room. I looked up from plumping the sofa cushions. "What?"

"My hair. I'm only half done. I look like one of those Victorian orphans." He turned his head so that I could better see my handiwork. "Unless this is one of your alternative-style statements."

"You want me to keep cutting?"

"Well, it seemed to keep you happy. And it would be nice not to look like I belong in an asylum."

I fetched a towel and scissors in silence.

"Nathan is definitely happier now that I apparently look like a bloke," he said. "Although he did point out that, having restored my face to its former state, I will now need shaving every day."

"Oh," I said.

"You don't mind, do you? Weekends I'll just have to put up with designer stubble."

I couldn't talk to him. I found it difficult even to meet his eye. It was like finding out your boyfriend had been unfaithful. I felt, weirdly, as if he had betrayed me.

"Clark?"

"Hmm?"

"You're having another unnervingly quiet day. What happened to 'chatty to the point of vaguely irritating'?"

"Sorry," I said.

"Running Man again? What's he done now? He hasn't gone and run off, has he?"

"No." I took a soft slice of Will's hair between my index and middle fingers and lifted the blades of the scissors to trim what lay exposed above them. They stilled in my hand. How would they do it? Would they give him an injection? Was it medicine? Or did they just leave you in a room with a load of razors?

"You look tired. I wasn't going to say anything when you came in, but —hell—you look terrible."

"Oh."

How did they assist someone who couldn't move their own limbs? I found myself gazing down at his wrists, which were always covered by long sleeves. I had assumed for weeks that this was because he felt the cold more than we did. Another lie.

"Clark?"

"Yes?"

I was glad I was behind him. I didn't want him to see my face.

He hesitated. Where the back of his neck had been covered by hair, it was even paler than the rest of his skin. It looked soft and white and oddly vulnerable.

"Look, I'm sorry about my sister. She was . . . she was very upset, but it didn't give her the right to be rude. She's a bit direct sometimes. Doesn't know how much she rubs people the wrong way." He paused. "It's why she likes living in Australia, I think."

"You mean, they tell each other the truth?"

"What?"

"Nothing. Lift your head up, please."

I snipped and combed, working my way methodically around his head until every single hair was chopped or trimmed and all that remained was a fine sprinkling on the floor.

It all became clear to me by the end of the day. While Will was watching television with his father, I took a sheet of paper from the printer and a pen from the jar by the kitchen window and wrote down what I wanted to say. I folded the paper, found an envelope, and left it on the kitchen table, addressed to his mother.

When I left for the evening, Will and his father were talking. Actually, Will was laughing. I paused in the hallway, my bag over my shoulder, listening. Why would he laugh? What could possibly provoke mirth, given that he had just a matter of weeks before he took his own life?

"I'm off," I called through the doorway, and started walking.

"Hey, Clark—" he began, but I had already closed the door behind me.

I spent the short bus ride trying to work out what I was going to tell my parents. They would be furious that I had left what they would see as a perfectly suitable and well-paid job. After her initial shock my mother would look pained and defend me, suggesting that it had all been too much. My father would probably ask why I couldn't be more like my sister. He often did, even though I was not the one who ruined her life by getting pregnant and having to rely on the rest of the family for financial support and babysitting. You weren't allowed to say anything like that in our house because, according to my mother, it was like implying that Thomas wasn't a blessing. And all babies were God's blessing, even those who said *bugger* quite a lot, and whose presence meant that half the potential wage earners in our family couldn't actually go and get a decent job.

I would not be able to tell them the truth. I knew I owed Will and his family nothing, but I wouldn't inflict the curious gaze of the neighborhood on him.

All these thoughts tumbled around my head as I got off the bus and walked down the hill. And then I got to the corner of our road and heard the shouting, felt the slight vibration in the air, and it was all briefly forgotten.

A small crowd had gathered around our house. I

picked up my pace, afraid that something had happened, but then I saw my parents on the porch, peering up, and realized it wasn't our house at all. It was just the latest in a long series of small wars that characterized our neighbors' marriage.

That Richard Grisham was not the most faithful of husbands was hardly news on our street. But judging by the scene in his front garden, it might have been to his wife.

"You must have thought I was bloody stupid. She was wearing your T-shirt! The one I had made for you for your birthday!"

"Baby . . . Dympna . . . it's not what you think."

"I went in for your bloody Scotch eggs! And there she was, wearing it! Bold as brass! And I don't even *like* Scotch eggs!"

I slowed my pace, pushing my way through the small crowd until I was able to get to our gate, watching as Richard ducked to avoid a DVD player. Next came a pair of shoes.

"How long have they been at it?"

My mother, her apron tucked neatly around her waist, unfolded her arms and glanced down at her watch. "It's a good three-quarters of an hour. Bernard, would you say it's a good three-quarters of an hour?"

"Depends if you time it from when she threw the clothes out or when he came back and found them."

"I'd say when he came home."

Dad considered this. "Then it's really closer to half an hour. She got a good lot out the window in the first fifteen minutes, though."

"Your dad says if she really does kick him out this time he's going to put in a bid for Richard's Black and Decker."

The crowd had grown, and Dympna Grisham showed no sign of letting up. If anything, she seemed encouraged by the increasing size of her audience.

"You can take her your filthy books," she yelled, hurling a shower of magazines out the window.

These prompted a small cheer among the crowd.

"See if she likes you sitting in the loo with *those* for half of Sunday afternoon, eh?" She disappeared inside, and then reappeared at the window, hauling the contents of a laundry basket down onto what remained of the lawn. "And your filthy underwear. See if she thinks you're such a—what was it?—*hot stud* when she's washing those for you every day!"

Richard was vainly scooping up armfuls of his stuff as it landed on the grass. He was yelling something up at the window, but against the general noise and catcalls it was hard to make it out. Oddly, whereas his CD collection and video games had been quite popular, no one made a move on his dirty laundry.

Crash. There was a brief hush as his stereo met the path.

He looked up in disbelief. "You crazy bitch!"

"You're shagging that disease-ridden cross-eyed troll from the garage, and *I'm* the crazy bitch?"

My mother turned to my father. "Would you like a cup of tea, Bernard? I think it's turning a little chilly."

My dad didn't take his eyes off next door. "That would be great, love. Thank you."

It was as my mother went indoors that I noticed the car. It was so unexpected that at first I didn't recognize it—Mrs. Traynor's Mercedes, navy blue, low-slung, and discreet. She pulled up, peering out at the scene on the pavement, and hesitated a moment before she climbed out. She stood, staring at the various houses, perhaps checking the numbers. And then she saw me.

I slid out from the porch and was down the path before Dad could ask where I was going. Mrs. Traynor stood to the side of the crowd, gazing at the chaos like Marie Antoinette viewing a load of rioting peasants.

"Domestic dispute," I said.

She looked away, as if almost embarrassed to have been caught looking. "I see."

"It's a fairly constructive one by their standards. They've been going to marriage counseling."

Her elegant wool suit, pearls, and expensive hair were enough to mark her out on our street, among the sweatpants and cheap fabrics in bright, chain-store colors. She appeared rigid, worse than the morning she had come home to find me sleeping in Will's room. I registered in some distant part of my mind that I was not going to miss Camilla Traynor.

"I was wondering if you and I could have a little talk." She had to lift her voice to be heard over the cheering.

I glanced over at the crowd and then behind me at the house. I could not imagine bringing Mrs. Traynor into our front room, with its litter of toy trains, Granddad snoring mutely in front of the television, Mum spraying air freshener around to hide the smell of Dad's socks, and Thomas popping by to murmur *bugger* at the new guest.

"Um . . . it's not a great time."

"Perhaps we could talk in my car? Look, just five minutes, Louisa. Surely you owe us that."

A couple of my neighbors glanced in my direction as I climbed into the car. I was lucky that the Grishams were the hot news of the evening, or I might have been the topic of conversation. On our street, if you climbed into an expensive car it meant you had either pulled a footballer or were being arrested by plainclothes police.

The doors closed with an expensive, muted clunk and suddenly there was silence. The car smelled of leather, and there was nothing in it apart from me and Mrs. Traynor. No candy wrappers, mud, lost toys, or perfumed dangly things to disguise the smell of the carton of milk that had been dropped in there three months earlier.

"I thought you and Will got on well." She spoke as if addressing someone straight ahead of her. When I didn't speak, she said, "Is there a problem with the money?"

"No."

"Do you need a longer lunch break? I am conscious that it's rather short. I could ask Nathan if he would—"

"It's not the hours. Or the money."

"Then—"

"I don't really want to—"

"Look, you cannot hand in your notice with immediate effect and expect me not even to ask what on earth's the matter."

I took a deep breath. "I overheard you. You and your daughter. Last night. And I don't want to . . . I don't want to be part of it."

"Ah."

We sat in silence. Mr. Grisham was now trying to bash his way in through the front door, and Mrs. Grisham was busy hurling anything she could locate through the window down onto his head. The choice of projectile missiles—loo roll, tampon boxes, toilet brush, shampoo bottles—suggested she was now in the bathroom.

"Please, don't leave," Mrs. Traynor said, quietly. "Will is comfortable with you. More so than he's been for some time. I . . . it would be very hard for us to replicate that with someone else."

"But you're . . . you're going to take him to that place where people commit suicide. Dignitas."

"No. I am going to do everything I can to ensure he doesn't do that."

"Like what—praying?"

Mrs. Traynor gave me what my mother would have termed an "old-fashioned" look. "You must know by now that if Will decides to make himself unreachable, there is little anybody can do about it."

"I worked it all out," I said. "I'm basically there just to make sure he doesn't cheat and do it before his six months are up. That's it, isn't it?"

"No. That's not it."

"Which is why you didn't care about my qualifications."

"I thought you were bright and cheerful and different. You didn't look like a nurse. You didn't behave . . . like any of the others. I thought . . . I thought you might cheer him up. And you do—you *do* cheer him up, Louisa. Seeing him without that awful beard yesterday . . . you seem to be one of the few people who are able to get through to him."

"Don't you think it would have been fair to mention that I was basically on suicide watch?"

The sigh Camilla Traynor gave was the sound of someone forced to explain something politely to an imbecile. I wondered if she knew that everything she said made the other person feel like an idiot. I wondered if it was something she'd actually cultivated deliberately. I didn't think I could ever manage to make someone feel inferior.

"That might have been the case when we first met you . . . but I'm confident Will is going to stick to his word. He has promised me six months, and that's what I'll get. We need this time, Louisa. We need this time to give him the idea of there being some *possibility*. I was hoping it might plant the idea that there is a life he could enjoy, even if it wasn't the life he had planned."

"But it's all lies. You've lied to me and you're all lying to each other."

She didn't seem to hear me. She turned to face me, pulling a checkbook from her handbag, a pen ready in her hand.

"Look, what do you want? I will double your money. Tell me how much you want."

"I don't want your money."

"A car. Some benefits. Bonuses—"

"No—"

"Then . . . what can I do that might change your mind?"

"I'm sorry. I just don't—"

I started to get out of the car. Her hand shot out. It sat there on my arm, strange and radioactive. We both stared at it.

"You signed a contract, Miss Clark," she said. "You signed a contract where you promised to work for us for six months. By my calculations you have done only two. I am simply requiring you to fulfill your contractual obligations."

Her voice had become brittle. I looked down at Mrs. Traynor's hand and saw that it was trembling.

She swallowed. "Please."

My parents were watching from the porch. I could see them, mugs poised in their hands, the only two people facing away from the theater next door. They turned away awkwardly when they saw that I had noticed them. Dad, I realized, was wearing the tartan slippers with the paint splotches.

I pushed the handle of the door. "Mrs. Traynor, I really can't sit by and watch . . . it's too weird. I don't want to be part of this."

"Just think about it. Tomorrow is Good Friday—I'll tell Will you have a family commitment if you really just need some time. Take the Bank Holiday weekend to think about it. But please. Come back. Come back and help him."

I walked back into the house without looking back. I sat down in the living room and stared at the television while my parents followed me in, exchanged glances, and pretended not to be watching me.

It was almost eleven minutes before I finally heard Mrs. Traynor's car start up and drive away.

———

My sister confronted me within five minutes of arriving home, thundering up the stairs and throwing open the door of my room.

"Yes, do come in," I said. I was lying on the bed, my legs stretched up the wall, staring at the ceiling. I was wearing tights and blue sequined shorts, which now looped unattractively around the tops of my legs.

Katrina stood in the doorway. "Is it true?"

"That Dympna Grisham has finally thrown out her cheating no-good philandering husband and—"

"Don't be smart. About your job."

I traced the pattern of the wallpaper with my big toe. "Yes, I handed in my notice. Yes, I know Mum and Dad are not too happy about it. Yes, yes, yes to whatever it is you're going to throw at me."

She closed the door carefully behind her, then sat down heavily on the end of my bed and swore lustily. "I don't bloody believe you."

She shoved my legs so that I slid down the wall, ending up almost lying on the bed. I pushed myself upright. "Ow."

Her face was puce. "I don't believe you. Mum's in bits downstairs. Dad's pretending not to be, but he is too. What are they supposed to do about money? You know Dad's already panicking about work. Why the hell would you throw away a perfectly good job?"

"Don't lecture me, Treen."

"Well, someone's got to! You're never going to get anything like that money anywhere else. And how's it going to look on your CV?"

"Oh, don't pretend this is about anything other than you and what you want."

"What?"

"You don't care what I do, as long as you can still go and resurrect your high-flying career. You just need me there propping up the family funds and providing the bloody child care. Sod everyone else." I knew I sounded mean and nasty but I couldn't help myself. It was my sister's plight that had got us into this mess, after all. Years of resentment began to ooze out of me. "We've all got to stick at jobs we hate just so that little Katrina can fulfill her bloody ambitions."

"It is not *about* me."

"No?"

"No, it's about you not being able to stick at the one decent job you've been offered in months."

"You know *nothing* about my job, okay?"

"I know it paid well above the minimum wage. Which is all I need to know about it."

"Not everything in life is about the money, you know."

"Yes? You go downstairs and tell Mum and Dad that."

"Don't you dare bloody lecture me about money when you haven't paid a sodding thing toward this house for years."

"You know I can't afford much because of Thomas."

I began to shove my sister out the door. I can't remember the last time I actually laid a hand on her, but right then I wanted to punch someone quite badly and I was afraid of what I would do if she stayed there in front of me. "Just piss off, Treen. Okay? Just piss off and leave me alone."

I slammed the door in my sister's face. And when I finally heard her walking slowly back down the stairs, I chose not to think about what she would say to my parents, about the way they would all treat this as further evidence of my catastrophic inability to do anything of any worth. I chose not to think about Syed at the Job Center and how I would explain my reasons for leaving this most well-paid of menial jobs. I chose not to think about the chicken factory and how somewhere, deep within its bowels, there was probably a set of plastic overalls and a hygiene cap with my name still on them.

I lay back and I thought about Will. I thought about his anger and his sadness. I thought about what his mother had said—that I was one of the only people able to get through to him. I thought about him trying not to laugh at the "Molahonkey Song" on a night when the snow drifted gold past the window. I thought about the warm skin and soft hair and hands of someone living, someone who was far cleverer and funnier than I would ever be and who still couldn't see a better future than to obliterate himself. And finally, my head pressed into the pillow, I cried, because my life suddenly seemed so much darker and more complicated than I could ever have imagined, and I wished I could go back, back to when my biggest worry was whether Frank and I had ordered in enough Chelsea buns.

There was a knock on the door.

I blew my nose. "Piss off, Katrina."

"I'm sorry."

I stared at the door.

Her voice was muffled, as if her lips were close up to the keyhole. "I've got wine. Look, let me in, for God's sake, or Mum will hear me. I've got two Bob the Builder mugs stuck up my sweater, and you know how she gets about us drinking upstairs."

I climbed off the bed and opened the door.

She glanced up at my tear-stained face, and swiftly closed the bedroom door behind her. "Okay," she said, wrenching off the screw top and pouring me a mug of wine, "what really happened?"

I looked at my sister hard. "You mustn't tell anyone what I'm about to tell you. Not Dad. Especially not Mum."

Then I told her.

I had to tell someone.

———

There were many ways in which I disliked my sister. A few years ago I could have shown you whole scribbled lists I had written on that very topic. I hated her for the fact that she's got thick, straight hair, while mine breaks off if it grows beyond my shoulders. I hated her for the fact that you can never tell her anything that she doesn't already know. I hated her for the fact that for my whole

school career teachers insisted on telling me in hushed
tones how bright she was, as if her brilliance wouldn't
mean that by default I lived in a permanent shadow. I
hated her for the fact that at the age of twenty-six I lived
in a box room in a semidetached house just so she could
have her illegitimate son in with her in the bigger bedroom. But every now and then I was very glad indeed
that she was my sister.

Because Katrina didn't shriek in horror. She didn't
look shocked, or insist that I tell Mum and Dad. She
didn't once tell me I'd done the wrong thing by walking
away.

She took a huge swig of her drink. "Jeez."

"Exactly."

"It's legal as well. It's not as if they can stop him."

"I know."

"Fuck. I can't even get my head around it."

We had downed two glasses just in the telling of it,
and I could feel the heat rising in my cheeks. "I hate the
thought of leaving him. But I can't be part of this, Treen.
I can't."

"Mmm." She was thinking. My sister actually has a
"thinking face." It makes people wait before speaking to
her. Dad says my thinking face makes it look like I want
to go to the loo.

"I don't know what to do," I said.

She looked up at me, her face suddenly brightening.
"It's simple."

"Simple."

She poured us another glass each. "Oops. We seem to
have finished this already. Yes. Simple. They've got
money, right?"

"I don't want their money. She offered me a raise. It's
not the point."

"Shut up. Not for you, idiot girl. They'll have their
own money. And he's probably got a shedload of insurance from the accident. Well, you tell them that you

want a budget and then you use that money, and you use the—what was it?—four months you've got left. And you change Will Traynor's mind."

"What?"

"You change his mind. You said he spends most of his time indoors, right? Well, start with something small, then once you've got him out and about again, you think of every fabulous thing you could do for him, everything that might make him want to live—adventures, foreign travel, swimming with dolphins, whatever—and then you do it. I can help you. I'll look things up on the Internet at the library. I bet we could come up with some brilliant things for him to do. Things that would really make him happy."

I stared at her.

"Katrina—"

"Yeah. I know." She grinned as I started to smile. "I'm a fucking genius."

10

They looked a bit surprised. Actually, that's an understatement. Mrs. Traynor looked stunned, and then a bit disconcerted, and then her whole face closed off. Her daughter, curled up next to her on the sofa, just glowered—the kind of face Mum used to warn me would stick in place if the wind changed. It wasn't quite the enthusiastic response I'd been hoping for.

"But what is it you actually want to do?"

"I don't know yet. My sister is good at researching stuff. She's trying to find out what's possible for quadriplegics. But I really wanted to find out from you whether you would be willing to go with it."

We were in their drawing room. It was the same room I had been interviewed in, except this time Mrs. Traynor and her daughter were perched on the sofa, their slobbery old dog between them. Mr. Traynor was standing by the fire. I was wearing my French peasant's jacket in indigo denim, a minidress, and a pair of army boots. With hindsight, I realized, I could have picked a more professional-looking uniform in which to outline my plan.

"Let me get this straight." Camilla Traynor leaned forward. "You want to take Will away from this house."

"Yes."

"And take him on a series of 'adventures.'" She said it like I was suggesting performing amateur keyhole surgery on him.

"Yes. Like I said, I'm not sure what's possible yet. But

it's about just getting him out and about, widening his horizons. There may be some local things we could do at first, and then hopefully something farther afield before too long."

"Are you talking about going abroad?"

"Abroad . . . ?" I blinked. "I was thinking more about maybe getting him to the pub. Or to a show, just for starters."

"Will has barely left this house in two years, apart from hospital appointments."

"Well, yes . . . I thought I'd try and persuade him otherwise."

"And you would, of course, go on all these adventures with him," Georgina Traynor said.

"Look. It's nothing extraordinary. I'm really talking about just getting him out of the house, to start with. A walk around the castle, or a visit to the pub. If we end up swimming with dolphins in Florida, then that's lovely. But really I just wanted to get him out of the house and thinking about something else." I didn't add that the mere thought of driving to the hospital in sole charge of Will was still enough to bring me out in a cold sweat. The thought of taking him abroad felt as likely as me running a marathon.

"I think it's a splendid idea," Mr. Traynor said. "I think it would be marvelous to get Will out and about. You know it can't have been good for him staring at the four walls day in and day out."

"We have tried to get him out, Steven," Mrs. Traynor said. "It's not as if we've left him in there to rot. I've tried again and again."

"I know that, darling, but we haven't been terribly successful, have we? If Louisa here can think up things that Will is prepared to try, then that can only be a good thing, surely?"

"Yes, well, 'prepared to try' being the operative phrase."

"It's just an idea," I said. I felt suddenly irritated. I

could see what she was thinking. "If you don't want me to do it—"

"You'll leave?" She looked straight at me.

I didn't look away. She didn't frighten me anymore. Because I knew now that she was no better than me. She was a woman who could sit back and let her son die right in front of her.

"Yes, I probably will."

"So it's blackmail."

"Georgina!"

"Well, let's not beat around the bush here, Daddy."

I sat up a little straighter. "No. Not blackmail. It's about what I'm prepared to be part of. I can't sit by and just quietly wait out the time until . . . Will . . . well . . ." My voice trailed off.

We all stared at our cups of tea.

"Like I said," Mr. Traynor said firmly, "I think it's a very good idea. If you can get Will to agree to it, I can't see that there's any harm at all. I'd love the idea of him going on holiday. Just . . . just let us know what you need us to do."

"I've got an idea." Mrs. Traynor put a hand on her daughter's shoulder. "Perhaps you could go on holiday with them, Georgina."

"Fine by me," I said. It was. Because my chances of getting Will away on holiday were about the same as me competing on *Mastermind*.

Georgina Traynor shifted uncomfortably in her seat. "I can't. You know I start my new job in two weeks. I won't be able to come over to England again for a bit once I've started."

"You're going back to Australia?"

"Don't sound so surprised. I did tell you this was just a visit."

"I just thought that . . . given . . . given recent events, you might want to stay here a bit longer." Camilla Traynor stared at her daughter in a way she never stared at Will, no matter how rude he was to her.

"It's a really good job, Mummy. It's the one I've been working toward for the last two years." She glanced over at her father. "I can't put my whole life on hold just because of Will's mental state."

There was a long silence.

"This isn't fair. If it was me in the chair, would you have asked Will to put all his plans on hold?"

Mrs. Traynor didn't look at her daughter. I glanced down at my list, reading and rereading the first paragraph.

"I have a life too, you know." It came out like a protest.

"Let's discuss this some other time." Mr. Traynor's hand landed on his daughter's shoulder and squeezed it gently.

"Yes, let's." Mrs. Traynor began to shuffle the papers in front of her. "Right, then. I propose we do it like this. I want to know everything you are planning," she said, looking up at me. "I want to do the estimates and, if possible, I'd like a schedule so that I can try and plan some time off to come along with you. I have some unused holiday entitlement left that I can—"

"No."

We all turned to look at Mr. Traynor. He was stroking the dog's head and his expression was gentle, but his voice was firm. "No. I don't think you should go, Camilla. Will should be allowed to do this by himself."

"Will can't do it by himself, Steven. There is an awful lot that needs to be considered when Will goes anywhere. It's complicated. I don't think we can really leave it to—"

"No, darling," he repeated. "Nathan can help, and Louisa can manage just fine."

"But—"

"Will needs to be allowed to feel like a man. That is

not going to be possible if his mother—or his sister, for that matter—is always on hand."

I felt briefly sorry for Mrs. Traynor then. She still wore that haughty look of hers, but I could see underneath that she seemed a little lost, as if she couldn't quite understand what her husband was doing. Her hand went to her necklace.

"I will make sure he's safe," I said. "And I will let you know everything we're planning on doing, well in advance."

Her jaw was so rigid that a little muscle was visible just underneath her cheekbone. I wondered if she actually hated me then.

"I want Will to want to live too," I said, finally.

"We do understand that," Mr. Traynor said. "And we do appreciate your determination. And discretion." I wondered whether that word was in relation to Will or to something else entirely, and then he stood up and I realized that it was my signal to leave. Georgina and her mother still sat on the sofa, saying nothing. I got the feeling there was going to be a whole lot more conversation once I was out of the room.

"Right, then," I said. "I'll draw you up the paperwork as soon as I've worked it all out in my head. It will be soon. We haven't much . . ."

Mr. Traynor patted my shoulder.

"I know. Just let us know what you come up with," he said.

———

Treena was blowing on her hands, her feet moving involuntarily up and down, as if marching on the spot. She was wearing my dark-green beret, which, annoyingly, looked much better on her than it did on me. She leaned over and pointed to the list she had just pulled from her pocket, and handed it to me.

"You're probably going to have to scratch number three, or at least put that off until it gets warmer."

I checked the list. "Quadriplegic basketball? I'm not even sure if he likes basketball."

"That's not the point. Bloody hell, it's cold up here." She pulled the beret lower over her ears. "The point is, it will give him a chance to see what's possible. He can see that there are other people just as bad off as he is who are doing sports and things."

"I'm not sure. He can't even lift a cup. I think these people must be paraplegic. I can't see that you could throw a ball without the use of your arms."

"You're missing the point. He doesn't have to actually *do* anything, but it's about widening his horizons, right? We're letting him see what other handicapped people are doing."

"If you say so."

A low murmur rose in the crowd. The runners had been sighted, some distance away. If I went onto tiptoes, I could just make them out, probably two miles away, down in the valley, a small block of bobbing white dots forcing their way through the cold along a damp, gray road. I glanced at my watch. We had been standing here on the brow of the aptly named Windy Hill for almost forty minutes, and I could no longer feel my feet.

"I've looked up what's local and, if you didn't want to drive too far, there's a match at the sports center in a couple of weeks. He could even have a bet on the result."

"Betting?"

"That way he could get a bit involved without even having to play. Oh look, there they are. How long do you think they'll take to get to us?"

We stood near the finish line. Above our heads a tarpaulin banner announcing the "Spring Triathlon Finish Line" flapped wanly in the stiff breeze.

"Dunno. Twenty minutes? Longer? I've got an emergency Mars bar if you want to share." I reached into my pocket. It was impossible to stop the list from flapping. "So what else did you come up with?"

"You said you wanted to go farther afield, right?" She pointed to my fingers. "You've given yourself the bigger bit."

"Take this bit then. I think the family thinks I'm freeloading."

"What, because you want to take him on a few crummy days out? Jesus. They should be grateful someone's making the effort. It's not like they are."

Treena took the other piece of Mars bar. "Anyway. Number five, I think it is. There's a computer course that he could do. They put a thing on their head with, like, a stick on it, and they nod their head to touch the keyboard. There are loads of quadriplegic groups online. He could make lots of new friends that way. It would mean he doesn't always have to actually leave the house. I even spoke to a couple in the chat rooms. They seemed nice. Quite"—she shrugged—"*normal*."

We ate our Mars bar halves in silence, watching as the group of miserable-looking runners drew closer. I couldn't see Patrick. I never could. He had the kind of face that became instantly invisible in crowds.

She pointed to the bit of paper.

"Anyway, head for the cultural section. There's a concert specially for people with disabilities here. You said he's cultured, right? Well, he could just sit there and be transported by the music. That's meant to take you out of yourself, right? Derek with the mustache, at work, told me about it. He said it can get noisy because of the really disabled people who yell a bit, but I'm sure he'd still enjoy it."

I wrinkled my nose. "I don't know, Treen—"

"You're just frightened because I said 'culture.' You only have to sit there with him. And not rustle your crisp packet. Or, if you fancied something a bit saucier . . ." She grinned at me. "There's a strip club. You could take him to London for that."

"Take my employer to watch a stripper?"

"Well, you say you do everything else for him—all the cleaning and feeding and stuff. I can't see why you wouldn't just sit by him while he gets a stiffy."

"Treena!"

"Well, he must miss it. You could even buy him a lap dance."

Several people around us in the crowd swiveled their heads. My sister was laughing. She could talk about sex like that. Like it was some kind of recreational activity. Like it didn't matter.

"And then on the other side, there are the bigger trips. Don't know what you fancied, but you could do wine tasting in the Loire . . . that's not too far for starters."

"Can quadriplegics get drunk?"

"I don't know. Ask him."

I frowned at the list. "So . . . I'll go back and tell the Traynors that I'm going to get their suicidal quadriplegic son drunk, spend their money on strippers and lap dancers, and then trundle him off to the Disability Olympics—"

Treena snatched the list back from me. "Well, I don't see *you* coming up with anything more bloody inspirational."

"I just thought . . . I don't know." I rubbed at my nose. "I'm feeling a bit daunted, to be honest. I have trouble even persuading him to go into the garden."

"Well, that's hardly the attitude, is it? Oh, look. Here they come. We'd better smile."

———

"Go, Patrick!" I yelled weakly. He didn't see me.

And he flashed by, toward the finish line.

———

Treena didn't talk to me for two days after I failed to show the required enthusiasm for her to-do list. My parents didn't notice; they were just overjoyed to hear that I had decided not to leave my job. Management had called a series of meetings at the furniture factory for the end of that week, and Dad was convinced that he would be among those made redundant. Nobody over the age of forty had yet survived the cull.

"We're very grateful for your housekeeping, love," Mum said, so often that it made me feel a bit uncomfortable.

It was a funny week. Treena began packing for her course, and each day I had to sneak upstairs to go through the bags she had already packed to see which of my possessions she planned to take with her. Most of my clothes were safe, but so far I had recovered a hair dryer, my fake Prada sunglasses, and my favorite washbag with the lemons on it. If I confronted her over any of it, she would just shrug and say, "Well, you never use it," as if that were entirely the point.

That was Treena all over. She felt entitled. Even though Thomas had come along, she had never quite lost that sense of being the baby of the family—the deep-rooted feeling that the whole world actually did revolve around her. When we were little and she threw a huge tantrum because she wanted something of mine, Mum would plead with me to "just let her have it," if only for some peace in the house. Nearly twenty years later, nothing had really changed. We had to babysit Thomas so that Treena could still go out, feed him so that Treena didn't have to worry, buy her extra-nice presents at birthdays and Christmas "because Thomas means she often goes without." Well, she could go without my bloody lemons washbag. I stuck a note on my door that read: "My stuff is MINE. GO AWAY." Treena ripped it off and told Mum I was the biggest child she had ever met and that Thomas had more maturity in his little finger than I did.

But it got me thinking. One evening, after Treena had gone out to her night class, I sat in the kitchen while Mum sorted Dad's shirts ready for ironing.

"Mum . . ."

"Yes, love."

"Do you think I could move into Treena's room once she's gone?"

Mum paused, a half-folded shirt pressed to her chest. "I don't know. I hadn't really thought about it."

"I mean, if she and Thomas are not going to be here, it's only fair that I should be allowed a proper-sized bedroom. It seems silly, it sitting empty, if they're going off to college."

Mum nodded, and placed the shirt carefully in the laundry basket. "I suppose you're right."

"And by rights, that room should have been mine, what with me being the elder and all. It's only because she had Thomas that she got it at all."

She could see the sense in it. "That's true. I'll talk to Treena about it," she said.

I suppose, with hindsight, it would have been a good idea to mention it to my sister first.

Three hours later she came bursting into the living room with a face like thunder.

"Would you jump in my grave so quickly?"

Granddad jerked awake in his chair, his hand reflexively clasped to his chest.

I looked up from the television. "What are you talking about?"

"Where are me and Thomas supposed to go on weekends? We can't both fit in the box room. There's not even enough room in there for two beds."

"Exactly. And I've been stuck in there for five years." The knowledge that I was ever so slightly in the wrong made me sound pricklier than I had intended.

"You can't take my room. It's not fair."

"You're not even going to be in it!"

"But I need it! There's no way me and Thomas can fit in the box room. Dad, tell her!"

Dad's chin descended to somewhere deep in his

collar, his arms folded across his chest. He hated it when we fought, and tended to leave it to Mum to sort out. "Turn it down a bit, girls," he said.

"I don't believe you. No wonder you were so keen to help me leave."

"What? So you begging me to keep my job so that I can help you out financially is now part of my sinister plan, is it?"

"You're *so* two-faced."

"Katrina, calm down." Mum appeared in the doorway, her rubber gloves dripping foamy water onto the living-room carpet. "We can talk about this calmly. I don't want you getting Granddad all wound up."

Katrina's face had gone blotchy, the way it did when she was small and she didn't get her way. "She actually wants me to go. That's what this is. She can't wait for me to go, because she's jealous that I'm actually doing something with my life. So she just wants to make it difficult for me to come home again."

"There's no guarantee you're even going to be coming home on the weekends," I yelled, stung. "I need a bedroom, not a cupboard, and you've had the best room the whole time, just because you were dumb enough to get yourself up the duff."

"Louisa!" said Mum.

"Yes, well, if you weren't so thick that you can't even get a proper job, you could have gotten your own bloody place. You're old enough. Or what's the matter? You've finally figured out that Patrick is never going to ask you?"

"That's it!" Dad's roar broke into the silence. "I've heard enough! Treena, go into the kitchen. Lou, sit down and shut up. I've got enough stress in my life without having to listen to you caterwauling at each other."

"If you think I'm helping you now with your stupid list, you've got another thing coming," Treena hissed at me, as Mum manhandled her out the door.

"Good. I didn't want your help anyway, *freeloader*," I

said, and then ducked as Dad threw a copy of the *Radio Times* at my head.

―――――――

On Saturday morning I went to the library. I think I probably hadn't been in there since I was at school— quite possibly out of fear that they would remember the Judy Blume I had lost in Year 7, and that a clammy, official hand would reach out as I passed through the building's Victorian pillared doors, demanding £3,853 in fines.

It wasn't what I remembered. Half the books seemed to have been replaced by CDs and DVDs, great bookshelves full of audiobooks, and even stands of greeting cards. And it was not silent. The sound of singing and clapping filtered through from the children's book corner, where some kind of mother and baby group was in full swing. People read magazines and chatted quietly. The section where old men used to fall asleep over the free newspapers had disappeared, replaced by a large oval table with computers dotted around the perimeter. I sat down gingerly at one of these, hoping that nobody was watching. Computers, like books, are my sister's thing. Luckily, they seemed to have anticipated the sheer terror felt by people like me. A librarian stopped by my table, and handed me a card and a laminated sheet with instructions on it. She didn't stand over my shoulder, just murmured that she would be at the desk if I needed any further help, and then it was just me and a chair with a wonky castor and the blank screen.

The only computer I have had any contact with in years is Patrick's. He only really uses it to download fitness plans, or to order sports technique books from Amazon. If there is other stuff he does on there, I don't really want to know about it. But I followed the librarian's instructions, double-checking every stage as I completed it. And, astonishingly, it worked. It didn't just work, but it was *easy*.

Four hours later I had the beginnings of my list.

And nobody mentioned the Judy Blume. Mind you, that was probably because I had used my sister's library card.

On the way home I nipped in to the stationer's and bought a wall calendar—the sort you might find in an office, with staff holiday entitlement marked on it in permanent pen. In my little room at home, I opened it out, pinned it carefully to the back of my door, and marked the date when I had started at the Traynors', way back at the beginning of February. Then I counted forward, and marked the date—August 12—now barely four months ahead. I took a step back and stared at it for a while, trying to make the little black ring bear some of the weight of what it heralded. And as I stared, I began to realize what I was taking on.

I would have to fill those little white rectangles with a lifetime of things that could generate happiness, contentment, satisfaction, or pleasure. I would have to fill them with every good experience I could summon up for a man whose powerless arms and legs meant he could no longer make them happen by himself. I had just under four months' worth of printed rectangles to pack with days out, trips away, visitors, lunches, and concerts. I had to come up with all the practical ways to make them happen, and do enough research to make sure that they didn't fail.

And then I had to convince Will to actually do them.

I stared at my calendar, the pen stilled in my hand. This little patch of paper suddenly bore a whole heap of responsibility.

I had a hundred and seventeen days in which to convince Will Traynor that he had a reason to live.

11

There are places where the changing seasons are marked by migrating birds, or the ebb and flow of tides. Here, in our little town, it was the return of the tourists. At first, a tentative trickle, stepping off trains or out of cars in brightly colored waterproof coats, clutching their guide-books and National Trust membership; then, as the air warmed and the season crept forward, disgorged along-side the belch and hiss of their coaches, clogging up the high street, Americans, Japanese, and packs of foreign schoolchildren dotted the perimeter of the castle.

In the winter, little stayed open. The wealthier shop owners took advantage of the long bleak months to disap-pear to holiday homes abroad, while the more deter-mined hosted Christmas events, capitalizing on occasional carol concerts on the grounds, or festive craft fairs. But then as the temperatures rose, the castle car parks would become studded with vehicles, the local pubs would chalk up an increase in requests for a ploughman's lunch, and, within a few sunny Sundays, we had morphed again from being a sleepy market town into a traditional English tour-ist destination.

I walked up the hill, dodging this season's hovering early few as they clutched their neoprene fanny packs and well-thumbed tourist guides, their cameras already poised to capture mementoes of the castle in spring. I smiled at a few, paused to take photographs of others with proffered cameras. Some locals complained about the tourist season—the traffic jams, the overwhelmed public toilets, the demands for strange comestibles in the Buttered Bun café ("You don't do sushi? Not even hand roll?"). But I didn't. I liked the breath of foreign air, the close-up glimpses of lives far removed from my own. I liked to hear the accents and work out where their owners came from, to study the clothes of people who had never seen a Next catalog or bought a five-pack of knickers at Marks and Spencer.

"You look cheerful," Will said, as I dropped my bag in the hallway. He said it as if it were almost an affront.

"That's because it's today."

"What is?"

"Our outing. We're taking Nathan to see the horse racing."

Will and Nathan looked at each other. I almost laughed. I had been so relieved at the sight of the weather; once I saw the sun, I knew everything was going to be all right.

"Horse racing?"

"Yup. Flat racing at"—I pulled my notepad from my pocket—"Longfield. If we leave now we can be there in time for the third race. And I have five pounds each way on Man Oh Man, so we'd better get a move on."

"Horse racing."

"Yes. Nathan's never been."

In honor of the occasion I was wearing my blue quilted minidress, with the scarf with horse bits around the edge knotted at my neck, and a pair of leather riding boots.

Will studied me carefully, then reversed his chair and swerved so that he could better see his male caregiver. "This is a long-held desire of yours, is it, Nathan?"

I gave Nathan a warning glare.

"Yiss," he said, and broke out in a smile. "Yes, it is. Let's head for the ponies."

I had primed him, of course. I had rung him on Friday and asked him which day I could borrow him. The Traynors had agreed to pay his extra hours (Will's sister had left for Australia, and I think they wanted to be sure that someone "sensible" was going to accompany me), but I hadn't been sure until Sunday what it actually was we were going to do. This seemed the ideal start—a nice day out, less than half an hour's drive away.

"And what if I say I don't want to go?"

"Then you owe me forty pounds," I said.

"Forty pounds? How do you work that out?"

"My winnings. Five pounds each way at eight to one." I shrugged. "Man Oh Man's a sure thing."

I seemed to have got him off balance.

Nathan clapped his hands onto his knees. "Sounds great. Nice day for it too," he said. "You want me to pack some lunch?"

"Nah," I said. "There's a nice restaurant. When my horse comes in, lunch is on me."

"You've been racing often, then?" Will said.

And then before he could say anything else, we had bundled him into his coat and I ran outside to reverse the car.

————

I had it all planned, you see. We would arrive at the racecourse on a beautiful sunny day. There would be burnished, stick-legged Thoroughbreds, their jockeys in billowing bright silks, careering past. Perhaps a brass band or two. The stands would be full of cheering people, and we would find a space from which to wave our winning betting slips. Will's competitive streak would kick in and he would be unable to resist calculating the odds and making sure he won more than either Nathan or me. I had worked it all out. And then, when we had had enough of watching the horses, we would go to the well-reviewed racecourse restaurant and have a slap-up meal.

I should have listened to my father. "Want to know the true definition of the triumph of hope over experience?" he would say. "Plan a fun family day out."

It started with the car park. I drove there without

incident, now a little more confident that I wasn't going to tip Will over if I went faster than 15 mph. I kept up a cheerful banter almost the whole way there, commenting on the beautiful blue sky, the countryside, the lack of traffic. There were no queues to enter the racecourse, which was, admittedly, a little less grand than I had expected, and the car park was clearly marked.

But nobody had warned me it was on grass, and grass that had been driven over for much of a wet winter at that. We backed into a space (not hard, as it was only half full) and almost as soon as the ramp was down Nathan looked worried.

"It's too soft," he said. "He's going to sink."

I glanced over at the stands. "Surely, if we can get him onto that pathway we'll be okay?"

"It weighs a ton, this chair," he said. "And that's forty feet away."

"Oh, come on. They must build these chairs to withstand a bit of soft ground."

I backed Will's chair down carefully and then watched as the wheels sank several inches into the mud.

Will said nothing. He looked uncomfortable, and had been silent for much of the half-hour drive. "Come on," I said. "We'll do it manually. I'm sure between us we can manage to get there."

We tilted Will backward. I took one handle and Nathan took the other and we dragged the chair toward the path. It was slow progress. I had to keep stopping because my arms hurt and my pristine boots grew thick with mud. When we finally made it to the pathway, Will's blanket had half slipped off him and had somehow got caught up in his wheels, leaving one corner torn and muddy.

"Don't worry," Will said drily. "It's only cashmere."

I ignored him. "*Right*. We've made it. Now for the fun bit."

Ah, yes. The fun bit. Who thought it would be a good

idea for racecourses to have turnstiles? It was hardly as if they needed crowd control. We looked at the turnstile, and then back at Will's chair, and then Nathan and I looked at each other.

Nathan stepped over to the ticket office and explained our plight to the woman inside. She tilted her head to look at Will, then pointed us toward the far end of the stand.

"The disabled entrance is over there," she said.

She said *disabled* like someone entering a diction contest. It was a good two hundred yards away. By the time we finally made it over there the blue skies had disappeared abruptly, replaced by a sudden squall. Naturally, I hadn't brought an umbrella. I kept up a relentless, cheerful commentary about how funny this was and how ridiculous, and even to my ears I had begun to sound brittle and irritating.

"Clark," said Will, finally. "Just chill out, okay? You're being exhausting."

We bought tickets for the stands, and then, almost faint with relief at finally having gotten there, I wheeled Will out to a sheltered area just to the side of the main stand. While Nathan sorted out Will's drink, I had some time to look at our fellow race-goers.

Above us, on a glass-fronted balcony, men in suits proffered champagne glasses to women in wedding outfits. They looked warm and cozy, and I guessed that was the Premier Area, listed next to some stratospheric price on the board in the ticket kiosk. They wore little badges on red thread, marking them out as special. I wondered briefly if it was possible to color our blue ones a different shade, but decided that being the only people with a wheelchair would probably make us a little conspicuous.

Beside us, dotted along the stands and clutching polystyrene cups of coffee and hip flasks, were men in tweedy suits and women in smart padded coats. They looked a little more everyday, and wore blue badges like ours. And then, like some parody of a class system, around the parade ring stood a group of men in striped polo shirts, who clutched beer cans and seemed to be on some kind of outing. Their shaved heads suggested military service. Periodically they would break out into song, or begin some noisy, physical altercation, ramming one another with blunt heads or wrapping their arms around one another's necks. As I passed to go to the loo, they catcalled and I flipped them the finger behind my back. And then they lost interest as seven or eight horses began skirting around one another, and they eased into the stands with workmanlike skill, all preparing for the next race.

And then I jumped as around us the small crowd roared into life and the horses bolted from the starting gate. I stood and watched them go, suddenly transfixed, unable to suppress a flurry of excitement at the tails suddenly streaming out behind them, the frantic efforts of the brightly colored men atop them, all jostling for position. When the winner crossed the finish line it was almost impossible not to cheer.

We watched the Sisterwood Cup, and then the Maiden Stakes, and Nathan won six pounds on a small each-way bet. Will declined to bet. He watched each race, but he was silent, his head retracted into the high collar of his jacket. I thought perhaps he had been indoors so long that it was all bound to feel a little weird for him, and I decided I was simply not going to acknowledge it.

"So how many races will it take to ensure we've fulfilled your long-held ambitions?"

"Don't be grumpy. They say you should try everything once," I said.

"I think horse racing falls into the 'except incest and morris dancing' category."

"You're the one always telling me to widen my horizons. You're loving it," I said. "And don't pretend otherwise."

And then they were off. Man Oh Man was in purple silks with a yellow diamond. I watched him flatten out around the white rail, the horse's head extended, the jockey's legs pumping, arms flailing backward and forward up the horse's neck.

"Go on, mate!" Nathan had gotten into it, despite himself. His fists were clenched, his eyes fixed on the blurred group of animals speeding around the far side of the track.

"Go on, Man Oh Man!" I yelled. "We've got a steak dinner riding on you!" I watched him vainly trying to make ground, his nostrils dilated, his ears back against his head. My own heart lurched into my mouth. And then, as they reached the final furlong, my yelling began to die away. "All right, a coffee," I said. "I'll settle for a coffee."

Around me the stands had erupted into shouting and screaming. A girl was bouncing up and down two seats away from us, her voice hoarse with screeching. I found I was bouncing on my toes. And then I looked down and saw that Will's eyes were closed, a faint furrow separating his brows. I tore my attention from the track, and knelt down.

"Are you okay, Will?" I said, moving close to him. "Do you need something?"

"Scotch," he said. "Large one."

He lifted his eyes to mine. He looked utterly fed up.

"Let's get some lunch," I said to Nathan.

Man Oh Man, that four-legged impostor, flashed past the finish line a miserable sixth. There was another cheer, and the announcer's voice came over the loudspeaker: *Ladies and gentlemen, an emphatic win there from Love Be a Lady, there in first place, followed by Winter Sun, and Barney Rubble two lengths behind in third place.*

I pushed Will's chair through the oblivious groups of

people, deliberately bashing into heels when they failed to react to my second "excuse me."

We were just at the lift when I heard Will's voice. "So, Clark, does this mean you owe me forty pounds?"

———

The restaurant had been refurbished, the food now under the auspices of a television chef whose face appeared on posters around the racecourse. I had looked up the menu beforehand.

"The signature dish is duck in orange sauce," I told the two men. "It's seventies retro, apparently."

"Like your outfit," said Will.

Out of the cold, and away from the crowds, he appeared to have cheered up a little. He had begun to look around him, instead of retreating back into his solitary world. My stomach began to rumble, already anticipating a good, hot lunch. Will's mother had given us eighty pounds as a "float." I had decided I would pay for my food myself, and show her the receipt, and as a result had no fears at all that I was going to order myself whatever I fancied on the menu—retro roast duck or otherwise.

"You like going out to eat, Nathan?" I said.

"I'm more of a beer and takeaway man myself," Nathan said. "Happy to come today, though."

"When did you last go out for a meal, Will?" I said.

He and Nathan looked at each other. "Not while I've been there," Nathan said.

"Strangely, I'm not overly fond of being spoon-fed in front of strangers."

"Then we'll get a table where we can face you away from the room," I said. I had anticipated this one. "And if any celebrities are here, that will be your loss."

"Because celebrities are thick on the ground at a muddy minor racecourse in March."

"You're not going to spoil this for me, Will Traynor," I said, as the lift doors opened. "The last time I ate out anywhere was a birthday party for four-year-olds at Hails-bury's only indoor bowling alley, and there wasn't a thing that wasn't covered in batter. Including the children."

We wheeled our way down the carpeted corridor. The restaurant ran along one side, behind a glass wall, and I could see there were plenty of free tables.

"Hello," I said, stepping up to the reception area. "I'd like a table for three, please." *Please don't look at Will*, I told the woman silently. *Don't make him feel awkward. It's important that he enjoy this.*

"Badge, please," she said.

"Sorry?"

"Your Premier Area badge?"

I looked at her blankly.

"This restaurant is for Premier badge holders only."

I glanced behind me at Will and Nathan. They couldn't hear me, but stood, expectantly, waiting. Nathan was helping remove Will's coat.

"Um . . . I didn't know we couldn't eat anywhere we wanted. We have the blue badges."

She smiled. "Sorry," she said. "Only Premier badge holders. It does say so on all our promotional material."

I took a deep breath. "Okay. Are there any other restaurants?"

"I'm afraid the Weighing Room, our relaxed dining area, is being refurbished right now, but there are stalls along the stands where you can get something to eat." She saw my face fall, and added, "The Pig in a Poke is pretty good. You get a hog roast in a bun. They do ap-plesauce too."

"A stall."

"Yes."

I leaned in toward her. "Please," I said. "We've come a long way, and my friend there isn't good in the cold. Is there any way at all that we could get a table in here? We just really need to get him into the warm. It's really im-portant that he has a good day."

She wrinkled her nose. "I'm really sorry," she said. "It's more than my job's worth to override the rules. But there is a disabled seating area downstairs that you can shut the doors on. You can't see the course, but it's quite snug."

I stared at her. I could feel the tension creeping upward from my shins. I studied her name badge. "Sharon," I said, "you haven't even begun to fill your tables. Surely it would be better to have more people eating than leaving half these tables empty? Just because of some arcane class-based regulation in a rule book?"

Her smile glinted under the recessed lighting. "Madam, I have explained the situation to you. If we relaxed the rules for you, we'd have to do it for everyone."

"It's a wet Monday lunchtime. You have empty tables. We want to buy a meal. A properly expensive meal, with napkins and everything. We don't want to eat pork rolls and sit in a cloakroom with no view, no matter how snug."

Other diners had begun to turn in their seats, curious about the altercation by the door. I could see Will looking embarrassed now. He and Nathan had worked out that something was going wrong.

"Then I'm afraid you should have bought a Premier Area badge."

"Okay." I reached for my handbag, and began to rifle through, searching for my purse. "How much is a Premier Area badge?" Tissues, old bus tickets, and one of Thomas's Hot Wheels toy cars flew out. I no longer cared. I was going to get Will his posh lunch in a restaurant. "Here. How much? Another ten? Twenty?" I thrust a fistful of notes at her.

She looked down at my hand. "I'm sorry, Madam, we don't sell badges here. This is a restaurant. You'll have to go back to the ticket office."

"The one that's all the way over at the other side of the racecourse."

"Yes."

We stared at each other.

Will's voice broke in. "Louisa, let's go."

I felt my eyes suddenly brim with tears. "No," I said. "This is ridiculous. We've come all this way. You stay here and I'll go and get us all Premier Area badges. And then we will have our meal."

"Louisa, I'm not hungry."

"We'll be fine once we've eaten. We can watch the horses and everything. It will be fine."

Nathan stepped forward and laid a hand on my arm. "Louisa, I think Will really just wants to go home."

We were now the focus of the whole restaurant. The gaze of the diners swept over us and traveled past me to Will, where they clouded with faint pity or distaste. I felt like an utter failure. I looked up at the woman, who did at least have the grace to look slightly embarrassed now that Will had actually spoken.

"Well, thank you," I said to her. "Thanks for being so fucking accommodating."

"Clark—" Will's voice carried a warning.

"So glad that you are so flexible. I'll certainly recommend you to everyone I know."

"Louisa!"

I grabbed my bag and thrust it under my arm.

"You've forgotten your little car," she called, as I swept through the door that Nathan held open for me.

"Why, does that need a bloody badge too?" I said, and followed them into the lift.

We descended in silence. I spent most of the short lift journey trying to stop my hands from shaking with rage.

———

We ordered three buns with pork, crackling, and applesauce, and sheltered under the striped awning while we ate them. I perched on a small dustbin, so that I could be at the same level as Will, and helped him to manageable bites of meat, shredding it with my fingers when necessary. The two women who served behind the counter pretended not to look at us. I could see them monitoring Will out of the corners of their eyes, periodically muttering to each other when they thought we weren't looking. *Poor man*, I could practically hear them saying. *What a terrible way to live.* I tried not to think too hard about what Will must be feeling.

The rain had stopped, but the windswept course felt suddenly bleak, its brown and green surface littered with discarded betting slips, its horizon flat and empty. The car park had thinned out with the rain, and in the distance we could just hear the distorted sound of the loudspeaker as some other race thundered past.

"I think maybe we should head back," Nathan said, wiping his mouth. "I mean, it was nice and all, but best to miss the traffic, eh?"

"Didn't he like it?" said one of the women, as Nathan began to wheel him away across the grass.

"I don't know. Perhaps he would have liked it better if it hadn't come with a side order of rubberneck," I said, and chucked the remnants hard into the bin.

But getting to the car and back up the ramp was easier said than done. In the few hours that we had spent at the racecourse, the arrivals and departures meant that the car park had turned into a sea of mud. Even with Nathan's impressive might, and my best shoulder, we couldn't get the chair even halfway across the grass to the car. The wheels skidded and whined, unable to get the purchase to make it up that last couple of inches. My feet and Nathan's slithered in the mud, which worked its way up the sides of our shoes.

"It's not going to happen," said Will.

"I think we're going to need some help," Nathan said. "I can't even get the chair back onto the path. It's stuck."

Will let out an audible sigh. He looked about as fed up as I had ever seen him.

"I could lift you into the front seat, Will, if I tilt it back a little. And then Louisa and I could see if we could get the chair in afterward."

Will's voice emerged through gritted teeth. "I am not ending today with a fireman's lift."

"Sorry, mate," Nathan said. "But Lou and I are not going to be able to manage this alone. Here, Lou, you're prettier than I am. Go and collar a few extra pairs of arms, will you?"

Will closed his eyes, set his jaw, and I ran toward the stands.

———

I am not usually good with strangers, but desperation made me fearless. I walked from group to group of race-goers in the grandstand, asking if anyone could just spare me a few minutes' help. They looked at me and my clothes as if I were plotting some kind of trap.

"We're just waiting on the next race," they said. Or, "Sorry." Or, "It'll have to wait till after the two thirty."

I even thought about collaring a jockey or two. But as I got near the enclosure, I saw that they were even smaller than I was.

By the time I got to the parade ring I was incandescent with suppressed rage. I suspect I was snarling at people then, not smiling. And there, finally, joy of joys, were the lads in striped polo shirts. The backs of their shirts referred to "Marky's Last Stand" and they clutched cans of Pilsner and Tennent's Extra. They cheered as I approached, and I fought the urge to give them the finger again.

"Gissa smile, sweetheart. It's Marky's stag weekend," one slurred, slamming a ham-sized hand on my shoulder.

"It's Monday." I tried not to flinch as I peeled it off.

"You're joking. Monday already?" He reeled backward.

"Actually," I said, "I've come over to ask you for help."

"Ah'll give you any help you need, pet." This was accompanied by a lascivious wink.

His mates swayed gently around him like aquatic plants.

"I need you to help my friend. Over in the car park."

"Ah'm sorry, ah'm not sure ah'm in any fit state to help youse, pet."

"Next race is up, Marky. You got money on this? I think I've got money on this."

They turned back toward the track, already losing interest. I looked over my shoulder at the car park, seeing the hunched figure of Will, Nathan pulling vainly at the handles of his chair. I pictured myself returning home to tell Will's parents that we had left Will's superexpensive chair in a car park. And then I saw the tattoo.

"He's a soldier," I said, loudly. "Ex-soldier."

One by one they turned around.

"He was injured. In Iraq. All we wanted to do was get him a nice day out. But nobody will help us." As I spoke the words, I felt my eyes welling up with tears.

"Where is he?"

"In the car park. I've asked lots of people, but they just don't want to help."

"C'mon, lads. We're not having that." They swayed after me in a wayward trail. When we reached them, Nathan was standing by Will, whose head had sunk deep into the collar of his coat with cold, even as Nathan covered his shoulders with another blanket.

"These very nice gentlemen have offered to help us," I said.

Nathan was staring at the cans of lager. I had to admit that you'd have had to look quite hard to see a suit of armor in any of them.

"Where do youse want to get him to?" said one.

The others stood around Will, nodding their hellos. One offered him a beer, apparently unable to grasp that Will could not pick it up.

Nathan motioned to our car. "Back in the car, ultimately. But to do that we need to get him over to the stand, and then reverse the car back to him."

"You don't need to do that," said one, clapping Nathan on the back. "We can take him to your car, can't we, lads?"

There was a chorus of agreement. They began to position themselves around Will's chair.

I shifted uncomfortably. "I don't know . . . that's a long way for you to carry him," I ventured. "And the chair's very heavy."

They were howlingly drunk. Some of them could barely hang on to their cans of drink. One thrust his Tennent's into my hand.

"Don't you worry, pet. Anything for a fellow soldier, isn't that right, lads?"

"We wouldn't leave you there, mate. We never leave a man down."

I saw Nathan's face and shook my head furiously at his quizzical expression. Will seemed unlikely to say anything. He just looked grim, and then—as the men clustered around his chair and with a shout hoisted it up between them—vaguely alarmed.

"What regiment, pet?"

I tried to smile, trawling my memory for names. "Rifles . . . ," I said. "Eleventh Rifles."

"I don't know the Eleventh Rifles," said another.

"It's a new regiment," I stuttered. "Top secret. Based in Iraq."

Their trainers slid in the mud, and I felt my heart lurch. Will's chair was hoisted several inches off the ground, like some kind of sedan. Nathan was running for Will's bag, and unlocking the car ahead of us.

"Did those boys train over in Catterick?"

"That's the one," I said, and then changed the subject. "So—which one of you is getting married?"

We had exchanged numbers by the time I finally got rid of Marky and his mates. They dug into their pockets, offering us almost forty pounds toward Will's rehabilitation fund, and only stopped insisting when I told them we would be happiest if they would have a drink on us instead. I had to kiss each and every one of them. I was nearly dizzy with fumes by the time I had finished. I continued to wave at them as they disappeared back into the stands, and Nathan sounded the horn to get me into the car.

"They were helpful, weren't they?" I said brightly, as I turned the ignition.

"The tall one dropped his entire beer down my right leg," said Will. "I smell like a brewery."

"I don't believe this," said Nathan, as I finally pulled out toward the main entrance. "Look. There's a whole disabled parking section right there, by the stand. And it's all on tarmac."

Will didn't say much of anything for the rest of the day. He bid Nathan good-bye when we dropped him off at home, and then grew silent as I negotiated the road up to the castle. The traffic had thinned out now that the temperature had dropped again, and finally I parked outside the annex.

I lowered Will's chair, got him inside, and made him a warm drink. I changed his shoes and trousers, put the beer-stained ones in the washing machine, and got the fire going. I put the television on, and drew the curtains so that the room grew cozy around us—perhaps cozier for the time spent out in the cold air. But it was only when I sat in the living room with him, sipping my tea, that I realized he wasn't talking—not out of exhaustion, or because he wanted to watch the television. He just wasn't talking to me.

"Is . . . something the matter?" I said, when he failed to respond to my third comment about the local news.

"You tell me, Clark."

"What?"

"Well, you know everything else there is to know about me. You tell me."

I stared at him. "I'm sorry," I said, finally. "I know today didn't turn out quite like I planned. But it was just meant to be a nice outing. I actually thought you'd enjoy it."

I didn't add that he was being determinedly grumpy, that he had no idea what I had gone through just to get him to try to enjoy himself, that he hadn't even tried to have a good time. I didn't tell him that if he'd let me buy the stupid badges we might have had a nice lunch and all the other stuff might have been forgotten.

"That's my point."

"What?"

"Oh, you're no different from the rest of them."

"What does that mean?"

"If you'd bothered to ask me, Clark, if you'd bothered to consult me just once about this so-called fun outing of ours, I could have told you. I hate horses, and horse racing. Always have. But you didn't bother to ask me. You decided what you thought you'd like me to do, and you went ahead and did it. You did what everyone else does. You decided for me."

I swallowed.

"I didn't mean to—"

"But you did."

He turned his chair away from me, and after another couple of minutes of silence, I realized I had been dismissed.

12

I can tell you the exact day I stopped being fearless.

It was almost seven years ago, in the last lazy, heat-slurred days of July, when the narrow streets around the castle were thick with tourists, and the air filled with the sound of their meandering footsteps and the chimes of the ever-present ice cream vans that lined the top of the hill.

My grandmother had died a month previously after a long illness, and that summer was veiled in a thin layer of sadness; it gently smothered everything we did, muting my and my sister's tendencies to the dramatic, and canceling our usual summer routines of brief holidays and days out. My mother stood most days at her washing-up bowl, her back rigid with the effort of trying to suppress her tears, while Dad disappeared to work each morning with a grimly determined expression, returning hours later shiny-faced from the heat and unable to speak before he had cracked open a beer. My sister was home from her first year at university, her head already somewhere far from our small town. I was twenty and would meet Patrick in less than three months. We were enjoying one of those rare summers of utter freedom—no financial responsibility, no debts, no time owing to anybody. I had a seasonal job and all the hours in the world to practice my makeup, put on heels that made my father wince, and just generally work out who I was.

I dressed normally, in those days. Or, I should say, I dressed like the other girls in town—long hair, flicked over the shoulder, indigo jeans, T-shirts tight enough to show off our tiny waists and high breasts. We spent hours perfecting our lip gloss, and the exact shade of a smoky eye. We looked good in anything, but spent hours complaining about nonexistent cellulite and invisible flaws in our skin.

And I had ideas. Things I wanted to do. One of the boys I knew at school had taken a round-the-world trip and come back somehow removed and unknowable, like he wasn't the same scuffed eleven-year-old who used to blow spit bubbles during double French. I had booked a cheap flight to Australia on a whim, and was trying to find someone who might come with me. I liked the exoticism his travels gave him, the unknownness. He had blown in with the soft breezes of a wider world, and it was weirdly seductive. Everyone here knew everything about me, after all. And with a sister like mine, I was never allowed to forget any of it.

It was a Friday, and I had spent the day working as a car park attendant with a group of girls I had known at school, steering visitors to a craft fair held on the grounds of the castle. The whole day was punctuated with laughter, with fizzy drinks guzzled under a hot sun, the blue sky's light glinting off the battlements. I don't think there was a single tourist who didn't smile at me that day. People find it very hard not to smile at a group of cheerful, giggling girls. We were paid thirty pounds, and the organizers were so pleased with the turnout that they gave us an extra fiver each. We celebrated by getting drunk with some boys who had been working on the far car park by the visitor center. They were well spoken, sporting rugby shirts and floppy hair. One was called Ed, two of them were at university—I still can't remember where—and they were working for holiday money too. They were flush with cash at the end of a whole week of stewarding, and when our money ran out they were happy to buy drinks for giddy local girls who flicked their hair and sat on one another's laps and shrieked and joked and called them posh. They spoke a different language; they talked of gap years and summers spent in South America, and the backpacker trail in Thailand and who was going to try for an internship abroad. While we listened, and drank, I remember my sister stopping by the beer garden where we lay sprawled on the grass. She was wearing the world's oldest hoody and no makeup, and I'd forgotten I was meant to be meeting her. I told her to tell Mum and Dad I'd be back sometime after I was thirty. For some reason I found this hysterically funny. She had lifted her eyebrows, and stalked off like I was the most irritating person ever born.

When the Red Lion closed we all went and sat in the center of the castle maze. Someone managed to scramble over the gates and, after much colliding and giggling, we all found our way to the middle and drank strong cider while someone passed around a joint. I remember staring up at the stars, feeling myself disappear into their infinite depths, as the ground gently swayed and lurched around me like the deck of a huge ship. Someone was playing a guitar, and I had on a pair of pink satin high heels, which I kicked into the long grass and never went back for. I thought I probably ruled the universe.

It was about half an hour before I realized that the other girls had gone.

My sister found me silent and shivering, in the center of the maze, sometime later, long after the stars had been obscured by the night clouds. As I said, she's pretty smart. Smarter than me, anyway.

She's the only person I ever knew who could find her way out of the maze safely.

———

"This will make you laugh. I've joined the library."

Will was over by his CD collection. He swiveled the chair around, and waited while I put his drink in his cup holder. "Really? What are you reading?"

"Oh, nothing sensible. You wouldn't like it. Just boy-meets-girl stuff. But I'm enjoying it."

"You were reading my Flannery O'Connor the other day." He took a sip of his drink. "When I was ill."

"The short stories? I can't believe you noticed that."

"I couldn't help but notice. You left the book out on the side. I can't pick it up."

"Ah."

"So don't read rubbish. Take the O'Connor stories home. Read them instead."

I was about to say no, and then I realized I didn't really know why I was refusing. "All right. I'll bring them back as soon as I've finished."

"Put some music on for me, Clark."

"What do you want?"

He told me, nodding at its rough location, and I flicked through until I found the CD.

"I have a friend who plays lead violin in the Albert Symphonia. He called to say he's playing near here next week. This piece of music. Do you know it?"

"I don't know anything about classical music. I mean, sometimes my dad accidentally tunes into Classic FM, but—"

"You've never been to a concert?"

"No."

He looked genuinely shocked.

"Well, I did go to see Westlife once. But I'm not sure if that counts. It was my sister's choice. Oh, and I was meant to go see Robbie Williams on my twenty-second birthday, but I got food poisoning."

Will gave me one of his looks—the kind of look that suggests I may actually have been locked up in somebody's cellar for several years.

"You should go. He's offered me tickets. This will be really good. Take your mother."

I laughed and shook my head. "I don't think so. My mum doesn't really go out. And it's not my cup of tea."

"Like films with subtitles weren't your cup of tea?"

I frowned at him. "I'm not your project, Will. This isn't *My Fair Lady*."

"*Pygmalion*."

"What?"

"The play you're referring to. It's *Pygmalion*. *My Fair Lady* is just its bastard offspring."

I glared at him. It didn't work. I put the CD on. When I turned around he was still shaking his head.

"You're the most terrible snob, Clark."

"What? *Me?*"

"You cut yourself off from all sorts of experiences because you tell yourself you are 'not that sort of person.'"

"But I'm not."

"How do you know? You've done nothing, been nowhere. How do you have the faintest idea what kind of person you are?"

How could someone like him have the slightest clue what it felt like to be me? I felt almost cross with him for willfully not getting it.

"Go on. Open your mind."

"No."

"Why?"

"Because I'd be uncomfortable. I feel like . . . I feel like they'd know."

"Who? Know what?"

"Everyone else would know that I didn't belong."

"How do you think I feel?"

We looked at each other.

"Clark, every single place I go to now people look at me like I don't belong."

We sat in silence as the music started. Will's father was on the telephone in his hall, and the sound of muffled laughter carried through it into the annex, as if from a long way away. *The disabled entrance is over there*, the woman at the racecourse had said. As if he were a different species.

I stared at the CD cover. "I'll go if you come with me."

"But you won't go on your own."

"Not a chance."

We sat there, while he digested this. "Jesus, you're a pain in the arse."

"So you keep telling me."

———

I made no plans this time. I expected nothing. I was just quietly hopeful that, after the racing debacle, Will was still prepared to leave the annex. His friend the violinist sent us the promised free tickets, with an information leaflet on the venue attached. It was a forty-minute drive away. I did my homework, checked the location of the disabled parking, rang the venue beforehand to assess the best way to get Will's chair to his seat. They would place us at the front, with me on a folding chair beside Will.

"It's actually the best location," the woman in the box office said cheerfully. "You somehow get more of an impact when you're right in the pit near the orchestra. I've often been tempted to sit there myself."

She even asked if I would like someone to meet us in the car park, to help us to our seats. Afraid that Will would feel too conspicuous, I thanked her and said no.

As the evening approached, I don't know who grew more nervous about it, Will or me. I felt the failure of our last outing keenly, and Mrs. Traynor didn't help, coming in and out of the annex fourteen times to confirm where and when the concert would be taking place and what exactly we would be doing.

Will's postconcert evening routine would also take some time, she said. She needed to ensure that someone was there to help. Nathan had other plans later. Mr. Traynor was apparently out for the evening. "It's an hour and a half minimum," she said.

"And it's incredibly tedious," Will said.

I realized he was looking for an excuse not to go. "I'll

do it," I said. "If Will tells me what to do. I don't mind staying to help." I said it almost before I realized what I was agreeing to.

"Well, that's something for us both to look forward to," Will said grumpily after his mother had left. "You get a good view of my backside, and I get a bed bath from someone who falls over at the sight of naked flesh."

"I do not fall over at the sight of naked flesh."

"Clark, I've never seen anyone more uncomfortable with a human body than you."

"Let your mum do it, then," I snapped back.

"Yes, because that makes the whole idea of going out so much more attractive."

And then there was the wardrobe problem. I didn't know what to wear.

I had worn the wrong thing to the races. How could I be sure I wouldn't do so again? I asked Will what would be best, and he looked at me as if I were mad. "The lights will be down," he explained. "Nobody will be looking at you. They'll be focused on the music."

"You know *nothing* about women," I said.

I brought three different outfits to work with me in the end, hauling them all onto the bus in my dad's ancient suit carrier. It was the only way I could convince myself to go at all.

Nathan arrived for the teatime shift at 5:30 P.M., and while he saw to Will I disappeared into the bathroom to get ready. First I put on what I thought of as my "artistic" outfit, a green smock dress with huge amber beads stitched into it. I imagined the kind of people who went to concerts might be quite arty and flamboyant. Will and Nathan both stared at me as I entered the living room.

"No," said Will flatly.

"That looks like something my mum would wear," said Nathan.

"You never told me your mum was Nana Mouskouri," Will said.

I could hear them both chuckling as I disappeared back into the bathroom.

The second outfit was a very severe black dress, cut on the bias and stitched with white collar and cuffs, which I had made myself. It looked, I thought, both chic and Parisian.

"You look like you're about to serve the ice creams," Will said.

"Aw, mate, but you'd make a great maid," Nathan said, approvingly. "Feel free to wear that one in the daytime. Really."

"You," I said, "are both going to get Mr. Muscle in your tea tomorrow."

I put on my third option, a vintage dress in dark-red satin. It was made for a more frugal generation and I always had to say a secret prayer that the zip would make it up past my waist, but it gave me the outline of a 1950s starlet, and it was a "results" dress, one of those outfits you couldn't help but feel good in. I put a silver bolero over my shoulders, tied a gray silk scarf around my neck to cover up my cleavage, applied some matching lipstick, and then stepped into the living room.

"*Ka-pow,*" said Nathan, admiringly.

Will's eyes traveled up and down my dress. It was only then that I realized he had changed into a shirt and suit jacket. Clean-shaven, and with his trimmed hair, he looked surprisingly handsome. I couldn't help but smile at the sight of him. It wasn't so much how he looked; it was the fact that he had made the effort.

"That's the one," he said. His voice was expressionless and oddly measured. And as I reached down to adjust my neckline, he said, "But lose the jacket."

He was right. I had known it wasn't quite right. I took it off, folded it carefully, and laid it on the back of the chair.

"And the scarf."

My hand shot to my neck. "The scarf? Why?"

"It doesn't go. And you look like you're trying to hide something behind it."

"But I'm . . . well, I'm all cleavage otherwise."

"So?" He shrugged. "Look, Clark, if you're going to wear a dress like that you need to wear it with confidence. You need to fill it mentally as well as physically."

"Only you, Will Traynor, could tell a woman how to wear a bloody dress."

But I took the scarf off.

Nathan went to pack Will's bag. I was working out what I could add about how patronizing he was when I turned and saw that he was still looking at me.

"You look great, Clark," he said, quietly. "Really."

With ordinary people—what Camilla Traynor would probably call "working-class" people—I had observed a few basic routines as far as Will was concerned. Most would stare. A few might smile sympathetically, express sympathy, or ask me in a stage whisper what had happened. I was often tempted to respond, "Unfortunate falling-out with MI6," just to see their reaction, but I never did.

Here's the thing about middle-class people. They pretend not to look, but they do. They're too polite to actually stare. Instead, they do this weird thing of catching sight of Will in their field of vision and then determinedly *not* looking at him. Until he's gone past, at which point their gaze flickers toward him, even while they remain in conversation with someone else. They won't talk about him, though. Because that would be rude.

As we moved through the foyer of the symphony hall, where clusters of smart people stood with handbags and programs in one hand, gin and tonics in the other, I saw this response pass through them in a gentle ripple that followed us to the stalls. I don't know if Will noticed it. Sometimes I thought the only way he could deal with it was to pretend he could see none of it.

We sat down, the only two people at the front in the center block of seats. To our right there was another man in a wheelchair, chatting cheerfully to two women who flanked him. I watched them, hoping that Will would notice them too. But he stared straight in front of him, his head dipped into his shoulders as if he were trying to become invisible.

This isn't going to work, a little voice said.

"Do you need anything?" I whispered.

"No." He shook his head. He swallowed. "Actually, yes. Something's digging into my collar."

I leaned over and ran my finger around the inside of it; a nylon tag had been left inside. I pulled at it, hoping to snap it, but it proved stubbornly resistant.

"New shirt. Is it really troubling you?"

"No. I just thought I'd bring it up for fun."

"Do we have any scissors in the bag?"

"I don't know, Clark. Believe it or not, I rarely pack it myself."

There were no scissors. I glanced behind me, where the other concertgoers were still settling themselves into their seats, murmuring and scanning their programs. If Will couldn't relax and focus on the music, the outing would be wasted. I couldn't afford a second disaster.

"Don't move," I said.

"Why—"

Before he could finish, I leaned across, gently peeled his collar from the side of his neck, placed my mouth against it, and took the offending tag between my front teeth. After a few seconds, I was able to bite through it, and I closed my eyes, trying to ignore the scent of clean male, the feel of his skin against mine, the incongruity of what I was doing. And then, finally, I felt it give. I pulled back my head and opened my eyes, triumphant, with the freed tag between my front teeth.

"Got it!" I said, pulling the tag from my teeth and flicking it across the seats.

Will stared at me.

"What?"

I swiveled in my chair to catch those audience members who suddenly seemed to find their programs absolutely fascinating. Then I turned back to Will.

"Oh, come on, it's not as if they've never seen a girl nibbling a bloke's collar before."

I seemed to have briefly silenced him. Will blinked a couple of times and made as if to shake his head. I noticed with amusement that his neck had colored a deep red.

I straightened my skirt. "Anyway," I said, "I think we should both just be grateful that it wasn't in your trousers."

And then, before he could respond, the orchestra musicians walked out in their dinner jackets and cocktail dresses and the audience grew quiet. I felt a little flutter of excitement despite myself. I placed my hands together on my lap and sat up in my seat. They began to tune up, and suddenly the auditorium was filled with a single sound—the most alive, three-dimensional thing I had ever heard. It made the hairs on my skin stand up, my breath catch in my throat.

Will looked sideways at me, his face still carrying the mirth of the last few moments. *Okay*, his expression said. *We're going to enjoy this*.

The conductor stepped up, tapped twice on the rostrum, and a great hush descended. I felt the stillness, the auditorium alive, expectant. Then he brought down his baton and suddenly everything was pure sound. I felt the music like a physical thing; it didn't just sit in my ears, it flowed through me, around me, made my senses vibrate. It made my skin prickle and my palms dampen. Will hadn't described any of it like this. I had thought I might be bored. It was the most beautiful thing I had ever heard.

And it made my imagination do unexpected things; as I sat there, I found myself thinking of things I hadn't thought of for years, old emotions washing over me, new thoughts and ideas being pulled from me as if my perception itself were being stretched out of shape. It was almost too much, but I didn't want it to stop. I wanted to sit there forever. I stole a look at Will. He was rapt, suddenly unself-conscious. I turned away, unexpectedly afraid to look at him. I was afraid of what he might be feeling, the depth of his loss, the extent of his fears. Will Traynor's life had been so far beyond the experiences of mine. Who was I to tell him how he should want to live it?

———

Will's friend left a note asking us to go backstage and see him afterward, but Will didn't want to. I urged him once, but I could see from the set of his jaw that he would not be budged. I couldn't blame him. I remembered how his former workmate Rupert had looked at him that day—that mixture of pity, revulsion, and, somewhere, deep relief that he himself had escaped this particular stroke of fate. I suspected there were only so many of those sorts of meetings he could stomach.

We waited until the auditorium was empty, then I wheeled him out, down to the car park in the lift, and loaded Will up without incident. I didn't say much; my head was still ringing with the music, and I didn't want it to fade. I kept thinking back to it, the way that Will's friend had been so lost in what he was playing. I hadn't realized that music could unlock things in you, could transport you to somewhere even the composer hadn't predicted. It left an imprint in the air around you, as if you carried its remnants with you when you went. For some time, as we sat there in the audience, I had completely forgotten Will was even beside me.

We pulled up outside the annex. In front of us, just visible above the wall, the castle sat, floodlit under the full moon, gazing serenely down from its position on the top of the hill.

"So you're not a classical music person."

I looked into the rearview mirror. Will was smiling.

"I didn't enjoy that in the slightest."

"I could tell."

"I especially didn't enjoy that bit near the end, the bit where the violin was singing by itself."

"I could see you didn't like that bit. In fact, I think you had tears in your eyes you hated it so much."

I grinned back at him. "I really loved it," I said. "I'm not sure I'd like *all* classical music, but I thought that was amazing." I rubbed my nose. "Thank you. Thank you for taking me."

We sat in silence, gazing at the castle. Normally, at night, it was bathed in a kind of orange glow from the lights dotted around the fortress wall. But tonight, under a full moon, it seemed flooded in an ethereal blue.

"What kind of music would they have played there, do you think?" I said. "They must have listened to something."

"The castle? Medieval stuff. Lutes, strings. Not my cup of tea, but I've got some I can lend you, if you like. You should walk around the castle with it on earphones, if you really want the full experience."

"Nah. I don't really go to the castle."

"It's always the way, when you live close by somewhere."

We sat there a moment longer, listening to the engine tick its way to silence.

"Right," I said, unfastening my belt. "We'd better get you in. The evening routine awaits."

"Just wait a minute, Clark."

I turned in my seat. Will's face was in shadow and I couldn't quite make it out.

"Just hold on. Just for a minute."

"Are you all right?" I found my gaze dropping toward his chair, afraid some part of him was pinched, or trapped, that I had gotten something wrong.

"I'm fine. I just . . ."

I could see his pale collar, his dark suit jacket a contrast against it.

"I don't want to go in just yet. I just want to sit and not have to think about . . ." He swallowed.

Even in the half-dark it seemed effortful.

"I just . . . want to be a man who has been to a concert with a girl in a red dress. Just for a few minutes more."

I released the door handle.

"Sure."

I closed my eyes and lay my head against the headrest, and we sat there together for a while longer, two people lost in remembered music, half hidden in the shadow of a castle on a moonlit hill.

———

My sister and I never really talked about what happened that night at the maze. I'm not entirely sure we had the words. She held me for a bit, then spent some time helping me find my clothes, and then searched in vain in the long grass for my shoes until I told her that it really didn't matter. I wouldn't have worn them again, anyway. And then we walked home slowly—me in my bare feet, her with her arm linked through mine, even though we hadn't walked like that since she was in her first year at school and Mum had insisted I never let her go.

When we got home, we stood on the porch and she wiped at my hair and then at my eyes with a damp tissue, and then we unlocked the front door and walked in as if nothing had happened.

Dad was still up, watching some football match. "You girls are a bit late," he called out. "I know it's a Friday, but still . . ."

"Okay, Dad," we called out, in unison.

Back then, I had the room that is now Granddad's. I walked swiftly upstairs and, before my sister could say a word, I closed the door behind me.

I chopped all my hair off the following week. I canceled

my plane ticket. I didn't go out with the girls from my old school again. Mum was too sunk in her own grief to notice, and Dad put any change in mood in our house, and my new habit of locking myself in my bedroom, down to "Women's problems." I had worked out who I was, and it was someone very different from the giggling girl who got drunk with strangers. It was someone who wore nothing that could be construed as suggestive. Clothes that would not appeal to the kind of men who went to the Red Lion, anyway.

Life returned to normal. I took a job at the hairdresser's, then the Buttered Bun, and put it all behind me.

I must have walked past the castle five thousand times since that day.

But I have never been to the maze since.

13

Patrick stood on the edge of the track, jogging on the spot, his new Nike T-shirt and shorts sticking slightly to his damp limbs. I had stopped by to say hello and to tell him that I wouldn't be at the Triathlon Terrors meeting at the pub that evening. Nathan was off, and I had stepped in to take over the evening routine.

"That's three meetings you've missed."

"Is it?" I counted back on my fingers. "I suppose it is."

"You'll have to come next week. It's all the travel plans for the Xtreme Viking. And you haven't told me what you want to do for your birthday." He began to do his stretches, lifting his leg high and pressing his chest to his knee. "I thought maybe the cinema? I don't want to do a big meal, not while I'm training."

"Ah. Mum and Dad are planning a special dinner."

He grabbed at his heel, pointing his knee to the ground.

I couldn't help but notice that his leg was becoming weirdly sinewy.

"It's not exactly a night out, is it?"

"Well, nor is the multiplex. Anyway, I feel like I should, Patrick. Mum's been a bit down."

Treena had moved out the previous weekend (minus my lemons washbag). Mum was devastated; it was actually worse than when Treena had gone to university the first time around. She missed Thomas like an amputated limb. His toys, which had littered the living-room floor since babyhood, were boxed up and put away. There were no chocolate fingers or small cartons of drink in the cupboard. She no longer had a reason to walk to the school at 3:15 P.M., nobody to chat to on the short walk home. It had been the only time Mum ever really spent outside the house. Now she went nowhere at all, apart from the weekly supermarket shopping with Dad.

She floated around the house looking a bit lost for three days, then she began spring cleaning with a vigor that frightened even Granddad. He would mouth gummy protests at her as she tried to vacuum under the chair that he was still sitting in or flick at his shoulders with her duster. Treena had said she wouldn't come home for the first few weeks, just to give Thomas a chance to settle in. When she rang each evening, Mum would speak to them and then cry for a full half hour in her bedroom afterward.

"You're always working late these days. I feel like I hardly see you."

"Well, you're always training. Anyway, it's good money, Patrick. I'm hardly going to say no to the overtime."

He couldn't argue with that.

I was earning more than I had ever earned in my life. I doubled the amount I gave my parents, put some aside into a savings account every month, and I was still left with more than I could spend. Part of it was, I worked so many hours that I was never away from Granta House when the shops were open. The other was, simply, that I didn't really have an appetite for spending. The spare hours I did have I had started to spend in the library, looking things up on the Internet.

There was a whole world available to me from that PC, layer upon layer of it, and it had begun to exert a siren call.

It had started with the thank-you letter. A couple of days after the concert, I told Will I thought we should write and thank his friend, the violinist.

"I bought a nice card on the way in," I said. "You tell

me what you want to say, and I'll write it. I've even brought in my good pen."

"I don't think so," Will said.

"What?"

"You heard me."

"You don't *think* so? That man gave us front-of-house seats. You said yourself it was fantastic. The least you could do is thank him."

Will's jaw was fixed, immovable.

I put down my pen. "Or are you just so used to people giving you stuff that you don't feel you have to?"

"You have no idea, Clark, how frustrating it is to rely on someone else to put your words down for you. The phrase 'written on behalf of' is . . . humiliating."

"Yeah? Well, it's still better than a great big fat nothing," I grumbled. "*I'm* going to thank him, anyway. I won't mention your name, if you really want to be an arse about it."

I wrote the card, and posted it. I said nothing more about it. But that evening, with Will's words still echoing around my head, I found myself diverting into the library. I looked up whether there were any devices that Will could use to do his own writing. Within an hour, I had come up with three—a piece of voice recognition software, another type of software that relied on the blinking of an eye, and, as my sister had mentioned, a tapping device that Will could wear on his head.

He was predictably sniffy about the head device, but he conceded that the voice recognition software might be useful, and within a week we managed, with Nathan's help, to install it on his computer, setting Will up so that with the computer tray fixed to his chair, he no longer needed someone else to type for him. He was self-conscious about it initially, but after I instructed him to begin everything with "Take a letter, Miss Clark," he got over it.

Even Mrs. Traynor couldn't find anything to complain about. "If there is any other equipment that you think might be useful," she said, her lips still pursed as if she couldn't quite believe this might have been a straightfor-wardly good thing, "do let us know." Three days later, just as I set off for work, the postman handed me a let-ter. I opened it on the bus, thinking it might be an early birthday card from some distant cousin. It read, in com-puterized text:

> *Dear Clark,*
> *This is to show you that I am not an entirely*
> *selfish arse. And I do appreciate your efforts.*
> *Thank you. Will*

I laughed so hard the bus driver asked me if my lot-tery numbers had come up.

———

After years in that box room, my clothes perched on a rail in the hallway outside, Treena's bedroom felt pala-tial. The first night I spent in it I spun around with my arms outstretched, just luxuriating in the fact that I couldn't touch both walls simultaneously. I went to the DIY store and bought paint and new blinds, as well as a new bedside light and some shelves, which I assembled myself. It's not that I'm good at that stuff; I guess I just wanted to see if I could do it.

I set about redecorating, painting for an hour a night after I came home from work, and at the end of the week even Dad had to admit I'd done a really good job. He stared for a bit at my cutting in, fingered the blinds that I had put up myself, and put his hand on my shoul-der. "This job has been the making of you, Lou."

I bought a new duvet cover, a rug, and some over-sized cushions—just in case anyone ever stopped by, and fancied lounging. Not that anyone did. The calendar went on the back of the new door. Nobody saw it except for me. Nobody else would have known what it meant, anyway.

I went to work each day thinking about other places I could take Will. I didn't have any overall plan, I just focused each day on getting him out and about and trying to keep him happy. There were some days—days when his limbs burned, or when infection claimed him and he lay miserable and feverish in bed—that were harder than others. But on the good days I had managed several times to get him out into the spring sunshine. I knew now that one of the things Will hated most was the pity of strangers, so I drove him to local beauty spots, where for an hour or so it could be just the two of us. I made picnics and we sat out on the edges of fields, just enjoying the breeze and being away from the annex.

"My boyfriend wants to meet you," I told him one afternoon, breaking off pieces of cheese-and-pickle sandwich for him.

I had driven several miles out of town, up onto a hill, and we could see the castle across the valley opposite, separated from us by fields of lambs.

"Why?"

"He wants to know who I'm spending all these late nights with."

Oddly, I could see he found this quite cheering.

"Running Man."

"I think my parents do too."

"I get nervous when a girl says she wants me to meet her parents. How is your mum, anyway?"

"The same."

"Your dad's job? Any news?"

"No. Next week, they're telling him now. Anyway, they said did I want to invite you to my birthday dinner on Friday? All very relaxed. Just family, really. But it's fine . . . I said you wouldn't want to."

"Who says I wouldn't want to?"

"You hate strangers. You don't like eating in front of people. And you don't like the sound of my boyfriend. It seems like a no-brainer to me."

I had worked him out now. The best way to get Will to do anything was to tell him you knew he wouldn't want to. Some obstinate, contrary part of him still couldn't bear it.

Will chewed for a minute. "No. I'll come to your birthday. It'll give your mother something to focus on, if nothing else."

"Really? Oh God, if I tell her she'll start polishing and dusting this evening."

"Are you sure she's your biological mother? Isn't there supposed to be some kind of genetic similarity there? Sandwich, please, Clark. And more pickle on the next bit."

I had been only half joking. Mum went into a complete tailspin at the thought of hosting a quadriplegic. Her hands flew to her face, and then she started rearranging stuff on the dresser, as if he were going to arrive within minutes of me telling her.

"But what if he needs to go to the loo? We don't have a downstairs bathroom. I don't think Daddy would be able to carry him upstairs. I could help . . . but I'd feel a bit worried about where to put my hands. Would Patrick do it?"

"You don't need to worry about that side of things. Really."

"And what about his food? Will he need his pureed? Is there anything he can't eat?"

"No, he just needs help picking it up."

"Who's going to do that?"

"I will. Relax, Mum. He's nice. You'll like him."

And so it was arranged. Nathan would pick up Will and drive him over, and would come by two hours later to take him home again and run through the nighttime routine. I had offered, but they both insisted I should "let my hair down" on my birthday. They plainly hadn't met my parents.

At half past seven on the dot, I opened the door to

find Will and Nathan on the front porch. Will was wearing his smart shirt and jacket. I didn't know whether to be pleased that he had made the effort or worried that my mum would now spend the first hour of the night worrying that she hadn't dressed smartly enough.

"Hey, you."

My dad emerged into the hallway behind me. "Aha. Was the ramp okay, lads?" He had spent all afternoon making the particleboard ramp for the outside steps.

Nathan carefully negotiated Will's chair up and into our narrow hallway. "Nice," Nathan said, as I closed the door behind him. "Very nice. I've seen worse in hospitals."

"Bernard Clark." Dad reached out and shook Nathan's hand. He held it out toward Will, before snatching it away again with a sudden flush of embarrassment. "Bernard. Sorry, um . . . I don't know how to greet a . . . I can't shake your—" He began to stutter.

"A curtsy will be fine."

Dad stared at him and then, when he realized Will was joking, he let out a great laugh of relief. "Hah!" he said, and clapped Will on the shoulder. "Yes. Curtsy. Nice one. Hah!"

It broke the ice. Nathan left with a wave and a wink, and I wheeled Will through to the kitchen. Mum, luckily, was holding a casserole dish, which absolved her of the same anxiety.

"Mum, this is Will. Will, Josephine."

"Josie, please." She beamed at him, her oven gloves up to her elbows. "Lovely to meet you finally, Will."

"Pleased to meet you," he said. "Don't let me interrupt."

She put down the dish and her hand went to her hair, always a good sign with my mother. It was a shame she hadn't remembered to take an oven glove off first.

"Sorry," she said. "Roast dinner. It's all in the timing, you know."

"Not really," Will said. "I'm not a cook. But I love good food. It's why I have been looking forward to tonight."

"So . . ." Dad opened the fridge. "How do we do this? Do you have a special beer . . . cup, Will?"

If it was Dad, I told Will, he would have had an adapted beer cup before he had a wheelchair.

"Got to get your priorities right," Dad said. I rummaged in Will's bag until I found his beaker.

"Beer will be fine. Thank you."

He took a sip and I stood in the kitchen, suddenly conscious of our tiny, shabby house with its 1980s wallpaper and dented kitchen cupboards. Will's home was elegantly furnished, its décor spare and beautiful. Our house looked as if 90 percent of its contents came from the local pound shop. Thomas's dog-eared paintings covered every unoccupied surface of wall. But if he had noticed, Will said nothing. He and Dad had quickly found a shared point of reference, which turned out to be my general uselessness. I didn't mind. It kept them both happy.

"Did you know, she once drove backward into a postbox and swore it was the postbox's fault . . ."

"You want to see her lowering my ramp. It's like *Ski Sunday* coming out of that car sometimes . . ."

Dad burst out laughing.

I left them to it. Mum followed me out, fretting. She put a tray of glasses on the dining table, then glanced up at the clock. "Where's Patrick?"

"He was coming straight from training," I said. "Perhaps he's been held up."

"He couldn't put it off just for your birthday? This chicken is going to be spoiled if he's much longer."

"Mum, it will be fine."

I waited until she had put the tray down, and then I slid my arms around her and gave her a hug. She was rigid with anxiety. I felt a sudden wave of sympathy for her. It couldn't be easy being my mother.

"Really. It will be fine."

She let go of me, kissed the top of my head, and brushed her hands down her apron. "I wish your sister was here. It seems wrong to have a celebration without her."

Not to me, it didn't. Just for once, I was quite enjoying being the focus of attention. It might sound childish, but it was true. I loved having Will and Dad laughing about me. I loved the fact that every element of supper—from roast chicken to chocolate mousse—was my favorite. I liked the fact that I could be who I wanted to be without my sister's voice reminding me of who I had been.

The doorbell rang, and Mum flapped her hands. "There he is. Lou, why don't you start serving?"

Patrick was still flushed from his exertions at the track. "Happy birthday, babe," he said, stooping to kiss me. He smelled of aftershave and deodorant and warm, recently showered skin.

"Best go straight through." I nodded toward the living room. "Mum's having a timing meltdown."

"Oh." He glanced down at his watch. "Sorry. Must have lost track of time."

"Not *your* time, though, eh?"

"What?"

"Nothing."

Dad had moved the big gateleg table into the living room. He had also, on my instruction, moved one of the sofas to the other wall so that Will would be able to enter the room unobstructed. Will maneuvered his wheelchair to the place I pointed to, and then elevated himself a little so that he would be the same height as everyone else. I sat on his left, and Patrick sat opposite. He and Will and Granddad nodded their hellos. I had already warned Patrick not to try to shake Will's hand. Even as I sat down I could feel Will studying Patrick, and I wondered, briefly, whether he would be as charming to my boyfriend as he had been to my parents.

Will inclined his head toward me. "If you look in

the back of the chair, there's a little something for the dinner."

I leaned back and reached my hand downward into his bag. I pulled it up again, retrieving a bottle of Laurent-Perrier champagne.

"You should always have champagne on your birthday," he said.

"Oh, look at that," Mum said, bringing in the plates. "How lovely! But we have no champagne glasses."

"These will be fine," Will said.

"I'll open it." Patrick reached for it, unwound the wire, and placed his thumbs under the cork. He kept glancing over at Will, as if Will were not what he had expected at all.

"If you do that," Will observed, "it's going to go everywhere." He lifted his arm an inch or so, gesturing vaguely. "I find that holding the cork and turning the bottle tends to be a safer bet."

"There's a man who knows his champagne," Dad said. "There you go, Patrick. Turning the bottle, you say? Well, who knew?"

"I knew," Patrick said. "That's how I was going to do it."

The champagne was safely popped and poured, and my birthday was toasted.

Granddad called out something that may well have been "Hear, hear."

I stood up and bowed. I was wearing a 1960s yellow A-line minidress I had got from the thrift shop. The woman had thought it might be Biba, although someone had cut the label out.

"May this be the year our Lou finally grows up," Dad said. "I was going to say 'does something with her life' but it seems like she finally is. I have to say, Will, since she's had the job with you she's—well, she's really come out of herself."

"We're very proud," Mum said. "And grateful. To you. For employing her, I mean."

"Gratitude's all mine," Will said. He glanced sideways at me.

"To Lou," Dad said. "And her continued success."

"And to absent family members," Mum said.

"Blimey," I said. "I should have a birthday more often. Most days you all just hurl abuse at me."

They began to talk, Dad telling some other story about me that made him and Mum laugh out loud. It was good to see them laughing. Dad had looked so worn down these last weeks, and Mum had been hollow-eyed and distracted, as if her real self were always elsewhere. I wanted to savor these moments, of them briefly forgetting their troubles, in shared jokes and familial fondness. Just for a moment, I realized I wouldn't have minded if Thomas was there. Or Treena, for that matter.

I was so lost in my thoughts that it took a minute to register Patrick's expression. I was feeding Will as I said something to Granddad, folding a piece of smoked salmon in my fingers and placing it to Will's lips. It was such an unthinking part of my daily life now that the intimacy of the gesture only struck me when I saw the shock on Patrick's face.

Will said something to Dad and I stared at Patrick, willing him to stop. On his left, Granddad was picking at his plate with greedy delight, letting out what we called his "food noises"—little grunts and murmurs of pleasure.

"Delicious salmon," Will said to my mother. "Really lovely flavor."

"Well, it's not something we would have every day," she said, smiling. "But we did want to make today special."

Stop staring, I told Patrick silently.

Finally, he caught my eye and looked away. He looked furious.

I fed Will another piece, and then some bread when I saw him glance at it. I had, I realized in that moment, become so attuned to Will's needs that I barely needed to look at him to work out what he wanted.

"So, Patrick," Will said, perhaps sensing my discomfort. "Louisa tells me you're a personal trainer. What does that involve?"

I so wished he hadn't asked. Patrick launched into his sales spiel, all about personal motivation and how a fit body made for a healthy mind. Then he segued into his training schedule for the Xtreme Viking. I normally tuned out at this point, but all I could think of now, with Will beside me, was how inappropriate it was. Why couldn't he have just said something vague and left it at that?

"In fact, when Lou said you were coming, I thought I'd take a look at my books and see if there was any physio I could recommend."

I choked on my champagne. "It's quite a specialist thing, Patrick. I'm not sure you'd really be the person."

"I can do specialist. I do sports injuries. I have medical training."

"This is not a sprained ankle, Pat. Really."

"There's a man I worked with a couple of years ago had a client who was paraplegic. He's almost fully recovered now, he says. Does triathlons and everything."

"Fancy," said my mother.

"He pointed me to this new research in Canada that says muscles can be trained to remember former activity. If you get them working enough, every day, it's like a brain synapse—it can come back. I bet you if we hooked you up with a really good regime, you could see a difference in your muscle memory. After all, Lou tells me you were quite the action man before."

"Patrick," I said loudly. "You know nothing about it."

"I was just trying to—"

"Well, *don't*. Really."

The table fell silent. Dad coughed, and excused

himself for it. Granddad peered around the table in wary silence.

Mum made as if to offer everyone more bread, and then seemed to change her mind.

When Patrick spoke again, there was a faint air of martyrdom in his tone. "It's just research that I thought might be helpful. But I'll say no more about it."

Will looked up and smiled, his face blank, polite. "I'll certainly bear it in mind."

I got up to clear the plates, wanting to escape the table. But Mum scolded me, telling me to sit down.

"You're the birthday girl," she said—as if she ever let anyone else do anything, anyway. "Bernard. Why don't you go and get the chicken?"

The rest of the meal passed without incident. My parents, I could see, were completely charmed by Will. Patrick, less so. He and Will barely exchanged another word. Somewhere around the point where Mum served up the roast potatoes—Dad doing his usual thing of trying to steal extras—I stopped worrying. Dad was asking Will all sorts of questions, about his life before, even about the accident, and he seemed comfortable enough to answer him directly. In fact, I learned a fair bit that he'd never told me. His job, for example, sounded pretty important, even if he played it down. He bought and sold companies and made sure he turned a profit while doing so. It took Dad a few attempts to prize out of him that his idea of profit ran into six or seven figures. I found myself staring at Will, trying to reconcile the man I knew with this ruthless financier that he now described. Dad told him about the company that was about to take over the furniture factory, and when he said the name, Will nodded almost apologetically, and said that, yes, he knew of them. Yes, he would probably have gone for it too. The way he said it didn't sound promising for Dad's job.

Mum just cooed at Will, and made a huge fuss over him. I realized, watching her smile, that at some stage during the meal he had just become a smart young man at her table. No wonder Patrick was pissed off.

"Birthday cake?" Granddad said, as Mum began to clear the dishes.

It was so distinct, so surprising, that Dad and I stared at each other in shock. The whole table went quiet.

"No." I walked around the table and kissed him. "No, Granddad. Sorry. But it is chocolate mousse. You like that."

He nodded in approval. My mother was beaming. I don't think any of us could have had a better present.

The mousse arrived on the table, and with it a large, square present, about the size of a telephone directory, wrapped in tissue.

"Presents, is it?" Patrick said. "Here. Here's mine." He smiled at me as he placed it in the middle of the table.

I raised a smile back. This was no time to argue, after all.

"Go on," said Dad. "Open it."

I opened theirs first, peeling the paper away carefully so that I didn't tear it. It was a photograph album, and on every page there was a picture from a year in my life. Me as a baby; me and Treena as solemn, chubby-faced girls; me on my first day at secondary school, all hair clips and oversized skirt. More recently, there was a picture of me and Patrick, the one where I was actually telling him to piss off. And me, dressed in a gray skirt, my first day on my new job. In between the pages were pictures of our family by Thomas, letters that Mum had kept from school trips, my childish handwriting telling of days on the beach, lost ice creams, and thieving gulls. I flipped through, and only hesitated briefly when I saw the girl with the long, dark, flicked-back hair. I turned the page.

"Can I see?" Will said.

"It's not been . . . the best year," Mum told him, as I turned the pages in front of him. "I mean, we're fine and everything. But, you know, things being what they are.

And then Granddad saw something on the daytime telly about making your own presents, and I thought that was something that would . . . you know . . . really mean something."

"It does, Mum." My eyes had filled with tears. "I love it. Thank you."

"Granddad picked out some of the pictures," she said.

"It's beautiful," said Will.

"I love it," I said again.

The look of utter relief she and Dad exchanged was the saddest thing I have ever seen.

"Mine next." Patrick pushed the little box across the table. I opened it slowly, feeling vaguely panicked for a moment that it might be an engagement ring. I wasn't ready. I had barely gotten my head around having my own bedroom. I opened the little box, and there, against the dark-blue velvet, was a thin gold chain with a little star pendant. It was sweet, delicate, and not remotely me. I didn't wear that kind of jewelry, never had.

I let my eyes rest on it while I worked out what to say. "It's lovely," I said, as he leaned across the table and fastened it around my neck.

"Glad you like it," Patrick said, and kissed me on the mouth. I swear he'd never kissed me like that in front of my parents before.

Will watched me, his face impassive.

"Well, I think we should eat pudding now," Dad said. "Before it gets too hot." He laughed out loud at his own joke. The champagne had boosted his spirits immeasurably.

"There's something in my bag for you too," Will said, quietly. "The one on the back of my chair. It's in orange wrapping."

I pulled the present from Will's backpack.

My mother paused, the serving spoon in her hand. "You got Lou a present, Will? That's ever so kind of you. Isn't that kind of him, Bernard?"

"It certainly is."

The wrapping paper had brightly colored Chinese kimonos on it. I didn't have to look at it to know I would save it. Perhaps even create something to wear based on it. I removed the ribbon, putting it to one side for later. I opened the paper, and then the tissue paper within it, and there, staring at me, was a strangely familiar black and yellow stripe.

I pulled the fabric from the parcel, and in my hands were two pairs of black and yellow tights. Adult-sized, opaque, in a wool so soft that it almost slid through my fingers.

"I don't believe it," I said. I had started to laugh—a joyous, unexpected thing. "Oh my God! Where did you get these?"

"I had them made. You'll be happy to know I instructed the woman via my brand-new voice recognition software."

"Tights?" Dad and Patrick said in unison.

"Only the best pair of tights ever."

My mother peered at them. "You know, Louisa, I'm pretty sure you had a pair just like that when you were very little."

Will and I exchanged a look.

I couldn't stop beaming. "I want to put them on now," I said.

"Jesus Christ, she'll look like Max Wall in a beehive," my father said, shaking his head.

"Ah, Bernard, it's her birthday. Sure, she can wear what she wants."

I ran out of the room and pulled on a pair in the hallway. I pointed a toe, admiring the silliness of them. I don't think a present had ever made me so happy in my life.

I walked back in. Will let out a small cheer. Granddad banged his hands on the table. Mum and Dad burst out laughing. Patrick just stared.

"I can't even begin to tell you how much I love these,"
I said. "Thank you. Thank you." I reached out a hand
and touched the back of his shoulder. "Really."

"There's a card in there too," he said. "Open it some
other time."

———

My parents made a huge fuss over Will as he was
leaving.

Dad, who was drunk, kept thanking him for employing me, and made him promise to come back. "If I lose
my job, maybe I'll come over and watch the footie with
you one day," he said.

"I'd like that," said Will, even though I'd never seen
him watch a football match.

My mum wrapped some leftover mousse in a Tupper-
ware container and pressed it on him. "Seeing as you
liked it so much."

What a gentleman, they would say, for a good hour
after he had gone. A real gentleman.

Patrick came out to the hallway, his hands shoved
deep in his pockets, as if perhaps to stop the urge to shake
Will's own. That was my more generous conclusion.

"Good to meet you, Patrick," Will said. "And thank
you for the . . . advice."

"Oh, just trying to help my girlfriend get the best out
of her job," he said. "That's all." There was a definite emphasis on the word *my*.

"Well, you're a lucky man," Will said, as Nathan began
to steer him out. "She certainly gives a good bed bath."
The words came out so quickly that the door was closed
before Patrick even realized what he had said.

———

"You never told me you were giving him bed baths."

We had gone back to Patrick's house, a new-build flat
on the edge of town. It had been marketed as "loft living," even though it overlooked the retail park and was
no more than three floors high.

"What does that mean? You wash his dick?"

"I don't wash his dick." I picked up the cleanser that was one of the few things I was allowed to keep at Patrick's place, and began to clean off my makeup with sweeping strokes.

"He just said you did."

"He's teasing you. And after you going on and on about how he *used* to be an action man, I don't blame him."

"So what is it you do for him? You've obviously not been giving me the full story."

"I do wash him, sometimes, but only down to his underwear."

Patrick's stare spoke volumes. Finally, he looked away from me, pulled off his socks, and hurled them into the laundry basket. "Your job isn't meant to be about this. No medical stuff, it said. No intimate stuff. It wasn't part of your job description." A sudden thought occurred to him. "You could sue. Constructive dismissal, I think it is, when they change the terms of your job."

"Don't be ridiculous. And I do it because Nathan can't always be there, and it's horrible for Will to have some complete stranger from an agency handling him. And besides, I'm used to it now. It really doesn't bother me."

How could I explain to him—how a body can become so familiar to you? I could change Will's tubes with a deft professionalism, sponge-bathe his naked top half without a break in our conversation. I didn't even balk at Will's scars now. For a while, all I had been able to see was a potential suicide. Now he was just Will— maddening, mercurial, clever, funny Will—who patronized me and liked to play Professor Higgins to my Eliza Doolittle. His body was just part of the whole package, a thing to be dealt with, at intervals, before we got back to the talking. It had become, I supposed, the least interesting part of him.

"I just can't believe . . . after all we went through . . .

how long it took you to let me come anywhere near you . . . and here's some stranger who you're quite happy to get up close and personal with—"

"Can we not talk about this tonight, Patrick? It's my birthday."

"I wasn't the one who started it, with talk of bed baths and whatnot."

"Is it because he's good-looking?" I demanded. "Is that it? Would it all be so much easier for you if he looked like—you know—a *proper* vegetable?"

"So you *do* think he's good-looking."

I pulled my dress over my head, and began peeling my tights carefully from my legs, the dregs of my good mood finally evaporating. "I can't believe you're doing this. I can't believe you're jealous of him."

"I'm not jealous of him." His tone was dismissive. "How could I be jealous of a cripple?"

Patrick made love to me that night. Perhaps "made love" is stretching it a bit. We had sex, a marathon session in which he seemed determined to show off his athleticism, his strength and vigor. It lasted for hours. If he could have swung me from a chandelier I think he would have done so. It was nice to feel so wanted, to find myself the focus of Patrick's attention after months of semidetachment. But a little part of me stayed aloof during the whole thing. I suspected it wasn't for me, after all. I had worked that out pretty quickly. This little show was for Will's benefit.

"How was that, eh?" He wrapped himself around me afterward, our skin sticking slightly with perspiration, and kissed my forehead.

"Great," I said.

"I love you, babe."

And, satisfied, he rolled off, threw an arm back over his head, and was asleep within minutes.

When sleep didn't come for me, I got out of bed and

went downstairs to my bag. I rifled through it, looking for the book of Flannery O'Connor short stories. It was as I pulled them from my bag that the envelope fell out.

I stared at it. Will's card. I hadn't opened it at the table. I did so now, feeling an unlikely sponginess at its center. I slid the card carefully from its envelope, and opened it. Inside were ten crisp fifty-pound notes. I counted them twice, unable to believe what I was seeing. Inside, it read:

Birthday bonus. Don't fuss. It's a legal requirement. W.

14

May was a strange month. The newspapers and television were full of headlines about what they termed "The right to die." A woman suffering from a degenerative disease had asked that the law be clarified to protect her husband, should he accompany her to Dignitas when her suffering became too much. A young football player had committed suicide after persuading his parents to take him there. The police were involved. There was to be a debate in the House of Lords.

I watched the news reports and listened to the legal arguments from pro-lifers and esteemed moral philosophers, and didn't quite know where I stood on any of it. It all seemed weirdly unrelated to Will.

We, in the meantime, had gradually been increasing Will's outings—and the distance that he was prepared to travel. We had been to the theater, down the road to see the morris dancers (Will kept a straight face at their bells and hankies, but he had gone slightly pink with the effort), driven one evening to an open-air concert at a nearby stately home (more his thing than mine), and gone once to the multiplex, where, due to inadequate research on my part, we ended up watching a film about a girl with a terminal illness.

But I knew he saw the headlines too. He had begun using the computer more since we got the new software, and he had worked out how to move a mouse by dragging his thumb across a track pad. This laborious exercise enabled him to read the day's newspapers online. I

brought him a cup of tea one morning to find him reading about the young football player—a detailed feature
about the steps he had gone through to bring about his
own death. He blanked the screen when he realized I
was behind him. That small action left me with a lump
somewhere high in my chest that took a full half hour to
go away.

I looked up the same piece at the library. I had begun
to read newspapers. I had worked out which of their arguments tended to go deeper—that information wasn't
always at its most useful boiled down to stark, skeletal
facts.

The football player's parents had been savaged by the
tabloid newspapers. HOW COULD THEY LET HIM DIE?
screamed the headlines. I couldn't help but feel the same
way. Leo McInerney was twenty-four. He had lived with
his injury for almost three years, so not much longer
than Will. Surely he was too young to decide that there
was nothing left to live for? And then I read what Will
had read—not an opinion piece, but a carefully researched feature about what had actually taken place in
this young man's life. The writer seemed to have had access to his parents.

Leo, they said, had played football since he was three
years old. His whole life was football. He had been injured in what they termed a "million-to-one" accident
when a tackle went wrong. They had tried everything to
encourage him, to give him a sense that his life would
still hold value. But he had retreated into depression. He
was an athlete not just without athleticism but without
even the ability to move or, on occasion, breathe without
assistance. He gleaned no pleasure from anything. His
life was painful, disrupted by infection, and dependent
on the constant ministrations of others. He missed his
friends, but refused to see them. He told his girlfriend he
wouldn't see her. He told his parents daily that he didn't

want to live. He told them that watching other people live even half the life he had planned for himself was unbearable, a kind of torture.

He had tried to commit suicide twice by starving himself until hospitalized, and when he returned home had begged his parents to smother him in his sleep. When I read that, I sat in the library and stuck the balls of my hands in my eyes until I could breathe without sobbing.

Dad lost his job. He was pretty brave about it. He came home that afternoon, got changed into a shirt and tie, and headed back into town on the next bus, to register at the Job Center.

He had already decided, he told Mum, that he would apply for anything, despite being a skilled craftsman with years of experience. "I don't think we can afford to be picky at the moment," he said, ignoring Mum's protestations.

But if I had found it hard to get employment, prospects for a fifty-five-year-old man who had only ever held one job were harder. He couldn't even get a job as a warehouseman or a security guard, he said, despairingly, as he returned home from another round of interviews. They would take some unreliable snot-nosed seventeen-year-old because the government would make up their wages, but they wouldn't take a mature man with a proven work record. After a fortnight of rejections, he and Mum admitted they would have to apply for benefits, just to tide them over, and spent their evenings poring over incomprehensible fifty-page forms that asked how many people used their washing machine, and when was the last time they had left the country (Dad thought it might have been 1988). I put Will's birthday money into the cash tin in the kitchen cupboard. I thought it might make them feel better to know they had a little security.

When I woke up in the morning, it had been pushed back under my door in an envelope.

The tourists came, and the town began to fill. Mr. Traynor was around less and less now; his hours lengthened as the visitor numbers to the castle grew. I saw him in town one Thursday afternoon, when I walked home via the dry cleaner's. That wouldn't have been unusual in itself, except for the fact that he had his arm around a red-haired woman who clearly wasn't Mrs. Traynor. When he saw me he dropped her like a hot potato.

I turned away, pretending to peer into a shop window, unsure if I wanted him to know that I had seen them, and tried very hard not to think about it again.

On the Friday after my dad lost his job, Will received an invitation—a wedding invitation from Alicia and Rupert. Well, strictly speaking, the invitation came from Colonel and Mrs. Timothy Dewar, Alicia's parents, inviting Will to celebrate their daughter's marriage to Rupert Freshwell. It arrived in a heavy parchment envelope with a schedule of celebrations, and a fat, folded list of things that people could buy them from stores I had never even heard of.

"She's got some nerve," I observed, studying the gilt lettering, the gold-edged piece of thick card. "Want me to throw it?"

"Whatever you want." Will's whole body was a study in determined indifference.

I stared at the list. "What the hell is a couscoussier anyway?"

Perhaps it was something to do with the speed with which he turned away and began busying himself with his computer keyboard. Perhaps it was his tone of voice. But for some reason I didn't throw it away. I put it carefully into his folder in the kitchen.

Will gave me another book of short stories, one that he'd ordered from Amazon, and a copy of *The Red Queen*. I knew it wasn't going to be my sort of book at all. "It hasn't even got a story," I said, after studying the back cover.

"So?" Will replied. "Challenge yourself a bit."

I tried—not because I really had an appetite for genetics—but because I couldn't bear the thought that Will would go on and on at me if I didn't. He was like that now. He was actually a bit of a bully. And, really annoyingly, he would quiz me on how much I had read of something, just to make sure I really had.

"You're not my teacher," I would grumble.

"Thank God," he would reply, with feeling.

This book—which was actually surprisingly readable— was all about a kind of battle for survival. It claimed that women didn't pick men because they loved them at all. It said that the female of the species would always go for the strongest male, in order to give her offspring the best chance. She couldn't help herself. It was just the way nature was.

I didn't agree with this. And I didn't like the argument. There was an uncomfortable undercurrent to what he was trying to persuade me of. Will was physically weak, damaged, in this author's eyes. That made him biologically irrelevant. It would have made his life worthless.

He had been going on and on about this for the better part of an afternoon when I butted in. "There's one thing this Matt Ridley bloke hasn't factored in," I said.

Will looked up from his computer screen. "Oh yes?"

"What if the genetically superior male is actually a bit of a dickhead?"

———

On the third Saturday of May, Treena and Thomas came home. My mother was out the door and up the garden path before they had made it halfway down the street. Thomas, she swore, clutching him to her, had grown several inches in the time they had been away. He had changed, was so grown-up, looked so much the •

little man. Treena had cut off her hair and looked oddly sophisticated. She was wearing a jacket I hadn't seen before, and strappy sandals. I found myself wondering, meanly, where she had found the money.

"So how is it?" I asked, while Mum walked Thomas around the garden, showing him the frogs in the tiny pond. Dad was watching football with Granddad, exclaiming in mild frustration at another supposed missed opportunity.

"Great. Really good. I mean, it's hard not having any help with Thomas, and it did take him a while to settle in at the crèche." She leaned forward. "Although you mustn't tell Mum—I told her he was fine."

"But you like the course."

Treena's face broke out into a smile. "It's the best. I can't tell you, Lou, the joy of just using my brain again. I feel like there's been this big chunk of me missing for ages . . . and it's like I've found it again. Does that sound wanky?"

I shook my head. I was actually glad for her. I wanted to tell her about the library, and the computers, and what I had done for Will. But I thought this should probably be her moment. We sat on the foldaway chairs, under the tattered sunshade, and sipped at our mugs of tea. Her fingers, I noticed, were all the right colors.

"She misses you," I said.

"We'll be back most weekends from now on. I just needed . . . Lou, it wasn't just about settling Thomas in. I just needed a bit of time to be away from it all. I just wanted time to be a different person."

She looked a bit like a different person. It was weird. Just a few weeks away from home could rub the familiarity right off someone. I felt like she was on the path to being someone I wasn't quite sure of. I felt, weirdly, as if I were being left behind.

"Mum told me your disabled bloke came to dinner."

"He's not my disabled bloke. His name's Will."

"Sorry. Will. So it's going well, then, the old anti—bucket list?"

"So-so. Some trips have been more successful than others." I told her about the horse racing disaster, and the unexpected triumph of the violin concert. I told her about our picnics, and she laughed when I told her about my birthday dinner.

"Do you think . . ." I could see her working out the best way to put it. "Do you think you'll win?"

Like it was some kind of contest.

I pulled a tendril from the honeysuckle and began picking off its leaves. "I don't know. I think I'm going to need to up my game." I told her what Mrs. Traynor had said to me about going abroad.

"I can't believe you went to a violin concert, though. You, of all people!"

"I liked it."

She raised an eyebrow.

"No. Really, I did. It was . . . emotional."

She looked at me carefully. "Mum says he's really nice."

"He is really nice."

"And handsome."

"A spinal injury doesn't mean you turn into Quasimodo." *Please don't say anything about it being a tragic waste*, I told her silently.

But perhaps my sister was smarter than that. "Anyway. She was definitely surprised. I think she was prepared for Quasimodo."

"That's the problem, Treen," I said, and threw the rest of my tea into the flower bed. "People always are."

———

Mum was cheerful over supper that night. She had cooked lasagna, Treena's favorite, and Thomas was allowed to stay up as a treat. We ate and laughed and talked about safe things, like the football team, and my job, and what Treena's fellow students were like. Mum must have asked Treena a hundred times if she was sure she was managing okay on her own, whether there was anything she needed for Thomas—as if they had anything spare they could have given her. I was glad I had warned Treena about how broke they were. She said no, gracefully and with conviction. It was only afterward I thought to ask if it was the truth.

That night I was woken at midnight by the sound of crying. It was Thomas, in the box room. I could hear Treena trying to comfort him, to reassure him, the sound of the light going on and off, a bed being rearranged. I lay in the dark, watching the sodium light filter through my blinds onto my newly painted ceiling, and waited for it to stop. But the same thin wail began again at two. This time, I heard Mum padding across the hallway, and murmured conversation. Then, finally, Thomas was silent again.

At four I woke to the sound of my door creaking open. I blinked groggily, turning toward the light. Thomas stood silhouetted against the doorway, his oversized pajamas loose around his legs, his comfort blanket half spooled on the floor. I couldn't see his face, but he stood there uncertainly, as if unsure what to do next.

"Come here, Thomas," I whispered. As he padded toward me, I could see he was still half asleep. His steps were halting, his thumb thrust into his mouth, his treasured blanket clutched to his side. I held the duvet open and he climbed into bed beside me, his tufty head burrowing into the other pillow, and curled up into a fetal ball. I pulled the duvet over him and lay there, gazing at him, marveling at the certainty and immediacy of his sleep.

"Night, night, sweetheart," I whispered, and kissed his forehead, and a fat little hand crept out and took a chunk of my T-shirt in its grasp, as if to reassure itself that I couldn't move away.

"What was the best place you've ever visited?"

We were sitting in the shelter, waiting for a sudden squall to stop so that we could walk around the rear gardens of the castle. Will didn't like going to the main area—too many people to gawk at him. But the vegetable gardens were one of its hidden treasures, visited by few. Its secluded orchards and fruit gardens were separated by honeyed pea-shingle paths that Will's chair could negotiate quite happily.

"In terms of what? And what's that?"

I poured some soup from a flask and held it up to his lips. "Tomato."

"Okay. Jesus, that's hot. Give me a minute." He squinted into the distance. "I climbed Mount Kilimanjaro when I hit thirty. That was pretty incredible."

"How high?"

"A little over nineteen thousand feet to Uhuru Peak. That said, I pretty much crawled the last thousand or so. The altitude hits you pretty hard."

"Was it cold?"

"No . . ." He smiled at me. "It's not like Everest. Not the time of year that I went, anyway." He gazed off into the distance, briefly lost in his remembrance. "It was beautiful. The roof of Africa, they call it. When you're up there, it's like you can actually see to the end of the world."

Will was silent for a moment. I watched him, wondering where he really was. When we had these conversations he became like the boy in my class, the boy who had distanced himself from us by venturing away.

"So where else have you liked?"

"Trou d'Eau Douce bay, Mauritius. Lovely people, beautiful beaches, great diving. Um . . . Tsavo National Park, Kenya, all red earth and wild animals. Yosemite. That's California. Rock faces so tall your brain can't quite process the scale of them."

He told me of a night he'd spent rock climbing, perched on a ledge several hundred feet up, how he'd had to pin himself into his sleeping bag, and attach it to the rock face, because to roll over in his sleep would have been disastrous.

"You've actually just described my worst nightmare, right there."

"I like more metropolitan places too. Sydney, I loved. The Northern Territories. Iceland. There's a place not far from the airport where you can bathe in the volcanic springs. It's like a strange, nuclear landscape. Oh, and riding across central China. I went to this place about two days' ride from the capital of Sichuan province, and the locals spat at me because they hadn't seen a white person before."

"Is there anywhere you haven't been?"

He took another sip of soup. "North Korea?" He pondered. "Oh, I've never been to Disneyland. Will that do? Not even Disneyland Paris."

"I once booked a ticket to Australia. Never went, though."

He turned to me in surprise.

"Stuff happened. It's fine. Perhaps I will go one day."

"Not 'perhaps.' You've got to get away from here, Clark. Promise me you won't spend the rest of your life stuck around this bloody parody of a place mat."

"Promise you? Why?" I tried to make my voice light. "Where are you going?"

"I just . . . can't bear the thought of you staying around here forever." He swallowed. "You're too bright. Too interesting." He looked away from me. "You only get one life. It's actually your duty to live it as fully as possible."

"Okay," I said, carefully. "Then tell me where I should go. Where would you go, if you could go anywhere?"

"Right now?"

"Right now. And you're not allowed to say Kilimanjaro. It has to be somewhere I can imagine going myself."

When Will's face relaxed, he looked like someone

quite different. A smile settled across his face now, his
eyes creasing with pleasure. "Paris. I would sit outside a
café in Le Marais and drink coffee and eat a plate of warm
croissants with unsalted butter and strawberry jam."

"Le Marais?"

"It's a little district in the center of Paris. It is full of
cobbled streets and teetering apartment blocks and gay
men and orthodox Jews and women of a certain age
who once looked like Brigitte Bardot. It's the only place
to stay."

I turned to face him, lowering my voice. "We could go,"
I said. "We could do it on the Eurostar. It would be easy. I
don't think we'd even need to ask Nathan to come. I've
never been to Paris. I'd love to go. Really love to go. Especially with someone who knows his way around. What do
you say, Will?"

I could see myself in that café. I was there, at that table, maybe admiring a new pair of French shoes, pur-
chased in a chic little boutique, or picking at a pastry with
Parisian red fingernails. I could taste the coffee, smell the
smoke from the next table's Gauloises.

"No."

"What?" It took me a moment to drag myself away
from that sidewalk table.

"No."

"But you just told me—"

"You don't get it, Clark. I don't want to go there in
this—this thing." He gestured at the chair, his voice dropping. "I want to be in Paris as *me*, the old me. I want to sit
in a chair, leaning back, my favorite clothes on, with
pretty French girls who pass by giving me the eye just as
they would any other man sitting there. Not looking away
hurriedly when they realize I'm a man in an overgrown
bloody pram."

"But we could try," I ventured. "It needn't be—"

"No. No, we couldn't. Because at the moment I can

shut my eyes and know exactly how it feels to be in the Rue des Francs Bourgeois, cigarette in hand, clementine juice in a tall, cold glass in front of me, the smell of someone's steak frites cooking, the sound of a moped in the distance. I know every sensation of it."

He swallowed. "The day we go and I'm in this bloody contraption, all those memories, those sensations, will be wiped out, erased by the struggle to get behind the table, up and down Parisian curbs, the taxi drivers who refuse to take us, and the wheelchair bloody power pack that wouldn't charge in a French socket. Okay?"

His voice had hardened. I screwed the top back on the vacuum flask. I examined my shoes quite carefully as I did it, because I didn't want him to see my face.

"Okay," I said.

"Okay." Will took a deep breath.

Below us a coach stopped to disgorge another load of visitors outside the castle gates. We watched in silence as they filed out of the vehicle and into the old fortress in a single, obedient line, primed to stare at the ruins of another age.

It's possible he realized I was a bit subdued, because he leaned into me a little. And his face softened. "So, Clark. The rain seems to have stopped. Where shall we go this afternoon. The maze?"

"No." It came out more quickly than I would have liked, and I caught the look Will gave me.

"You claustrophobic?"

"Something like that." I began to gather up our things. "Let's just go back to the house."

———

The following weekend, I came down in the middle of the night to fetch some water. I had been having trouble sleeping, and had found that actually getting up was marginally preferable to lying in my bed batting away the swirling mess of my thoughts.

I didn't like being awake at night. I couldn't help but wonder whether Will was awake, on the other side of the castle, and my imagination kept prying its way into his thoughts. It was a dark place to go to.

Here was the truth of it: I was getting nowhere with him. Time was running out. I couldn't even persuade him to take a trip to Paris. And when he told me why, it was hard for me to argue. He had a good reason for turning down almost every single longer trip I suggested to him. And without telling him why I was so anxious to take him, I had little leverage at all.

I was walking past the living room when I heard the sound—a muffled cough, or perhaps an exclamation. I stopped, retraced my steps, and stood in the doorway. I pushed gently at the door. On the living-room floor, the sofa cushions arranged into a sort of haphazard bed, lay my parents, under the guest quilt, their heads level with the gas fire. We stared at each other for a moment in the half-light, my glass motionless in my hand.

"What—what are you doing there?"

My mother pushed herself up onto her elbow. "Shh. Don't raise your voice. We . . ." She looked at my father. "We fancied a change."

"What?"

"We fancied a change." My mother glanced at my father for backup.

"We've given Treena our bed," Dad said. He was wearing an old blue T-shirt with a rip in the shoulder, and his hair stuck up on one side. "She and Thomas, they weren't getting on too well in the box room. We said they could have ours."

"But you can't sleep down here! You can't be comfortable like this."

"We're fine, love," Dad said. "Really."

And then, as I stood, dumbly struggling to comprehend, he added, "It's only at weekends. And you can't sleep in that box room. You need your sleep, what with . . ." He swallowed. "What with you being the only one of us at work and all."

My father, the great lump, couldn't meet my eye.

"Go on back to bed now, Lou. Go on. We're fine." Mum practically shooed me away.

I walked back up the stairs, my bare feet silent on the carpet, dimly aware of the brief murmured conversation below.

I hesitated outside Mum and Dad's room, now hearing what I had not heard before—Thomas's muffled snoring within. Then I walked slowly back across the landing to my own room, and I closed the door carefully behind me. I lay in my oversized bed and stared out the window at the sodium lights of the street, until dawn—finally, thankfully—brought me a few precious hours of sleep.

There were seventy-nine days left on my calendar. I started to feel anxious again.

And I wasn't alone.

Mrs. Traynor had waited until Nathan was taking care of Will one lunchtime, then asked me to accompany her to the big house. She sat me down in the living room and asked me how I thought things were going.

"Well, we're going out a lot more," I said.

She nodded, as if in agreement.

"He talks more than he did."

"To you, perhaps." She gave a half-laugh that wasn't really a laugh at all. "Have you mentioned going abroad to him?"

"Not yet. I will. It's just . . . you know what he's like."

"I really don't mind," she said, "if you want to go somewhere. I know we probably weren't the most enthusiastic advocates of your idea, but we've been talking a lot, and we both agree . . ."

We sat there in silence. She had brought me coffee in

a cup and saucer. I took a sip of it. It always made me feel about sixty, having a saucer balanced on my lap.

"So—Will tells me he went to your house."

"Yes, it was my birthday. My parents were doing a special dinner."

"How was he?"

"Good. Really good. He was really sweet with my mum." I couldn't help but smile when I thought back to it. "I mean, she's a bit sad because my sister and her son moved out. Mum misses them. I think he . . . he just wanted to take her mind off it."

Mrs. Traynor looked surprised. "That was . . . thoughtful of him."

"My mum thought so."

She stirred her coffee. "I can't remember the last time Will agreed to have supper with us."

She probed a little more. Never asking a direct question, of course—that wasn't her way. But I couldn't give her the answers she wanted. Some days I thought Will was happier—he went out with me without a fuss, he teased me, prodded me mentally, seemed a little more engaged with the world outside the annex—but what did I really know? With Will I sensed a vast internal hinterland, a world he wouldn't give me even a glimpse of. These last couple of weeks I'd had the uncomfortable feeling that hinterland was growing.

"He seems a little happier," she said. It sounded almost as if she were trying to reassure herself.

"I think so."

"It has been very"—her gaze flickered toward me— "rewarding, to see him a little more like his old self. I am very well aware that all these improvements are due to you."

"Not all of them."

"I couldn't reach him. I couldn't get anywhere near him." She placed her cup and saucer on her knee. "He's a singular person, Will. From the time he hit adolescence, I always had to fight the feeling that in his eyes I had somehow done something wrong. I've never been quite sure what it was." She tried to laugh, but it wasn't really a laugh at all, glancing briefly at me and then looking away.

I pretended to sip my coffee, even though there was nothing in my cup.

"Do you get on well with your mother, Louisa?"

"Yes," I said, then added, "It's my sister who drives me nuts."

Mrs. Traynor gazed out the windows, to where her precious garden had begun to bloom, its blossoms a pale and tasteful melding of pinks, mauves, and blues.

"We have just two and a half months." She spoke without turning her head.

I put my coffee cup on the table. I did it carefully, so that it didn't clatter. "I'm doing my best, Mrs. Traynor."

"I know, Louisa." She nodded.

I let myself out.

———

Leo McInerney died on May 22, in the anonymous room of a flat in Switzerland, wearing his favorite football shirt, with both his parents at his side. His younger brother refused to come, but issued a statement saying that no one could have been more loved or more supported than his brother. Leo drank the milky solution of lethal barbiturate at 3:47 P.M., and his parents said that within minutes he was in what appeared to be a deep sleep. He was pronounced dead at a little after four o'clock that afternoon by an observer who had witnessed the whole thing, alongside a video camera there to forestall any suggestion of wrongdoing.

"He looked at peace," his mother was quoted as saying. "It's the only thing I can hold on to."

She and Leo's father had been interviewed three times by police and faced the threat of prosecution. Hate mail had been sent to their house. She looked almost twenty years older than her given age. And yet, there was something else in her expression when she spoke; something that, alongside the grief and the anger and the anxiety and the exhaustion, told of a deep, deep relief.

"He finally looked like Leo again."

15

"So come on then, Clark. What exciting events have you got planned for this evening?"

We were in the garden. Nathan was doing Will's physio, gently moving his knees up and down toward his chest, while Will lay on a blanket, his face turned to the sun, his arms spread out as though he were sunbathing. I sat on the grass alongside them and ate my sandwiches. I rarely went out at lunchtime anymore.

"Why?"

"Curiosity. I'm interested in how you spend your time when you're not here."

"Well . . . tonight it's a quick bout of advanced martial arts, then a helicopter is flying me to Monte Carlo for supper. And then I might take in a cocktail in Cannes on the way home. If you look up at around—ooh—2 A.M., I'll give you a wave on my way over," I said. I peeled the two sides of my sandwich apart, checking the filling. "I'm probably finishing my book."

Will glanced up at Nathan. "Tenner," he said, grinning.

Nathan reached into his pocket. "Every time," he said.

I stared at them. "Every time what?" I said, as Nathan put the money into Will's hand.

"He said you'd be reading a book. I said you'd be watching telly. He always wins."

My sandwich stilled at my lips. "Always? You've been betting on how boring my life is?"

"That's not a word we would use," Will said. The faintly guilty look in his eyes told me otherwise.

I sat up straight. "Let me get this straight. You two are betting actual money that on a Friday night I would be at home either reading a book or watching television?"

"No," said Will. "I had each way on you seeing Running Man down at the track."

Nathan released Will's leg. He pulled Will's arm straight and began massaging it from the wrist up.

"What if I said I was actually doing something completely different?"

"But you never do," Nathan said.

"Actually, I'll have that." I plucked the tenner from Will's hand. "Because tonight you're wrong."

"You said you were going to read your book!" he protested.

"Now I have this," I said, brandishing the ten-pound note. "I'll be going to the pictures. So there. Law of unintended consequences, or whatever it is you call it."

I stood up, pocketed the money, and shoved the remains of my lunch into its brown paper bag. I was smiling as I walked away from them but, weirdly, and for no reason that I could immediately understand, my eyes were prickling with tears.

I had spent an hour working on the calendar before coming to Granta House that morning. Some days I just sat and stared at it from my bed, Magic Marker in hand, trying to work out what I could take Will to. I wasn't yet convinced that I could get Will to go much farther afield, and even with Nathan's help the thought of an overnight visit seemed daunting.

I scanned the local paper, glancing at football matches and village fêtes, but was afraid after the racing debacle that Will's chair might get stuck in the grass. I was concerned that crowds might leave him feeling exposed. I had to rule out all horse-related activities, which in an area like ours meant a surprising amount of outdoor stuff. I knew he wouldn't want to watch Patrick running, and cricket and rugby left him cold. Some days I felt crippled by my own inability to think up new ideas.

Perhaps Will and Nathan were right. Perhaps I was boring. Perhaps I was the least well-equipped person in the world to try to come up with things that might inflame Will's appetite for life.

A book, or the television.

Put like that, it was hard to believe any differently.

———

After Nathan left, Will found me in the kitchen. I was sitting at the small table, peeling potatoes for his evening meal, and didn't look up when he positioned his wheelchair in the doorway. He watched me long enough for my ears to turn pink with the scrutiny.

"You know," I said, finally, "I could have been horrible to you back there. I could have pointed out that you do nothing either."

"I'm not sure Nathan would have offered particularly good odds on me going out dancing," Will said.

"I know it's a joke," I continued, discarding a long piece of potato peel. "But you just made me feel really like crap. If you were going to bet on my boring life, did you have to make me aware of it? Couldn't you and Nathan just have had it as some kind of private joke?"

He didn't say anything for a bit. When I finally looked up, he was watching me. "Sorry," he said.

"You don't look sorry."

"Well . . . okay . . . maybe I wanted you to hear it. I wanted you to think about what you're doing."

"What, how I'm letting my life slip by . . . ?"

"Yes, actually."

"God, Will. I wish you'd stop telling me what to do. What if I like watching television? What if I don't want to do much else other than read a book?" My voice had become shrill. "What if I'm tired when I get home? What if I don't need to fill my days with frenetic activity?"

"But one day you might wish you had," he said, quietly. "Do you know what I would do if I were you?"

I put down my peeler. "I suspect you're going to tell me."

"Yes. And I'm completely unembarrassed about telling you. I'd be doing night school. I'd be training as a seamstress or a fashion designer or whatever it is that taps into what you really love." He gestured at my minidress, a sixties-inspired Pucci-type dress, made with fabric that had once been a pair of Granddad's curtains.

The first time Dad had seen it he had pointed at me and yelled, "Hey, Lou, pull yourself together!" It had taken him a full five minutes to stop laughing.

Will continued, "I'd be finding out what I could do that didn't cost much—keep-fit classes, swimming, volunteering, whatever. I'd be teaching myself music or going for long walks with somebody else's dog, or—"

"Okay, okay, I get the message," I said irritably. "But I'm not you, Will."

"Luckily for you."

We sat there for a bit. Will wheeled himself in, and raised the height of his chair so that we faced each other over the table.

"Okay," I said. "So what did you do after work? That was so valuable?"

"Well, there wasn't much time left after work, but I tried to do something every day. I did rock climbing at an indoor center, and squash, and I went to concerts, and tried new restaurants—"

"It's easy to do those things if you have money," I protested.

"And I went running. Yes, really," he said, as I raised an eyebrow. "And I tried to learn new languages for places I thought I might visit one day. And I saw my friends—or people I thought were my friends . . ." He hesitated for a moment. "And I planned trips. I looked for places I'd never been, things that would frighten me or push me to my limit. I swam the Channel once. Yes—" he said, as I made to interrupt, "I know a lot of these need money, but a lot of them don't. And besides, how do you think I made money?"

"Ripping people off through your job?"

"I worked out what would make me happy, and I worked out what I wanted to do, and I trained myself to do the job that would make those two things happen."

"You make it sound so simple."

"It is simple," he said. "The thing is, it's also a lot of hard work. And people don't want to put in a lot of work."

I had finished the potatoes. I threw the peels into the bin, and put the pan on the stove ready for later. I turned and pushed up, using my arms, so that I was sitting on the table facing him, my legs dangling.

"You had a big life, didn't you?"

"Yeah, I did." He moved a bit closer, and raised his chair so that he was almost at eye level. "That's why you piss me off, Clark. Because I see all this talent, all this . . ." He shrugged. "This energy and brightness, and—"

"Don't say potential . . ."

"Potential. Yes. Potential. And I cannot for the life of me see how you can be content to live this tiny life. This life that will take place almost entirely within a five-mile radius and contain nobody who will ever surprise you or push you or show you things that will leave your head spinning and unable to sleep at night."

"This is your way of telling me I should be doing something far more worthwhile than peeling your potatoes."

"I'm telling you there's a whole world out there. But that I'd be very grateful if you'd do me some potatoes first." He smiled at me, and I couldn't help but smile back.

"Don't you think—" I started, and then broke off.

"Go on."

"Don't you think it's actually harder for you . . . to adapt, I mean? Because you've done all that stuff?"

"Are you asking me if I wish I'd never done it?"

"I'm just wondering if it would have been easier for you. If you'd led a smaller life. To live like this, I mean."

"I will never, ever regret the things I've done. Because most days, if you're stuck in one of these, all you have are the places in your memory that you can go to." He smiled. It was tight, as if it cost him. "So if you're asking me would I rather be reminiscing about the view of the castle from the minimart, or that lovely row of shops down off the roundabout, then, no. My life was just fine, thanks."

I slid off the table. I wasn't entirely sure how, but I felt, yet again, like I'd somehow been argued into a corner. I reached for the chopping board on the drainer.

"And Lou, I'm sorry. About the money thing."

"Yeah. Well." I turned, and began rinsing the chopping board under the faucet. "Don't think that's going to get you your tenner back."

———

Two days later Will ended up in hospital with an infection. A precautionary measure, they called it, although it was obvious to everyone that he was in a lot of pain. Some quadriplegics had no sensation, but, while he was impervious to temperature, below his chest Will could feel both pain and touch. I went in to see him twice, bringing him music and nice things to eat, and offering to keep him company, but peculiarly I felt in the way, and realized quite quickly that Will didn't actually want the extra attention in there. He told me to go home and enjoy some time to myself.

A year previously, I would have wasted those free days; I would have trawled the shops, maybe gone over to meet Patrick for lunch. I would probably have watched some daytime television, and maybe made a vague attempt to sort out my clothes. I might have slept a lot.

Now, however, I felt oddly restless and dislocated. I missed having a reason to get up early, a purpose to my day.

It took me half a morning to work out that this time could be useful. I went to the library and began to research. I looked up every Web site about quadriplegics that I could find, and worked out things we could do when Will was better. I wrote lists, adding to each entry the equipment or things I might need to consider for each event.

I discovered chat rooms for those with spinal injuries, and found there were thousands of men and women out there just like Will—leading hidden lives in London, Sydney, Vancouver, or just down the road—aided by friends or family, or sometimes heartbreakingly alone.

I wasn't the only caregiver interested in these sites. There were girlfriends asking how they could help their partners gain the confidence to go out again, husbands seeking advice on the latest medical equipment. There were advertisements for wheelchairs that would go on sand or off-road, clever hoists, and inflatable bathing aids.

There were codes to their discussions. I worked out that SCI was a spinal cord injury, AB the able-bodied, a UTI an infection. I saw that a C4-5 spinal injury was far more severe than a C11-12, which seemed to allow most the use of their arms or torso. There were stories of love and loss, of partners struggling to cope with disabled spouses as well as young children. There were wives who felt guilty that they had prayed their husbands would stop beating them—and then found they never would again. There were husbands who wanted to leave disabled wives but were afraid of the reaction of their community. There was exhaustion and despair, and a lot of black humor—jokes about exploding catheter bags, other people's well-meaning idiocy, or drunken misadventures. Falling out of chairs seemed to be a common theme. And there were threads about suicide—those who wanted to, those who encouraged them to give themselves more time, to learn to look at their lives in a different way. I read each thread, and felt like I was getting a secret insight into the workings of Will's brain.

I took a breath and typed a message.

> *Hi—I am the friend/caregiver of a 35 yo C5-6 quadriplegic. He was very successful and dynamic in his former life and is having trouble adjusting to his new one. In fact, I know that he does not want to live, and I am trying to think of ways of changing his mind. Please could anyone tell me how I could do this? Any ideas for things he might enjoy, or ways I could get him to think differently? All advice gratefully received.*

I called myself Busy Bee. Then I sat back in my chair, chewed at my thumbnail for a bit, and finally pressed Send.

————

When I sat down at the terminal the next morning, I had fourteen answers. I logged into the chat room, and blinked as I saw the list of names, the responses that had come from people worldwide, throughout the day and night. The first one said:

> *Dear Busy Bee,*
> *Welcome to our board. I'm sure your friend will gain a lot of comfort from having someone looking out for him.*

I'm not so sure about that, I thought.

Most of us on here have hit a definite hump at some point in our lives. It may be that your friend has hit his. Don't let him push you away. Stay positive. And remind him that it is not his place to decide when we enter and depart this world, but that of the Lord. He decided to change your friend's life, in His own wisdom, and there may be a lesson in it that He—

I scanned down to the next one.

Dear Bee,
There is no way around it, being a quad can suck. If your guy was a bit of a player too, then he is going to find it extra hard. These are the things that helped me. A lot of company, even when I didn't feel like it. Good food. Good docs. Good meds, depression meds when necessary. You didn't say where you were based, but if you can get him talking to others in the SCI community it may help. I was pretty reluctant at first (I think some part of me didn't want to admit I was actually a quad) but it does help to know you're not alone out there.

Oh, and DON'T let him watch any films like The Diving Bell and the Butterfly. Major downer!
Let us know how you get on.
All best,
Ritchie

I looked up *The Diving Bell and the Butterfly*. "The story of a man who suffers a paralyzing stroke, and his attempts to communicate with the outside world," the Web site said. I wrote the title down on my pad, uncertain whether I was doing so to make sure Will avoided it or to remind myself to watch it.

The next two responses were from a Seventh-day Adventist and a man whose suggested ways in which I could cheer Will up were certainly not covered by my working contract. I blushed and hurriedly scrolled down, afraid that someone might glance at the screen from behind me. And then I hesitated on the next reply.

> *Hi Busy Bee,*
> *Why do you think your friend/charge/whatever needs his mind changed? If I could work out a way of dying with dignity, and if I didn't know it would devastate my family, I would take it. I have been stuck in this chair eight years now, and my life is a constant round of humiliations and frustrations. Can you really put yourself in his shoes? Do you know how it feels to not even be able to empty your bowels without help? To know that forever after you are going to be stuck in your bed unable to eat, dress, communicate with the outside world without someone to help you? To never have sex again? To face the prospect of sores and ill health and even ventilators? You sound like a nice person, and I'm sure you mean well. But it may not be you looking after him next week. It may be someone who depresses him, or even doesn't like him very much. That, like everything else, is out of his control. We SCIs know that very little is under our control—who feeds us, dresses us, washes us, dictates our medication. Living with that knowledge is very hard.*
> *So I think you are asking the wrong question. Who are the AB to decide what our lives should be? If this is the wrong life for your friend, shouldn't the question be: How do I help him to end it?*
> *Best wishes,*
> *Gforce, Missouri, US*

I stared at the message, my fingers briefly stilled on the keyboard. Then I scrolled down. The next few were from other quadriplegics, criticizing Gforce for his bleak words, protesting that they had found a way forward, that theirs was a life worth living. There was a brief argument going on that seemed to have little to do with Will at all.

And then the thread dragged itself back to my request. There were suggestions of antidepressants, massage, miracle recoveries, stories of how members' own lives had been given new value. There were a few practical suggestions: wine tasting, music, art, specially adapted keyboards.

"A partner," said Grace31 from Birmingham. "If he has love, he will feel he can go on. Without it, I would have sunk many times over."

That phrase echoed in my head long after I had left the library.

———

Will came out of the hospital on Thursday. I picked him up in the adapted car, and brought him home. He was pale and exhausted, and stared out the window listlessly for the whole journey.

"No sleep in these places," he explained when I asked him if he was okay. "There's always someone moaning in the next bed."

I told him he would have the weekend to recover, but after that I had a series of outings planned. I told him I was taking his advice and trying new things, and he would have to come with me. It was a subtle change in emphasis, but I knew that was the only way I could get him to accompany me.

In fact, I had devised a detailed schedule for the next couple of weeks. Each event was carefully marked on my calendar in black, with red pen outlining the precautions I should take, and green for the accessories I would need. Every time I looked at the back of my door I felt a little glimmer of excitement, both that I had been so organized and that one of these events might actually be the thing that changed Will's view of the world.

As my dad always says, my sister is the brains of our family.

The art gallery trip lasted a shade under twenty minutes. And that included driving around the block three times in search of a suitable parking space. We got there, and almost before I had closed the door behind him he said all the work was terrible. I asked him why and he said if I couldn't see it he couldn't explain it. The cinema had to be abandoned after the staff told us, apologetically, that their lift was out of order. Others, such as the failed attempt to go swimming, required more time and organization—ringing up the swimming pool beforehand, booking Nathan for overtime—and then, when we got to the leisure center, after the flask of hot chocolate was drunk in silence in the car park, Will resolutely refused to go in.

The following Wednesday evening, we went to hear a singer he had once seen live in New York. That was a good trip.

And then the following day I took him to a wine tasting, part of a promotional event held by a vineyard in a specialist wine shop. I had to promise Nathan I wouldn't get him drunk. I held up each glass for Will to sniff, and he knew what it was even before he'd tasted it. I tried quite hard not to snort when Will spat it into the beaker (it did look really funny), and he looked at me and said I was a complete child. The shop owner went from being weirdly disconcerted by having a man in a wheelchair in his shop to being quite impressed. As the afternoon went on, he sat down and started opening other bottles, discussing region and grape with Will, while I wandered up and down looking at the labels, becoming, frankly, a little bored.

"Come on, Clark. Get an education," he said, nodding at me to sit down beside him.

"I can't. My mum told me it was rude to spit."

The two men looked at each other as if I were the mad one. And yet he didn't spit every time. I watched him. And he was suspiciously talkative for the rest of the afternoon—swift to laugh, and even more combative than usual.

And then, on the way home, we were driving through a town we didn't normally go to and, as we sat in traffic, I glanced over and saw the Tattoo and Piercing Parlor.

"I always quite fancied a tattoo," I said.

I should have known that you couldn't just say stuff like that in Will's presence. He didn't do small talk, or shooting the breeze. He immediately wanted to know why I hadn't gotten one.

"Oh, the thought of what everyone would say, I guess."

"Why? What would they say?"

"My dad hates them."

"How old are you again?"

"Patrick hates them too."

"And he *never* does anything that you might not like."

"I might get claustrophobic. I might change my mind once it was done."

"Then you·get it removed by laser, surely?"

I looked at him in my rearview mirror. His eyes were merry.

"Come on, then," he said. "What would you have?"

I realized I was smiling. "Not a snake. Or anyone's name."

"I wasn't expecting a heart with a banner saying 'Mother.'"

"You· promise not to laugh?"

"You know I can't do that. Oh God, you're not going to have some Indian Sanskrit proverb or something, are you? *What doesn't kill me makes me stronger.*"

"No. I'd have a bee. A little black and yellow bee. I love them."

He nodded, as if that were a perfectly reasonable

thing to want. "And where would you have it? Or daren't I ask?"

I shrugged. "Dunno. My shoulder? Lower hip?"

"Pull over," he said.

"Why, are you okay?"

"Just pull over. There's a space there. Look, on your left."

I pulled the car up to the curb and glanced back at him. "Go on, then," he said. "We've got nothing else on today."

"Go on where?"

"To the tattoo parlor."

I started to laugh. "Yeah. Right."

"Why not?"

"You *have* been swallowing instead of spitting."

"You haven't answered my question."

I turned in my seat. He was serious.

"I can't just go and get a tattoo. Just like that."

"Why not?"

"Because . . ."

I stared down the road at the tattoo parlor frontage. The slightly grimy window bore a large neon heart, and some framed photographs of Angelina Jolie and Mickey Rourke.

Will's voice broke into my calculations. "Okay. I will, if you will."

I turned back to him. "You'd get a tattoo?"

"If it persuaded you, just once, to climb out of your little box."

I switched off the engine. We sat, listening to it tick its way down, the dull murmur of the cars queuing along the road beside us.

"It's quite permanent."

"No 'quite' about it."

"Patrick will hate it."

"So you keep saying."

"And we'll probably get hepatitis from dirty needles.

And die slow, horrible, painful deaths." I turned to Will. "They probably wouldn't be able to do it now. Not actually right now."

"Probably not. But shall we just go and check?"

———

Two hours later we exited the tattoo parlor, me eighty pounds lighter and bearing a surgical patch over my hip where the ink was still drying. Its relatively small size, the tattoo artist said, meant that I could have it lined and colored in one visit, so there I was. Finished. Tattooed. Or, as Patrick would no doubt say, scarred for life. Under that white dressing sat a fat little bumblebee, culled from the laminated ring binder of images that the tattoo artist had handed us when we walked in. I felt almost hysterical with excitement. I kept reaching around to peek at it until Will told me to stop or I was going to dislocate something.

Will had been relaxed and happy in there, oddly enough. They had not given him a second look. They had done a few quads, they said, which explained the ease with which they had handled him. They were surprised when Will said he could feel the needle. Six weeks earlier they had finished inking a paraplegic who had had trompe l'oeil bionics inked the whole way down one side of his leg.

The tattooist with the bolt through his ear had taken Will into the next room and, with my tattooist's help, laid him down on a special table so that all I could see through the open door were his lower legs. I could hear the two men murmuring and laughing over the buzz of the tattooing needle, the smell of antiseptic sharp in my nostrils.

When the needle first bit into my skin, I chewed my lip, determined not to let Will hear me squeal. I kept my mind on what he was doing next door, trying to eavesdrop on his conversation, wondering what it was he was having done.

"You're a bad bloody influence on me, Will Traynor," I said, opening the car door and lowering the ramp. I couldn't stop grinning.

"Show me."

I glanced down the street, then turned and peeled a little of the dressing down from my hip.

"It's great. I like your little bee. Really."

"I'm going to have to wear high-waisted trousers around my parents for the rest of my life." I helped him steer his chair onto the ramp and raised it. "Mind you, if your mum gets to hear you've had one too . . ."

"I'm going to tell her the girl from the council estate led me astray."

"Okay then, Traynor, you show me yours."

He gazed at me steadily, half smiling. "You'll have to put a new dressing on it when we get home."

"Yeah. Like that never happens. Go on. I'm not driving off until you do."

"Lift my shirt, then. To the right. Your right."

I leaned through the front seats, and tugged at his shirt, peeling back the piece of gauze beneath. There, dark against his pale skin, was a black-and-white-striped ink rectangle, small enough that I had to look twice before I realized what it said.

Best before: 19 March 2007

I stared at it. I half laughed, and then my eyes filled with tears. "Is that the—"

"Date of my accident. Yes." He raised his eyes to the heavens. "Oh, for Christ's sake, don't get maudlin, Clark. It was meant to be funny."

"It is funny. In a crappy sort of way."

"Nathan will enjoy it. Oh, come on, don't look like that. It's not as if I'm ruining my perfect body, is it?"

I pulled Will's shirt back down and then turned and fired up the ignition. I had no idea what to say. I didn't know what any of this meant. Was this him coming to terms with his state? Or just another way of showing his contempt for his own body?

"Hey, Clark, do me a favor," he said, just as I was about to pull away. "Reach into the backpack for me. The zipped pocket."

I glanced into the rearview mirror, and put the hand brake on again. I leaned through the front seats and put my hand in the bag, rummaging around according to his instructions.

"You want painkillers?" I was inches from his face. He had more color in his skin than at any time since he'd come back from the hospital. "I've got some in my—"

"No. Keep looking."

I pulled out a piece of paper and sat back. It was a folded ten-pound note.

"There you go. The emergency tenner."

"So?"

"It's yours."

"For what?"

"That tattoo." He grinned at me. "Right up until you were in that chair, I didn't think for a minute you were going to actually do it."

16

There was no way around it. The sleeping arrangements just weren't working. Every weekend that Treena came home, the Clark family began a lengthy nocturnal game of musical beds. After supper on Friday night Mum and Dad would offer up their bedroom, and Treena would accept it, after they had reassured her that no, they were not in the least bit put out, and how much better Thomas was at sleeping in a room he knew. It would mean, they said, that everyone got a good night's sleep.

But Mum sleeping downstairs also involved her and Dad needing their own quilt, their own pillows and even undersheet, as Mum couldn't sleep properly unless her bed was just as she liked it. So after supper she and Treena would strip Mum and Dad's bed and put on a new set of sheets, together with a mattress protector, just in case Thomas had an accident. Mum and Dad's bedding, meanwhile, would be folded and placed in the corner of the living room, where Thomas would dive into it and onto it and string the sheet across the dining chairs to turn it into a tent.

Granddad offered his room, but nobody took it. It smelled of yellowing copies of the *Racing Post* and Old Holborn, and it would have taken all weekend to clear out. I would alternately feel guilty—all this was my fault, after all—while knowing I would not offer to return to the box room. It had become a kind of specter for me, that airless little room with no windows. The thought of sleeping in there again made my chest feel tight. I was twenty-seven years old. I was the main earner of the family. I could not sleep in what was essentially a cupboard.

One weekend I offered to sleep at Patrick's, and everyone looked secretly relieved. But then, while I was away, Thomas put sticky fingers all over my new blinds and drew on my new duvet cover in permanent pen, at which point Mum and Dad decided it would be best if *they* slept in my room, while Treena and Thomas went into theirs, where the odd bit of felt tip apparently didn't matter.

Once you had accounted for all the extra bed stripping and laundry, me spending Friday and Saturday nights at Pat's, Mum admitted, wasn't actually much help at all.

And then there was Patrick. Patrick was now a man obsessed. He ate, drank, lived, and breathed the Xtreme Viking. His flat, normally sparsely furnished and immaculate, was strung with training schedules and dietary sheets. He had a new lightweight bike which lived in the hallway and which I wasn't allowed to touch, in case I interfered with its finely balanced lightweight racing capabilities.

And he was rarely home, even on a Friday or Saturday night. What with his training and my work hours we seemed to have become used to spending less time together. I could follow him down to the track and watch him push himself around and around in circles until he had completed the requisite number of miles, or I could stay home and watch television by myself, curled up in a corner of his vast leather settee. There was no food in the fridge, apart from strips of turkey breast and vile energy drinks the consistency of frog spawn. Treena and I had tried one once and spat it out, gagging theatrically, like children.

The truth of it was I didn't like Patrick's flat. He had bought it a year ago, when he finally felt his mother would be okay by herself. His business had done well, and he had told me it was important that one of us get on the property ladder. I suppose that would have been the cue for us to have a conversation about whether we were going to live together, but somehow it didn't happen, and neither of us is the type to bring up subjects that make us feel a bit uncomfortable. As a result, there was nothing of me in that flat, despite our years together. I had never quite been able to tell him, but I would rather live in my house, with all its noise and clutter, than in that soulless, featureless bachelor pad, with its allocated parking spaces and executive view of the castle.

And besides, it was a bit lonely.

"Got to stick to the schedule, babe," he would say, if I told him. "If I do any fewer than twenty-three miles at this stage of the game, I'll never make it back on schedule." Then he would give me the latest update on his shin splints or ask me to pass him the heat spray.

When he wasn't training, he was at endless meetings with other members of his team, comparing equipment and finalizing travel arrangements. Sitting among them was like being with a bunch of Korean speakers. I had no idea what any of it meant, and no great desire to immerse myself.

And I was supposed to be going with them to Norway in seven weeks' time. I hadn't yet worked out how to tell Patrick that I hadn't asked the Traynors for the time off. How could I? By the time the Xtreme Viking took place, there would be less than one week of my contract left to run. I suppose I was childishly refusing to deal with it all, but truthfully, all I could see was Will and a ticking clock. Not a lot else seemed to register.

The great irony of all this was that I didn't even sleep well at Patrick's flat. I don't know what it was, but I came to work from there feeling like I was speaking through a glass jar, and looking like I had been punched in both eyes. I began painting concealer on my dark shadows with slapdash abandon.

———

"What's going on, Clark?" Will said.

I opened my eyes. He was right beside me, his head cocked to one side, watching me. I got the feeling he might have been there for some time. My hand went automatically for my mouth in case I had been dribbling.

The film I was supposed to have been watching was now a series of slow-moving credits.

"Nothing. Sorry. It's just warm in here." I pushed myself upright.

"It's the second time you've fallen asleep in three days." He studied my face. "And you look bloody awful."

So I told him. I told him about my sister, and our sleeping arrangements, and how I didn't want to make a fuss because every time I looked at Dad's face I saw his barely concealed despair that he could not even provide his family with a house we could all sleep in.

"He's still not found anything?"

"No. I think it's his age. But we don't talk about it. It's . . ." I shrugged. "It's too uncomfortable for everyone."

It felt somehow wrong, telling Will my problems. They seemed embarrassingly trivial next to his.

"I'll get used to it," I said. "It'll be fine. Really."

Will seemed preoccupied for the rest of the afternoon. I washed up, then came through and set up his computer for him. When I brought him a drink, he swiveled his chair toward me.

"It's quite simple," he said, as if we had been in conversation. "You can sleep here on weekends. There's a room going spare—it might as well get some use."

I stopped, the beaker in my hand. "I can't do that."

"Why not? I'm not going to pay you for the extra hours you're here."

I placed the beaker in his holder. "But what would your mum think?"

"I have no idea."

I must have looked troubled, because he added, "It's okay. I'm safe in taxis."

"What?"

"If you're worried I have some devious secret plan to seduce you, you can just pull my plug out."

"Funny."

"Seriously. Think about it. You could have it as your backup option. Things might change faster than you think. Your sister might decide she doesn't want to spend every weekend at home after all. Or she might meet someone. A million things might change."

And you might not be here in two months, I told him silently, and immediately hated myself for thinking it.

"Tell me something," he said as he went to leave the room. "Why isn't Running Man offering you his place?"

"Oh, he has," I said.

He looked at me, as if he were about to pursue the conversation.

And then he seemed to change his mind. "Like I said." He shrugged. "The offer's there."

———

"You saw my dad in town the other week."

"Oh. Yes." I was hanging washing out on a line. The line itself was hidden in what Mrs. Traynor called the Kitchen Garden. I think she didn't want anything as mundane as laundry polluting the view of her herbaceous borders. My own mother pegged her whites out almost as a badge of pride. It was like a challenge to her neighbors: *Beat this, ladies!* It was all Dad could do to stop her putting a second revolving clothes dryer out front.

"He asked me if you'd said anything about it."

"Oh." I kept my face a studied blank. And then, because he seemed to be waiting, "Evidently not."

"Was he with someone?"

I put the last peg back in the peg bag. I rolled it up and placed it in the empty laundry basket. I turned to him.

"Yes."

"A woman."

"Yes."

"Red-haired?"

"Yes."

Will thought about this for a minute.

"I'm sorry if you think I should have told you," I said. "But it . . . it didn't seem like my business."

"And it's never an easy conversation to have."

"No."

"If it's any consolation, Clark, it's not the first time," he said, and headed back into the house.

Every day, while he was watching television, or otherwise engaged, I sat in front of Will's computer and worked on coming up with the magic event that might Make Will Happy. But as time went on, I found that my list of things we couldn't do, places we couldn't go to, had begun to exceed my ideas for those we could by a significant factor. When the one figure first exceeded the other, I went back onto the chat room sites, and asked their advice.

"Ha!" said Ritchie. "Welcome to our world, Bee."

From the ensuing conversations I learned that getting drunk in a wheelchair came with its own hazards, including catheter disasters, falling down curbs, and being steered to the wrong home by other drunks. I learned that there was no single place where nonquads were more or less helpful than anywhere else, but that Paris was singled out as the least wheelchair-friendly place on earth. This was disappointing, as some small, optimistic part of me had still hoped we might make it there.

I began to compile a new list—things you cannot do with a quadriplegic.

Go on a tube train (most underground stations don't have lifts), which pretty much ruled out activities in half of London unless we wanted to pay for taxis. And there was no way I was going to drive around the capital city.

Go swimming, without help, and unless the temperature was warm enough to stop involuntary shivering within minutes. Even disabled changing rooms are not much use without a pool hoist. Not that Will would have allowed himself into a pool hoist.

Go to the cinema, unless guaranteed a seat at the front, or unless Will's spasms were low-grade that day. I had spent at least twenty minutes of *Rear Window* on my hands and knees picking up the popcorn that Will's unexpected knee jerk had sent flying into the air.

Go on a beach, unless your chair had been adapted with "fat wheels." Will's hadn't.

Go shopping, unless all the shops had gotten their statutory ramps in place. Many around the castle used their listed-building status to say they couldn't fit them. Some were even telling the truth.

Go anywhere too hot, or too cold (temperature issues).

Go anywhere spontaneously (bags needed to be packed, routes to be double-checked for accessibility).

Go out to eat, if feeling self-conscious about being fed, or—depending on the catheter situation— if the restaurant's bathroom was down a flight of stairs.

Go to friends' houses, unless they had wheelchair ramps. Most houses have stairs. Most people do not have ramps. Will said there was nobody he wanted to see anyway.

Go anywhere hilly in heavy rain (the brakes

were not always safe, and the chair was too heavy for me to hold).

Go anywhere where there were likely to be drunks. Will was a magnet for drunks. They would crouch down, breathe fumes all over him, and make big, sympathetic eyes. Sometimes they would, indeed, try to wheel him off.

Go anywhere where there might be crowds. This meant that, as summer approached, outings around the castle were getting harder, and half the places I thought we might be able to go—fairs, outdoor theater, concerts—were ruled out.

When, struggling for ideas, I asked the online quads what was the thing they would like to do most in all the world, the answer that nearly always came back was, "Have sex." I got quite a lot of unsolicited detail on that one.

But essentially it was not a huge help. There were eight weeks to go, and I had run out of ideas.

———

A couple of days after our discussion under the clothesline, I returned home to find Dad standing in the hallway. This would have been unusual in itself (the last few weeks he seemed to have retreated to the sofa in the daytime, supposedly to keep Granddad company), but he was wearing an ironed shirt, had shaved, and the hallway was filled with the scent of Old Spice. I am pretty sure he'd had that bottle of aftershave since 1974.

"There you are."

I closed the door behind me. "Here I am."

I was feeling tired and anxious. I had spent the whole bus journey home talking on my mobile phone to a travel agent about places to take Will, but we were both stumped.

"Are you okay getting your own tea tonight?"

"Sure. I can join Patrick at the pub later. Why?" I

hung up my coat on a free peg. The rack was so much emptier with all of Treena's and Thomas's coats gone.

"I am taking your mother out for dinner."

I did a quick mental calculation. "Did I miss her birthday?"

"Nope. We're celebrating." He lowered his voice, as if it were some kind of secret. "I got a job."

"You didn't!" And now I could see it; his whole body had lightened. He was standing straighter again, his face wreathed in smiles. He looked years younger.

"Dad, that's fantastic."

"I know. Your mother's over the moon. And, you know, she's had a tough few months what with Treena going and Granddad and all. So I want to take her out tonight, treat her a bit."

"So what's the job?"

"I'm going to be head of maintenance. Up at the castle."

I blinked. "But that's—"

"Mr. Traynor. That's right. He rang me and said he was looking for someone, and your man, Will there, had told him that I was available. I went this afternoon and showed him what I could do, and I'm on a month's trial. Beginning Saturday."

"You're going to work for Will's dad?"

"Well, he said they have to do a month's trial, to go through the proper procedures and all, but he said he couldn't think of any reason why I shouldn't get it."

"That—that's great," I said. I felt weirdly unbalanced by the news. "I didn't even know there was a job open."

"Nor me. It's great, though. He's a man who understands quality, Lou. I talked to him about green oak, and he showed me some of the work done by the previous man. You wouldn't believe it. Shocking. He said he was very impressed by my work."

He was animated, more so than I had seen him for months.

Mum had appeared beside him. She was wearing lip-stick, and her good pair of heels. "There's a van. He gets his own van. And the pay is good, Lou. It's more than your dad was getting at the furniture factory."

She was looking up at him as though he were some kind of all-conquering hero. Her face, when she turned to me, told me I should do the same. It could contain a million messages, my mother's face, and this one told me Dad should be allowed his moment.

"That's great, Dad. Really." I stepped forward and gave him a hug.

"Well, it's really Will you should thank. What a smashing bloke. I'm just bloody grateful that he thought of me."

I listened to them leave the house, the sound of Mum fussing in the hall mirror, Dad's repeated reassurances that she looked lovely, that she was just fine as she was. I heard him patting his pockets for keys, wallet, loose change, followed by a brief burst of laughter. The door slammed. I heard the hum of the car pulling away, and then there was just the distant sound of the television in Granddad's room. I sat on the stairs. And then I pulled out my phone and rang Will's number.

It took him a while to answer. I pictured him heading to the hands-free device, depressing the button with his thumb.

"Hello?"

"Is this your doing?"

There was a brief pause. "Is that you, Clark?"

"Did you get my dad a job?"

He sounded a little breathless. I wondered, absently, whether he was sitting up okay.

"I thought you'd be pleased."

"I am pleased. It's just . . . I don't know. I feel weird."

"You shouldn't. Your dad needed a job. Mine needed a skilled maintenance man."

"Really?" I couldn't keep the skepticism from my voice. "What?"

"This has nothing to do with what you asked me the other day? About him and the other woman?"

There was a long pause. I could see him there, in his living room, looking out through the French windows.

His voice, when it came, was careful. "You think I'd blackmail my father into giving yours a job?"

Put like that, it did sound far-fetched.

"Sorry. I don't know. It's just weird. The timing. It's all a bit convenient."

"Then be pleased, Clark. It's good news. Your dad will be great. And it means . . ." He hesitated.

"It means what?"

"That one day you can go off and spread your wings without worrying about how your parents are going to be able to support themselves."

It was as if he had punched me. I felt the air disappear from my lungs.

"Lou?"

"Yes?"

"You're awfully quiet."

"I'm . . ." I swallowed. "Sorry. Distracted by something. Granddad's calling me. But yes. Thanks for—for putting a word in for him." I had to get off the phone. Because out of nowhere a huge lump had lodged itself somewhere in my throat and I wasn't sure I could say anything else.

———

I walked to the pub. The air was thick with the smell of blossoms, and people smiled as they passed me on the street. I couldn't raise a single greeting in return. I just knew I couldn't stay in that house, alone with my thoughts. I found the Triathlon Terrors all in the beer garden, their two tables pushed together in a dappled corner, arms and legs spilling off the ends in sinewy pink angles. I got a few polite nods (none from the women) and Patrick stood, creating a small space for me beside him. I realized I really wished Treena was around.

"I wasn't expecting you. Do you want a drink?"

"In a minute." I just wanted to sit there, to let my head rest against Patrick. I wanted to feel like I used to feel— normal, untroubled. I wanted not to think about death.

"I broke my best time today. Fifteen miles in just 79.2 minutes."

"Great."

"Cooking with gas now, eh, Pat?" someone said.

Patrick bunched both his fists and made a revving noise with his mouth.

"That's great. Really." I tried to look pleased for him.

I had a drink, and then another. I listened to their talk of mileage, of the skinned knees and hypothermic swimming bouts. I tuned out, and watched the other people in the pub, wondering about their lives. Each of them would have huge events in their own families—babies loved and lost, dark secrets, great joys and tragedies. If they could put it into perspective, if they could just enjoy a sunny evening in a pub garden, then surely I should too.

And then I told Patrick about Dad's job. His face looked a little like I imagine mine had. I had to repeat it, just so he could be sure he had heard me right.

"That's . . . very cozy. You both working for him."

I wanted to tell him then, I really did. I wanted to explain that so much of everything was tied up in my battle to keep Will alive. I wanted to tell him how afraid I was that Will seemed to be trying to buy me my freedom. But I knew I could say nothing. I might as well get the rest of it over while I could.

"Um . . . that's not the only thing. He says I can stay there when I want, in the spare room. To get past the whole bed problem at home."

Patrick looked at me. "You're going to live at his house?"

"I might. It's a nice offer, Pat. You know what it's been

like at home. And you're never here. I like coming to your house, but . . . well, if I'm honest, it doesn't feel like home."

He was still staring at me. "Then make it home."

"What?"

"Move in. Make it home. Put your stuff up. Bring your clothes. It's about time we moved in together."

It was only afterward, when I thought about it, that I realized he had actually looked really unhappy as he said this. Not like a man who had finally worked out he could not live without his girlfriend close by him, and wanted to make a joyous union of our two lives. He looked like someone who felt outmaneuvered.

"You really want me to move in?"

"Yes. Sure." He rubbed at his ear. "I mean, I'm not saying let's get married or anything. But it does make sense, right?"

"You old romantic."

"I mean it, Lou. It's time. It's probably been time for ages, but I guess I've just been wrapped up in one thing and another. Move in. It'll be good." He hugged me. "It will be really good."

Around us the Triathlon Terrors had diplomatically resumed their chatter. A small cheer went up as a group of Japanese tourists got the photograph they had wanted. Birds sang, the sun dipped, the world turned. I wanted to be part of it, not stuck in a silent room, worrying about a man in a wheelchair.

"Yes," I said. "It will be good."

17

The worst thing about working as a caregiver is not what you might think. It's not the lifting and cleaning, the medicines and wipes, and the distant but somehow always perceptible smell of disinfectant. It's not even the fact that most people assume you're only doing it because you really aren't smart enough to do anything else. It's the fact that when you spend all day in proximity to someone, there is no escape from their moods. Or your own.

Will had been distant with me all morning, since I had first told him my plans. It was nothing an outsider could have put their finger on, but there were fewer jokes, perhaps less casual conversation. He asked me nothing about the contents of the day's newspapers.

"That's . . . what you want to do?" His eyes had flickered, but his face betrayed nothing.

I shrugged. Then I nodded more emphatically. I felt there was something childishly noncommittal about my response. "It's about time, really," I said. "I mean, I *am* twenty-seven."

He studied my face. Something tightened in his jaw.

I felt suddenly, unbearably tired. I felt this peculiar urge to say I was sorry, and I wasn't sure what for.

He gave a little nod, raised a smile. "Glad you've got it all sorted out," he said, and wheeled himself into the kitchen.

I was starting to feel really cross with him. I had never felt as judged by anyone as I felt judged by Will now. It was as if my deciding to settle down with my boyfriend had made me less interesting to him. Like I could no longer be his pet project. I couldn't say any of this to him, of course, but I was just as cool with him as he was with me.

It was, frankly, exhausting.

In the afternoon, there was a knock at the back door. I hurried down the corridor, my hands still wet from washing up, and opened it to find a man standing there in a dark suit, a briefcase in hand.

"Oh no. We're Buddhist," I said firmly, closing the door as the man began to protest.

Two weeks previously a pair of Jehovah's Witnesses had kept Will captive at the back door for almost fifteen minutes, while he struggled to reverse his chair over the dislodged doormat. When I finally shut the door, they had called out that "he more than anyone" should understand what it was to look forward to the afterlife.

"Um . . . I'm here to see Mr. Traynor?" the man said, and I opened the door cautiously. In all my time at Granta House nobody had ever come to see Will via the back door.

"Let him in," Will said, appearing behind me. "I asked him to come." When I still stood there, he added, "It's okay, Clark . . . he's a friend."

The man stepped over the threshold, held out his hand, and shook mine. "Michael Lawler," he said.

He was about to say something else, but Will moved his chair between us, effectively cutting off any further conversation.

"We'll be in the living room. Could you make some coffee, then leave us for a while?"

"Um . . . okay."

Mr. Lawler smiled at me, a little awkwardly, and followed Will into the living room. When I walked in with a tray of coffee some minutes later, they were discussing cricket. The conversation about legs and runs continued until I had no further reason to lurk.

Brushing invisible dust from my skirt, I straightened up and said, "Well. I'll leave you to it."

"Thanks, Louisa."

"You sure you don't want anything else? A snack?"

"Thank you, Louisa."

Will never called me Louisa. And he had never banished me from anything before.

Mr. Lawler stayed almost an hour. I did my chores, then hung around in the kitchen, wondering if I was brave enough to eavesdrop. I wasn't. I sat, ate two Bourbon creams, chewed my nails, listened to the low hum of their voices, and wondered for the fifteenth time why Will had asked this man not to use the front entrance.

He didn't look like a doctor, or a consultant. He could have been a financial adviser, but he somehow didn't have the right air about him. He certainly didn't look like a physiotherapist, occupational therapist, or dietitian—or one of the legions of other people employed by the local authority to pop by and assess Will's ever-changing needs. You could spot those a mile off. They always looked exhausted, but were briskly, determinedly cheerful. They wore woolens in muted colors, with sensible shoes, and drove dusty estate cars full of folders and boxes of equipment. Mr. Lawler had a navy blue BMW. His gleaming 5-series was not a local authority sort of a car.

Finally, Mr. Lawler emerged. He closed his briefcase, and his jacket hung over his arm. He no longer looked awkward.

I was in the hallway within seconds.

"Ah. Would you mind pointing me toward the bathroom?"

I did so, mutely, and stood there, fidgeting, until he emerged.

"Right. So that's all for now."

"Thank you, Michael." Will didn't look at me. "I'll wait to hear from you."

"I should be in touch later this week," Mr. Lawler said.

"E-mail would be preferable to a letter—at least for now."

"Yes. Of course."

I opened the back door to see him out. Then, as Will disappeared back into the living room, I followed Lawler into the courtyard and said lightly, "So—do you have far to go?"

His clothes were beautifully cut; they carried the sharp edge of the city in their tailoring, serious money in their thread count.

"London, unfortunately. Still, hope the traffic won't be too bad at this time of the afternoon."

The sun was high in the sky and I had to squint to see him. "So . . . um . . . where in London are you based?"

"Regent Street."

"*The* Regent Street? Nice."

"Yes. Not a bad place to be. Right. Thank you for the coffee, Miss . . ."

"Clark. Louisa Clark."

He stopped then and looked at me for a moment, and I wondered whether he had sussed my inadequate attempts to work out who he might be.

"Ah. Miss Clark," he said, his professional smile swiftly reinstated. "Thank you, anyway."

He put his briefcase carefully on the backseat, climbed into his car, and was gone.

That night, I stopped off at the library on my way home to Patrick's. I could have used his computer, but I still felt obliged to ask, and this just seemed easier. I sat down, and typed "Michael Lawler" and "Regent Street, London" into the search engine. *Knowledge is power, Will,* I told him silently.

There were 3,290 results, the first three of which revealed a "Michael Lawler, practitioner at law, specialist in wills, probate, and power of attorney" based on that same street. I stared at the screen for a few minutes, then I typed in his name again, this time against the search engine of images, and there he was, at some Round Table function, in a dark suit—Michael Lawler, specialist in wills and probate, the same man who had spent an hour with Will.

I moved into Patrick's that night, in the hour and a half between my finishing work and his heading off to the track. I took everything except my bed and the new blinds. He arrived with his car, and we loaded my belongings into bin bags. Within two trips we had it all— barring my school books in the loft—at his.

Mum cried; she thought she was forcing me out.

"For goodness' sake, love. It's time she moved on. She's twenty-seven years old," my father told her.

"She's still my baby," she said, pressing two tins of fruitcake and a tote bag of cleaning products into my arms.

I didn't know what to say to her. I don't even like fruitcake.

It was surprisingly easy, fitting my belongings into Patrick's flat. He had next to nothing anyway, and I had almost nothing from years spent in the box room. The only thing we fell out over was my CD collection, which apparently could only be combined with his once I had stickered the backs of mine and sorted them into alphabetical order.

"Make yourself at home," he kept saying, as if I were some kind of guest. We were nervous, strangely awkward with each other, like two people on a first date. While I was unpacking, he brought me tea and said, "I thought this could be your mug." He showed me where everything lived in the kitchen, then said, several times, "Of course, put stuff where you want. I don't mind."

He had cleared two drawers and the wardrobe in the spare room. The other two drawers were filled with his fitness clothes. I didn't know there were so many permutations of Lycra and fleece. My wildly colorful clothes left several feet of closet space still empty, the wire hangers jangling mournfully.

"I'll have to buy more stuff just to fill it up," I said, looking at it.

He laughed nervously. "What's that?"

He looked at my calendar, tacked up on the spare-room wall, with its ideas in green and its actual planned events in black. When something had worked (music, wine tasting), I put a smiley face next to it. When it hadn't (horse racing, art galleries), it stayed blank. There was little marked in for the next two weeks—Will had become bored of the places nearby, and as yet I could not persuade him to venture farther afield. I glanced over at Patrick. I could see him eyeing the August 12 date, which was now underlined with exclamation marks in black.

"Um . . . it's just reminding me about my job."

"You don't think they're going to renew your contract?"

"I don't know, Patrick."

Patrick took the pen from its clip, looked at the next month, and scribbled under week twenty-eight: Time to start job hunting.

"That way you're covered for whatever happens," he said. He kissed me and left me to it.

I laid out my creams carefully in the bathroom, tucked my razors, moisturizer, and tampons neatly into his mirrored cabinet. I put some books in a neat row along the spare-room floor under the window, including the new titles that Will had ordered from Amazon for me. Patrick promised to put up some shelves when he had a spare moment.

And then, as he left to go running, I sat and looked out over the industrial estate toward the castle, and practiced saying the word *home*, silently under my breath.

I am pretty hopeless at keeping secrets. Treena says I touch my nose as soon as I even think of lying. It's a pretty straightforward giveaway. My parents still joke about the time I wrote absence notes for myself after bunking off school. "Dear Miss Trowbridge," they read. "Please excuse Louisa Clark from today's lessons as I am very poorly with women's problems." Dad had struggled to keep a straight face even while he was supposed to be tearing a strip off me.

Keeping Will's plan from my family had been one thing—I was good at keeping secrets from my parents (it's one of the things we learn while growing up, after all)—but coping with the anxiety by myself was something else entirely.

I spent the next couple of nights trying to work out what Will was up to, and what I could do to stop him, my thoughts racing even as Patrick and I chatted, cooking together in the little galley kitchen. (I was already discovering new things about him—like, he really *did* know a hundred different things to do with turkey breast.) At night we made love—it seemed almost obligatory at the moment, as if we should take full advantage of our freedom. It was like Patrick somehow felt I owed him something, given my constant physical proximity to Will. But as soon as he dropped off to sleep, I was lost in my thoughts again.

There were just seven weeks left.

And Will was making plans, even if I wasn't.

The following week, if Will noticed that I was preoccupied, he didn't say anything. We went through the motions of our daily routine—I took him for short drives into the country, cooked his meals, saw to him when we were in his house. He didn't make jokes about Running Man anymore.

I talked to him about the latest books he had recommended: we discussed *The English Patient* (I had loved this), and a Swedish thriller (which I hadn't). We were solicitous with each other, almost excessively polite. I missed his insults, his crabbiness—their absence just added to the looming sense of threat that hung over me.

Nathan watched us both, as if he were observing some kind of new species.

"You two had a row?" he asked me one day in the kitchen, as I unpacked the groceries.

"You'd better ask him," I said.

"That's exactly what he said."

He looked at me sideways, and disappeared into the bathroom to unlock Will's medical cabinet.

Meanwhile, I'd lasted three days after Michael Lawler's visit before I rang Mrs. Traynor. I asked if we could meet somewhere other than her house, and we agreed on a little café that had opened on the grounds of the castle. The same café, ironically, that had cost me my job.

It was a much smarter affair than the Buttered Bun— all limed oak and bleached wood tables and chairs. It sold homemade soup full of actual vegetables, and fancy cakes. And you couldn't buy a normal coffee, only lattes, cappuccinos, and macchiatos. There were no builders, or girls from the hairdresser's. I sat nursing my tea, and wondered about the Dandelion Lady and whether she would feel comfortable enough to sit in here and read a newspaper all morning.

"Louisa, I'm sorry I'm late." Camilla Traynor entered briskly, her handbag tucked under her arm, dressed in a gray silk shirt and navy trousers.

I fought the urge to stand up. There was never a time when I spoke to her that I didn't still feel like I was engaged in some kind of interview.

"I was held up in court."

"Sorry. To get you out of work, I mean. I just . . . well, I wasn't sure it could wait."

She held up her hand, and mouthed something at the waitress. Then she sat across from me. I felt her gaze as if I were transparent.

"Will had a lawyer come to the house," I said. "I found out he is a specialist in wills and probate." I couldn't think of any gentler way to open the conversation.

She looked as if I'd just smacked her in the face. I realized, too late, that she might actually have thought I'd have something good to tell her.

"A lawyer? Are you sure?"

"I looked him up on the Internet. He's based on Regent Street. In London," I added unnecessarily. "His name is Michael Lawler."

She blinked hard, as if trying to take this in. "Did Will tell you this?"

"No. I don't think he wanted me to know. I . . . I got his name and looked him up."

Her coffee arrived. The waitress put it on the table in front of her, but Mrs. Traynor didn't seem to notice.

"Did you want anything else?" the girl said.

"No, thank you."

"We have carrot cake on special today. We make it here ourselves. It's got a lovely buttercream fill—"

"*No.*" Mrs. Traynor's voice was sharp. "Thank you."

The girl stood there just long enough to let us know she was offended and then stalked off, her notepad swinging conspicuously from one hand.

"I'm sorry," I said. "You told me before that I should let you know anything important. I stayed awake half the night trying to work out whether to say anything."

Her face looked almost leached of color.

I knew how she felt.

"How is he himself? Have you . . . have you come up with any other ideas? Outings?"

"He's not keen." I told her about Paris, and my list of things I had compiled.

All the while I spoke, I could see her mind working ahead of me, calculating, assessing.

"Anywhere," she said, finally. "I'll finance it. Any trip

you want. I'll pay for you. For Nathan. Just—just see if you can get him to agree to it."

I nodded.

"If there's anything else you can think of . . . just to buy us some time. I'll pay your wages beyond the six months, obviously."

"That's . . . that's really not an issue."

We finished our coffees in silence, both lost in our thoughts. As I watched her surreptitiously, I noticed that her immaculate hairstyle was now flecked with gray, her eyes as shadowed as my own. I realized I didn't feel any better for having told her, to have passed my own heightened anxiety on to her—but what choice did I have? The stakes were getting higher with every day that passed. The sound of the clock striking two seemed to spur her out of her stasis.

"I suppose I should get back to work. Please let me know anything that you . . . you can come up with, Louisa. It might be better if we have these conversations away from the annex."

I stood up. "Oh," I said, "you'll need my new number. I just moved." As she reached into her handbag for a pen, I added, "I moved in with Patrick . . . my boyfriend."

I don't know why this news surprised her so much. She looked startled, and then she handed me her pen.

"I didn't know you had a boyfriend."

"I didn't know I needed to tell you."

She stood, one hand resting on the table. "Will mentioned the other day that you . . . he thought you might be moving into the annex. On weekends."

I scribbled Patrick's home number.

"Well, I thought it might be more straightforward for everyone if I moved in with Patrick." I handed her the slip of paper. "But I'm not far away. Just by the industrial estate. It won't affect my hours. Or my punctuality."

We stood there. Mrs. Traynor seemed agitated, her

hand running through her hair, then reaching down for the chain around her neck. Finally—as if she could not help herself—she blurted out, "Would it really have hurt you to have waited? Just a few weeks?"

"I'm sorry?"

"Will . . . I think Will is very fond of you." She bit her lip. "I can't see . . . I can't see how this really helps."

"Hold on. Are you telling me I shouldn't have moved in with my boyfriend?"

"I'm just saying that the timing is not ideal. Will is in a very vulnerable state. We're all doing our best to keep him optimistic . . . and you—"

"I what?" I could see the waitress watching us, her notepad stilled in her hand. "I what? Dared to have a life away from work?"

She lowered her voice. "I am doing everything I can, Louisa, to stop this . . . thing. You know the task we're facing. And I'm just saying that I wish—given the fact he is very fond of you—that you had waited a while longer before rubbing your . . . your happiness in his face."

I could hardly believe what I was hearing. I felt the color rise to my face, and took a deep breath before I spoke again.

"How dare you suggest I would do anything to hurt Will's feelings. I have done everything," I hissed. "I have done everything I can think of. I've come up with ideas, got him out, talked to him, read to him, looked after him." My last words exploded out of my chest. "I've cleaned up after him. I've changed his bloody catheter. I've made him laugh. I've done more than your bloody family has done."

Mrs. Traynor stood very still. She drew herself up to her full height, tucked her handbag under her arm. "I think this conversation has probably ended, Miss Clark."

"Yes. Yes, Mrs. Traynor. I think it probably has."

She turned, and walked swiftly out of the café.

When the door slammed shut, I realized I too was shaking.

————

That conversation with Mrs. Traynor kept me jangling for the next couple of days. I kept hearing her words, the idea that I was *rubbing my happiness in his face*. I didn't think Will could be affected by anything that I did. When he had seemed disapproving about my decision to move in with Patrick, I had thought it was about him not liking Patrick rather than any feelings he had for me. More important, I didn't think I had looked particularly happy.

At home, I couldn't shake this feeling of anxiety. It was like a low-level current running through me, and it fed into everything I did. I asked Patrick, "Would we have done this if my sister hadn't needed my room at home?"

He looked at me as if I were daft. He leaned over and pulled me to him, kissing the top of my head. Then he glanced down. "Do you have to wear these pajamas? I hate you in pajamas."

"They're comfortable."

"They look like something my mum would wear."

"I'm not going to wear a corset and stockings every night just to keep you happy. And you're not answering my question."

"I don't know. Probably. Yes."

"But we weren't talking about it, were we?"

"Lou, most people move in with each other because it's sensible. You can love someone and still see the financial and practical advantages."

"I just . . . don't want you to think I made this happen. I don't want to feel like I made this happen."

He sighed, and rolled onto his back. "Why do women always have to go over and over a situation until it becomes a problem? I love you, you love me, we've been together nearly seven years, and there was no room at your parents' house anymore. It's actually pretty simple."

But it didn't feel simple.

It felt like I was living a life I hadn't had a chance to anticipate.

That Friday it rained all day—warm, heavy sheets of it, like we were in the tropics, making the guttering gurgle and bowing the stems of the flowering shrubs as if in supplication. Will stared out the windows like a dog denied a walk. Nathan came and went, a plastic bag lifted above his head. Will watched a documentary about penguins, and afterward, while he logged on to his computer, I busied myself, so that we didn't have to talk to each other. I felt our discomfort with each other keenly, and being in the same room as him all the time made it that much worse.

I had finally begun to understand the consolations of cleaning. I mopped, cleaned windows, and changed duvets. I was a constant whirl of activity. No dust mite escaped my eye, no tea ring my forensic attentions. I was dislodging the lime scale on the bathroom taps using paper towels soaked in vinegar (my mother's tip) when I heard Will's chair behind me.

"What are you doing?"

I was bent low over the bath. I didn't turn around. "I'm descaling your taps."

I could feel him watching me.

"Say that again," he said, after a beat.

"What?"

"Say that again."

I straightened up. "Why? Are you having problems with your hearing? I'm descaling your taps."

"No, I just want you to listen to what you're saying. There is no reason to descale my taps, Clark. My mother won't notice it, I won't care, and it's making the bathroom stink like a fish and chips shop. Besides, I'd like to go out."

I wiped a lock of hair from my face. It was true. There was a definite waft of large haddock in the atmosphere.

"Come on. It's finally stopped raining. I just spoke to my dad. He said he'll give us the keys to the castle after five o'clock, once all the tourists are out."

I didn't feel great about the idea of us having to make polite conversation during a walk around the grounds. But the thought of being out of the annex was appealing.

"Okay. Give me five minutes. I need to try and get the smell of vinegar off my hands."

The difference between growing up like me and growing up like Will was that he wore his sense of entitlement lightly. I think if you grow up as he had done, with wealthy parents, in a nice house, if you go to good schools and nice restaurants as a matter of course, you probably just have this sense that good things will fall into place, that your position in the world is naturally an elevated one.

Will had escaped into the empty grounds of the castle his whole childhood, he said. His dad let him roam the place, trusting him not to touch anything. After 5:30 P.M., when the last of the tourists had gone, as the gardeners began to trim and tidy, as the cleaners emptied the bins and swept up the empty cartons of drink and commemorative toffee fudge, it had become his private playground. "First girl I ever kissed was in front of the drawbridge," he said, slowing to look toward it as we walked along the gravel path.

"Did you tell her it was your place?"

"No. Perhaps I should have. She dumped me a week later for the boy who worked in the minimart."

I turned and stared at him in shock. "Not Terry Rowlands? Dark slicked-back hair, tattoos up to his elbows?"

He raised an eyebrow. "That's him."

"He still works there, you know. In the minimart. If that makes you feel any better."

"I'm not sure he'd feel entirely envious of where I ended up," Will said, and I stopped talking again.

It was strange seeing the castle like this, in silence, the two of us the only people there apart from the odd gardener in the distance. Instead of gazing at the tourists, being distracted by their accents and their alien lives, I found myself looking at the castle for perhaps the first time, beginning to absorb some of its history. Its flinted walls had stood there for more than eight hundred years. People had been born and died there, hearts filled and broken. Now, in the silence, you could almost hear their voices, their own footsteps on the path.

"Okay, confession time," I said. "Did you ever walk around here and pretend secretly that you were some kind of warrior prince?"

Will looked sideways at me. "Honestly?"

"Of course."

"Yes. I even borrowed one of the swords off the walls of the Great Hall once. It weighed a ton. I remember being petrified that I wouldn't be able to lift it back onto its stand."

We had reached the swell of the hill, and from here, at the front of the moat, we could look down the long sweep of grass to the ruined wall that had marked the boundary. Beyond it lay the town, the neon signs and queues of traffic, the bustle that marked the rush hour. Up here it was silent apart from the birds and the soft hum of Will's chair.

He stopped the chair briefly and swiveled it so that we looked down at the grounds. "I'm surprised we never met each other," he said. "When I was growing up, I mean. Our paths must have crossed."

"Why would they? We didn't exactly move in the same circles. And I would just have been the baby you passed in the pram, while swinging your sword."

"Ah. I forgot—I am positively ancient compared to you."

"Eight years would definitely have qualified you as an 'older man,'" I said. "Even when I was a teenager my dad would never have let me go out with an older man."

"Not even if he had his own castle?"

"Well, that would change things, obviously."

The sweet smell of the grass rose up around us as we walked, Will's wheels hissing through the clear puddles on the path. I felt relieved. Our conversation wasn't quite as it had been, but perhaps that was only to be expected. Mrs. Traynor had been right—it would always be hard for Will to watch other people moving on with their lives. I made a mental note to think more carefully about how my actions might make an impact on his life. I didn't want to be angry anymore.

"Let's do the maze. I haven't done it for ages."

I was pulled back from my thoughts. "Oh. No, thanks." I glanced over, noticing suddenly where we were.

"Why? Are you afraid of getting lost? C'mon, Clark. It'll be a challenge for you. See if you can memorize the route you take in, then take the reverse one out. I'll time you. I used to do it all the time."

I glanced back toward the house. "I'd really rather not." Even the thought of it had brought a knot to my stomach.

"Ah. Playing it safe again."

"That's not it."

"No problem. We'll just take our boring little walk and go back to the boring little annex."

I knew he was joking. But something in his tone really got to me. I thought of my parents, my sister with her big new life. Mine was to be the small life, my ambitions the petty ones.

I glanced over at the maze, at its dark, dense box hedging. I was being ridiculous. Perhaps I had been behaving ridiculously for years. It was all over, after all. And I was moving on.

"Just remember which turn you take, then reverse it to come out. It's not as hard as it looks. Really."

I left him on the path before I could think about it. I took a breath, and walked in past the sign that warned NO UNACCOMPANIED CHILDREN, striding briskly between the dark, damp hedging which still glistened with raindrops.

It's not so bad, it's not so bad, I found myself murmuring under my breath. *It's just a load of old hedges*. I took a right turn, then a left through a break in the hedge. I took another right, a left, and as I went I rehearsed in my head the reverse of where I had been. *Right. Left. Break. Right. Left.*

My heart rate began to rise a little, so that I could hear the blood pumping in my ears. I forced myself to think about Will on the other side of the hedge, glancing down at his watch. It was just a silly test. I was no longer that naive young woman. I was twenty-seven. I lived with my boyfriend. I had a responsible job. I was a different person.

I turned, went straight on, and turned again.

And then, almost from nowhere, the panic rose within me like bile. I thought I saw a man darting at the end of the hedge. Even though I told myself it was just my imagination, the act of reassuring myself made me forget my reversed instructions. *Right. Left. Break. Right. Right?* Had I got that the wrong way around? My breath caught in my throat. I forced myself onward, only to realize that I had completely lost my bearings. I stopped and glanced around me at the direction of the shadows, trying to work out which direction was west.

And as I stood there, it dawned on me that I couldn't do it. I couldn't stay in there. I whipped around, and began to walk in what I thought was a southerly direction. I would get out. I was twenty-seven years old. It was fine. But then I heard their voices, the catcalling, the mocking laughter. I saw them, darting in and out of the gaps in the hedge, felt my own feet sway drunkenly in my high heels, the unforgiving prickle of the hedge as I fell against it, trying to steady myself.

"I want to get out now," I had told them, my voice slurring and unsteady. "I've had enough, guys."

And they had all vanished. The maze was silent, just the distant whispers that might have been them on the other side of the hedge—or might have been the wind dislodging the leaves.

"I want to go out now," I had said, my voice sounding uncertain even to me. I had gazed up at the sky, briefly unbalanced by the vast, studded black of the space above me. And then I jumped as someone caught me around my waist—the dark-haired one. The one who had been to Africa.

"You can't go yet," he said. "You'll spoil the game."

I had known then, just from the feel of his hands on my waist. I had realized that some balance had shifted, that some restraint on behavior had begun to evaporate. And I had laughed, pushed at his hands as if they were a joke, unwilling to let him know that I knew. I heard him shout for his friends. And I broke away from him, running suddenly, trying to fight my way to the exit, my feet sinking into the damp grass. I heard them all around me, their raised voices, their bodies unseen, and felt my throat constrict in panic. I was too disorientated to work out where I was. The tall hedges kept swaying, pitching toward me. I kept going, pushing my way around corners, stumbling, ducking into openings, trying to get away from their voices. But the exit never came. Everywhere I turned there was just another expanse of hedge, another mocking voice.

I stumbled into an opening, briefly exultant that I was near freedom. But then I saw I was back at the center again, back where I had started. I reeled as I saw them all standing there, as if they had simply been waiting for me.

"There you go," one of them said, as his hand grabbed my arm. "I told you she was up for it. Come on, Lou-lou, give me a kiss and I'll show you the way out." His voice was soft and drawling.

"Give us all a kiss and we'll all show you the way out."
Their faces were a blur.

"I just . . . I just want you to—"

"Come on, Lou. You like me, don't you? You've been sitting on my lap all evening. One kiss. How hard is that?"

I heard a snigger.

"And you'll show me how to get out?" My voice sounded pathetic, even to me.

"Just one." He moved closer.

I felt his mouth on mine, a hand squeezing my thigh.

He broke away, and I heard the tenor of his breathing change. "And now Jake's turn."

I don't know what I said then. Someone had my arm. I heard the laughter, felt a hand in my hair, another mouth on mine, insistent, invasive, and then—

"Will . . ."

I was sobbing now, crouched over myself. "Will . . ." I was saying his name, over and over again, my voice ragged, emerging somewhere from my chest. I heard him somewhere far off, beyond the hedge.

"Louisa? Louisa, where are you? What's the matter?"

I was in the corner, as far under the hedge as I could get. Tears blurred my eyes, my arms wrapped tightly around me. I couldn't get out. I would be stuck here forever. Nobody would find me.

"Will . . ."

"Where are—"

And there he was, in front of me.

"I'm sorry," I said, looking up, my face contorted. "I'm sorry. I can't . . . do it."

He lifted his arm a couple of inches—the maximum he could manage. "Oh Jesus, what the—? Come here, Clark." He moved forward, then glanced down at his arm in frustration. "Bloody useless thing . . . It's okay. Just breathe. Come here. Just breathe. Slowly."

I wiped my eyes. At the sight of him, the panic had begun to subside. I stood up, unsteadily, and tried to straighten my face. "I'm sorry. I . . . don't know what happened."

"Are you claustrophobic?" His face, inches from mine, was etched with worry. "I could see you didn't want to go in. I just . . . I just thought you were being—"

I shut my eyes. "I just want to go now."

"Hold on to my hand. We'll go out."

He had me out of there within minutes. He knew the maze backward, he told me as we walked, his voice calm, reassuring. It had been a challenge for him as a boy to learn his way through. I entwined my fingers with his and felt the warmth of his hand as something comforting. I felt foolish when I realized how close to the entrance I had been all along.

We stopped at a bench just outside, and I rummaged in the back of his chair for a tissue. We sat there in silence, me on the end of the bench beside him, both of us waiting for my hiccoughing to subside.

He sat, sneaking sideways glances at me.

"So . . . ?" he said, finally, when I must have looked as if I could speak without falling apart again. "You want to tell me what's going on?"

I twisted the tissue in my hands. "I can't."

He closed his mouth.

I swallowed. "It's not you," I said, hurriedly. "I haven't talked to anyone about . . . It's . . . it's stupid. And a long time ago. I didn't think . . . I would . . ."

I felt his eyes on me, and wished he wouldn't look. My hands wouldn't stop trembling, and my stomach felt as if it were made of a million knots.

I shook my head, trying to tell him that there were things I couldn't say. I wanted to reach for his hand again, but I didn't feel I could. I was conscious of his gaze, could almost hear his unspoken questions.

Below us, two cars had pulled up near the gates. Two figures got out—from here it was impossible to see who—and embraced. They stood there for a few minutes, perhaps talking, and then got back into their cars and drove off in the opposite direction. I watched them but I couldn't think. My mind felt frozen. I didn't know what to say about anything anymore.

"Okay. Here's the thing," he said, finally. I turned around, but he wasn't looking at me. "I'll tell you something that I never tell anyone. All right?"

"All right." I screwed the tissue into a ball in my hands, waiting.

He took a deep breath.

"I get really, really scared of how this is going to go." He let that settle in the air between us, and then, in a low, calm voice, he carried on. "I know most people think living like me is about the worst thing that could happen. But it could get worse. I could end up not being able to breathe by myself, not being able to talk. I could get circulatory problems that mean my limbs have to be amputated. I could be hospitalized indefinitely. This isn't much of a life, Clark. But when I think about how much worse it could get—some nights I lie in my bed and I can't actually breathe."

He swallowed. "And you know what? Nobody wants to hear that stuff. Nobody wants you to talk about being afraid, or in pain, or being scared of dying through some stupid, random infection. Nobody wants to know how it feels to know you will never have sex again, never eat food you've made with your own hands again, never hold your own child. Nobody wants to know that sometimes I feel so claustrophobic, being in this chair, I just want to scream like a madman at the thought of spending another day in it. My mother is hanging on by a thread and can't forgive me for still loving my father. My sister resents me for the fact that yet again I have overshadowed her—and because my injuries mean she can't properly hate me, like she has since we were children. My father just wants it all to go away. Ultimately, they want to look on the bright side. They need me to look on the bright side."

He paused. "They need to believe there *is* a bright side."

I blinked into the darkness. "Do I do that?" I said, quietly.

"You, Clark," he looked down at his hands, "are the only person I have felt able to talk to since I ended up in this bloody thing."

And so I told him.

I reached for his hand, the same one that had led me out of the maze, and I looked straight down at my feet and I took a breath and I told him about the whole night, and how they had laughed at me and made fun of how drunk and stoned I was, and how I had passed out and later my sister had said it might actually be a good thing, the not remembering all of what they had done, but how that half hour of not knowing had haunted me ever since. I filled it, you see. I filled it with their laughter, their bodies, and their words. I filled it with my own humiliation. I told him how I saw their faces every time I went anywhere beyond the town, and how Patrick and Mum and Dad and my small life had been just fine for me, with all their problems and limitations. They had let me feel safe.

By the time we finished talking the sky had grown dark, and there were fourteen messages on my mobile phone wondering where we were.

"You don't need me to tell you it wasn't your fault," he said quietly.

Above us the sky had become endless and infinite.

I twisted the tissue in my hand. "Yes. Well. I still feel . . . responsible. I drank too much to show off. I was a terrible flirt. I was—"

"No. They were responsible."

Nobody had ever said those words aloud to me. Even

Treena's look of sympathy had held some mute accusation. *Well, if you will get drunk and silly with men you don't know . . .*

His fingers squeezed mine. A faint movement, but there it was.

"Louisa. It wasn't your fault."

I cried then. Not sobbing, this time. The tears left me silently, and told me something else was leaving me. Guilt. Fear. A few other things I hadn't yet found words for. I leaned my head gently on his shoulder and he tilted his head until it rested against mine.

"Right. Are you listening to me?"

I murmured a yes.

"Then I'll tell you something good," he said, and then he waited, as if he wanted to be sure he had my attention. "Some mistakes . . . just have greater consequences than others. But you don't have to let that night be the thing that defines you."

I felt his head still pressed against mine.

"You, Clark, have the choice not to let that happen."

The sigh that left me then was long, and shuddering. We sat there in silence, letting his words sink in. I could have stayed there all night, above the rest of the world, the warmth of Will's hand in mine, feeling the worst of myself slowly begin to ebb away.

"We'd better get back," he said eventually. "Before they call out a search party."

I released his hand and stood, a little reluctantly, feeling the cool breezes on my skin. And then, almost luxuriously, I stretched my arms high above my head. I let my fingers straighten in the evening air, the tension of weeks, months, perhaps years, easing a little, and let out a deep breath.

Below me the lights of the town winked, a circle of light amid the black countryside below us. I turned back toward him. "Will?"

"Yes?"

I could barely see him in the dim light, but I knew he was watching me. "Thank you. Thank you for coming to get me."

He shook his head, and turned his chair back toward the path.

18

"Disney World is good."

"I told you, no theme parks."

"I know you said that, but it's not just roller coasters and whirling teacups. In Florida you've got the film studios and the science center. It's actually quite educational."

"I don't think a thirty-five-year-old former company head needs educating."

"There are disabled loos on every corner. And the members of the staff are incredibly caring. Nothing is too much trouble."

"You're going to say there are rides especially for handicapped people next, aren't you?"

"They accommodate everyone. Why don't you try Florida, Miss Clark? If you don't like it you could go on to SeaWorld. And the weather is lovely."

"In Will versus killer whale I think I know who would come off worst."

He didn't seem to hear me. "And they are one of the top-rated companies for dealing with disability. You know they do a lot of stuff for people who are dying?"

"He is *not* dying." I put the phone down on the travel agent just as Will came in. I fumbled with the receiver, trying to set it back in its cradle, and snapped my note-pad shut.

"Everything all right, Clark?"

"Fine." I smiled brightly.

"Good. Got a nice frock?"

"What?"

"What are you doing on Saturday?"

He was waiting expectantly. My brain was still stalled on killer whale versus travel agent.

"Um . . . nothing. Patrick's away all day training. Why?"

He waited just a few seconds before he said it, as if it actually gave him some pleasure to surprise me.

"We're going to a wedding."

———

Afterward, I was never entirely sure why Will changed his mind about Alicia and Rupert's nuptials. I suspected there was probably a large dose of natural contrariness in his decision—nobody expected him to go, probably least of all Alicia and Rupert themselves. Perhaps it was about finally getting closure. But I think in the last couple of months she had lost the power to wound him.

We decided we could manage without Nathan's help. I called up to make sure the marquee was suitable for Will's wheelchair, and Alicia sounded so flustered when she realized we weren't actually declining the invitation that it dawned on me that her embossed correspondence really had been for appearance's sake.

"Um . . . well . . . there is a very small step up into the marquee, but I suppose the people who are putting it up did say they could provide a ramp . . ." She trailed off.

"That will be lovely, then. Thank you," I said. "We'll see you on the day."

We went online and picked out a wedding present. Will spent £120 on a silver picture frame, and a vase that he said was "absolutely vile" for another £60. I was shocked that he would spend that much money on someone he didn't even like, but I had worked out within weeks of being employed by the Traynors that they had different ideas about money than I did.

I decided to wear my red dress—partly because I knew Will liked it (and I figured today he was going to need all the minor boosts he could get)—but also because I didn't actually have any other dresses that I felt brave enough to wear at such a gathering. Will had no idea of the fear I felt at the thought of going to a society wedding, let alone as "the help." Every time I thought of the braying voices, the assessing glances in our direction, I wanted to spend the day watching Patrick run in circles instead. Perhaps it was shallow of me to even care, but I couldn't help it. The thought of those guests looking down on both of us was already tying my stomach in knots.

I didn't say anything to Will, but I was afraid for him. Going to the wedding of an ex seemed a masochistic act at the best of times, but to go to a public gathering, one that would be full of his old friends and work colleagues, to watch her marry his former friend, seemed to me a surefire route to depression. I tried to suggest as much the day before we left, but he brushed it off.

"If I'm not worried about it, Clark, I don't think you should be," he said.

I rang Treena and told her.

"Check his wheelchair for anthrax and ammunition," was all she said.

"It's the first time I've gotten him a proper distance from home and it's going to be a bloody disaster."

"Maybe he just wants to remind himself that there are worse things than dying?"

"Funny."

"Okay. Have fun. Oh, and don't wear that red dress. It shows way too much cleavage."

———

The morning of the wedding dawned bright and balmy, as I had secretly known it would. Girls like Alicia always got their way.

"That's remarkably bitter of you, Clark," Will said when I told him.

"Yes, well, I've learned from the best."

Nathan had come early to get Will ready so that we could leave the house by nine. It was a two-hour drive, and I had built in rest stops, planning our route carefully to ensure we had the best facilities available. I got ready in the bathroom, pulling stockings over my newly shaved legs, painting on makeup and then rubbing it off again in case the posh guests thought I looked like a call girl. I dared not put a scarf around my neck, but I had brought a wrap, which I could use as a shawl if I felt overexposed.

"Not bad, eh?" Nathan stepped back, and there was Will in a dark suit, a cornflower-blue shirt, and a tie. He was clean-shaven, and carried a faint tan on his face. The shirt made his eyes look peculiarly vivid. They seemed, suddenly, to carry a glint of the sun.

"Not bad," I said—because, weirdly, I didn't want to say how handsome he actually looked. "She'll certainly be sorry she's marrying that braying bucket of lard, anyway."

Will raised his eyes heavenward. "Nathan, do we have everything in the bag?"

"Yup. All set and ready to go." He turned to Will. "No snogging the bridesmaids, now."

"As if he'd want to," I said. "They'll all be wearing piecrust collars and smell of horse."

Will's parents came out to see him off. I suspected they had just had an argument, as Mrs. Traynor could not have stood farther away from her husband unless they had actually been in separate counties. She kept her arms folded firmly, even as I reversed the car for Will to get in. She didn't once look at me.

"Don't get him too drunk, Louisa," she said, brushing imaginary lint from Will's shoulder.

"Why?" Will said. "I'm not driving."

"You're quite right, Will," his father said. "I always needed a good stiff drink or two to get through a wedding."

"Even your own," Mrs. Traynor murmured, adding more audibly, "You look very smart, darling." She knelt down, adjusting the hem of Will's trousers. "Really, very smart."

"So do you." Mr. Traynor eyed me approvingly as I stepped out of the driver's seat. "Very eye-catching. Give us a twirl, then, Louisa."

Will turned his chair away. "She doesn't have time, Dad. Let's get on the road, Clark. I'm guessing it's bad form to wheel yourself in behind the bride."

I climbed back into the car with relief. With Will's chair secured in the back, and his smart jacket hung neatly over the passenger's seat so that it wouldn't crease, we set off.

———

I could have told you what Alicia's parents' house would be like even before I got there. In fact, my imagination got it so nearly spot on that Will asked me why I was laughing as I slowed the car. A large Georgian rectory, its tall windows partly obscured by showers of pale wisteria, its drive a caramel pea shingle, it was the perfect house for a colonel. I could already picture her growing up within it, her hair in two neat blond plaits as she sat astride her first fat pony on the lawn.

Two men in reflective tabards were directing traffic into a field between the house and the church beside it. I wound down the window. "Is there a car park beside the church?"

"Guests are this way, Madam."

"Well, we have a wheelchair, and it will sink into the grass here," I said. "We need to be right beside the church. I'll go just there."

The two men looked at each other, and murmured something between themselves. Before they could say anything else, I drove up and parked in the secluded spot beside the church. *And here it starts*, I told myself, catching Will's eye in the mirror as I turned off the ignition.

"Chill out, Clark. It's all going to be fine," he said.

"I'm perfectly relaxed. Why would you think I wasn't?"

"You're ridiculously transparent. Plus you've chewed off four of your fingernails while you've been driving."

"So . . . how are we playing today?"

Will followed my line of vision. "Honestly?"

"Yup. I need to know. And please don't say Shock and Awe. Are you planning something terrible?"

Will's eyes met mine. Blue, unfathomable. A small cloud of butterflies landed in my stomach.

"We're going to be incredibly well behaved, Clark."

The butterflies' wings began to beat wildly, as if trapped against my rib cage. I began to speak, but he interrupted me.

"Look, we'll just do whatever it takes to make it fun," he said.

Fun. As if going to an ex's wedding could ever be less painful than root canal surgery. But it was Will's choice. Will's day. I took a breath, trying to pull myself together.

"One exception," I said, adjusting the wrap around my shoulders for the fourteenth time.

"What?"

"You're not to do the Christy Brown. If you do the Christy Brown I will drive home and leave you stuck here with the pointy-heads."

As Will turned and began making his way toward the church, I thought I heard him murmur, "Spoilsport."

We sat through the ceremony without incident. Alicia looked as ridiculously beautiful as I had known she would, her skin polished a pale caramel, the bias-cut off-white silk skimming her slim figure as if it wouldn't dare rest there without permission. I stared at her as she floated down the aisle, wondering how it would feel to be tall and long-legged and look like something most of us only saw on airbrushed posters. I wondered if she was wearing control pants. Of course not. She would be wearing pale wisps of something lacy—underwear for women who didn't need anything actually supported, and which cost more than my weekly salary.

While the vicar droned on, and the little ballet-shod bridesmaids shuffled in their pews, I gazed around me at the other guests. There was barely a woman there who didn't look like she might appear in the pages of a glossy magazine. Their shoes, which matched their outfits to the exact hue, looked as if they had never been worn before. The younger women stood elegantly in four- or five-inch heels, with perfectly manicured toenails. The older women, in kitten heels, wore structured suits, with padded shoulders and silk linings in contrasting colors, and hats that looked as if they defied gravity.

The men were less interesting to look at, but nearly all had that air about them that I could sometimes detect in Will—of wealth and entitlement, a sense that life would settle itself agreeably around them. I wondered about the companies they ran, the worlds they inhabited. I wondered if they noticed people like me, who nannied their children, or served them in restaurants. *Or pole-danced for their business colleagues*, I thought, remembering my interviews at the Job Center.

The weddings I went to usually had to separate the bride's and groom's families for fear of someone breaching the terms of their parole.

And then it was over. Will was already making his way out toward the exit of the church. I watched the back of his head, upright and curiously dignified, and wanted to ask him if it had been a mistake to come. I wanted to ask him if he still had feelings for her. I wanted to tell him that he was too good for that silly caramel woman, no matter what appearances might suggest, and that . . . I didn't know what else I wanted to say.

I just wanted to make it better.

"You okay?" I said, as I caught up.

The bottom line was, it should have been him.

He blinked a couple of times. "Fine," he said. He let

out a little breath, as if he had been holding it. Then he looked up at me. "Come on, let's go and get a drink."

The marquee was situated in a walled garden, the wrought-iron gateway into it intertwined with garlands of pale-pink flowers. The bar, positioned at the far end, was already crowded, so I suggested that Will wait outside while I went and got him a drink. I weaved my way through tables clad in white linen cloths and laden with more cutlery and glassware than I had ever seen. The chairs had gilt backs, like the ones you see at fashion shows, and white lanterns hung above each centerpiece of freesias and lilies. The air was thick with the scent of flowers, to the point that I found it almost stifling.

"Pimm's?" the barman said when I got to the front.

"Um . . ." I looked around, seeing that this was actually the only drink on offer. "Oh. Okay. Two, please."

He smiled at me. "The other drinks come out later, apparently. But Miss Dewar wanted everyone to start with Pimm's." The look he gave me was slightly conspiratorial. It told me with the faintest lift of an eyebrow what he thought of that.

I stared at the pink lemonade drink. My dad said it was always the richest people who were the tightest, but I was amazed that they wouldn't even start the wedding reception with alcohol. "I guess that'll have to do, then," I said, and took the glasses from him.

When I found Will, there was a man talking to him. Young, bespectacled, he was half crouching, one arm resting on the arm of Will's chair. The sun was now high in the sky, and I had to squint to see them properly. I could suddenly see the point of all those wide-brimmed hats.

"So bloody good to see you out again, Will," he was saying. "The office isn't the same without you. I shouldn't say as much . . . but it's not the same. It just isn't."

He looked like a young accountant—the kind of man who is only really comfortable in a suit.

"It's nice of you to say so."

"It was just so odd. Like you fell off a cliff. One day you were there, directing everything, the next we were just supposed to . . ."

He glanced up as he noticed me standing there. "Oh," he said, and I felt his eyes settle on my chest. "Hello."

"Louisa Clark, meet Freddie Derwent."

I put Will's glass in his holder and shook the younger man's hand.

He adjusted his sightline. "Oh," he said again. "And—"

"I'm a friend of Will's," I said, and then, not entirely sure why, let my hand rest lightly on Will's shoulder.

"Life not all bad, then," Freddie Derwent said with a laugh that was a bit like a cough. He flushed a little as he spoke. "Anyway . . . must mingle. You know these things—apparently, we're meant to see them as a net-working opportunity. But good to see you, Will. Really. And . . . and you, Miss Clark."

"He seemed nice," I said as we moved away. I lifted my hand from Will's shoulder and took a long sip of my Pimm's. It was actually tastier than it looked. I had been slightly alarmed by the presence of cucumber.

"Yes. Yes, he's a nice kid."

"Not too awkward, then."

"No." Will's eyes flickered up to meet mine. "No, Clark, not too awkward at all."

As if freed by the sight of Freddie Derwent doing so, over the next hour several more people approached Will to say hello. Some stood a little way back from him, as if this absolved them of the handshake dilemma, while others hoisted the knees of their trousers and crouched down almost at his feet. I stood by Will and said little. I watched him stiffen slightly at the approach of two of them.

One—a big, bluff man with a cigar—seemed not to know what to say when he was actually there in front of Will, and settled for "Bloody nice wedding, wasn't it?

Thought the bride looked splendid." I guessed he hadn't known Alicia's romantic history.

Another, who seemed to be some business rival of Will's, hit a more diplomatic note, but there was something in his very direct gaze, his straightforward questions about Will's condition, that I could see made Will tense. They were like two dogs circling each other, deciding whether to bare their teeth.

"New CEO of my old company," Will said, as the man finally departed with a wave. "I think he was just making sure that I wouldn't be trying to stage a takeover."

Alicia, floating around the garden—an ethereal vision, air-kissing and exclaiming—didn't approach us.

I watched Will drain two glasses of Pimm's and was secretly glad.

———

Lunch was served at 4 P.M. I thought that was a pretty odd time to serve lunch but, as Will pointed out, it was a wedding. Time seemed to have stretched and become meaningless anyway, its passage blurred by endless drinks and meandering conversations. I don't know if it was the heat or the atmosphere, but by the time we arrived at our table I felt almost drunk. When I found myself babbling incoherently to the elderly man on my left, I realized it was actually a possibility.

"Is there any alcohol in that Pimm's stuff?" I said to Will after I had managed to tip the contents of the salt cellar into my lap.

"About the same as a glass of wine. In each one."

I stared at him in horror. Both of him. "You're kidding. It had fruit in it! I thought that meant it was alcohol-free. How am I going to drive you home?"

"Some caregiver you are," he said. He raised an eyebrow. "What's it worth for me not to tell my mother?"

I was stunned by Will's reaction to the whole day. I had thought I was going to get Taciturn Will, Sarcastic

Will. At the very least, Silent Will. But he had been charming to everybody. Even the arrival of soup at lunch didn't faze him. He just asked politely whether anybody would like to swap his soup for their bread, and the two girls on the far side of the table—who professed themselves "wheat intolerant"—nearly threw their rolls at him.

The more anxious I grew about how I was going to sober up, the more upbeat and carefree Will became. The elderly woman on his right turned out to be a former MP who had campaigned on the rights of the disabled, and she was one of the few people I had seen talk to Will without the slightest discomfort. At one point I watched her feed him a slice of roulade. When she briefly got up to leave the table, he muttered that she had once climbed Kilimanjaro. "I love old birds like that," he said. "I could just picture her with a mule and a pack of sandwiches. Tough as old boots."

I was less fortunate with the man on my left. He took about four minutes—the briefest of quizzes about who I was, where I lived, who I knew there—to work out that there was nothing I had to say that might be of interest to him. He turned back to the woman on his left, leaving me to plow silently through what remained of my lunch. At one point, when I started to feel properly awkward, I felt Will's arm slide off the chair beside me, and his hand landed on my arm. I glanced up and he winked at me. I took his hand and squeezed it, grateful that he could see it. And then he moved his chair back six inches, and brought me into the conversation with Mary Rawlinson.

"So Will tells me you're in charge of him," she said. She had piercing blue eyes, and wrinkles that told of a life impervious to skin-care routines.

"I try," I said, glancing at him.

"And have you always worked in this field?"

"No. I used to . . . work in a café." I'm not sure I would have told anybody else at this wedding that fact, but Mary Rawlinson nodded approvingly.

"I always thought that might be rather an interesting job. If you like people, and are rather nosy, which I am." She beamed.

Will moved his arm back onto his chair. "I'm trying to encourage Louisa to do something else, to widen her horizons a bit."

"What did you have in mind?" she asked me.

"She doesn't know," Will said. "Louisa is one of the smartest people I know, but I can't make her see her own possibilities."

Mary Rawlinson gave him a sharp look. "Don't patronize her, dear. She's quite capable of answering for herself."

I blinked.

"I rather think that you of all people should know that," she added.

Will looked as if he were about to say something, and then closed his mouth. He stared at the table and shook his head a little, but he was smiling.

"Well, Louisa, I imagine your job at the moment takes up an awful lot of mental energy. And I don't suppose this young man is the easiest of clients."

"You can say that again."

"But Will is quite right about seeing possibilities. Here's my card. I'm on the board of a charitable organization that encourages retraining. Perhaps you would like to consider something different in the future?"

"I'm very happy working with Will, thank you."

I took the card that she proffered regardless, a little stunned that this woman would have the slightest interest in what I did with my life. But even as I took it, I felt like an impostor. There was no way I would be able to give up work, even if I knew what I wanted to learn. I wasn't convinced I was the kind of person who would suit retraining. And besides, keeping Will alive was my priority. I was so lost in my thoughts that I briefly stopped listening to the two of them beside me.

". . . it's very good that you've got over the hump, so to speak. I know it can be crushing to have to readjust your life so dramatically around new expectations."

I stared at the remains of my poached salmon. I had never heard anyone speak to Will like that.

He frowned at the table, and then turned back to her. "I'm not sure I am over the hump," he said quietly.

She eyed him for a moment, and glanced over at me.

I wondered if my face betrayed me.

"Everything takes time, Will," she said, placing her hand briefly on his arm. "And that's something that your generation find it a lot harder to adjust to. You have all grown up expecting things to go your way almost instantaneously. You all expect to live the lives you chose. Especially a successful young man like yourself. But it takes time."

"Mrs. Rawlinson—Mary—I'm not expecting to recover," he said.

"I'm not talking about physically," she said. "I'm talking about learning to embrace a new life."

And then, just as I waited to hear what Will was going to say next, there was a loud tapping of a spoon on a glass, and the room hushed for the speeches.

I barely heard what they said. It seemed to me to be one puffed-up penguin-suited man after another, referring to people and places I didn't know, provoking polite laughter. I sat and chewed my way through the dark-chocolate truffles that had arrived in silver baskets on the table, and drank three cups of coffee in quick succession so that as well as feeling drunk I felt jittery and wired. Will, on the other hand, was a picture of stillness. He sat and watched the guests applaud his ex-girlfriend, and listened to Rupert drone on about what a perfectly wonderful woman Alicia was. Nobody acknowledged Will. I don't know if that was because they wanted to spare his feelings, or because his presence there was actually a bit of an embarrassment. Occasionally Mary Rawlinson leaned in and muttered something into his ear and he nodded slightly, as if in agreement.

When the speeches finally ended, an army of staff appeared and began clearing the center of the room for dancing. Will leaned in to me. "Mary reminded me there is a very good hotel up the road. Ring them and see if we can stay there."

"What?"

Mary handed me a name and a telephone number scribbled on a napkin.

"It's okay, Clark," he said, quietly, so that she couldn't hear. "I'll pay. Go on, and then you can stop worrying about how much you've drunk. Grab my credit card from my bag. They'll probably want to take the number."

I took it, reached for my mobile phone, and walked off into the farther reaches of the garden. They had two rooms available, they said—a single, and a double on the ground floor. Yes, it was suitable for disabled access. "Perfect," I said, and then had to swallow a small yelp when they told me the price. I gave them Will's credit card number, feeling slightly sick as I read the numbers.

"So?" he said, when I reappeared.

"I've done it, but . . ." I told him how much the two rooms had come to.

"That's fine," he said. "Now ring that bloke of yours to tell him you're staying out all night, then have another drink. In fact, have six. It would please me no end to see you get hammered on Alicia's father's bill."

———

And so I did.

Something happened that evening. The lights dropped, so that our little table was less conspicuous, the overpowering fragrance of the flowers was tempered by the evening breezes, and the music and the wine and the dancing meant that in the most unlikely of places, we all began to actually enjoy ourselves. Will was the most relaxed I had seen him. Sandwiched between me and Mary, he talked and smiled at her, and there was something about the sight of him being briefly happy that repelled those people who might otherwise have looked at him askance, or offered pitying glances. He made me lose my wrap and sit up straight. I took off his jacket and loosened his tie, and we both tried not to giggle at the sight of the dancing. I cannot tell you how much better I felt once I saw the way posh people danced. The men looked as if they had been electrocuted, the women did little pointy fingers at the stars and looked horribly self-conscious even as they twirled.

Mary Rawlinson muttered, "Dear God," several times. She glanced over at me. Her language had gotten saltier with every drink. "You don't want to go and strut your stuff, Louisa?"

"God, no."

"Jolly sensible of you. I've seen better dancing at a bloody Young Farmers Club disco."

At nine, I got a text from Nathan.

All okay?

I responded:

Yes. Lovely, believe it or not. Will having great time.

And he was. I watched him laughing hard at something Mary had said, and something in me grew strange and tight. This had shown me it could work. He could be happy, if surrounded by the right people, if allowed to be Will, instead of The Man in the Wheelchair, the list of symptoms, the object of pity.

And then, at 10 P.M., the slow dances began. We watched Rupert guide Alicia around the dance floor, applauded politely by onlookers. Her hair had begun to droop, and she wrapped her arms around his neck as if she needed the support. Rupert's arms encircled her, his hands resting on the small of her back. Beautiful and wealthy as she was, I felt a little sorry for her. I thought she probably wouldn't realize what she had lost until it was much too late.

Halfway through the song, other couples joined them so that they were partially obscured from view, and I got distracted by Mary talking about caregivers' allowances, until suddenly I looked up and there she was, standing right in front of us, the supermodel in her white silk dress. My heart lodged in my throat.

Alicia nodded a greeting to Mary, and dipped a little from her waist so that Will could hear her over the music. Her face was a little tense, as if she had had to prime herself to come over.

"Thank you for coming, Will. Really." She glanced sideways at me but said nothing.

"Pleasure," Will said smoothly. "You look lovely, Alicia. It was a great day."

A flicker of surprise passed across her face. And then a faint wistfulness. "Really? You think so? I do think . . . I mean, there's so much I want to say—"

"There's no need," Will said. "You remember Louisa?"

"I do."

There was a brief silence.

I could see Rupert hovering in the background, eyeing us all warily. She glanced back at him, and then held out a hand in a half-wave. "Well, thank you anyway, Will. You are a superstar for coming. And thank you for the . . ."

"Mirror."

"Of course. I absolutely loved the mirror." She stood up and walked back to her husband, who turned away, already clasping her arm.

We watched them cross the dance floor.

"You didn't buy her a mirror."

"I know."

They were still talking, Rupert's gaze flickering back

to us. It was as if he couldn't believe Will had simply been nice. Mind you, neither could I.

"Does it . . . did it bother you?" I said to him.

He looked away from them. "No," he said, and he smiled at me. His smile had gone a bit lopsided with drink and his eyes were sad and contemplative at the same time.

And then, as the dance floor briefly emptied for the next dance, I found myself saying, "What do you say, Will? Going to give me a whirl?"

"What?"

"Come on. Let's give these fuckers something to talk about."

"Oh good," Mary said, raising a glass. "Fucking marvelous."

"Come on. While the music is slow. Because I don't think you can pogo in that thing."

I didn't give him any choice. I sat down carefully on Will's lap, draped my arms around his neck to hold myself in place. He looked into my eyes for a minute, as if working out whether he could refuse me. Then, astonishingly, Will wheeled us out onto the dance floor, and began moving in small circles under the sparkling lights of the mirrorballs.

I felt simultaneously acutely self-conscious and mildly hysterical. I was sitting at an angle that meant my dress had risen halfway up my thighs.

"Leave it," Will murmured into my ear.

"This is . . ."

"Come on, Clark. Don't let me down now."

I closed my eyes and wrapped my arms around his neck, letting my cheek rest against his, breathing in the citrus smell of his aftershave. I could feel him humming along with the music.

"Are they all appalled yet?" he said. I opened one eye, and glanced out into the dim light.

A couple of people were smiling encouragingly, but

most seemed not to know what to make of it. Mary saluted me with her drink. And then I saw Alicia staring at us, her face briefly falling. When she saw me looking, she turned away and muttered something to Rupert. He shook his head, as if we were doing something disgraceful.

I felt a mischievous smile creeping across my face. "Oh yes," I said.

"Hah. Move in closer. You smell fantastic."

"So do you. Although, if you keep turning in left-hand circles I may throw up."

Will changed direction. My arms looped around his neck, I pulled back a little to look at him, no longer self-conscious. He glanced down at my chest. To be fair, with me positioned where I was, there wasn't anywhere else he could look. He lifted his gaze from my cleavage and raised an eyebrow. "You know, you would never have let those breasts get so close to me if I weren't in a wheelchair," he murmured.

I looked back at him steadily. "You would never have looked at my breasts if you hadn't been in a wheelchair."

"What? Of course I would."

"Nope. You would have been far too busy looking at the tall blond girls with the endless legs and the big hair, the ones who can smell an expense account at forty paces. And anyway, I wouldn't have been here. I would have been serving the drinks over there. One of the invisibles."

He blinked.

"Well? I'm right, aren't I?"

Will glanced over at the bar, then back at me. "Yes. But in my defense, Clark, I was an arse."

I burst out laughing so hard that even more people looked over in our direction.

I tried to straighten my face. "Sorry," I mumbled. "I think I'm getting hysterical."

"Do you know something?"

I could have looked at his face all night. The way his eyes wrinkled at the corners. That place where his neck met his shoulder. "What?"

"Sometimes, Clark, you are pretty much the only thing that makes me want to get up in the morning."

"Then let's·go somewhere." The words were out almost before I knew what I wanted to say.

"What?"

"Let's go somewhere. Let's have a week where we just have fun. You and me. None of these . . ."

He waited. "Arses?"

"Arses. Say yes, Will. Go on."

His eyes didn't leave mine.

I don't know what I was telling him. I don't know where it all came from. I just knew if I didn't get him to say yes tonight, with the stars and the freesias and the laughter and Mary, then I had no chance at all.

"Please."

The seconds before he answered me seemed to take forever.

"Okay," he said.

19

NATHAN

They thought we couldn't tell. They finally got back from the wedding around lunchtime the following day and Mrs. Traynor was so mad she could barely even speak.

"You could have rung," she said.

She had stayed in just to make sure they arrived back okay. I had listened to her pacing up and down the tiled corridor next door since I got there at 8 A.M.

"I must have called or texted you both eighteen times. It was only when I managed to call the Dewars' house and somebody told me 'the man in the wheelchair' had gone to a hotel that I could be sure you hadn't both had some terrible accident on the motorway."

"'The man in the wheelchair.' Nice," Will observed.

But you could see he wasn't bothered. He was all loose and relaxed, carried his hangover with humor, even though I had the feeling he was in some pain. It was only when his mum started to have a go at Louisa that he stopped smiling. He jumped in and just said that if she had anything to say she should say it to him, as it had been his decision to stay overnight, and Louisa had simply gone along with it.

"And as far as I can see, Mother, as a thirty-five-year-old man I'm not strictly answerable to anybody when it comes to choosing to spend a night at a hotel. Even to my parents."

She had stared at them both, muttered something about "common courtesy," and then left the room.

Louisa looked a bit shaken but he had gone over and

murmured something to her, and that was the point at which I saw it. She went kind of pink and laughed, the kind of laugh you do when you know you shouldn't be laughing. The kind of laugh that spoke of a conspiracy. And then Will turned to her and told her to take it easy for the rest of the day. Go home, get changed, maybe catch forty winks.

"I can't be walking around the castle with someone who has so clearly just done the walk of shame," he said.

"Walk of shame?" I couldn't keep the surprise from my voice.

"Not *that* walk of shame," Louisa said, flicking me with her scarf, and grabbed her coat to leave.

"Take the car," he called out. "It'll be easier for you to get back."

I watched Will's eyes follow her all the way to the back door.

I would have offered you seven-to-four just on the basis of that look alone.

He deflated a little after she left. It was as if he had been holding on until both his mum and Louisa had left the annex. I had been watching him carefully now, and once his smile left his face I realized I didn't like the look of him. His skin held a faint blotchiness, he had winced twice when he thought no one was looking, and I could see even from here that he had goosebumps. A little alarm bell had started to sound, distant but shrill, inside my head.

"You feeling okay, Will?"

"I'm fine. Don't fuss."

"You want to tell me where it hurts?"

He looked a bit resigned then, as if he knew I saw straight through him. We had worked together a long time.

"Okay. Bit of a headache. And . . . um . . . I need my tubes changed. Probably quite sharpish."

I had transferred him from his chair onto his bed and now I began getting the equipment together. "What time did Lou do them this morning?"

"She didn't." He winced. And he looked a little guilty. "Or last night."

"What?"

I took his pulse, and grabbed the blood pressure equipment. Sure enough, it was sky-high. When I put my hand on his forehead it came away with a faint sheen of sweat. I went for the medicine cabinet, and crushed some vasodilator drugs. I gave them to him in water, making sure he drank every last bit. Then I propped him up, placing his legs over the side of the bed, and I changed his tubes swiftly, watching him all the while.

"AD?"

"Yeah. Not your most sensible move, Will."

Autonomic dysreflexia was pretty much our worst nightmare. It was Will's body's massive overreaction against pain, discomfort—or, say, an unemptied catheter—his damaged nervous system's vain and misguided attempt to stay in control. It could come out of nowhere and send his body into meltdown. He looked pale, his breathing labored.

"How's your skin?"

"Bit prickly."

"Sight?"

"Fine."

"Aw, man. You think we need help?"

"Give me ten minutes, Nathan. I'm sure you've done everything we need. Give me ten minutes."

He closed his eyes. I checked his blood pressure again, wondering how long I should leave it before calling an ambulance. AD scared the hell out of me because you never knew which way it was going to go. He had had it once before, when I had first started working with him, and he had ended up in the hospital for two days.

"Really, Nathan. I'll tell you if I think we're in trouble."

He sighed, and I helped him backward so that he was leaning against his headboard.

He told me Louisa had been so drunk he hadn't wanted to risk letting her loose on his equipment. "God knows where she might have stuck the ruddy tubes." He half laughed as he said it. It had taken Louisa almost half an hour just to get him out of his chair and into bed, he said. They had both ended up on the floor twice. "Luckily we were both so drunk by then I don't think either of us felt a thing." She had had the presence of mind to call down to reception, and they had asked a porter to help lift him. "Nice chap. I have a vague memory of insisting Louisa give him a fifty-pound tip. I knew she was properly drunk because she agreed to it."

Will had been afraid when she finally left his room that she wouldn't actually make it to hers. He'd had visions of her curled up in a little red ball on the stairs.

My own view of Louisa Clark was a little less generous just at that moment. "Will, mate, I think maybe next time you should worry a little more about yourself, yeah?"

"I'm all right, Nathan. I'm fine. Feeling better already."

I felt his eyes on me as I checked his pulse.

"Really. It wasn't her fault."

His blood pressure was down. His color was returning to normal in front of me. I let out a breath I hadn't realized I had been holding.

We chatted a bit, passing the time while everything settled down, discussing the previous day's events. He didn't seem a bit bothered about his ex. He didn't say much, but for all he was obviously exhausted, he looked okay.

I let go of his wrist. "Nice tattoo, by the way."

He gave me a wry look.

"Make sure you don't graduate to an 'End by,' yeah?"

Despite the sweats and the pain and the infection, he

looked for once like there was something else on his mind other than the thing that consumed him. I couldn't help thinking that if Mrs. Traynor had known this, she might not have kicked off as hard as she did.

———————

We didn't tell her anything of the lunchtime events—Will made me promise not to—but when Lou came back later that afternoon she was pretty quiet. She looked pale, with her hair washed and pulled back like she was trying to look sensible.

But it became clear after a while that it wasn't just a hangover troubling her.

Will kept on and on at her about why she was being so quiet, and then she said, "Yes, well, I've discovered it's not the most sensible thing to stay out all night when you've just moved in with your boyfriend."

She was smiling as she said it, but it was a forced smile, and Will and I both knew that there must have been some serious words.

I couldn't blame the guy. I wouldn't have wanted my missus staying out all night with some bloke, even if he was a quad. And he hadn't seen the way Will looked at her.

We didn't do much that afternoon. Louisa emptied Will's backpack, revealing every free hotel shampoo, conditioner, miniature sewing kit, and shower cap she could lay her hands on. ("Don't laugh," she said. "At those prices, Will paid for a bloody shampoo factory.") We watched some Japanese animated film that Will said was perfect hangover viewing, and I stuck around—partly because I wanted to keep an eye on his blood pressure and partly, to be honest, because I was being a bit mischievous. I wanted to see his reaction when I announced I was going to keep them both company.

"Really?" he said. "You like Miyazaki?"

He caught himself immediately, saying that of course I would love it . . . it was a great film . . . blah, blah, blah.

But there it was. I was glad for him, on one level. He had thought about one thing for too long, that man.

So we watched the film. Pulled down the blinds, took the phone off the hook, and watched this weird cartoon about a girl who ends up in a parallel universe, with all these weird creatures, half of whom you couldn't tell if they were good or bad. Lou sat right up close to Will, handing him his drink or, at one point, wiping his eye when he got something in it. It was quite sweet, really, although a little bit of me wondered what on earth this was going to lead to.

And then, as Louisa pulled up the blinds and made us all some tea, they looked at each other like two people wondering whether to let you in on a secret, and they told me about going away. Ten days. Not sure where yet, but it would probably be long haul and it would be good. Would I come and help?

Does a bear shit in the woods?

I had to take my hat off to the girl. If you had told me four months ago that we'd get Will off on a long-haul holiday—hell, that we would get him out of this house—I would have told you that you were a few sandwiches short of a picnic. Mind you, I'd have a quiet word with her about Will's medical care before we went. We couldn't afford a near miss like that again if we were stuck in the middle of nowhere.

They even told Mrs. T as she popped by, just as Louisa was leaving. Will said it as though it was no more remarkable than him going for a walk around the castle.

I have to tell you, I was really pleased. That ruddy online poker site had eaten all my money, and I wasn't even planning on a holiday this year. I even forgave Louisa for being stupid enough to listen to Will when he said he hadn't wanted her to do his tubes. And believe me, I had been pretty pissed about that. So it was all looking great, and I was whistling when I shouldered my way into my coat, already looking forward to white sands and blue seas. I was even trying to work out if I could tie in a short visit home to Auckland.

And then I saw them—Mrs. Traynor standing outside the back door as Lou waited to set off down the road. I don't know what sort of a chat they'd had already, but they both looked grim.

I only caught the last line but, to be honest, that was enough for me.

"I hope you know what you're doing, Louisa."

20

"You what?"

We were on the hills just outside town when I told him. Patrick was halfway through a sixteen-mile run and wanted me to time him while following behind on the bicycle. As I was marginally less proficient on a bicycle than I was at particle physics, this involved a lot of swearing and swerving on my part, and a lot of exasperated shouting on his.

As we reached the top of Sheepcote Hill, me puffing, my legs like lead, I decided to just throw it out there. I figured we still had ten miles home for him to recover his good mood.

"I'm not coming to the Xtreme Viking."

He didn't stop, but he came close. He turned to face me, his legs still moving under him, and he looked so shocked that I nearly swerved into a tree.

"What? Why?"

"I'm . . . working."

He turned back to the road and picked up speed. We had reached the brow of the hill, and I had to close my fingers around the brakes a little to stop myself overtaking him.

"So when did you decide this?" Fine beads of sweat had broken out on his forehead, and tendons stood out on his calves. I couldn't look at them too long or I would start wobbling.

"On the weekend. I just wanted to be sure."

"But we've booked your flights and everything."

"It's only easyJet. I'll reimburse you the thirty-nine pounds if you're that bothered."

"It's not the cost. I thought you were going to support me. You said you were coming to support me."

He could look quite sulky, Patrick. When we were first together, I used to tease him about it. I called him Mr. Grumpy Trousers. It made me laugh and him so cross that he usually stopped sulking just to shut me up.

"Oh, come on. I'm hardly not supporting you now, am I? I hate cycling, Patrick. You know I do. But I'm supporting you."

We went on another mile before he spoke again. It might have been me, but the pounding of Patrick's feet on the road seemed to have taken on a grim, resolute tone. We were high above the little town now, me puffing on the uphill stretches, trying and failing to stop my heart racing every time a car came past. I was on Mum's old bike (Patrick wouldn't let me anywhere near his racing demon) and it had no gears, so I was frequently left trailing him.

He glanced behind, and slowed his pace a fraction so that I could draw level. "So why can't they get an agency person in?" he said.

"An agency person?"

"To come to the Traynors' house. I mean, if you're there for six months you must be entitled to a holiday."

"It's not that simple."

"I don't see why not. You started work there knowing nothing, after all."

I held my breath. This was quite hard given that I was completely breathless from cycling. "Because he needs to go on a trip."

"What?"

"He needs to go on a trip. So they need me and Nathan there to help him."

"Nathan? Who's Nathan?"

"His medical caregiver. The guy you met when Will

came to Mum's. And before you ask," I added, "no, I am not having an affair with Nathan."

He slowed, and glanced down at the tarmac, until he was practically jogging on the spot. "What is this, Lou? Because . . . because it seems to me that there is a line being blurred here between what is work and what is"— he shrugged—"normal."

"It's not a normal job. You know that."

"But Will Traynor seems to take priority over everything these days."

"Oh, and this doesn't?" I took my hand off the handlebars and gestured toward his shifting feet.

"That's different. He calls, you come running."

"And you go running, I come running." I tried to smile.

"Very funny." He turned away.

"It's six months, Pat. Six months. You were the one who thought I should take this job, after all. You can't have a go at me for taking it seriously."

"I don't think . . . I don't think it's about the job . . . I just . . . I think there's something you're not telling me."

I hesitated, just a moment too long. "That's not true."

"But you won't come to the Viking."

"I've told you, I—"

He shook his head slightly, as if he couldn't hear me properly. Then he began to run down the road, away from me. I could see from the set of his back how angry he was.

"Oh, come on, Patrick. Can't we just stop for a minute and discuss this?"

His tone was mulish. "No. It will throw out my time."

"Then let's stop the clock. Just for five minutes."

"No. I have to do it in real conditions."

He began to run faster, as if he had gained a new momentum.

"Patrick?" I said, struggling suddenly to keep up with him. My feet slipped on the pedals, and I cursed, kicking a pedal back to try to set off again. "Patrick? Patrick!"

I stared at the back of his head and the words were out of my mouth almost before I knew what I was saying. "Okay. Will wants to die. He wants to commit suicide. And this trip is my last attempt to change his mind."

Patrick's stride shortened and then slowed. He stopped on the road ahead, his back straight, still facing away from me. He turned slowly. He had finally stopped jogging.

"Say that again."

"He wants to go to Dignitas. In August. I'm trying to change his mind. This is the last chance I have."

He was staring at me like he didn't know quite whether to believe me.

"I know it sounds mad. But I have to change his mind. So . . . so I can't come to the Viking."

"Why didn't you tell me this before?"

"I had to promise his family I wouldn't tell anyone. It would be awful for them if it got out. Awful. Look, even he doesn't know I know. It's all been . . . tricky. I'm sorry." I reached out my hand to him. "I would have told you if I could."

He didn't answer. He looked crushed, as if I had done something terrible. There was a faint frown on his face, and he swallowed twice, hard.

"Pat—"

"No. Just . . . I just need to run now, Lou. By myself." He ran a hand across his hair. "Okay?"

I swallowed. "Okay."

He looked for a moment as if he had forgotten why we were even out there. Then he struck off again, and I watched him disappear down the road in front of me, his head facing resolutely forward, his legs eating up the road beneath him.

I had put the request out on the day after we returned from the wedding.

> *Can anyone tell me a good place to go where*
> *quadriplegics can have adventures? I am looking*
> *for things that an able-bodied person might be*
> *able to do, things that might make my depressed*
> *friend forget for a while that his life is a bit limited.*
> *I don't really know what I'm hoping for, but all*
> *suggestions gratefully received. This is quite ur-*
> *gent. Busy Bee*

As I logged on I found myself staring at the screen in disbelief. There were eighty-nine replies. I scrolled up and down the screen, unsure at first whether they could all possibly be in response to my request. Then I glanced around me at the other computer users in the library, desperate for one of them to look at me so that I could tell them. Eighty-nine responses! To a single question!

There were tales of bungee jumping for quadriplegics, of swimming, canoeing, even horseback riding, with the aid of a special frame. (When I watched the online video this linked to, I was a little disappointed that Will had said he couldn't stand horses. It looked ace.)

There was swimming with dolphins, and scuba diving with supporters. There were floating chairs that would enable him to go fishing, and adapted quad bikes that would allow him to off-road. Some of them had posted photographs or videos of themselves taking part in these activities. A few of them, including Ritchie, had remembered my previous posts, and wanted to know how Will was doing.

> *This all sounds like good news. Is he feeling better?*

I typed a quick response:

> *Maybe. But I'm hoping this trip will really make a*
> *difference.*

Ritchie responded:

> *Attagirl! If you've got the funds to sort it all out,
> the sky's the limit!*

Scootagirl wrote:

> *Make sure you post up some pics of him in the
> bungee harness. Love the look on guys' faces when
> they're upside down!*

I loved them—these quads and their caregivers—for
their courage and their generosity and their imagina-
tions. I spent two hours that evening writing down their
suggestions, following their links to related Web sites
they had tried and tested, even talking to a few in the
chat rooms. By the time I left, I had a destination; we
would head to California, to the Four Winds Ranch, a
specialist center that offered experienced help "in a way
that will make you forget you ever needed help," according to its Web site. The ranch itself, a low-slung
timber building set into a forest clearing near Yosemite,
had been set up by a former stuntman who refused to
let his spinal injury limit the things he could do, and the
online visitors book was full of happy and grateful holi-
daymakers who swore that he had changed the way
they felt about their disabilities—and themselves. At
least six of the chat-room users had been there, and all
said it had turned their lives around.

It was wheelchair-friendly but with all the facilities
you would expect from a luxury hotel. There were outside sunken baths with discreet hoists, and specialist
masseurs. There was trained medical help on-site, and a
cinema with spaces for wheelchairs beside the normal
seats. There was an accessible outdoor hot tub where
you could sit and stare up at the stars. We would spend a

week there, and then a few days on the coast at a hotel complex where Will could swim, and get a good look at the rugged coastline. Best of all, I had found a climax to the holiday that Will would never forget—a skydive, with the help of parachute instructors who were trained in helping quads jump. They had special equipment that would strap Will to them (apparently, the most important thing was securing their legs so that their knees didn't fly up and bash them in the face).

I would show him the hotel brochure, but I wasn't going to tell him about this. I was just going to turn up there with him and then watch him do it. For those few, precious minutes Will would be weightless, and free. He would escape the dreaded chair. He would escape gravity.

I printed out all the information and kept that one sheet at the top. Whenever I looked at it I felt a germ of excitement building—both at the thought of my first ever long-haul trip and at the thought that this might just be it.

This might be the thing that would change Will's mind.

———

I showed Nathan the next morning, the two of us stooping furtively over our coffees in the kitchen as if we were doing something properly clandestine. He flicked through the papers that I had printed out.

"I have spoken to other quads about the skydiving. There's no medical reason he can't do it. And the bungee jumping. They have special harnesses to relieve any potential pressure points on his spine."

I studied his face anxiously. I knew Nathan didn't rate my capabilities when it came to Will's medical well-being. It was important to me that he was happy with what I'd planned.

"The place here has everything we might need. They say if we call ahead and bring a doctor's prescription, they can even get any generic drugs that we might need, so that there is no chance of us running out."

He frowned. "Looks good," he said finally. "You did a great job."

"You think he'll like it?"

He shrugged. "I haven't got a clue. But"—he handed me the papers—"you've surprised us so far, Lou." His smile was a sly thing, breaking in from the side of his face. "No reason you couldn't do it again."

I showed Mrs. Traynor before I left for the evening.

She had just pulled into the drive in her car and I hesitated, out of sight of Will's window, before I approached her. "I know this is expensive," I said. "But . . . I think it looks amazing. I really think Will could have the time of his life. If . . . if you know what I mean."

She glanced through it all in silence, and then studied the figures that I had compiled.

"I'll pay for myself, if you like. For my board and lodging. I don't want anyone thinking—"

"It's fine," she said, cutting me off. "Do what you have to do. If you think you can get him to go then just book it."

I understood what she was saying. There was no time for anything else.

"Do you think you can persuade him?" she said.

"Well . . . if I . . . if I make out that it's"—I swallowed—"partly for my benefit. He thinks I've never done enough with my life. He keeps telling me I should travel. That I should . . . do things."

She looked at me very carefully. She nodded. "Yes. That sounds like Will." She handed back the paperwork.

"I am . . ." I took a breath, and then, to my surprise, I found that I couldn't speak. I swallowed hard, twice. "What you said before. I never meant . . . Will's happiness is important to me. I—I—"

She didn't seem to want to wait for me to speak. She

ducked her head, her slim fingers reaching for the chain around her neck. "Yes. Well, I'd better go in. I'll see you tomorrow. Let me know what he says."

———

I didn't go back to Patrick's that evening. I had meant to, but something led me away from the industrial park and, instead, I crossed the road and boarded the bus that led toward home. I walked the 180 steps to our house, and let myself in. It was a warm evening, and all the windows were open in an attempt to catch the breeze. Mum was cooking, singing away in the kitchen. Dad was on the sofa with a mug of tea, Granddad napping in his chair, his head lolling to one side. Thomas was carefully drawing in black felt-tip on his shoes. I said hello and walked past them, wondering how it could feel so swiftly as if I didn't quite belong here anymore.

Treena was working in my room. I knocked on the door, and walked in to find her at the desk, hunched over a pile of textbooks, glasses that I didn't recognize perched on her nose. It was strange to see her surrounded by the things I had chosen for myself, with Thomas's pictures already obscuring the walls I had painted so carefully, his pen drawing still scrawled over the corner of my blind. I had to gather my thoughts so that I didn't feel instinctively resentful.

She glanced over her shoulder at me. "Does Mum want me?" she said. She looked up at the clock. "I thought she was going to do Thomas's tea."

"She is. He's having fish fingers."

She looked at me, then removed the glasses. "You okay? You look like shit."

"So do you."

"I know. I went on this stupid detox diet. It's given me hives." She reached a hand up to her chin.

"You don't need to diet."

"Yeah. Well . . . there's this bloke I like in Accountancy 2. I thought I might start making the effort. Huge hives all over your face is always a good look, right?"

I sat down on the bed. It was my duvet cover. I had known Patrick would hate it, with its crazy geometric pattern. I was surprised Katrina didn't.

She closed her book, and leaned back in her chair. "So what's going on?"

I bit my lip, until she asked me again.

"Treen, do you think I could retrain?"

"Retrain? As what?"

"I don't know. Something to do with fashion. Design. Or maybe just tailoring."

"Well . . . there are definitely courses. I'm pretty sure my uni has one. I could look it up, if you want."

"But would they take people like me? People who don't have qualifications?"

She threw her pen up in the air and caught it. "Oh, they love mature students. Especially mature students with a proven work ethic. You might have to do a conversion course, but I don't see why not. Why? What's going on?"

"I don't know. It's just something Will said a while back. About . . . about what I should do with my life."

"And?"

"And I keep thinking . . . maybe it's time I did what you're doing. Now that Dad can support himself again, maybe you're not the only one capable of making something of herself?"

"You'd have to pay."

"I know. I've been saving."

"I think it's probably a bit more than you've managed to save."

"I could apply for a grant. Or maybe a loan. And I've got enough to see me through for a bit. I met this MP woman who said she has links to some agency that could help me. She gave me her card."

"Hang on," Katrina said, swiveling on her chair, "I

don't really get this. I thought you wanted to stay with Will. I thought the whole point of this was that you wanted to keep him alive and keep working with him."

"I do, but . . ." I stared up at the ceiling.

"But what?"

"It's complicated."

"So's quantitative easing. But I still get that it means printing money."

She rose from her chair and walked over to shut the bedroom door. She lowered her voice so that nobody outside could possibly hear.

"You think you're going to lose? You think he's going to . . ."

"No," I said hurriedly. "Well, I hope not. I've got plans. Big plans. I'll show you in a bit."

"But . . ."

I stretched my arms above me, twisting my fingers together. "But, I like Will. A lot."

She studied me. She was wearing her thinking face. There is nothing more terrifying than my sister's thinking face when it is trained directly on you.

"Oh, shit."

"Don't . . ."

"So *this* is interesting," she said.

"I know." I dropped my arms.

"You want a job. So that . . ."

"It's what the other quads tell me. The ones who I talk to on the message boards. You can't be both. You can't be caregiver and . . ." I lifted my hands to cover my face.

I could feel her eyes on me.

"Does he know?"

"No. I'm not sure *I* know. I just . . ." I threw myself down on her bed, face first. It smelled of Thomas. Underlaid with a faint hint of Marmite. "I don't know what I think. All I know is that most of the time I would rather be with him than anyone else I know."

"Including Patrick."

And there it was, out there. The truth that I could barely admit to myself.

I felt my cheeks flood with color. "Yes," I said into the duvet. "Sometimes, yes."

"Fuck," she said, after a minute. "And I thought *I* liked to make my life complicated."

She lay down beside me on the bed, and we stared up at the ceiling. Downstairs we could hear Granddad whistling tunelessly, accompanied by the whine and clunk of Thomas driving some remote-controlled vehicle backward and forward into a piece of skirting. For some unexplained reason my eyes filled with tears. After a minute, I felt my sister's arm snake around me.

"You fucking madwoman," she said, and we both began to laugh.

"Don't worry," I said, wiping at my face. "I'm not going to do anything stupid."

"Good. Because the more I think about this, the more I think it's about the intensity of the situation. It's not real, it's about the drama."

"What?"

"Well, this is actual life or death, after all, and you're locked into this man's life every day, locked into his weird secret. That's got to create a kind of false intimacy. Either that or you're getting some weird Florence Nightingale complex."

"Believe me, that is definitely not it."

We lay there, staring at the ceiling.

"But it is a bit mad, thinking about loving someone who can't . . . you know, love you back. Maybe this is just a panic reaction to the fact that you and Patrick have finally moved in together."

"I know. You're right."

"And you two have been together a long time. You're bound to get crushes on other people."

"Especially while Patrick is obsessed with being Marathon Man."

"And you might go off Will again. I mean, I remember when you thought he was an arse."

"I still do sometimes."

My sister reached for a tissue and dabbed at my eyes. Then she thumbed at something on my cheek.

"All that said, the college idea is good. Because—let's be blunt—whether it all goes tits up with Will or whether it doesn't, you're still going to need a proper job. You're not going to want to be a caregiver forever."

"It's not going to go 'tits up,' as you call it, with Will. He's . . . he's going to be okay."

"Sure he is."

Mum was calling Thomas. We could hear her, singing it beneath us in the kitchen: "Thomas. Tomtomtomtom Thomas . . ."

Treena sighed and rubbed at her eyes. "You going back to Patrick's tonight?"

"Yes."

"You want to grab a quick drink at the Spotted Dog and show me these plans, then? I'll see if Mum will put Thomas to bed for me. Come on, you can treat me, seeing as you're now loaded enough to go to college."

———————

It was a quarter to ten by the time I got back to Patrick's.

My holiday plans, astonishingly, had met with Katrina's complete approval. She hadn't even done her usual thing of adding, "Yes, but it would be even better if you . . ." There had been a point where I wondered if she was doing it just to be nice, because I was obviously going a bit nuts. But she kept saying things like, "Wow, I can't believe you found this! You've got to take lots of pictures of him bungee jumping." And, "Imagine his face when you tell him about the skydiving! It's going to be brilliant."

Anyone watching us at the pub might have thought that we were two friends who actually really quite liked each other.

Still mulling this over, I let myself in quietly. The flat was dark from outside and I wondered if Patrick was having an early night as part of his intensive training. I dropped my bag on the floor in the hall and pushed at the living-room door, thinking as I did so that it was nice of him to have left a light on for me.

And then I saw him. He was sitting at a table laid with two places, a candle flickering between them. As I closed the door behind me, he stood up. The candle was burned halfway down to the base.

"I'm sorry," he said.

I stared at him.

"I was an idiot. You're right. This job of yours is only for six months, and I have been behaving like a child. I should be proud that you're doing something so worthwhile, and taking it all so seriously. I was just a bit . . . thrown. So I'm sorry. Really."

He held out his hand. I took it.

"It's good that you're trying to help him. It's admirable."

"Thank you." I squeezed his hand.

When he spoke again, it was after a short breath, as if he had successfully managed some prerehearsed speech. "I've made supper. I'm afraid it's salad again." He reached past me into the fridge, and pulled out two plates. "I promise we'll go somewhere for a blowout meal once the Viking is over. Or maybe once I'm on to carb loading. I just . . ." He blew out his cheeks. "I guess I haven't been able to think about much else lately. I guess that's been part of the problem. And you're right. There's no reason you should follow me about. It's my thing. You have every right to work instead."

"Patrick . . . ," I said.

"I don't want to argue with you, Lou. Forgive me?"

His eyes were anxious and he smelled of cologne. Those two facts descended upon me slowly like a weight.

"Sit down, anyway," he said. "Let's eat, and then . . . I

don't know. Enjoy ourselves. Talk about something else. Not running." He forced a laugh.

I sat down and looked at the table.

Then I smiled. "This is really nice," I said.

Patrick could do 101 things with turkey breast.

We ate the green salad, the pasta salad, the seafood salad, and an exotic fruit salad that he had prepared for pudding, and I drank wine while he stuck to mineral water. It took us a while, but we did begin to relax. There, in front of me, was a Patrick I hadn't seen for some time. He was funny, attentive. He policed himself rigidly so that he didn't say anything about running or marathons, and laughed whenever he caught the conversation veering in that direction. I felt his feet meet mine under the table and our legs entwine, and slowly I felt something that had felt tight and uncomfortable begin to ease in my chest.

My sister was right. My life had become strange and disconnected from everyone I knew—Will's plight and his secrets had swamped me. I had to make sure that I didn't lose sight of the rest of me.

I began to feel guilty about the conversation I had had earlier with my sister. Patrick wouldn't let me get up, not even to help him clear the dishes. At a quarter past eleven he rose and moved the plates and bowls to the kitchenette and began to load the dishwasher. I sat, listening to him as he talked to me through the little doorway. I was rubbing at the point where my neck met my shoulder, trying to release some of the knots that seemed to be firmly embedded there. I closed my eyes, trying to relax into it, so that it was a few minutes before I realized the conversation had stopped.

I opened my eyes. Patrick was standing, holding my holiday folder. He held up several pieces of paper. "What's all this?"

"It's . . . the trip. The one I told you about."

I watched him flick through the paperwork I had

shown my sister, taking in the itinerary, the pictures, the California beach.

"I thought . . ." His voice, when it emerged, sounded strangely strangled. "I thought you were talking about Lourdes."

"What?"

"Or . . . I don't know . . . Stoke Mandeville . . . or somewhere. I thought, when you said you couldn't come because you had to help him, it was actual work. Physio, or faith healing, or something. This looks like . . ." He shook his head disbelievingly. "This looks like the holiday of a lifetime."

"Well . . . it kind of is. But not for me. For him."

Patrick grimaced. "No . . . ," he said, shaking his head. "You wouldn't enjoy this *at all*. Hot tubs under the stars, swimming with dolphins . . . Oh, look, 'five-star luxury' and 'twenty-four-hour room service.'" He looked up at me. "This isn't a work trip. This is a bloody honeymoon."

"Don't be ridiculous."

"But this is. You . . . you really expect me to just sit here while you swan off with another man on a holiday like *this*?"

"His caregiver is coming too."

"Oh. Oh yes, *Nathan*. That makes it all right, then."

"Patrick, come on—it's complicated."

"So explain it to me." He thrust the papers toward me. "Explain this to me, Lou. Explain it in a way that I can possibly understand."

"It matters to me that Will wants to live, that he sees good things in his future."

"And those good things would include you?"

"That's not fair. Look, have I ever asked you to stop doing the job you love?"

"My job doesn't involve hot tubs with strange men."

"Well, I don't mind if it does. You can have hot tubs with strange men! As often as you like! There!" I tried to smile, hoping he would too.

But he wasn't having any of it. "How would you feel, Lou? How would you feel if I said I was going to some keep-fit convention with—I don't know—Leanne from the Terrors because she needed cheering up?"

"Cheering up?" I thought of Leanne, with her flicky blond hair and her perfect legs, and I wondered absently why he had thought of her name first.

"And then how would you feel if I said she and I were going to eat out together all the time, and maybe sit in a hot tub or go on days out together. In some destination six thousand miles away, just because she had been a bit down. That really wouldn't bother you?"

"He's not 'a bit down,' Pat. He wants to kill himself. He wants to take himself off to Dignitas, and end his own bloody life." I could hear my blood thumping in my ears. "And you can't turn it around like this. You were the one who called Will a cripple. You were the one who made out he couldn't possibly be a threat to you. 'The perfect boss,' you said. Someone not even worth worrying about."

He put the folder back down on the table.

"Well, Lou . . . I'm worrying now."

I sank my face into my hands and let it rest there for a minute. Out in the corridor I heard a fire door swing and the voices of people swallowed up as a door was unlocked and closed behind them.

Patrick slid his hand slowly backward and forward along the edge of the table. A little muscle worked in his jaw. "You know how this feels, Lou? It feels like I might be running, but I feel like I'm permanently just a little bit behind the rest of the field. I feel like . . ." He took a deep breath, as if he were trying to compose himself. "I feel like there's something bad around the bend, and everyone else seems to know what it is except me."

He lifted his eyes to mine. "I don't think I'm being unreasonable. But I don't want you to go. I don't care if you don't want to do the Viking, but I don't want you to go on this . . . this holiday. With him."

"But I—"

"Nearly seven years we've been together. And you've known this man, had this job, for five months. Five months. If you go with him now, you're telling me something about our relationship. About how you feel about us."

"It doesn't have to say anything about us," I protested.

"It does if I can say all this and you're still going to go."

The little flat seemed so still around us. He was looking at me with an expression I had never seen before.

When my voice emerged, it did so as a whisper. "But he needs me."

I realized almost as soon as I said it, heard the words and how they twisted and regrouped in the air, knew already how I would have felt if he had said the same to me.

He swallowed, shook his head a little as if he were having trouble taking in what I said. His hand came to rest on the side of the table, and then he looked up at me.

"Whatever I say isn't going to make a difference, is it?"

That was the thing about Patrick. He always was smarter than I gave him credit for.

"Patrick, I—"

He closed his eyes, just for a moment, and then he turned and walked out of the living room, leaving the last of the dirty dishes on the sideboard.

21

STEVEN

The girl moved in over the weekend. Will didn't say anything to Camilla or me, but I walked into the annex on Saturday morning still in my pajamas to see if Will needed any help, as Nathan was delayed, and there she was, walking up the hallway with a bowlful of cereal in one hand and the newspaper in the other. She blushed when she saw me. I don't know why—I was wearing my dressing gown, all perfectly decent. I remember thinking afterward that there had been a time when it had been perfectly normal to find pretty young things creeping out of Will's bedroom in the morning.

"Just bringing Will his post," I said, waving it.

"He's not up yet. Do you want me to give him a shout?" Her hand went to her chest, shielding herself with the newspaper. She was wearing a Minnie Mouse T-shirt and the kind of embroidered trousers you used to see Chinese women wearing in Hong Kong.

"No, no. Not if he's sleeping. Let him rest."

When I told Camilla, I thought she'd be pleased. She had been so wretchedly cross about the girl moving in with her boyfriend, after all. But she just looked a bit surprised, and then adopted that tense expression that meant she was already imagining all sorts of possible and undesirable consequences. She didn't say as much, but I was pretty sure she was not keen on Louisa Clark. That said, I didn't know who it was Camilla approved of these days. Her default setting seemed to be stuck on Disapprove.

We never got to the bottom of what had prompted

Louisa to stay—Will just said "family issues"—but she was a busy little thing. When she wasn't looking after Will, she was dashing around, cleaning and washing, whizzing backward and forward to the travel agent's and to the library. I would have known her anywhere in town because she was so conspicuous. She wore the brightest-colored clothing of anyone I'd seen outside the tropics— little jewel-hued dresses and strange-looking shoes.

I would have said to Camilla that she brightened the place up. But I couldn't make that sort of remark to Camilla anymore.

Will had apparently told her that she could use his computer, but she refused, in favor of using those at the library. I don't know if she was afraid of being seen to be taking advantage, or if it was because she didn't want him to see whatever it was she was doing.

Whichever it was, Will seemed a little happier when she was around. A couple of times I heard their conversations filtering through my open window, and I'm sure I heard Will laugh. I spoke to Bernard Clark, just to make sure he was quite happy with the arrangement, and he said it was a bit tricky as she had split up with her long-term boyfriend, and all sorts of things seemed to be up in the air at their home. He also mentioned that she had applied for some conversion course to continue her education. I decided not to tell Camilla about that one. I didn't want her to think what that might mean. Will said she was into fashion and that sort of thing. She was certainly easy on the eye, and had a lovely figure—but, honestly, I wasn't sure who on earth would buy the kinds of things she wore.

On Monday evening, she asked if Camilla and I would come with Nathan into the annex. She had laid out the table with brochures, printed timetables, insurance documents, and other things that she'd printed off the Internet. There were copies for each of us, in clear plastic folders. It was all terribly organized.

She wanted, she said, to present us and Will with her plans for a holiday. (She had warned Camilla that she would make it sound like she was the one gleaning all the benefit, but I could still see Camilla's eyes grow a little steely as she detailed all the things she had booked for them.)

It was an extraordinary trip that seemed to involve all sorts of unusual activities, things I couldn't imagine Will doing even before his accident. But every time she mentioned something—white-water rafting, or bungee jumping, or what have you—she would hold up a document in front of Will, showing other injured young men taking part, and say, "If I'm going to try all these things you keep saying I should, then you have to do them with me."

I have to admit, I was secretly rather impressed by her. She was a resourceful little thing.

Will listened to her, and I could see him reading the documents she laid out in front of him.

"Where did you find all this information?" he said finally.

She raised her eyebrows at him. "Knowledge is power, Will," she said.

And my son smiled, as if she had said something particularly clever.

"So," Louisa said, when all the questions had been asked, "we will be leaving in eight days' time. Are you happy, Mrs. Traynor?" There was a faint air of defiance in the way she said it, as if she were daring Camilla to say no.

"If that's what you all want to do, then it's quite all right by me," Camilla said.

"Nathan? Are you still up for it?"

"You bet."

"And . . . Will?"

We all looked at him. There was a time, not that long ago, when any one of these activities would have been unthinkable. There was a time when Will would have taken pleasure in saying no just to upset his mother. He had always been like that, our son—quite capable of doing the opposite of what was right, simply because he didn't want to be seen to be complying in some way. I don't know where it came from, this urge to subvert. Perhaps it was what made him such a brilliant negotiator.

He looked up at me, his eyes unreadable, and I felt my jaw tense. And then he looked at the girl, and smiled. "Why not?" he said. "I'm quite looking forward to seeing Clark throw herself into some rapids."

The girl seemed to physically deflate a little—with relief—as if she had half expected him to say no.

It's funny. I admit that when she first wound her way into our lives I was a little suspicious of her. Will, despite all his bluster, had been vulnerable. I was rather afraid that he could be manipulated. He's a wealthy young man, despite it all, and that wretched Alicia running off with his friend had made him feel about as worthless as anyone in his position could feel.

But I saw the way Louisa looked at him that day she presented the trip, a strange mixture of pride and gratitude on her face, and I was suddenly immensely glad that she was there. My son, although we never said as much, was in the most untenable of situations. Whatever it was she was doing, it seemed to be giving him just a small respite from that.

There was, for a few days, a faint but definitely celebratory air in the house. Camilla seemed quietly hopeful, although she refused to admit to me that that was what it was. I knew her subtext: what did we really have to celebrate, when all was said and done? I heard her on the telephone to Georgina late at night, justifying what she had agreed to. Her mother's daughter, Georgina was already looking for any way in which Louisa might have used Will's situation to advantage herself.

"She offered to pay for herself, Georgina," Camilla said. And, "No, darling. I don't really think we have a choice. We have very little time and Will has agreed to it, so I'm just going to hope for the best. I think you really have to do the same now."

I knew what it cost her to defend Louisa, to even be nice to her. But she tolerated that girl because she knew, as I did, that Louisa was our only chance of keeping our son even halfway happy.

Louisa Clark had become, although neither of us said it, our only chance of keeping him alive.

———

I went for a drink with Della last night. Camilla was visiting her sister, so we went for a walk down by the river on the way back.

"Will's going to take a holiday," I said.

"How wonderful," she replied.

Poor Della. I could see her fighting her instinctive urge to ask me about our future—to consider how this unexpected development might affect it—but I didn't suppose she ever would. Not until this was all resolved.

We walked, watching the swans, smiling at the tourists splashing around in their boats in the early evening sun, and she chatted away about how this might all be actually rather wonderful for Will, and probably showed that he was really learning to adapt to his situation. It was a sweet thing for her to say, as I knew that, in some respects, she might legitimately have hoped for an end to it all. It was Will's accident that had curtailed our plans for a life together, after all. She must have secretly hoped that my responsibilities toward Will would one day end so that I could be free.

And I walked along beside her, feeling her hand resting in the crook of my arm, listening to her singsong voice. I couldn't tell her the truth—the truth that just a handful of us knew. That if the girl failed with her ranches and her bungee jumping and hot tubs and what have you, she would paradoxically be setting me free. Because the only way I would ever be able to leave my family was if Will decided, after all, that he was still determined to go to this infernal place in Switzerland.

I knew it, and Camilla knew it. Even if neither of us would admit it to ourselves. Only on my son's death would I be free to live the life of my choosing.

"Don't," she said, catching my expression.

Dear Della. She could tell what I was thinking, even when I didn't know myself.

"It's good news, Steven. Really. You never know, this might be the start of a whole new independent life for Will."

I placed my hand over hers. A braver man might have told her what I really thought. A braver man would have let her go long ago—her, and maybe even my wife too.

"You're right," I said, forcing a smile. "Let's hope he comes back full of tales of bungee ropes or whatever horror it is the young people like to inflict upon each other."

She nudged me. "He might make you put one up in the castle."

"White-water rafting in the moat?" I said. "I shall file it away as a possible attraction for next summer's season."

Sustained by this unlikely picture, we walked, occasionally chuckling, all the way down to the boathouse.

And then Will got pneumonia.

22

I ran into Accident and Emergency. I had to ask three times before someone pointed me in the right direction. I finally swung open the doors to Ward C12, breathless and gasping, and there, in the corridor, was Nathan, sitting reading a newspaper. He looked up as I approached him.

"How is he?"

"On oxygen. Stable."

"I don't understand. He was fine on Friday night. He had a bit of a cough Saturday morning, but . . . but this? What happened?"

My heart was racing. I sat down for a moment, trying to catch my breath. I had been running pretty much since I received Nathan's text message an hour earlier. He sat up, and folded his newspaper.

"It's not the first time, Lou. He gets a bit of bacteria in his lungs, his cough mechanism doesn't work like it should, he goes down pretty fast. I tried to do some clearing techniques on him Saturday afternoon but he was in too much pain. He got a fever out of nowhere, then he got a stabbing pain in his chest. We had to call an ambulance Saturday night. Sorry—should have called you, but Will was insistent that we shouldn't bother you."

"Shit," I said, bending over. "Shit, shit, shit. Can I go in?"

"He's pretty groggy. Not sure you'll get much out of him. And Mrs. T is with him."

I left my bag with Nathan, cleaned my hands with

antibacterial lotion, then pushed at the door and entered.

Will was in the middle of the hospital bed, his body covered with a blue blanket, wired up to a drip and surrounded by various intermittently bleeping machines. His face was partially obscured by an oxygen mask and his eyes were closed. His skin looked gray, tinged with a blue-whiteness that made something in me constrict. Mrs. Traynor sat next to him, one hand resting on his covered arm. She was staring, unseeing, at the wall opposite.

"Mrs. Traynor," I said.

She glanced up with a start. "Oh. Louisa."

"How . . . how is he doing?" I wanted to go and take Will's other hand, but I didn't feel like I could sit down. I hovered there by the door. There was an expression of such dejection on her face that even to be in the room felt like intruding.

"A bit better. They have him on some very strong antibiotics."

"Is there . . . anything I can do?"

"I don't think so, no. We . . . we just have to wait. The consultant will be making his rounds in an hour or so. He'll be able to give us more information, hopefully."

The world seemed to have stopped. I stood there a little longer, letting the steady beep of the machines burn a rhythm into my consciousness.

"Would you like me to take over for a while? So you can have a break?"

"No. I think I'll stay, actually."

A bit of me was hoping that Will would hear my voice. A bit of me was hoping his eyes would open above that clear plastic mask, and he would mutter, "Clark. Come and sit down, for God's sake. You're making the place look untidy."

But he just lay there.

I wiped at my face. "Would . . . would you like me to get you a drink?"

Mrs. Traynor looked up. "What time is it?"

"A quarter to ten."

"Is it really?" She shook her head, as if she found that hard to believe. "Thank you, Louisa. That would be . . . that would be very kind. I seem to have been here rather a long time."

I had been off on Friday—in part because the Traynors insisted I was owed a day off, but mostly because there was no way I could get a passport other than by heading to London on the train and queuing up at Petty France. I had popped by their house on Friday night, on my return, to show Will my spoils and to make sure his own passport was still valid. I thought he had been a little quiet, but there had been nothing particularly unusual in that. Some days he was in more discomfort than others. I had assumed it was one of those days. If I'm honest, my mind was so full of our travel plans that I didn't have a lot of room to think about anything else.

I spent Saturday morning picking up my belongings from Patrick's house with Dad, and then I went shopping in the high street with Mum in the afternoon to pick up a swimsuit and some holiday necessities, and I stayed over at my parents' house Saturday and Sunday nights. It was a tight squeeze, with Treena and Thomas there as well. On Monday morning I got up at seven, ready to be at the Traynors' by eight. I arrived there to find the whole place closed up, the front and back doors locked. There was no note. I stood on the front porch and rang Nathan's phone three times without an answer. Mrs. Traynor's phone was set to voice mail. Finally, as I sat on the steps for forty-five minutes, Nathan's text arrived.

We are at county hospital. Will has pneumonia.
Ward C12.

Once I arrived at the hospital, Nathan left, and I sat outside Will's room for a further hour. I flipped through the magazines that somebody had apparently left on the table in 1982, and then pulled a paperback from my bag and tried to read that, but it was impossible to concentrate.

The consultant came around, but I didn't feel that I could follow him into the room while Will's mother was there. When he emerged, fifteen minutes later, Mrs. Traynor came out behind him. I'm not sure if she told me simply because she had to talk to somebody and I was the only person available, but she said in a voice thick with relief that the consultant was fairly confident that they had got the infection under control. It had been a particularly virulent bacterial strain. It was lucky that Will had gone to the hospital when he had, or . . .

That "or . . ." hung in the silence between us.

"So what do we do now?" I said.

She shrugged. "We wait."

"Would you like me to get you some lunch? Or perhaps I could sit with Will while you go and get some?"

Just occasionally, something like understanding passed between me and Mrs. Traynor. Her face softened briefly and—without that customary, rigid expression—I could see suddenly how desperately tired she looked. I think she had aged ten years in the time that I had been with them.

"Thank you, Louisa," she said. "I would very much like to nip home and change my clothes, if you wouldn't mind staying with him. I don't really want Will to be left alone right now."

After she'd gone I went in, closing the door behind me, and sat down beside him. He seemed curiously absent, as if the Will I knew had gone on a brief trip somewhere else and left only a shell. I wondered, briefly, if that was how it was when people died. Then I told myself to stop thinking about death.

I sat and watched the clock tick and heard the occasional murmuring voices outside and the soft squeak of shoes on the linoleum. Twice a nurse came in and checked various levels, pressed a couple of buttons, took his temperature, but still Will didn't stir.

"He is . . . okay, isn't he?" I asked her.

"He's asleep," she said reassuringly. "It's probably the best thing for him right now. Try not to worry."

It's an easy thing to say. But I had a lot of time to think in that hospital room. I thought about Will and the frightening speed with which he had become dangerously ill. I thought about Patrick, and the fact that even as I had collected my things from his flat, unpeeled and rolled up my wall calendar, folded and packed the clothes I had laid so carefully in his chest of drawers, my sadness was never the crippling thing I should have expected. I didn't feel desolate, or overwhelmed, or any of the things you should feel when you split apart a love of several years. I felt quite calm, and a bit sad, and perhaps a little guilty—both at my part in the split and at the fact that I didn't feel the things I probably should. I had sent him two text messages, to say I was really, really sorry, and that I hoped he would do really well in the Xtreme Viking. But he hadn't replied.

After an hour, I leaned over, lifted the blanket from Will's arm, and there, pale brown against the white sheet, lay his hand. A cannula was taped to the back of it with surgical tape. When I turned it over, the scars were still livid on his wrists. I wondered, briefly, if they would ever fade, or if he would be permanently reminded of what he had tried to do.

I took his fingers gently in mine and closed my own around them. They were warm, the fingers of someone very much living. I was so oddly reassured by how they felt in my own that I kept them there, gazing at them, at the calluses that told of a life not entirely lived behind a desk, at the pink seashell nails that would always have to be trimmed by somebody else.

Will's were good man's hands—attractive and even, with squared-off fingers. It was hard to look at them and believe that they held no strength, that they would never again pick something up from a table, stroke an arm, or make a fist.

I traced his knuckles with my finger. Some small part of me wondered whether I should be embarrassed if Will opened his eyes at this point, but I couldn't feel it. I felt with some certainty that it was good for him to have his hand in mine. Hoping that in some way, through the barrier of his drugged sleep, he knew this too, I closed my eyes and waited.

———

Will finally woke up shortly after four. I was outside in the corridor, lying across the chairs, reading a discarded newspaper, and I jumped when Mrs. Traynor came out to tell me. She looked a little lighter when she mentioned he was talking, and that he wanted to see me. She said she was going to go downstairs and ring Mr. Traynor.

And then, as if she couldn't quite help herself, she added, "Please don't tire him."

"Of course not," I said.

My smile was charming.

"Hey," I said, peeping my head around the door.

He turned his face slowly toward me. "Hey, yourself."

His voice was hoarse, as if he had spent the past thirty-six hours not sleeping but shouting. I sat down and looked at him. His eyes flickered downward.

"You want me to lift the mask for a minute?"

He nodded. I took it and carefully slid it up over his head. There was a fine film of moisture where it had met his skin, and I took a tissue and wiped gently around his face.

"So how are you feeling?"

"Been better."

A great lump had risen, unbidden, to my throat, and I tried to swallow it. "I don't know. You'll do anything for attention, Will Traynor. I bet this was all just a—"

He closed his eyes, cutting me off in midsentence. When he opened them again, they held a hint of an apology. "Sorry, Clark. I don't think I can do witty today."

We sat. And I talked, letting my voice rattle away in the little pale-green room, telling him about getting my things back from Patrick's—how much easier it had been getting my CDs out of his collection given his insistence on a proper cataloging system.

"You okay?" he said, when I had finished. His eyes were sympathetic, like he expected it to hurt more than it actually did.

"Yeah. Sure." I shrugged. "It's really not so bad. I've got other things to think about anyway."

Will was silent. "The thing is," he said, eventually, "I'm not sure I'm going to be bungee jumping anytime soon."

I knew it. I had half expected this ever since I had first received Nathan's text. But hearing the words fall from his mouth felt like a blow.

"Don't worry," I said, trying to keep my voice even. "It's fine. We'll go some other time."

"I'm sorry. I know you were really looking forward to it."

I placed a hand on his forehead, and smoothed his hair back. "Shh. Really. It's not important. Just get well."

He closed his eyes with a faint wince. I knew what they said—those lines around his eyes, that resigned expression. They said there wasn't necessarily going to be another time. They said he thought he would never be well again.

I stopped off at Granta House on the way back from the hospital. Will's father let me in, looking almost as tired as

Mrs. Traynor did. He was carrying a battered wax jacket, as if he were just on his way out. I told him Mrs. Traynor was with Will again, and that the antibiotics were considered to be working well, but that she had asked me to let him know that she would be spending the night at the hospital again. Why she couldn't tell him herself, I don't know. Perhaps she just had too much to think about.

"How does he look?"

"Bit better than this morning," I said. "He had a drink while I was there. Oh, and he said something rude about one of the nurses."

"Still his impossible self."

"Yeah, still his impossible self."

Just for a moment I saw Mr. Traynor's mouth compress and his eyes glisten. He looked away at the window and then back at me. I didn't know whether he would have preferred it if I'd looked away.

"Third bout. In two years."

It took me a minute to catch up. "Of pneumonia?"

He nodded. "Wretched thing. He's pretty brave, you know. Under all that bluster." He swallowed and nodded, as if to himself. "It's good you can see it, Louisa."

I didn't know what to do. I reached out my hand and touched his arm. "I do see it."

He gave me a faint nod, then took his Panama hat from the coat hooks in the hall. Muttering something that might have been a thank-you or a good-bye, Mr. Traynor moved past me and out the front door.

The annex felt oddly silent without Will in it. I realized how much I had become used to the distant sound of his motorized chair moving backward and forward, his murmured conversations with Nathan in the next room, the low hum of the radio. Now the annex was still, the air like a vacuum around me.

I packed an overnight bag with all the things he might want the next day, including clean clothes, his toothbrush, hairbrush, and medication, plus earphones in case he was well enough to listen to music. As I did so I had to fight a peculiar sense of panic. A subversive little voice kept rising up inside me, saying, *This is how it would feel if he were dead.* To drown it out, I turned on the radio, trying to bring the annex back to life. I did some cleaning, made Will's bed with fresh sheets, and picked some flowers from the garden, which I put in the living room. And then, when I had gotten everything ready, I glanced over and saw the holiday folder on the table.

I would spend the following day going through all the paperwork and canceling every trip, every excursion I had booked. There was no saying when Will would be well enough to do any of them. The consultant had stressed that he had to rest, to complete his course of antibiotics, to stay warm and dry. White-water rafting and scuba diving were not part of his plan for convalescence.

I stared at my folder, at all the effort and work and imagination that had gone into compiling it. I stared at the passport that I had queued to collect, remembering my mounting sense of excitement even as I sat on the train heading into the city, and for the first time since I had embarked upon my plan, I felt properly despondent. There were just over three weeks to go, and I had failed. My contract was due to end, and I had done nothing to noticeably change Will's mind. I was afraid to even ask Mrs. Traynor where on earth we went from here. I felt suddenly overwhelmed. I dropped my head into my hands and, in the silent little house, I left it there.

"Evening."

My head shot up. Nathan was standing there, filling the little kitchen with his bulk. He had his backpack over his shoulder.

"I just came to drop off some prescription meds for when he gets back. You . . . okay?"

I wiped briskly at my eyes. "Sure. Sorry. Just . . . just a little daunted about canceling this lot."

Nathan swung his backpack off his shoulder and sat down opposite me. "It's a pisser, that's for sure." He picked up the folder, and began flipping through. "You want a hand tomorrow? They don't want me at the hospital, so I could stop by for an hour in the morning. Help you put in the calls."

"That's kind of you. But no. I'll be fine. Probably simpler if I do it all."

Nathan made tea, and we sat opposite each other and drank it. I think it was the first time Nathan and I had really talked to each other—at least, without Will between us. He told me about a previous client of his, C3-4 quadriplegic with a ventilator, who had been ill at least once a month for the whole time he worked there. He told me about Will's previous bouts of pneumonia, the first of which had nearly killed him, and from which it had taken him weeks to recover.

"He gets this look in his eye . . . ," he said. "When he's really sick. It's pretty scary. Like he just . . . retreats. Like he's almost not even there."

"I know. I hate that look."

"He's a—" he began. And then, abruptly, his eyes slid away from me and he closed his mouth.

We sat holding our mugs. From the corner of my eye I studied Nathan, looking at his friendly open face that seemed briefly to have closed off. And I realized I was about to ask a question to which I already knew the answer.

"You know, don't you?"

"Know what?"

"About . . . what he wants to do."

The silence in the room was sudden and intense.

Nathan looked at me carefully, as if weighing how to reply.

"I know," I said. "I'm not meant to, but I do. That's what . . . that's what the holiday was meant to be about. That's what the outings were all about. Me trying to change his mind."

Nathan put his mug on the table. "I did wonder," he said. "You seemed . . . to be on a mission."

"I was. Am."

He shook his head, whether to say I shouldn't give up or to tell me that nothing could be done, I wasn't sure.

"What are we going to do, Nathan?"

It took him a moment or two before he spoke again. "You know what, Lou? I really like Will. I don't mind telling you, I love the guy. I've been with him two years now. I've seen him at his worst, and I've seen him on his good days, and all I can say to you is I wouldn't be in his shoes for all the money in the world."

He took a swig of his tea. "There have been times when I've stayed over and he's woken up screaming because in his dreams he's still walking and skiing and doing stuff and just for those few minutes, when his defenses are down and it's all a bit raw, he literally can't bear the thought of never doing it again. He can't bear it. I've sat there with him and there is nothing I can say to the guy, nothing that is going to make it any better. He's been dealt the shittiest hand of cards you can imagine. And you know what? I looked at him last night and I thought about his life and what it's likely to become . . . and although there is nothing I'd like more in the world than for the big guy to be happy, I . . . I can't judge him for what he wants to do. It's his choice. It should be his choice."

My breath had started to catch in my throat. "But . . . that was before. You've all admitted that it was before I came. He's different now. He's different with me, right?"

"Sure, but—"

"But if we don't have faith that he can feel better, even

get better, then how is he supposed to keep the faith that good things might happen?"

Nathan put his mug on the table. He looked straight into my eyes.

"Lou. He's not going to get better."

"You don't know that."

"I do. Unless there is some massive breakthrough in stem cell research, Will is looking at another decade in that chair. Minimum. He knows it, even if his folks don't want to admit it. And this is half the trouble. She wants to keep him alive at any cost. Mr. T thinks there is a point where we have to let him decide."

"Of course he gets to decide, Nathan. But he has to see what his actual choices are."

"He's a bright guy. He knows exactly what his choices are."

My voice lifted in the little room. "No. You're wrong. You tell me he was in the same place before I came. You tell me he hasn't changed his outlook even a little bit just through me being here."

"I can't see inside his head, Lou."

"You know I've changed the way he thinks."

"No, I know that he will do pretty much anything to make you happy."

I stared at him. "You think he's going through the motions just to keep me happy?" I felt furious with Nathan, furious with them all. "So if you don't believe any of this can do any good, why were you going to come at all? Why did you even want to come on this trip? Just a nice holiday, was it?"

"No. I want him to live."

"But—"

"But I want him to live if *he* wants to live. If he doesn't, then by forcing him to carry on, you, me—no matter how much we love him—we become just another shitty bunch of people taking away his choices."

Nathan's words reverberated into the silence. I wiped a solitary tear from my cheek and tried to make my heart rate return to normal. Nathan, apparently embarrassed by my tears, scratched absently at his neck, and then, after a minute, silently handed me a paper towel.

"I can't just let it happen, Nathan."

He said nothing.

"I can't."

I stared at my passport, sitting on the kitchen table. It was a terrible picture. It looked like someone else entirely. Someone whose life, whose way of being, might actually be nothing like my own. I stared at it, thinking.

"Nathan?"

"What?"

"If I could fix some other kind of trip, something the doctors would agree to, would you still come? Would you still help me?"

"Course I would." He stood, rinsed his mug, and hauled his backpack over his shoulder. He turned to face me before he left the kitchen. "But I've got to be honest, Lou. I'm not sure even you are going to be able to pull this one off."

23

Exactly ten days later, Will's father disgorged us from the car at Gatwick Airport, Nathan wrestling our luggage onto a trolley, and me checking and checking again that Will was comfortable—until even he became irritated.

"Take care of yourselves. And have a good trip," Mr. Traynor said, placing a hand on Will's shoulder. "Don't get up to too much mischief." He actually winked at me when he said this.

Mrs. Traynor hadn't been able to leave work to come too. I suspected that actually meant she hadn't wanted to spend two hours in a car with her husband.

Will nodded but said nothing. He had been disarmingly quiet in the car, gazing out the window with his impenetrable stare, ignoring Nathan and me as we chatted about traffic and what we already knew we had forgotten.

Even as we walked across the concourse I wasn't sure we were doing the right thing. Mrs. Traynor had not wanted him to go at all. But from the day he agreed to my revised plan, I knew she had been afraid to tell him he shouldn't. She seemed to be afraid of talking to us at all that last week. She sat with Will in silence, talking only to the medical professionals. Or busied herself in her garden, cutting things down with frightening efficiency.

"The airline is meant to meet us. They're meant to

come and meet us," I said, as we made our way to the check-in desk, flipping through my paperwork.

"Chill out. They're hardly going to post someone at the doors," Nathan said.

"But the chair has to travel as a 'fragile medical device.' I checked with the woman on the phone three times. And we need to make sure they're not going to get funny about Will's onboard medical equipment."

The online quad community had given me reams of information, warnings, legal rights, and checklists. I had subsequently triple-checked with the airline that we would be given bulkhead seats, and that Will would be boarded first, and not moved from his power chair until we were actually at the gate. Nathan would remain on the ground, remove the joystick and turn it to manual, and then carefully tie and bolster the chair, securing the pedals. He would personally oversee its loading to protect against damage. It would be pink-tagged to warn luggage handlers of its extreme delicacy. We had been allocated three seats in a row so that Nathan could complete any medical assistance that Will needed without prying eyes. The airline had assured me that the armrests lifted so that we wouldn't bruise Will's hips while transferring him from the wheelchair to his aircraft seat. We would keep him between us at all times. And we would be the first allowed off the aircraft.

All this was on my "airport" checklist. That was the sheet in front of my "hotel" checklist but behind my "day before we leave" checklist and the itinerary. Even with all these safeguards in place, I felt sick.

Every time I looked at Will I wondered if I had done the right thing. He had been cleared by his GP for travel only the night before. He ate little and spent much of every day asleep. He seemed not just weary from his illness, but exhausted with life, tired of our interference, our upbeat attempts at conversation, our relentless determination to try to make things better for him. He tolerated me, but I got the feeling that he often wanted to be left alone. He didn't know that this was the one thing I could not do.

"There's the airline woman," I said, as a uniformed girl with a bright smile and a clipboard walked briskly toward us.

"Well, she's going to be a lot of use on transfer," Nathan muttered. "She doesn't look like she could lift a frozen prawn."

"We'll manage," I said. "Between us, we will manage."

It had become my catchphrase ever since I had worked out what I wanted to do. Since my conversation with Nathan in the annex, I had been filled with a renewed zeal to prove them all wrong. Just because we couldn't do the holiday I'd planned did not mean that Will could not do anything at all.

I hit the message boards, firing out questions. Where might be a good place for a far weaker Will to convalesce? Did anyone else know where we could go? Temperature was my main consideration—the English climate was too changeable (there was nothing more depressing than an English seaside resort in the rain). Much of Europe was too hot in late July, ruling out Italy, Greece, the south of France, and other coastal areas. I had a vision, you see. I saw Will relaxing by the sea. The problem was, with only a few days to plan it and go, there was a diminishing chance of making it a reality.

There were commiserations from the others, and many, many stories about pneumonia. It seemed to be the specter that haunted them all. There were a few suggestions as to places we could go, but none that inspired me. Or, more important, none that I felt Will would be inspired by. I didn't really know what I wanted, but I scrolled backward through the list of their suggestions and knew that nothing was right.

It was Ritchie, that chat-room stalwart, who had come to my aid in the end. The afternoon that Will was released from hospital, he typed:

> *Give me your e-mail address. Cousin is travel*
> *agent. I have got him on the case.*

I had rung the number he gave me and spoken to a middle-aged man with a broad Yorkshire accent. When he told me what he had in mind, a little bell of recognition rang somewhere deep in my memory. And within two hours, we had it sorted. I was so grateful to him that I could have cried.

"Think nothing of it, pet," he said. "You just make sure that bloke of yours has a good time."

That said, by the time we left I was almost as exhausted as Will was. I had spent days wrangling with the finer requirements of quadriplegic travel, and right up until the morning we left I had not been convinced that Will would be well enough to come. Now, seated with the bags, I gazed at him, withdrawn and pale in the bustling airport, and wondered again if I had been wrong. I had a sudden moment of panic. What if he got ill again? What if he hated every minute, as he had with the horse racing? What if I had misread this whole situation, and what Will needed was not an epic journey, but ten days at home in his own bed?

But we didn't have ten days to spare. This was it. This was my only chance.

"They're calling our flight," Nathan said, as he strolled back from the duty-free. He looked at me, raised an eyebrow, and I took a breath.

"Okay," I replied. "Let's go."

The flight itself, despite twelve long hours in the air, was not the ordeal I had feared. Nathan proved himself dexterous at doing Will's routine changes under cover of a blanket. The airline staff was solicitous and discreet, and careful with the chair. Will was, as promised, loaded first, achieved transfer to his seat with no bruising, and then settled in between us.

Within an hour of being in the air I realized that, oddly enough, above the clouds, provided his seat was tilted and he was wedged in enough to be stable, Will was pretty much equal to anyone in the cabin. Stuck in front of a screen, with nowhere to move and nothing to do, there was very little, at thirty thousand feet up, that separated him from any of the other passengers. He ate and watched a film, and mostly he slept.

Nathan and I smiled cautiously at each other and tried to behave as if this were fine, all good. I gazed out the window, my thoughts as jumbled as the clouds beneath us, unable yet to think about the fact that this was not just a logistical challenge but an adventure for me—that I, Lou Clark, was actually headed to the other side of the world. I couldn't see it. I couldn't see anything beyond Will by then. I felt like my sister, when she had first given birth to Thomas. "It's like I'm looking through a funnel," she had said, gazing at his newborn form. "The world has just shrunk to me and him."

She had texted me when I was in the airport.

You can do this. Am bloody proud of you xxx

I called it up now, just to look at it, feeling suddenly emotional, perhaps because of her choice of words. Or perhaps because I was tired and afraid and still finding it hard to believe that I had even gotten us this far. Finally, to block my thoughts, I turned on my little television screen, gazing unseeing at some American comedy series until the skies around us grew dark.

And then I woke to find that the flight attendant was standing over us with breakfast, that Will was talking to Nathan about a film they had just watched together, and that—astonishingly, and against all the odds—the three of us were less than an hour away from landing in Mauritius.

I don't think I believed that any of this could actually

happen until we touched down at Sir Seewoosagur Ramgoolam International Airport. We emerged groggily through Arrivals, still stiff from our time in the air, and I could have wept with relief at the sight of the operator's specially adapted taxi. That first morning, as the driver sped us toward the resort, I registered little of the island. True, the colors seemed brighter than in England, the sky more vivid, an azure blue that just disappeared and grew deeper and deeper to infinity. I saw that the island was lush and green, fringed with acres of sugarcane crops, the sea visible like a strip of mercury through the volcanic hills. The air was tinged with something smoky and gingery, the sun so high in the sky that I had to squint into the white light. In my exhausted state it was as if someone had woken me up in the pages of a glossy magazine.

But even as my senses wrestled with the unfamiliar, my gaze returned repeatedly to Will, to his pale, weary face, to the way his head seemed oddly slumped on his shoulders. And then we pulled into a palm-tree-lined driveway, stopped outside a low-framed building, and the driver was already out and unloading our bags.

We declined the offer of iced tea, of a tour around the hotel. We found Will's room, dumped his bags, settled him into his bed, and almost before we had drawn the curtains, he was asleep again. And then there we were. I had done it. I stood outside his room, finally letting out a deep breath, while Nathan gazed out the window at the white surf on the coral reef beyond. I don't know if it was the journey, or because this was the most beautiful place I had ever been in my life, but I felt suddenly tearful.

"It's okay," Nathan said, catching sight of my expression. And then, totally unexpectedly, he walked up to me and enveloped me in a huge bear hug. "Relax, Lou. It's going to be okay. Really. You did good."

———

It was almost three days before I started to believe him. Will slept for most of the first forty-eight hours—and then, astonishingly, he began to look better. His skin regained its color and he lost the blue shadows around his eyes. His spasms lessened and he began to eat again, wheeling his way slowly along the endless, extravagant buffet and telling me what he wanted on his plate. I knew he was feeling more like himself when he bullied me into trying things I would never have eaten—spicy creole curries and seafood whose names I did not recognize. He swiftly seemed more at home in this place than I did. And no wonder. I had to remind myself that, for most of his life, this had been Will's domain—this globe, these wide shores—not the little annex in the shadow of the castle.

The hotel had, as promised, come up with the special wheelchair with wide wheels, and most mornings Nathan transferred Will into it and we all three walked down to the beach, me carrying a parasol so that I could protect him if the sun grew too fierce. But it never did; that southern part of the island was renowned for sea breezes and, out of season, the resort temperatures rarely rose past 75 degrees Fahrenheit. We would stop at a small beach near a rocky outcrop, just out of view of the main hotel. I would unfold my chair, place myself next to Will under a palm tree, and we would watch Nathan attempt to windsurf, or water-ski—occasionally shouting encouragement, plus the odd word of abuse—from our spot on the sand.

At first the hotel staff wanted to do almost too much for Will, offering to push his chair, constantly pressing cool drinks upon him. We explained what we didn't need from them, and they cheerfully backed off. It was good, though, during the moments when I wasn't with him, to see porters or reception staff stopping by to chat with him, or sharing with him some place that they thought we should go. There was one gangly young man, Nadil, who seemed to take it upon himself to act as Will's unofficial caregiver when Nathan was not around. One day I came out to find him and a friend gently lowering Will out of his chair onto a cushioned sunbed he had positioned by "our" tree.

"This better," he said, giving me a thumbs-up as I walked across the sand. "You just call me when Mr. Will want to go back in his chair."

I was about to protest, and tell them they should not have moved him. But Will had closed his eyes and lay there with a look of such unexpected contentment that I just closed my mouth and nodded.

As for me, as my anxiety about Will's health began to ebb, I slowly began to suspect that I was actually in paradise. I had never, in my life, imagined I would spend time somewhere like this. Every morning I woke to the sound of the sea breaking gently on the shore, unfamiliar birds calling to one another from the trees. I gazed up at my ceiling, watching the sunlight playing through the leaves, and from next door heard the murmured conversation that told me Will and Nathan had already been up long before me. I dressed in sarongs and swimsuits, enjoying the feeling of the warm sun on my shoulders and back. My skin grew freckled, my nails bleached, and I began to feel a rare happiness at the simple pleasures of existing here—of walking on a beach, eating unfamiliar foods, swimming in warm, clear water where black fish gazed shyly from under volcanic rocks, or watching the sun sink fiery red into the horizon. Slowly the past few months began to slip away. To my shame, I hardly thought of Patrick at all.

Our days fell into a pattern. We ate breakfast together, all three of us, at the gently shaded tables around the pool. Will usually had fruit salad, which I fed to him by hand, and sometimes followed up with a banana pancake as his appetite grew. We then went down to the beach, where we stayed—me reading, Will listening to music—while Nathan practiced his watersport skills. Will kept telling me to try something too, but at first I said no. I just wanted to stay next to him. When Will insisted, I spent one morning windsurfing and kayaking, but I was happiest just hanging out next to him.

Occasionally if Nadil was around, and the resort was quiet, he and Nathan would ease Will into the warm water of the smaller pool, Nathan holding him under his head so that he could float. He didn't say much when they did this, but he looked quietly contented, as if his body were remembering long-forgotten sensations. His torso, long pale, grew golden. His scars silvered and began to fade. He grew comfortable without a shirt.

At lunchtime we would wheel our way over to one of the resort's three restaurants. The surface of the whole complex was tiled, with only a few small steps and slopes, which meant that Will could move in his chair with complete autonomy. It was a small thing, but his being able to get himself a drink without one of us accompanying him meant not so much a rest for me and Nathan as the brief removal of one of Will's daily frustrations—being entirely dependent on other people. Not that any of us had to move much anywhere. It seemed wherever you were, beach or poolside, or even the spa, one of the smiling staff would pop up with some drink they thought you might like, usually decorated with a fragrant pink flower. Even as you lay on the beach, a small buggy would pass, and a smiling waiter would offer you water, fruit juice, or something stronger.

In the afternoons, when the temperatures were at their highest, Will would return to his room and sleep for a couple of hours. I would swim in the pool, or read my book, and then in the evening we would all meet again to eat supper at the beachside restaurant. I swiftly developed a taste for cocktails. Nadil had worked out that if he gave Will the correct size straw and placed a tall glass in his holder, Nathan and I need not be involved at all. As dusk fell, the three of us talked of our childhoods and our first significant others and our first jobs and our families and other holidays we had had, and slowly I saw Will reemerge.

Except this Will was different. This place seemed to have granted him a peace that had been missing the whole time I had known him.

"He's doing good, huh?" said Nathan, as he met me by the buffet.

"Yes, I think he is."

"You know"—Nathan leaned toward me, reluctant for Will to see we were talking about him—"I think the ranch thing and all the adventures would have been great. But looking at him now, I can't help thinking this place has worked out better."

I didn't tell him what I had decided on the first day, when we checked in, my stomach knotted with anxiety, already calculating how many days I had until the return home. I had to try for each of those ten days to forget why we were actually there—the six-month contract, my carefully plotted calendar, everything that had come before. I had to just live in the moment and try to encourage Will to do the same. I had to be happy, in the hope that Will would be too.

I helped myself to another slice of melon, and smiled. "So what's on later? Are we doing the karaoke? Or have your ears not yet recovered from last night?"

On the fourth night, Nathan announced with only faint embarrassment that he had a date. Karen was a fellow Kiwi staying in the next hotel, and he had agreed to go down to the town with her.

"Just to make sure she's all right. You know . . . I'm not sure if it's a good place for her to go alone."

"No," Will said, nodding his head sagely. "Very chivalrous of you, Nate."

"I think that is a very responsible thing to do. Very civic-minded," I agreed.

"I have always admired Nathan for his selflessness. Especially when it comes to the fairer sex."

"Piss off, you two." Nathan grinned, and disappeared.

Karen swiftly became a fixture. Nathan disappeared with her most evenings and, although he returned for late duties, we tacitly gave him as much time as possible to enjoy himself.

Besides, I was secretly glad. I liked Nathan, and I was grateful that he had come, but I preferred it when it was just Will and me. I liked the shorthand we seemed to fall into when nobody else was around, the easy intimacy that had sprung up between us. I liked the way he turned his face and looked at me with amusement, like I had somehow turned out to be so much more than he had expected.

On the penultimate night, I told Nathan that I didn't mind if he wanted to bring Karen back to the complex. He had been spending nights in her hotel, and I knew it made it difficult for him, walking the twenty minutes each way in order to sort Will out last thing at night.

"I don't mind. If it will . . . you know . . . give you a bit of privacy."

He was cheerful, already lost in the prospect of the night ahead, and didn't give me another thought beyond an enthusiastic "Thanks, mate."

"Nice of you," said Will, when I told him.

"Nice of you, you mean," I said. "It's your room I've donated to the cause."

That night we got him into mine, and Nathan helped Will into bed and gave him his medication while Karen waited next door. In the bathroom I changed into my T-shirt and knickers and then opened the bathroom door and pottered over to the sofa with my pillow under my arm. I felt Will's eyes on me, and felt oddly self-conscious for someone who had spent most of the previous week walking around in front of him in a bikini. I plumped my pillow down on the sofa arm.

"Clark?"

"What?"

"You really don't have to sleep over there. This bed is large enough for an entire football team as it is."

The thing is, I didn't really even think about it. That was how it was, by then. Perhaps the days spent near-naked on the beach had loosened us all up a little. Perhaps it was the thought of Nathan and Karen on the other side of the wall, wrapped up in each other, a co-coon of exclusion. Perhaps I did just want to be near him. I began to walk toward the bed, then flinched at a sudden crash of thunder. The lights stuttered, someone shouted outside. From next door we heard Nathan and Karen burst out laughing.

I walked to the window and pulled back the curtain, feeling the sudden breeze, the abrupt drop in temperature. Out at sea a storm had exploded into life. Dramatic flashes of forked lightning briefly illuminated the sky, and then, as if in afterthought, the heavy drumbeat roll of a deluge hit the roof of our little bungalow, so fierce that at first it drowned out sound.

"I'd better close the shutters," I said.

"No, don't."

I turned.

"Throw the doors open." Will nodded toward the outside. "I want to see it."

I hesitated, then slowly opened the glass doors out onto the terrace. The rain hammered down on the hotel complex, dripping from our roof, sending rivers running away from our terrace and out toward the sea. I felt the moisture on my face, the electricity in the air. The hairs on my arms stood bolt upright.

"Can you feel it?" he said, from behind me.

"It's like the end of the world."

I stood there, letting the charge flow through me, the white flashes imprinting themselves on my eyelids. It caused my breath to catch in my throat.

I turned back, and walked over to the bed, seating myself on its edge. As he watched, I leaned forward and gently pulled his sun-browned neck toward me. I knew just how to move him now, how I could make his weight, his solidity, work with me. Holding him close to me, I leaned across and placed a fat white pillow behind his shoulders before releasing him back into its soft embrace. He smelled of the sun, as if it had seeped deep into his skin, and I found myself inhaling silently, as if he were something delicious.

Then, still a little damp, I climbed in beside him, so close that my legs touched his, and together we gazed out at the blue-white scorch as the lightning hit the waves, at the silvered stair rods of rain, the gently shifting mass of turquoise that lay only a hundred feet away.

The world around us shrank, until it was just the sound of the storm, the gently billowing gauze curtains, my shallow breath. I smelled the lotus flowers on the night breeze, heard the distant sounds of clinking glasses and hastily drawn-back chairs, of music from some far-off celebration, felt the charge of nature unleashed. I reached across for Will's hand, and took it in my own. I thought, briefly, that I would never feel as intensely connected to the world, to another human being, as I did at that moment.

"Not bad, eh, Clark?" Will said into the silence. In the face of the storm, his face was still and calm. He turned briefly and smiled at me, and there was something in his eyes then, something triumphant.

"No," I said. "Not bad at all."

I lay still, listening to his breathing slow and deepen, the sound of the rain below it, felt his warm fingers entwined with mine. I did not want to go home. I thought I might never go home. Here Will and I were safe, locked in our little paradise. Every time I thought about heading back to England, a great claw of fear gripped my stomach and began to tighten its hold.

It's going to be okay. I tried to repeat Nathan's words to myself. *It's going to be okay.*

Finally, I turned onto my side, away from the sea, and gazed at Will. He turned his head to look back at me in the dim light, and I felt he was telling me the same thing. *It's going to be okay.* For the first time in my life I tried not to think about the future. I tried to just be, to simply let the evening's sensations travel through me. I can't say how long we stayed like that, just gazing at each other, but gradually Will's eyelids grew heavier, until he murmured apologetically that he thought he might . . . His breathing deepened, he tipped over that small crevasse into sleep, and then it was just me watching his face, looking at the way his eyelashes separated into little points near the corners of his eyes, at the new freckles on his nose.

I told myself I had to be right. I had to be right.

The storm finally blew itself out sometime after 1 A.M., disappearing somewhere out at sea, its flashes of anger growing fainter and then finally disappearing altogether, off to bring meteorological tyranny to some other unseen place. The air slowly grew still around us, the curtains settling, the last of the water draining away with a gurgle. Sometime in the early hours I got up, gently releasing my hand from Will's, and closed the French windows, muffling the room in silence. Will slept—a sound, peaceful sleep that he rarely slept at home.

I didn't. I lay there and watched him and tried to make myself think nothing at all.

———

Two things happened on the last day. One was that, under pressure from Will, I agreed to try scuba diving. He had been at me for days, stating that I couldn't possibly come all this way and not go under the water. I had been hopeless at windsurfing, barely able to lift my sail from the waves, and had spent most of my attempts at waterskiing face-planting my way along the bay. But he was insistent and, the day before, had arrived at lunch announcing that he had booked me in for a half-day beginners' diving course.

It didn't get off to a good start. Will and Nathan sat on the side of the pool as my instructor tried to get me to believe I would continue to breathe underwater, but the knowledge that they were watching me made me hopeless. I'm not stupid—I understood that the tanks on my back would supply me with plenty of air, that my equipment was working, that I was not about to drown—but every time my head went under, I panicked and burst through the surface. It was as if my body refused to believe that it could still breathe underneath several thousand gallons of Mauritius's finest chlorinated.

"I don't think I can do this," I said, as I emerged for the seventh time, spluttering.

James, my diving instructor, glanced behind me at Will and Nathan.

"I can't," I said crossly. "It's just not me."

James turned his back on the two men, tapped me on the shoulder, and gestured toward the open water. "Some people actually find it easier out there," he said quietly.

"In the sea?"

"Some people are better thrown in at the deep end. Come on. Let's go out on the boat."

Three-quarters of an hour later, I was gazing underwater at the brightly colored landscape that had been hidden from view, forgetting to be afraid that my equipment might fail, that against all evidence I would sink to the bottom and die a watery death, even that I was afraid at all. I was distracted by the secrets of a new world. In the silence, broken only by the exaggerated *oosh shoo* of my own breath, I watched shoals of tiny iridescent fish, and larger black-and-white fish, that stared at me with blank, inquisitive faces, and gently swaying anemones filtering the gentle currents of their tiny, unseen haul. I saw distant landscapes twice as brightly colored and

Jojo Moyes

varied as they were above land. I saw caves and hollows where unknown creatures lurked, distant shapes that shimmered in the rays of the sun. I didn't want to come up. I could have stayed there forever, in that silent world. It was only when James started gesticulating toward the dial of his watch that I realized I didn't have a choice.

I could barely speak when I finally walked up the beach toward Will and Nathan, beaming. My mind was still humming with the images I had seen, my limbs somehow still propelling me under the water.

"Good, eh?" said Nathan.

"Why didn't you tell me?" I exclaimed to Will, throwing my flippers down on the sand in front of him. "Why didn't you make me do that earlier? All that! It was all there, all the time! Just right under my nose!"

Will gazed at me steadily. He said nothing at first, but his smile was slow and wide. "I don't know, Clark. Some people just won't be told."

———

I let myself get drunk that last night. It wasn't just that we were leaving the next day. It was the first time I had felt truly that Will was well and that I could let go. I wore a white cotton dress (my skin had colored now, so that wearing white didn't automatically make me resemble a corpse wearing a shroud) and a pair of silvery strappy sandals, and when Nadil gave me a scarlet flower and instructed me to put it in my hair, I didn't scoff at him as I might have done a week earlier.

"Well, hello, Carmen Miranda," Will said, when I met them at the bar. "Don't you look glamorous."

I was about to make some sarcastic reply, and then I realized he was looking at me with genuine pleasure.

"Thank you," I said. "You're not looking too shabby yourself."

There was a disco at the main hotel complex, so shortly before 10 P.M.—when Nathan left to be with Karen—we headed down to the beach with the music in our ears and the pleasant buzz of three cocktails sweetening my movements.

Oh, but it was so beautiful down there. The night was warm, carrying on its breezes the scents of distant barbecues, of warm oils on skin, of the faint salt tang of the sea. Will and I stopped near our favorite tree. Someone had built a fire on the beach, perhaps for cooking, and all that was left was a pile of glowing embers.

"I don't want to go home," I said into the darkness.

"It's a hard place to leave."

"I didn't think places like this existed outside films," I said, turning so that I faced him. "It has actually made me wonder if you might have been telling the truth about all the other stuff."

He was smiling. His whole face seemed relaxed and happy, his eyes crinkling as he looked at me. I looked at him, and for the first time it wasn't with a faint fear gnawing away at my insides.

"You're glad you came, right?" I said tentatively.

He nodded. "Oh yes."

"Hah!" I punched the air.

And then, as someone turned the music up by the bar, I kicked off my shoes and I began to dance. It sounds stupid—the kind of behavior that on another day you might be embarrassed by. But there, in the inky dark, half drunk from lack of sleep, with the fire and the endless sea and infinite sky, with the sounds of the music in our ears and Will smiling and my heart bursting with something I couldn't quite identify, I just needed to dance. I danced, laughing, not self-conscious, not worrying about whether anybody could see us. I felt Will's eyes on me and I knew he knew—that this was the only possible response to the last ten days. Hell, to the last six months.

The song ended, and I flopped, breathless, at his feet.

"You . . ." he said.

"What?" My smile was mischievous. I felt fluid, electrified. I barely felt responsible for myself.

He shook his head.

I rose, slowly, onto my bare feet, walked right up to his chair, and then slid onto his lap so that my face was inches from his. After the previous evening, it somehow didn't seem like such a leap to make.

"You . . ." His blue eyes, glinting with the light of the fire, locked onto mine. He smelled of the sun, and the bonfire, and something sharp and citrusy.

I felt something give, deep inside me.

"You . . . are something else, Clark."

I did the only thing I could think of. I leaned forward, and I placed my lips on his. He hesitated, just for a moment, and then he kissed me. And just for a moment I forgot everything—the million and one reasons I shouldn't, my fears, the reason we were here. I kissed him, breathing in the scent of his skin, feeling his soft hair under my fingertips, and when he kissed me back all of this vanished and it was just Will and me, on an island in the middle of nowhere, under a thousand twinkling stars.

And then he pulled back. "I . . . I'm sorry. No—"

My eyes opened. I lifted my hand to his face and let it trace his beautiful bones. I felt the faint grit of salt under my fingertips. "Will . . . ," I began. "You can. You—"

"No." It held a hint of metal, that word. "I can't."

"I don't understand."

"I don't want to go into it."

"Um . . . I think you have to go into it."

"I can't do this because I can't . . ." He swallowed. "I can't be the man I want to be with you. And that means that this"—he looked up into my face—"This just becomes . . . another reminder of what I am not."

I didn't let go of his face. I tipped my forehead forward so that it touched his, so that our breath mingled, and I said, quietly, so that only he could have heard me, "I don't care what you . . . what you think you can and can't do. It's not black and white. Honestly . . . I've talked to other people in the same situation and . . . and there are things that are possible. Ways that we can both be happy . . ." I had begun to stammer a little. I looked up and into his eyes. "Will Traynor," I said, softly. "Here's the thing. I think we can do—"

"No, Clark—" he began.

"I think we can do all sorts of things. I know this isn't a conventional love story. I know there are all sorts of reasons I shouldn't even be saying what I am. But I love you. I do. I knew it when I left Patrick. And I think you might even love me a little bit."

He didn't speak. His eyes searched my own, and there was this huge weight of sadness within them. I stroked the hair away from his temples, as if I could somehow lift his sorrow, and he tilted his head to meet the palm of my hand, so that it rested there.

He swallowed. "I have to tell you something."

"I know," I whispered. "I know everything."

Will's mouth closed on his words. The air seemed to still around us.

"I know about Switzerland. I know . . . why I was employed on a six-month contract."

He lifted his head away from my hand. He looked at me, then gazed upward at the skies. His shoulders sagged.

"I know it all, Will. I've known for months. And, Will, please listen to me . . ." I took his right hand in mine, and I brought it up close to my chest. "I know we can do this. I know it's not how you would have chosen it, but I know I can make you happy. And all I can say is that you make me . . . you make me into someone I couldn't even imagine. You make me happy, even when you're awful. I would rather be with you—even the you that you seem to think is diminished—than with anyone else in the world."

I felt his fingers tighten a fraction around mine, and it gave me courage.

"If you think it's too weird with me being employed by you, then I'll leave and I'll work somewhere else. I wanted to tell you—I've applied for a college course. I've done loads of research on the Internet, talking to other quads and caregivers of quads, and I have learned so much, so much about how to make this work. So I can do that, and just be with you. You see? I've thought of everything, researched everything. This is how I am now. This is your fault. You changed me." I was half laughing. "You've turned me into my sister. But with better dress sense."

He had closed his eyes. I placed both my hands around his, lifted his knuckles to my mouth, and I kissed them. I felt his skin against mine, and knew as I had never known anything that I could not let him go.

"What do you say?" I whispered.

I could have looked into his eyes forever.

He said it so quietly that for a minute I could not be sure I had heard him correctly.

"What?"

"No, Clark."

"No?"

"I'm sorry. It's not enough."

I lowered his hand. "I don't understand."

He waited before he spoke, as if he were struggling, for once, to find the right words. "It's not enough for me. This—my world—even with you in it. And believe me, Clark, my whole life has changed for the better since you came. But it's not enough for me. It's not the life I want."

Now it was my turn to pull away.

"The thing is, I get that this could be a good life. I get that with you around, perhaps it could even be a very good life. But it's not *my* life. I am not the same as these people you speak to. It's nothing like the life I want. Not even close." His voice was halting, broken. His expression frightened me.

I swallowed, shaking my head. "You . . . you once told me that the night in the maze didn't have to be the thing that defined me. You said I could choose what it was that defined me. Well, you don't have to let that . . . that chair define you."

"But it does define me, Clark. You don't know me, not really. You never saw me before this thing. I loved my life, Clark. Really loved it. I loved my job, my travels, the things I was. I loved being a physical person. I liked riding my motorbike, hurling myself off great heights. I liked crushing people in business deals. I liked having sex. Lots of sex. I led a *big life*." His voice had lifted now. "I am not designed to exist in this thing—and yet for all intents and purposes it is now the thing that defines me. It is the only thing that defines me."

"But you're not even giving it a chance," I whispered. My voice didn't seem to want to emerge from my chest. "You're not giving *me* a chance."

"It's not a matter of giving you a chance. I've watched you these six months becoming a whole different person, someone who is only just beginning to see her possibilities. You have no idea how happy that has made me. I don't want you to be tied to me, to my hospital appointments, to the restrictions on my life. I don't want you to miss out on all the things someone else could give you. And, selfishly, I don't want you to look at me one day and feel even the tiniest bit of regret or pity that—"

"I would *never* think that!"

"You don't know that, Clark. You have no idea how this would play out. You have no idea how you're going to feel even six months from now. And I don't want to look at you every day, to see you naked, to watch you wandering around the annex in your crazy dresses and not . . . not be able to do what I want with you. Oh, Clark, if you had any idea what I want to do to you right now. And I . . . I can't live with that knowledge. I can't.

It's not who I am. I can't be the kind of man who just . . . *accepts*."

He glanced down at his chair, his voice breaking. "I will never accept this."

I had begun to cry. "Please, Will. Please don't say this. Just give me a chance. Give us a chance."

"Shhhh. Just listen. You, of all people. Listen to what I'm saying. This . . . tonight . . . is the most wonderful thing you could have done for me. What you have told me, what you have done in bringing me here . . . knowing that, somehow, from that complete arse I was at the start of this, you managed to salvage something to love is astonishing to me. But"—I felt his fingers close on mine—"I need it to end here. No more chair. No more pneumonia. No more burning limbs. No more pain and tiredness and waking up every morning already wishing it was over. When we get back, I am still going to go to Switzerland. And if you do love me, Clark, as you say you do, the thing that would make me happier than anything is if you would come with me."

My head whipped back.

"What?"

"It's not going to get any better than this. The odds are I'm only going to get increasingly unwell and my life, reduced as it is, is going to get smaller. The doctors have said as much. There are a host of conditions encroaching on me. I can feel it. I don't want to be in pain anymore, or trapped in this thing, or dependent on everyone, or afraid. So I'm asking you—if you feel the things you say you feel—then do it. Be with me. Give me the end I'm hoping for."

I looked at him in horror, my blood thumping in my ears. I could barely take it in.

"How can you ask me that?"

"I know, it's—"

"I tell you I love you and I want to build a future with

you, and you ask me to come and watch you kill your-self?"

"I'm sorry. I don't mean it to sound blunt. But I haven't got the luxury of time."

"Wha—what? Why, are you actually booked in? Is there some appointment you're afraid of missing?"

I could see people at the hotel stopping, perhaps hearing our raised voices, but I didn't care.

"Yes," Will said, after a pause. "Yes, there is. I've had the consultations. The clinic agreed that I am a suitable case for them. And my parents agreed to the thirteenth of August. We're due to fly out the day before."

My head had begun to spin. It was less than a week away.

"I don't believe this."

"Louisa—"

"I thought . . . I thought I was changing your mind."

He tilted his head sideways and gazed at me. His voice was soft, his eyes gentle. "Louisa, nothing was ever going to change my mind. I promised my parents six months, and that's what I've given them. You have made that time more precious than you can imagine. You stopped it from being an endurance test—"

"Don't!"

"What?"

"Don't say another word." I was choking. "You are so selfish, Will. So stupid. Even if there was the remotest possibility of me coming with you to Switzerland . . . even if you thought I might, after all I've done for you, be someone who could do that, is that all you can say to me? I tore my heart out in front of you. And all you can say is, 'No, you're not enough for me. And now I want you to come watch the worst thing you can possibly imagine.' The thing I have dreaded ever since I first found out about it. Do you have any idea what you are asking of me?"

I was raging now. Standing in front of him, shouting

like a madwoman. "Fuck you, Will Traynor. Fuck you. I wish I'd never taken this stupid job. I wish I'd never met you." I burst into tears, ran up the beach and back to my hotel room, away from him.

His voice, calling my name, rang in my ears long after I had closed the door.

24

There is nothing more disconcerting to passers-by than to see a man in a wheelchair pleading with a woman who is meant to be looking after him. It's apparently not really the done thing to be angry with your disabled charge.

Especially when he is plainly unable to move, and is saying, gently, "Clark. Please. Just come over here. *Please*."

But I couldn't. I couldn't look at him. Nathan had packed up Will's stuff, and I had met them both in the lobby the following morning—Nathan still groggy from his hangover—and from the moment we had to be in each other's company again, I refused to have anything to do with Will. I was furious and miserable. There was an insistent, raging voice inside my head that demanded to be as far as possible from him. To go home. To never see him again.

"You okay?" Nathan said, appearing at my shoulder.

As soon as we arrived at the airport, I marched away from them to the check-in desk.

"No," I said. "And I don't want to talk about it."

"Hungover?"

"No."

There was a short silence.

"This mean what I think it does?" He was suddenly somber.

I couldn't speak. I nodded, and I watched Nathan's jaw stiffen briefly. He was stronger than I was, though. He was, after all, a professional. Within minutes he was back with Will, showing him something he had seen in a magazine, wondering aloud about the prospects for some football team they both knew of. Watching them, you would know nothing of the momentousness of the news I had just imparted.

I managed to make myself busy for the entire wait at the airport. I found a thousand small tasks to do— attending to the luggage labels, buying coffee, perusing newspapers, going to the loo—all of which meant that I didn't have to look at him. I didn't have to talk to him. But every now and then Nathan would disappear and we were left alone, sitting beside each other, the short distance between us jangling with unspoken recriminations.

"Clark—" he would begin.

"Don't," I would cut him off. "I don't want to talk to you."

I surprised myself with how cold I could be. I certainly surprised the flight attendants. I saw them on the flight, muttering among themselves at the way I turned rigidly away from Will, plugging my earphones in or resolutely staring out the window.

For once, he didn't get angry. That was almost the worst of it. He didn't get angry, and he didn't get sarcastic, and he simply grew quieter until he barely spoke. It was left to poor Nathan to bounce the conversation along, to ask questions about tea or coffee or spare packets of dry-roasted peanuts or whether anyone minded if he climbed past us to go to the loo.

It probably sounds childish now, but it was not just a matter of pride. I couldn't bear it. I couldn't bear the thought that I would lose him, that he was so stubborn, and determined not to see what was good, what could be good, that he would not change his mind. I couldn't believe that he would stick to that one date, as if it were cast in stone. A million silent arguments rattled around my head. *Why is this not enough for you? Why am I not enough for you? Why could you not have confided in me? If we'd had more time, would this have been different?* Every now and then I would catch myself staring down at his tanned hands, those squared-off fingers, just inches from my own, and I would remember how our fingers felt entwined—the warmth of him, the illusion, even in stillness, of a kind of strength—and a lump would rise in my throat until I thought I could barely breathe and I had to retreat to the WC, where I would lean over the sink and sob silently under the strip lighting. There were a few occasions when I thought about what Will still intended to do that I actually had to fight the urge to scream; I felt overcome by a kind of madness and thought I might just sit down in the aisle and howl and howl until someone else stepped in. Until someone else made sure he couldn't do it.

So although I looked childish—although I seemed to the cabin staff (as I declined to talk to Will, to look at him, to feed him) as if I were the most heartless of women—I knew that pretending he was not there was about the only way I could cope with these hours of enforced proximity. If I had believed Nathan capable of handling everything alone I would honestly have changed my flight, perhaps even disappeared until I could make sure that there was a whole continent between us, not just a few impossible inches.

The two men slept, and it came as something of a relief—a brief respite from the tension. I stared at the television screen and, with every mile that we flew toward home, I felt my heart grow heavier, my anxiety greater. It began to occur to me then that my failure was not just my own; Will's parents were going to be devastated. They would probably blame me. Will's sister would probably sue me. And it was my failure for Will too. I had failed to persuade him. I had offered him everything I could, including myself, and nothing I had shown him had convinced him of a reason to keep living.

Perhaps, I found myself thinking, he deserved some-one better than me. Someone cleverer. Someone like Treena might have thought of better things to do. They might have found some rare piece of medical research or something that could have helped him. They might have changed his mind. The fact that I was going to have to live with this knowledge for the rest of my life made me feel almost dizzy.

"Want a drink, Clark?" Will's voice would break into my thoughts.

"No. Thank you."

"Is my elbow too far over your armrest?"

"No. It's fine."

It was only in those last few hours, in the dark, that I allowed myself to look at him. My gaze slid slowly side-ways from my glowing television screen until I gazed at him surreptitiously in the dim light of the little cabin. And as I took in his face, so tanned and handsome, so peaceful in sleep, a solitary tear rolled down my cheek. Perhaps in some way conscious of my scrutiny, Will stirred, but didn't wake. And unseen by the cabin staff, by Nathan, I pulled his blanket slowly up around his neck, tucking it in carefully, to make sure, in the chill of the cabin air-conditioning, that Will would not feel the cold.

———

They were waiting at the Arrivals gate. I had somehow known they would be. I had felt the faintly sick sensa-tion expanding inside me even as we wheeled Will through passport control, fast-tracked by some well-meaning official even as I prayed that we would be forced to wait, stuck in a queue that lasted hours, prefer-ably days. But no, we crossed the vast expanse of lino-leum, me pushing the baggage trolley, Nathan pushing Will, and as the glass doors opened, there they were, standing at the barrier, side by side in some rare sem-blance of unity. I saw Mrs. Traynor's face briefly light up as she saw Will, and I thought, absently, *Of course—he looks so well.* And, to my shame, I put on my sunglasses—not to hide my exhaustion, but so that she wouldn't immediately see from my naked expression what it was I was going to have to tell her.

"Look at you!" she was exclaiming. "Will, you look wonderful. Really wonderful."

Will's father had stooped, his face wreathed in smiles; he was patting his son's chair, his knee. "We couldn't believe it when Nathan told us you were down on the beach every day. And swimming! What was the water like, then—lovely and warm? It's been raining cats and dogs here. Typical August!"

Of course. Nathan would have been texting them or calling them. As if they would have let us go all that time without some kind of contact.

"It . . . it was a pretty amazing place," said Nathan. He had grown quiet too, but now tried to smile, to seem his normal self.

I felt frozen, my hand clutching my passport like I was about to go somewhere else. I had to remind myself to breathe.

"Well, we thought you might like a special dinner," Will's father said. "There's a jolly nice restaurant at the Intercontinental. Champagne on us. What do you think? Your mother and I thought it might be a nice treat."

"Sure," said Will. He was smiling at his mother and she was looking back at him as if she wanted to bottle it. *How can you?* I wanted to yell at him. *How can you look at her like that when you already know what you are going to do to her?*

"Come on, then. I've got the car in disabled parking. It's only a short ride from here. I was pretty sure you'd all be a bit jet-lagged. Nathan, do you want me to take any of those bags?"

My voice broke into the conversation. "Actually," I

said—I was already pulling my luggage from the trolley— "I think I'm going to head off. Thank you, anyway."

I was focused on my bag, deliberately not looking at them, but even above the hubbub of the airport I could detect the brief silence my words provoked.

Mr. Traynor's voice was the first to break it. "Come on, Louisa. Let's have a little celebration. We want to hear all about your adventures. I want to know all about the island. And I promise you don't have to tell us *everything*." He almost chuckled.

"Yes." Mrs. Traynor's voice had a faint edge to it. "Do come, Louisa."

"No." I swallowed, tried to raise a bland smile. My sunglasses were a shield. "Thank you. I'd really rather get back."

"To where?" said Will.

I realized what he was saying. I didn't really have anywhere to go.

"I'll go to my parents' house. It will be fine."

"Come with us," he said. His voice was gentle. "Don't go, Clark. Please."

I wanted to cry then. But I knew with utter certainty that I couldn't be anywhere near him. "No. Thank you. I hope you have a lovely meal." I hoisted my bag over my shoulder and, before anyone could say anything else, I was walking away from them, swallowed up by the crowds in the terminal.

I was almost at the bus stop when I heard her. Camilla Traynor, her heels clipping on the pavement, half walked, half ran toward me.

"Stop. Louisa. Please stop."

I turned, and she was forcing her way through a coach party, casting the backpacking teenagers aside like Moses parting the waves. The airport lights were bright on her hair, turning it a kind of copper color. She was wearing a fine gray pashmina, which draped artistically over one shoulder. I remember thinking absently how beautiful she must have been only a few years earlier.

"Please. Please stop."

I stopped, glancing behind me at the road, wishing that the bus would appear now, that it would scoop me up and take me away. That anything would happen. A small earthquake, maybe.

"Louisa?"

"He had a good time." My voice sounded clipped. Oddly like her own, I found myself thinking.

"He does look well. Very well." She stared at me, standing there on the pavement. She was suddenly acutely still, despite the sea of people moving around her.

We didn't speak.

And then I said, "Mrs. Traynor, I'd like to hand in my notice. I can't . . . I can't do these last few days. I'll forfeit any money owed to me. In fact, I don't want this month's money. I don't want anything. I just—"

She went pale then. I saw the color drain from her face, the way she swayed a little in the morning sunshine. I saw Mr. Traynor coming up behind her, his stride brisk, one hand holding his Panama hat firmly on his head. He was muttering his apologies as he pushed through the crowds, his eyes fixed on me and his wife as we stood rigidly a few feet apart.

"You . . . you said you thought he was happy. You said you thought this might change his mind." She sounded desperate, as if she were pleading with me to say something else, to give her some different result.

I couldn't speak. I stared at her, and the most I could manage was a small shake of my head.

"I'm sorry," I whispered, so quietly that she could not have heard me.

He was almost there as she fell. It was as if her legs just gave way under her, and Mr. Traynor's left arm shot out and caught her as she went down, her mouth a great O, her body slumped against his.

His hat fell to the pavement. He glanced up at me, his face confused, not yet registering what had just taken place.

And I couldn't look. I turned, numb, and I began to walk, one foot in front of the other, my legs moving almost before I knew what they were doing, away from the airport, not yet even knowing where it was I was going to go.

25

KATRINA

Louisa didn't come out of her room for a whole thirty-six hours after she got back from her holiday. She arrived back from the airport late Sunday evening, pale as a ghost under her suntan—and we couldn't work that out, for a start, as she had definitely said she'd see us first thing Monday morning. *I just need to sleep*, she had said, then shut herself in her room and gone straight to bed. We had thought it a little odd, but what did we know? Lou has been peculiar since birth, after all.

Mum had taken up a mug of tea in the morning, and Lou had not stirred. By supper, Mum had become worried and shaken her, checking that she was alive. (She can be a bit melodramatic, Mum—although, to be fair, she had made fish pie and she probably just wanted to make sure Lou wasn't going to miss it.) But Lou wouldn't eat, and she wouldn't talk and she wouldn't come downstairs. *I just want to stay here for a bit, Mum*, she said into her pillow. Finally, Mum left her alone.

"She's not herself," said Mum. "Do you think it's some kind of delayed reaction to the thing with Patrick?"

"She couldn't give a stuff about Patrick," Dad said. "I told her he rang to tell us he came in 157th in the Viking thing, and she couldn't have looked less interested." He sipped his tea. "Mind you, to be fair to her, even I found it pretty hard to get excited about 157th."

"Do you think she's ill? All that sleeping isn't like her. She might have some terrible tropical disease."

"She's just jet-lagged," I said. I said it with some

authority, knowing that Mum and Dad tended to treat me as an expert on all sorts of matters that none of us really knew anything about.

"Jet lag! Well, if that's what long-haul travel does to you, I think I'll stick with Tenby. What do you think, Josie, love?"

"I don't know . . . who would have thought a holiday could make you look so ill?" Mum shook her head.

I went upstairs after supper. I didn't knock. (It was still, strictly speaking, my room, after all, and given that I was here for a whole week's break it should by rights have been me in there.) The air was thick and stale, and I pulled the blind up and opened a window, so that Lou turned groggily from under the duvet, shielding her eyes from the light, dust particles swirling around her.

"You going to tell me what happened?" I put a mug of tea on the bedside table.

She blinked at me.

"Mum thinks you've got Ebola virus. She's busy warning all the neighbors who have booked onto the Bingo Club trip to PortAventura."

She didn't say anything.

"Lou?"

"I quit," she said quietly.

"Why?"

"Why do you think?" She pushed herself upright, and reached clumsily for the mug, taking a long sip of tea.

For someone who had just spent almost two weeks in Mauritius, she looked bloody awful. Her eyes were tiny and red-rimmed, and her skin, without the tan, would have been even blotchier. Her hair stuck up on one side. She looked like she'd been awake for several years. But most of all she looked sad. I had never seen my sister look so sad.

"You think he's really going to go through with it?"

She nodded. Then she swallowed, hard.

"Shit. Oh, Lou. I'm really sorry."

I motioned to her to shove over, and I climbed into bed beside her. She took another sip of her tea, and then leaned her head on my shoulder. She was wearing my T-shirt. I didn't say anything about it. That was how bad I felt for her.

"What do I do, Treen?"

Her voice was small, like Thomas's when he hurts himself and is trying to be really brave. Outside we could hear the neighbors' dog running up and down alongside the garden fence, chasing the neighborhood cats. Every now and then we could hear a burst of manic barking; the dog's head would be popping up over the top right now, its eyes bulging with frustration.

"I'm not sure there's anything you can do. God. All that stuff you fixed up for him. All that effort . . ."

"I told him I loved him," she said, her voice dropping to a whisper. "And he just said it wasn't enough." Her eyes were wide and bleak. "How am I supposed to live with that?"

I am the one in the family who knows everything. I read more than anyone else. I go to the university. I am the one who is supposed to have all the answers.

But I looked at my big sister, and I shook my head. "I haven't got a clue," I said.

———

She finally emerged the following day, showered and wearing clean clothes, and I told Mum and Dad not to say a word. I implied it was boyfriend trouble, and Dad raised his eyebrows and made a face as if that explained everything and God only knew what we had been working ourselves into such a fuss over. Mum ran off to ring the Bingo Club and tell them she'd had second thoughts about the risks of air travel.

Lou ate a piece of toast (she didn't want lunch) and she put on a big floppy sunhat and we walked up to the castle with Thomas to feed the ducks. I don't think she really wanted to go out, but Mum insisted that we all needed some fresh air. This, in my mother's vocabulary, meant she was itching to get into the bedroom and air it and change the bedding. Thomas skipped and hopped ahead of us, clutching a plastic bag full of crusts, and we negotiated the meandering tourists with an ease born of years of practice, ducking out of the way of swinging backpacks, separating around posing couples and rejoining on the other side. The castle baked in the high heat of summer, the ground cracked and the grass wispy, like the last hairs on the head of a balding man. The flowers in the tubs looked defeated, as if they were already half preparing for autumn.

Lou and I didn't say much. What was there to say?

As we walked past the tourist car park I saw her glance under her brim at the Traynors' house. It stood elegant and redbrick, its tall blank windows disguising whatever life-changing drama was being played out in there, perhaps even at this moment.

"You could go and talk to him, you know," I said. "I'll wait here for you."

She looked at the ground, folded her arms across her chest, and we kept walking. "There's no point," she said. I knew the other bit, the bit she didn't say aloud. *He's probably not even there.*

We did a slow circuit of the castle, watching Thomas roll down the steep parts of the hill, feeding the ducks that by this stage in the season were so well stuffed they could barely be bothered to come over for mere bread. I watched my sister as we walked, seeing her brown back exposed by her halter-neck top, her stooped shoulders, and I realized that even if she didn't know it yet, everything had changed for her. She wouldn't stay here now, no matter what happened with Will Traynor. She had an air about her, a new air of knowledge, of things seen, places she had been. My sister finally had new horizons.

"Oh," I said, as we headed back toward the gates, "you got a letter. From the college, while you were away. Sorry—I opened it. I thought it must be for me."

"You opened it?"

I had been hoping it was extra grant money.

"You got an interview."

She blinked, as if receiving news from some long-distant past.

"Yeah. And the big news is, it's tomorrow," I said. "So I thought maybe we should go over some possible questions tonight."

She shook her head. "I can't go to an interview tomorrow."

"What else are you going to do?"

"I can't, Treen," she said sorrowfully. "How am I supposed to think about anything at a time like this?"

"Listen, Lou. They don't give interviews out like bread for ducks, you idiot. This is a big deal. They know you're a mature student, you're applying at the wrong time of year, and they're still going to see you. You can't muck them around."

"I don't care. I can't think about it."

"But you—"

"Just leave me alone, Treen. Okay? I *can't do it*."

"Hey," I said. I stepped in front of her so that she couldn't keep walking. Thomas was talking to a pigeon, a few paces up ahead. "This is exactly the time you have to think about it. This is the time when, like it or not, you finally have to work out what you are going to do with the rest of your life."

We were blocking the path. Now the tourists had to separate to walk around us—they did so, heads down or eyeing with mild curiosity the arguing sisters.

"I can't."

"Well, tough. Because, in case you forgot, you have no job anymore. No Patrick to pick up the pieces. And if you miss this interview, then in two days' time you are headed back down to the Job Center to decide whether you want to be a chicken processor or a lap dancer or wipe some other person's bum for a living. And believe it or not, because you are now headed for thirty, that's your life pretty well mapped out. And all of this—everything you've learned over the past six months—will have been a waste of time. All of it."

She stared at me, wearing that look of mute fury she wears when she knows I am right and she can't say anything back. Thomas appeared beside us now and pulled at my hand.

"Mum . . . you said *bum*."

My sister was still glaring at me. But I could see her thinking.

I turned to my son. "No, sweetheart, I said *bun*. We're going to go home for tea now—aren't we, Lou?—and see if we can have some *buns*. And then, while Granny gives you a bath, I'm going to help Auntie Lou do her homework."

———

Mum looked after Thomas the next day, so I saw Lou off on the bus. I didn't hold out a lot of hope for the interview, so I spent the day at the library worrying about my own future instead of hers. Over dinner that night, I glanced over at Lou. She was gazing at her plate, pushing the roast chicken around as if trying to disguise it. *Uh-oh*, I thought.

"You not hungry, love?" said Mum, following the line of my gaze.

"Not very," she said.

"It is very warm for chicken," Mum conceded. "I just thought you needed perking up a bit."

"So . . . you going to tell us how you got on at this interview?" Dad's fork stopped halfway to his mouth.

"Oh, that." She looked distracted, as if he had just dredged up something she did five years ago.

"Yes, that."

She speared a tiny piece of chicken. "It was okay."

Dad glanced at me.

I gave a tiny shrug. "Just okay? They must have given you some idea how you did."

"I got it."

"What?"

She was still looking down at her plate. I stopped chewing.

"They said I was exactly the kind of applicant they were looking for. I've got to do some kind of foundation course, which takes a year, and then I can convert it."

Dad sat back in his chair. "That's fantastic news."

Mum reached over and patted her shoulder. "Oh, well done, love. That's brilliant."

"Not really. I don't think I can afford four years of study."

"Don't you worry about that just now. Really. Look how well Treena's managing. Hey"—he nudged her—"We'll find a way. We always find a way, don't we?" Dad beamed at us both. "I think everything's turning around for us now, girls. I think this is going to be a good time for this family."

And then, out of nowhere, she burst into tears. Real tears. She cried like Thomas cries, wailing, all snot and tears and not caring who hears, her sobs breaking through the silence of the little room like a knife.

Thomas stared at her, open-mouthed, so that I had to haul him onto my lap and distract him so that he didn't get upset too. And while I fiddled with bits of potato and talking peas and made silly voices, she told them.

She told them everything—about Will and the six-month contract and what had happened when they went to Mauritius. As she spoke, Mum's hands went to her mouth. Granddad looked solemn. The chicken grew cold, the gravy congealing in its boat.

Dad shook his head in disbelief. And then, as my sister detailed her flight home from the Indian Ocean, her voice dropping to a whisper as she spoke of her last words to Mrs. Traynor, he pushed his chair back and stood up. He walked slowly around the table and he took her in his arms, like he had when we were little. He stood there and held her really, really tightly to him.

"Oh Jesus Christ, the poor fella. And poor you. Oh Jesus."

I'm not sure I ever saw Dad look so shocked.

"What a bloody mess."

"You went through all this? Without saying anything? And all we got was a postcard about scuba diving?" My mother was incredulous. "We thought you were having the holiday of a lifetime."

"I wasn't alone. Treena knew," she said, looking at me. "Treena was great."

"I didn't do anything," I said, hugging Thomas. He had lost interest in the conversation now that Mum had put an open tin of Celebrations in front of him. "I was just an ear. You did the lot. You came up with all the ideas."

"And some ideas they turned out to be." She leaned against Dad, sounding bereft.

Dad tilted her chin so that she had to look at him. "But you did everything you could."

"And I failed."

"Who says you failed?" Dad stroked her hair back from her face. His expression was tender. "I'm just thinking of what I know about Will Traynor, what I know about men like him. And I'll say one thing to you. I'm not sure anyone in the world was ever going to persuade that man once he'd set his mind to something. He's who he is. You can't make people change who they are."

"But his parents! They can't let him kill himself," said Mum. "What kind of people are they?"

"They're normal people, Mum. Mrs. Traynor just doesn't know what else she can do."

"Well, not bloody taking him to this clinic would be a start." Mum was angry. Two points of color had risen to her cheekbones. "I would fight for you two, for Thomas, until my dying breath."

"Even if he'd already tried to kill himself?" I said. "In really grim ways?"

"He's ill, Katrina. He's depressed. People who are vulnerable should not be given the chance to do something that they'll . . ." She trailed off in mute fury and dabbed at her eyes with a napkin. "That woman must be heartless. *Heartless*. And to think they got Louisa involved in all this. She's a magistrate, for goodness' sake. You'd think a magistrate would know what was right or wrong. Of all people. I've a good mind to head down there now and bring him back here."

"It's complicated, Mum."

"No. It's not. He's vulnerable and there is no way on earth she should entertain the thought of it. I'm shocked. That poor man. That *poor* man." She got up from the table, taking the remains of the chicken with her, and stalked out to the kitchen.

Louisa watched her go, her expression a little stunned. Mum was never angry. I think the last time we heard her raise her voice was 1993.

Dad shook his head, his mind apparently elsewhere. "I've just thought—no wonder I haven't seen Mr. Traynor. I wondered where he was. I assumed they were all off on some family holiday."

"They've . . . they've gone?"

"He's not been in these last two days."

Lou sat back down and slumped in her chair.

"Oh shit," I said, and then clamped my hands around Thomas's ears.

"It's tomorrow."

Lou looked at me, and I glanced up at the calendar on the wall.

"The thirteenth of August. It's tomorrow."

Lou did nothing that last day. She was up before me, staring out the kitchen window. It rained, and then it cleared, and then it rained again. She lay on the sofa with Granddad, and she drank the tea that Mum made her, and every half an hour or so I watched her gaze slide silently toward the mantelpiece and check the clock. It was awful to watch. I took Thomas swimming and I tried to make her come with us. I said Mum would mind him if she wanted to go to the shops with me later. I said I'd take her to the pub, just the two of us, but she refused every offer.

"What if I made a mistake, Treen?" she said, so quietly that only I could hear it.

I glanced up at Granddad, but he had eyes only for the racing. I think Dad was still putting on a sneaky bet each way for him, even though he denied it to Mum.

"What do you mean?"

"What if I should have gone with him?"

"But . . . you said you couldn't."

Outside, the skies were gray. She stared through our immaculate windows at the miserable day beyond.

"I know what I said. But I just can't bear not knowing what's happening." Her face crumpled a little. "I can't bear not knowing how he's feeling. I can't bear the fact that I never even got to say good-bye."

"Couldn't you go now? Maybe try and get a flight?"

"It's too late," she said. And then she closed her eyes. "I'd never get there in time. There's only two hours left until . . . until it stops for the day. I looked it up. On the Internet."

I waited.

"They don't . . . do . . . it . . . after five thirty." She shook her head in bemusement. "Something to do with the Swiss officials who have to be there. They don't like . . . certifying . . . things outside office hours."

I almost laughed. But I didn't know what to say to her. I couldn't imagine having to wait, as she was waiting, knowing what might be happening in some far-off place. I had never loved a man like she seemed to love Will. I had liked men, sure, and wanted to sleep with them, but sometimes I wondered if I was missing some sensitivity chip. I couldn't imagine crying over anyone I'd been with. The only equivalent was if I thought about Thomas waiting to die in some strange country, and as soon as that thought came to mind it made something inside me actually flip over, it was so hideous. So I stuck that in the back of my mental filing cabinet too, under the drawer labeled: *Unthinkable.*

I sat down beside my sister on the sofa and we stared in silence at the three-thirty Maiden Stakes, then the four o'clock handicap stakes, and the four races that followed it, with the fixed intensity of people who might actually have all the money in the world on the winner.

And then the doorbell rang.

Louisa was off the sofa and in the hallway in seconds. The way she wrenched the door open made even my heart stop.

But it wasn't Will there on the doorstep. It was a young woman, her makeup thick and perfectly applied, her hair cut in a neat bob around her chin. She folded her umbrella and smiled, reaching around toward the large bag she had over her shoulder. I wondered briefly if this was Will Traynor's sister.

"Louisa Clark?"

"Yes?"

"I'm from the *Globe.* I wondered if I could have a quick word?"

"The *Globe*?"

I could hear the confusion in Lou's voice.

"The newspaper?" I stepped behind my sister. I saw then the notepad in the woman's hand.

"Can I come in? I'd just like to have a little chat with you about William Traynor. You do work for William Traynor, don't you?"

"No comment," I said. And before the woman had a chance to say anything else, I slammed the door in her face.

My sister stood stunned in the hallway. She flinched as the doorbell rang again.

"Don't answer it," I hissed.

"But how—"

I began to push her up the stairs. God, she was impossibly slow. It was like she was half asleep. "Grand-dad, don't answer the door!" I yelled. "Who have you told?" I said when we reached the landing. "Someone must have told them. Who knows?"

"Miss Clark," the woman's voice came through the letter box. "If you just give me ten minutes . . . we do understand this is a very sensitive issue. We'd like you to put your side of the story . . ."

"Does this mean he's dead?" Her eyes had filled with tears.

"No, it just means some arse is trying to cash in." I thought for a minute.

"Who was that, girls?" Mum's voice came up the stairwell.

"No one, Mum. Just don't answer the door."

I peered over the banister. Mum was holding a tea towel in her hands and gazing at the shadowy figure visible through the glass panels of the front door.

"Don't answer the door?"

I took my sister's elbow. "Lou . . . you didn't say anything to Patrick, did you?"

She didn't need to say anything. Her stricken face said it all.

"Okay. Don't have a baby. Just don't go near the door. Don't answer the phone. Don't say a word to them, okay?"

———

Mum was not amused. She was even less amused after the phone started ringing. After the fifth call we put all calls through to the answering machine, but we still had to listen to them, their voices invading our little hallway. There were four or five of them, all the same. All offering Lou the chance to tell her side of "the story," as they called it. Like Will Traynor was now some commodity that they were all scrabbling over. The telephone rang and the doorbell rang. We sat with the curtains closed, listening to the reporters on the pavement just outside our gate, chatting to one another and speaking on their mobile phones.

It was like being under siege. Mum wrung her hands and shouted through the letter box for them to get the hell out of our front garden whenever one of them ventured past the gate. Thomas gazed out the upstairs bathroom window and wanted to know why there were people in our garden. Four of our neighbors rang, wanting to know what was going on. Dad parked on Ivy Street and came home via the back garden, and we had a fairly serious talk about castles and boiling oil.

Then, after I'd thought a bit longer, I rang Patrick and asked him how much he had got for his sordid little tip. The slight delay before he denied everything told me all I needed to know.

"You shitbag," I yelled. "I'm going to kick your stupid marathon-running shins so hard you're going to think 157th was actually a good result."

Lou just sat in the kitchen and cried. Not proper sobbing, just silent tears that ran down her face and which she wiped away with the palm of her hand. I couldn't think what to say to her.

Which was fine. I had plenty to say to everyone else.

All but one of the reporters cleared off by half past seven. I didn't know if they had given up or if Thomas's habit of posting bits of Lego out of the letter box every time they passed another note through had become boring. I told Louisa to bathe Thomas for me, mainly because I wanted her to get out of the kitchen, but also because that way I could go through all the messages on our answering machine and delete the newspaper ones while she couldn't hear me. Twenty-six. Twenty-six of the buggers. And all sounding so nice, so understanding. Some of them even offered her money.

I pressed delete on every one. Even those offering money, although I admit I was a teeny bit tempted to see how much they were offering. All the while, I heard Lou talking to Thomas in the bathroom, alongside the whine and splash of him dive-bombing his six inches of soapsuds with the Batmobile. That's the thing you don't know about children unless you have them—bath time, Lego, and fish fingers don't allow you to dwell on tragedy for too long. And then I hit the last message.

"Louisa? It's Camilla Traynor. Will you call me? As soon as possible?"

I stared at the answering machine. I rewound and replayed it. Then I ran upstairs and whipped Thomas out of the bath so fast my boy didn't even know what hit him. He was standing there, the towel wrapped tightly around him like a compression bandage, and Lou, stumbling and confused, was already halfway down the stairs, me pushing her by the shoulder.

"What if she hates me?"

"She didn't sound like she hated you."

"But what if the press are surrounding them there? What if they think it's all my fault?" Her eyes were wide and terrified. "What if she's ringing to tell me he's done it?"

"Oh, for Christ's sake, Lou. For once in your life, just get a grip. You won't know anything unless you call. Call her. Just call. You don't have a bloody choice."

I ran back into the bathroom to set Thomas free. I shoved him into his pajamas, told him that Granny had a biscuit for him if he ran to the kitchen superfast. And then I peered out the bathroom door to peek at my sister on the phone in the hallway.

She was turned away from me, one hand smoothing the hair at the back of her head. She reached out a hand to steady herself.

"Yes," she was saying. "I see." And then, "Okay."

And after a pause, "Yes."

She looked down at her feet for a good minute after she'd put the phone down.

"Well?" I said.

She looked up as if she'd only just seen me there, and shook her head.

"It was nothing about the newspapers," she said, her voice still numb with shock. "He's—he's still alive." Lou smiled shakily. "She asked me—begged me—to come to Switzerland. And she's booked me onto the last flight out this evening."

26

In other circumstances I suppose it might have seemed strange that I, Lou Clark, a girl who had rarely been more than a bus ride from her home town in twenty years, was now flying to her third country in less than a week. But I packed an overnight case with the swift efficiency of a flight attendant, rejecting all but the barest necessities. Treena ran around silently fetching any other things she thought I might need, and then we headed downstairs. We stopped halfway down. Mum and Dad were already in the hall, standing side by side in the ominous way they used to do when we sneaked back late from a night out.

"What's going on?" Mum was staring at my case.

Treena had stopped in front of me.

"Lou's going to Switzerland," she said. "And she needs to leave now. There's only one flight left today."

We were about to move when Mum stepped forward.

"No." Her mouth was set into an unfamiliar line, her arms folded awkwardly in front of her. "Really. I don't want you involved. If this is what I think it is, then no."

"But—" Treena began, glancing behind at me.

"No," said Mum, and her voice held an unusually steely quality. "No buts. I've been thinking about this, about everything you told us. It's wrong. Morally wrong. And if you get embroiled in it and you're seen to be helping a man kill himself, then you could end up in all sorts of trouble."

"Your mum's right," Dad said.

"We've seen it in the news. This could affect your whole life, Lou. This college interview, everything. If you get a criminal record, you'll never get a college degree or a good job or anything—"

"He's asked for her to come. She can't just ignore him," Treena interrupted.

"Yes. Yes, she can. She's given six months of her life to this family. And a fat lot of good it's brought her, judging by the state of things. A fat lot of good it's brought this family, with people banging on the door and all the neighbors thinking we've been done for benefit fraud or some such. No, she's finally got the chance to make something of herself, and now they want her to go to that dreadful place in Switzerland and get involved in God knows what. Well, I say no. No, Louisa."

"But she has to go," Treena said.

"No, she doesn't. She's done enough. She said herself last night, she's done everything she could." Mum shook her head. "Whatever mess the Traynors are going to make of their lives going to this . . . this . . . whatever they're going to do to their own son, I don't want Louisa involved. I don't want her ruining her whole life."

"I think I can make up my own mind," I said.

"I'm not sure you can. This is your friend, Louisa. This is a young man with his whole life ahead of him. You cannot be part of this. I'm . . . I'm shocked that you could even consider it." Mum's voice had a new, hard edge. "I didn't bring you up to help someone end his life! Would you end Granddad's life? Do you think we should shove him off to Dignitas too?"

"Granddad is different."

"No, he isn't. He can't do what he used to. But his life is precious. Just as Will's is precious."

"It's not my decision, Mum. It's Will's. The whole point of this is to support Will."

"Support Will? I've never heard such rubbish. You are a child, Louisa. You've seen nothing, done nothing. And you have no idea what this is going to do to you. How in God's name will you ever be able to sleep at night if you help him to go through with it? You'd be helping a man to *die*. Do you really understand that? You'd be helping Will, that lovely, clever young man, to *die*."

"I'd sleep at night because I trust Will to know what is right for him, and because what has been the worst thing for him has been losing the ability to make a single decision, to do a single thing for himself . . ." I looked at my parents, trying to make them understand. "I'm not a child. I love him. I love him, and I shouldn't have left him alone, and I can't bear not being there and not knowing what . . . what he's . . ." I swallowed. "So yes. I'm going. I don't need you to look out for me or understand. I'll deal with it. But I'm going to Switzerland—whatever either of you says."

The little hallway grew silent. Mum stared at me like she had no idea who I was. I took a step closer to her, trying to make her understand. But as I did, she took a step back.

"Mum? I *owe* Will. I owe it to him to go. Who do you think got me to apply to college? Who do you think encouraged me to make something of myself, to travel places, to have ambitions? Who changed the way I think about everything? About myself even? Will did. I've done more, lived more, in the last six months than in the last twenty-seven years of my life. So if he wants me to go to Switzerland, then yes, I'm going to go. Whatever the outcome."

We all stood staring at one another. Dad and Treena were shooting glances at each other, as if each of them was waiting for the other to say something.

But Mum broke the silence. "If you go, Louisa, you needn't come back."

The words fell out of her mouth like pebbles. I looked at my mother in shock. Her gaze was unyielding. It tensed as she watched for my reaction. It was as if a wall I had never known was there had sprung up between us.

"Mum?"

"I mean it. This is no better than murder."

"Josie . . ."

"That's the truth, Bernard. I can't be part of this."

I remember thinking, as if at a distance, that I had never seen Katrina look so uncertain as she did now. I saw Dad's hand reach out to Mum's arm, whether in reproach or comfort I couldn't tell. My mind went briefly blank. Then almost without knowing what I was doing, I walked slowly down the stairs and past my parents to the front door. And after a second, my sister followed me.

The corners of Dad's mouth turned down, as if he were struggling to contain all sorts of things. Then he turned to Mum, and placed one hand on her shoulder. Her eyes searched his face and it was as if she already knew what he was going to say.

And then he threw Treena his keys. She caught them one-handed.

"Here," he said. "Go out the back door, through Mrs. Doherty's garden, and take the van. They won't see you in the van. If you go now and the traffic's not too bad you might just make it."

———

"You have any idea where this is all headed?" Katrina said.

She glanced sideways at me as we sped down the motorway.

"Nope."

I couldn't look at her for long—I was rifling through my handbag, trying to work out what I had forgotten. I kept hearing the sound of Mrs. Traynor's voice on the line. *Louisa? Please will you come? I know we've had our differences, but please . . . It's vital that you come now.*

"Shit. I've never seen Mum like that," Treena continued.

Passport, wallet, door keys. Door keys? For what? I no longer had a home.

Katrina glanced sideways at me. "I mean, she's mad now, but she's in shock. You know she'll be all right in the end, right? I mean, when I came home and told her I was knocked up I thought she was never going to speak to me again. But it only took her—what?—two days to come around."

I could hear her babbling away beside me, but I wasn't really paying attention. I could barely focus on anything. My nerve endings seemed to have come alive; they almost jangled with anticipation. I was going to see Will. Whatever else, I had that. I could almost feel the miles between us shrinking, as if we were at two ends of some invisible elastic thread.

"Treen?"

"Yes?"

I swallowed. "Don't let me miss this flight."

My sister is nothing if not determined. We queue-jumped, sped up the inside lane, broke the speed limit, and scanned the radio for the traffic reports, and finally the airport came into view. She screeched to a halt and I was halfway out of the car before I heard her.

"Hey! Lou!"

"Sorry." I turned back and ran the few steps to her.

She hugged me, really tightly. "You're doing the right thing," she said. She looked almost close to tears. "Now fuck off. If you miss the bloody plane on top of me getting six points on my license, I'm never talking to you again."

I didn't look back. I ran all the way to the Swiss Air desk and it took me three goes to say my name clearly enough to request my tickets.

———

I arrived in Zurich shortly before midnight. Given the late hour, Mrs. Traynor had, as promised, booked me into a hotel at the airport and said she would send a car for me at nine the following morning. I had thought I wouldn't sleep, but I did—an odd, heavy, and disjointed trawl through the hours—waking up at seven the next morning with no idea where I was.

I stared groggily around the unfamiliar room, at the heavy burgundy drapes, designed to block out light, at the large flat-screen television, at my overnight bag, which I hadn't even bothered to unpack. I checked the clock, which said it was shortly after seven Swiss time. And as I realized where I was, I suddenly felt my stomach clench with fear.

I scrambled out of bed just in time to be sick in the little bathroom. I sank down on the tiled floor, my hair sticking to my forehead, my cheek pressed against the cold porcelain. I heard my mother's voice, her protests, and I felt a dark fear creeping over me. I wasn't up to this. I didn't want to fail again. I didn't want to have to watch Will die. With an audible groan, I scrambled up to be sick again.

I couldn't eat. I managed to swallow a cup of black coffee and showered and dressed, and that took me to 8 A.M. I stared at the pale-green dress I had thrown in last night and wondered if it was appropriate for where I was going. Would everyone wear black? Should I have worn something more vibrant and alive, like the red dress I knew Will liked? Why had Mrs. Traynor called me here? I checked my mobile phone, wondering whether I could call Katrina. It would be seven in the morning there now. But she would probably be dressing Thomas, and the thought of talking to Mum was too much. I put on some makeup and then sat down by the window, and the minutes ticked slowly past.

I don't think I had ever felt lonelier in my life.

When I couldn't bear being in the little room any longer, I threw the last of my things into my bag and left. I would buy a newspaper, and wait in the lobby. It couldn't be worse than sitting in my room with the silence or the satellite news channel and the suffocating darkness of the curtains. It was as I was passing reception that I saw the computer terminal, discreetly placed in a corner. It was marked: FOR USE OF GUESTS. PLEASE ASK AT RECEPTION.

"Can I use this?" I said to the receptionist.

She nodded, and I bought an hour's token. I knew suddenly very clearly who I wanted to speak to. I knew in my gut that he was one of the few people I could rely on to be online at this time. I logged on to the chat room and typed on the message board:

> *Ritchie. Are you there?*
> *Morning, Bee. You're early today.*

I hesitated for just a moment before typing:

> *I am about to begin the strangest day of my life. I am in Switzerland.*

He knew what it meant. They all knew what it meant. The clinic had been the subject of many heated debates. I typed:

> *I'm frightened.*
> *Then why are you there?*
> *Because I can't not be here. He asked me. Am in hotel waiting to go see him.*

I hesitated, then typed:

> *I have no idea how this day is going to end.*
> *Oh, Bee.*
> *What do I say to him? How do I change his mind?*

There was a delay before he typed again. His words appeared on the screen more slowly than usual, as if he were taking great care.

If he's in Switzerland, Bee, I'm not sure he's going to change his mind.

I felt a huge lump in my throat, and swallowed it. Ritchie was still typing.

It's not my choice. It's not the choice of most of us on this board. I love my life, even if I wish it was different. But I understand why your friend might well have had enough. It's tiring, leading this life, tiring in a way the AB can never truly understand. If he is determined, if he really can't see a way of things being better for him, then I guess the best thing you can do is just be there. You don't have to think he's right. But you do have to be there.

I realized I was holding my breath.

Good luck, Bee. And come see me after. Things may get a little bumpy for you afterward. Either way, I could do with a friend like you.

My fingers stilled on the keyboard. I typed:

I will.

And then the receptionist told me that my car had arrived outside.

———

I don't know what I expected—maybe some white building next to a lake, or snow-capped mountains. Perhaps some medical-looking marble frontage with a gold-plated plaque on the wall. What I didn't expect was to be driven through an industrial estate until I arrived at what looked remarkably like an ordinary house, surrounded by factories and, weirdly, a football pitch. I walked across decking, past a goldfish pond, and then I was in.

The woman who opened the door knew immediately who I was looking for. "He is here. Would you like me to show you?"

I stalled then. I stared at the closed door, oddly similar to the one I had stood outside in Will's annex all those months ago, and I took a breath. And nodded.

I saw the bed before I saw him; it dominated the room with its mahogany wood, its quaintly flowered quilt and pillows out of place in that setting. Mr. Traynor sat on one side of it, Mrs. Traynor on the other.

She looked ghostly pale, and stood up when she saw me. "Louisa."

Georgina was seated on a wooden chair in the corner, bent over her knees, her hands pressed together as if in prayer. She lifted her gaze as I walked in, revealing shadowed eyes, reddened with grief, and I felt a brief spasm of sympathy for her.

What would I have done if Katrina had insisted on her right to do the same?

The room itself was light and airy, like an upmarket holiday home. There was a tiled floor and expensive rugs, and a sofa at the end that looked out onto a little garden. I didn't know what to say. It was such a ridiculous, mundane sight, the three of them sitting there, as if they were a family trying to work out where to go sightseeing that day.

I turned toward the bed. "So," I said, my bag over my shoulder, "I'm guessing the room service isn't up to much?"

Will's eyes locked onto mine and despite everything, despite all my fears, the fact that I had thrown up twice, that I felt like I hadn't slept for a year, I was suddenly glad I had come. Not glad, relieved. Like I had excised some painful, nagging part of myself, and given it over.

And then he smiled. It was lovely, his smile—a slow thing, full of recognition.

Weirdly, I found myself smiling back. "Nice room," I

said, and immediately realized the idiocy of the remark. I saw Georgina Traynor close her eyes, and I blushed.

Will turned toward his mother. "I want to talk to Lou. Is that okay?"

She tried to smile. I saw a million things in the way she looked at me then—relief, gratitude, a faint resentment at being shut out of these few minutes, perhaps even a distant hope that my appearance meant something, that this fate might yet be twisted from its tracks.

"Of course."

She moved past me into the corridor, and as I stood back from the doorway to let her pass, she reached out a hand and touched my upper arm, just lightly. Our eyes met, and hers softened, so that briefly she looked like someone else entirely, and then she turned away from me.

"Come, Georgina," she said, when her daughter made no attempt to move.

Georgina stood slowly and walked out silently, her very back broadcasting her reluctance. Mr. Traynor placed his hand on her back as they passed.

And then it was just us.

Will was half propped up in the bed, able to see out of the window to his left, where the water feature in the little garden merrily trickled a thin stream of clear water below the decking. On the wall was a badly framed print picture of dahlias. I remember thinking that was a really crummy print to have to look at in your last hours.

"So . . ."

"You're not going to—"

"I'm not going to try and change your mind."

"If you're here, you accept it's my choice. This is the first thing I've been in control of since the accident."

"I know."

And there it was. He knew it, and I knew it. There was nothing left for me to do.

Do you know how hard it is to say nothing? When

every atom of you strains to do the opposite? I had practiced not saying anything the whole way from the airport, and it was still nearly killing me. I nodded. When I finally spoke, my voice was a small, broken thing. What emerged was the only thing I could safely say.

"I missed you."

He seemed to relax then. "Come over here." And then, when I hesitated. "Please. Come on. Right here, on the bed. Right next to me."

I realized then that there was actual relief in his expression. That he was pleased to see me in a way he wasn't actually going to be able to say. And I told myself that it was going to have to be enough. I would do the thing he had asked for. That would have to be enough.

I lay down on the bed beside him and I placed my arm across him. I rested my head on his chest, letting my body absorb the gentle rise and fall of it. I could feel the faint pressure of Will's fingertips on my back, his warm breath in my hair. I closed my eyes, breathing in the scent of him, still the same expensive cedar-wood smell, despite the bland freshness of the room, the slightly disturbing scent of disinfectant underneath. I tried not to think of anything at all. I just tried to be, tried to absorb the man I loved through osmosis, tried to imprint what I had left of him on myself. I did not speak. And then I heard his voice. I was so close to him that when he spoke it seemed to vibrate gently through me.

"Hey, Clark," he said. "Tell me something good."

I stared out the window at the bright-blue Swiss sky and I told him a story of two people. Two people who shouldn't have met, and who didn't like each other much when they did, but who found they were the only two people in the world who could possibly have understood each other. And I told him of the adventures they had, the places they had gone, and the things they had seen that they had never expected to. I conjured for him electric skies and iridescent seas and evenings full of laughter and silly jokes. I drew a world for him, a world far from a Swiss industrial estate, a world in which he was still somehow the person he had wanted to be. I drew the world he had created for me, full of wonder and possibility. I let him know a hurt had been mended in a way that he couldn't have known, and for that alone there would always be a piece of me indebted to him. And as I spoke I knew these would be the most important words I would ever say and that it was important that they were the right words, that they were not propaganda, an attempt to change his mind, but respectful of what Will had said.

I told him something good.

Time slowed, and stilled. It was just the two of us, me murmuring in the empty, sunlit room. Will didn't say much. He didn't answer back, or add a dry comment, or scoff. He nodded occasionally, his head pressed against mine, and murmured, or let out a small sound that could have been satisfaction at another good memory.

"It has been," I told him, "the best six months of my entire life."

There was a long silence.

"Funnily enough, Clark, mine too."

And then, just like that, my heart broke. My face crumpled, my composure went and I held him tightly and I stopped caring that he could feel the shudder of my sobbing body because grief swamped me. It overwhelmed me and tore at my heart and my stomach and my head and it pulled me under, and I couldn't bear it. I honestly thought I couldn't bear it.

"Don't, Clark," he murmured. I felt his lips on my hair. "Oh, please. Don't. Look at me."

I screwed my eyes shut and shook my head.

"Look at me. Please."

I couldn't.

"You're angry. Please. I don't want to hurt you or make you—"

"No . . ." I shook my head again. "It's not that. I don't want . . ." My cheek was pressed to his chest. "I don't want the last thing you see to be my miserable, blotchy face."

"You still don't get it, Clark, do you?" I could hear the smile in his voice. "It's not your choice."

It took some time to regain my composure. I blew my nose, took a long, deep breath. Finally, I raised myself on my elbow, and I looked back at him. His eyes, so long strained and unhappy, looked oddly clear and relaxed.

"You look absolutely beautiful."

"Funny."

"Come here," he said. "Right up close to me."

I lay down again, facing him. I saw the clock above the door and had a sudden sense of time running out. I took his arm and wrapped it tightly around me, threading my own arms and legs around him so that we were tightly entwined. I took his hand—the good one—and wrapped my fingers in his, kissing the knuckles as I felt him squeeze mine. His body was so familiar to me now. I knew it in a way I had never known Patrick's—its strengths and vulnerabilities, its scars and scents. I placed my face so close to his that his features became indistinct, and I began to lose myself in them. I stroked his hair, his skin, his brow with my fingertips, tears sliding unchecked down my cheeks, my nose against his, and all the time he watched me silently, studying me intently as if he were storing each molecule of me away. He was already retreating, withdrawing to somewhere I couldn't reach him.

I kissed him, trying to bring him back. I kissed him and let my lips rest against his so that our breath mingled and the tears from my eyes became salt on his skin, and I told myself that, somewhere, tiny particles of him would become tiny particles of me, ingested, swallowed, alive, perpetual. I wanted to press every bit of me against him. I wanted to will something into him. I wanted to give him every bit of life I felt and force him to live.

I realized I was afraid of living without him. *How is it you have the right to destroy my life*, I wanted to demand of him, *but I'm not allowed a say in yours?*

But I had promised.

So I held him, Will Traynor, ex–financial whiz kid, ex–stunt diver, sportsman, traveler, lover. I held him close and said nothing, all the while telling him silently that he was loved. Oh, but he was loved.

I couldn't say how long we stayed like that. I was dimly aware of soft conversation outside, of the shuffle of shoes, a distant church bell ringing in some far-off place. Finally, I felt him loosen a great breath, almost a shudder, and he drew his head back just an inch so that we could see each other clearly.

I blinked at him.

He gave me a small smile, almost an apology.

"Clark," he said, quietly. "Can you call my parents in?"

27

CROWN PROSECUTION SERVICE
FAO: DIRECTOR OF PUBLIC PROSECUTIONS
CONFIDENTIAL ADVISORY
RE: WILLIAM JOHN TRAYNOR
9.4.2009

Detectives have now interviewed everyone involved in the above case, and I attach files containing all related documents accordingly.

The subject at the center of the investigation is Mr. William Traynor, a thirty-five-year-old former partner in the firm Madingley Lewins, based in the City of London. Mr. Traynor suffered a spinal injury in a road accident in 2007 and had been diagnosed C5-6 quadriplegic with very limited movement in one arm only, requiring twenty-four-hour care. His medical history is attached.

The papers show that Mr. Traynor had been at pains to regularize his legal affairs sometime before his trip to Switzerland. We have been forwarded a signed and witnessed statement of intent by his lawyer, Mr. Michael Lawler, as well as copies of all relevant documentation relating to his consultations with the clinic beforehand.

Mr. Traynor's family and friends had all expressed their opposition to his stated desire to end his life prematurely but given his medical history and previous attempt on his own life (detailed in his attached hospital records), his intellect and strength of character, they were apparently unable to dissuade him, even during an extended six-month period which was negotiated with him specifically for this purpose.

It will be noted that one of the beneficiaries of Mr. Traynor's will is his paid female caregiver, Miss Louisa Clark. Given the limited length of her association with Mr. Traynor some questions may be asked about the extent of his generosity toward her, but all parties say they do not wish to contest Mr. Traynor's stated wishes, which are legally documented. She has been interviewed at length several times and police are satisfied that she made every effort to deter Mr. Traynor from his intention (please see her "calendar of adventures" included in the evidence).

It should also be noted that Mrs. Camilla Traynor, his mother, who has been a respected JP for many years, has tendered her resignation in light of the publicity surrounding the case. It is understood that she and Mr. Traynor separated soon after their son's death.

While the use of assisted suicide at foreign clinics is not something the CPS can be seen to encourage, judging by the evidence gathered, it is evident that the actions of Mr. Traynor's family and caregivers fall well within current guidelines as laid out relating to assisted suicide and the possible prosecution of those close to the deceased.

> Mr. Traynor was deemed competent and had a "voluntary, clear, settled, and informed" wish to make such a decision.
>
> There is no evidence of mental illness, or of coercion on any part.
>
> Mr. Traynor had indicated unequivocally that he wished to commit suicide.
>
> Mr. Traynor's disability was severe and incurable.
>
> The actions of those accompanying Mr. Traynor were of only minor assistance or influence.
>
> The actions of those accompanying Mr. Traynor may be characterized as reluctant assistance in the face of a determined wish on the part of the victim.

*All parties involved have offered every assistance to the
    police investigating this case.*

Given these facts as outlined, the previous good character of
all parties, and the evidence enclosed, I would advise that it
does not serve the public interest to pursue a prosecution in this
case.

I suggest that if and when any public statement is made to
this effect, the Director of Public Prosecutions makes it clear
that the Traynor case sets no kind of precedent, and that the
CPS will continue to judge each case on its individual merits
and circumstances.

With best wishes
Sheilagh Mackinnon
Crown Prosecution Service

Epilogue

SEPTEMBER 29

I was just following instructions.

I sat in the shadow of the dark-green café awning, staring down the length of the Rue des Francs Bourgeois, the tepid sun of a Parisian autumn warming the side of my face. In front of me the waiter had, with Gallic efficiency, deposited a plate of croissants and a large cup of filter coffee. A hundred yards down the street two cyclists stopped near the traffic lights and struck up a conversation. One wore a blue backpack from which two large baguettes poked at odd angles. The air, still and muggy, held the scents of coffee and patisserie and the acrid tang of someone's cigarettes.

I finished Treena's letter (she would have called, she said, but she couldn't afford the overseas charges). She had finished at the top of her class in Accountancy 2 and had a new boyfriend, Sundeep, who was trying to decide whether to work for his dad's import-export business outside Heathrow and had even worse taste in music than she did. Thomas was excited about moving up a class at school. Dad was still going great guns at his job, and sent his love. She was pretty confident that Mum would forgive me soon. *She definitely got your letter*, she said. *I know she read it. Give her time.*

I took a sip of my coffee, briefly transported to Renfrew Road and a home that seemed a million miles away. I thought about the letter I had received from Mrs. Traynor a week earlier. "I suspect desperation may have made me ungracious," she had written. "But I want you to know that I will always be grateful for your efforts, Louisa. I am comforted by the thought that Will had someone he could be honest with. I know you miss him as desperately as I do." I sat and squinted a little against the low sun, watching a woman in sunglasses adjust her hair in the mirror of a shop window. She pursed her lips at her reflection, straightened up a little, and then continued her path down the road.

I put down the cup, took a deep breath, and then picked up the other letter, the letter that I had carried around with me for almost six weeks now.

On the front of the envelope, in typed capitals, it said, under my name:

> *ONLY TO BE READ IN THE CAFÉ MARQUIS,*
> *RUE DES FRANCS BOURGEOIS,*
> *ACCOMPANIED BY CROISSANTS AND A*
> *LARGE CAFÉ CRÈME.*

I had laughed, even as I wept, on first reading the envelope—typical Will, bossy to the last.

The waiter—a tall, brisk man with a dozen bits of paper sticking out of the top of his apron—turned back and caught my eye. *All okay?* his raised eyebrows said.

"Yes," I said. And then, a little self-consciously, "*Oui.*"

The letter was typewritten. I recognized the font from a card he had sent me long ago. I settled back in my chair, and I began to read.

> *Clark,*
> *A few weeks will have passed by the time you read this (even given your newfound organizational skills, I doubt you will have made it to Paris before early September). I hope the coffee is good and strong and the croissants fresh and that the*

*weather is still sunny enough to sit outside on one
of those metallic chairs that never sit quite level on
the pavement. It's not bad, the Marquis. The
steak is also good, if you fancy coming back for
lunch. And if you look down the road to your left
you will hopefully see L'Artisan Parfumeur where,
after you read this, you should go and try the scent
called something like Papillons Extrême (can't
quite remember). I always did think it would smell
great on you.*

*Okay, instructions over. There are a few things
I wanted to say and would have told you in person, but (a) you would have got all emotional and
(b) you wouldn't have let me say all this out loud.
You always did talk too much.*

*So here it is: the check you got in the initial enve-
lope from Michael Lawler was not the full amount,
but just a small gift, to help you through your first
weeks of unemployment, and to get you to Paris.*

*When you get back to England, take this letter
to Michael in his London office and he will give
you the relevant documents so you can access an
account he has set up for me in your name. This
account contains enough for you to buy someplace
nice to live and to pay for your degree course and
your living expenses while you are in full-time education.*

*My parents will have been told all about it. I
hope that this, and Michael Lawler's legal work,
will ensure there is as little fuss as possible.*

*Clark, I can practically hear you starting to
hyperventilate from here. Don't start panicking, or
trying to give it away—it's not enough for you to
sit on your arse for the rest of your life. But it
should buy you your freedom, both from that
claustrophobic little town we both call home and*

from the kinds of choices you have so far felt you had to make.

I'm not giving the money to you because I want you to feel wistful, or indebted to me, or to feel that it's some kind of bloody memorial.

I'm giving you this because there is not much that makes me happy anymore, but you do.

I am conscious that knowing me has caused you pain, and grief, and I hope that one day when you are less angry with me and less upset you will see not just that I could only have done the thing that I did, but also that this will help you live a really good life, a better life, than if you hadn't met me.

You're going to feel uncomfortable in your new world for a bit. It always does feel strange to be knocked out of your comfort zone. But I hope you feel a bit exhilarated too. Your face when you came back from diving that time told me everything; there is a hunger in you, Clark. A fearlessness. You just buried it, like most people do.

I'm not really telling you to jump off tall buildings, or swim with whales or anything (although I would secretly love to think you were), but to live boldly. Push yourself. Don't settle. Wear those stripy legs with pride. And if you insist on settling down with some ridiculous bloke, make sure some of this is squirreled away somewhere. Knowing you still have possibilities is a luxury. Knowing I might have given them to you has alleviated something for me.

So this is it. You are scored on my heart, Clark. You were from the first day you walked in, with your ridiculous clothes and your bad jokes and your complete inability to ever hide a single thing you felt. You changed my life so much more than this money will ever change yours.

> *Don't think of me too often. I don't want to*
> *think of you getting all maudlin. Just live well.*
> *Just live.*
> *Love,*
> *Will*

A tear had plopped onto the rickety table in front of me. I wiped at my cheek with my palm, and put the letter down on the table. It took me some minutes to see clearly again.

"Another coffee?" said the waiter, who had reappeared in front of me.

I blinked at him. He was younger than I had thought, and had dropped his faint air of haughtiness. Perhaps Parisian waiters were trained to be kind to weeping women in their cafés.

"Maybe . . . a cognac?" He glanced at the letter and smiled, with something resembling understanding.

"No," I said, smiling back. "Thank you. I've . . . I've got things to do."

I paid the bill, and tucked the letter carefully into my pocket.

And stepping out from behind the table, I straightened my bag on my shoulder and set off down the street toward the parfumerie and the whole of Paris beyond.

Jojo Moyes's unforgettable sequel to
Me Before You is available
from Pamela Dorman Books.

Read on for the first chapter of . . .

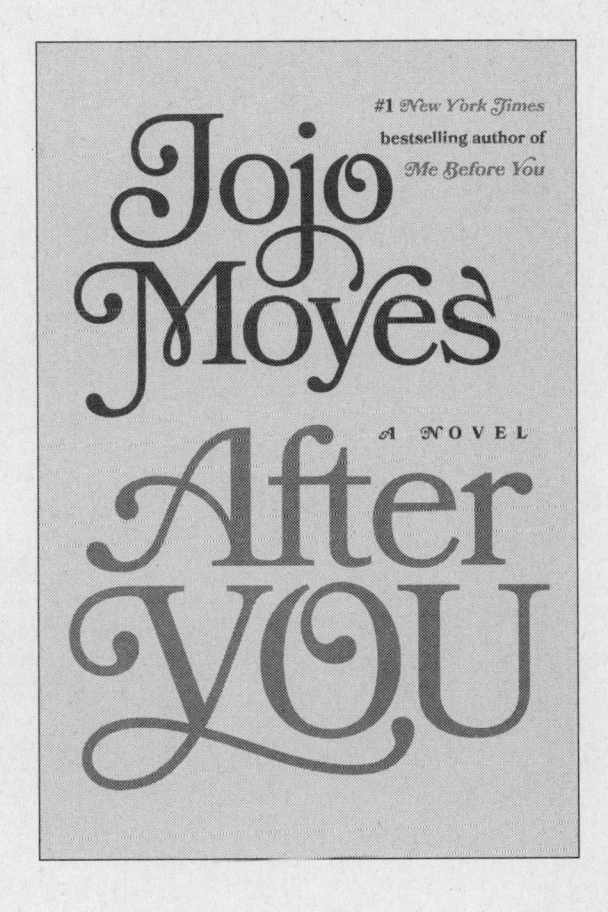

#1 *New York Times*
bestselling author of
Me Before You

Jojo
Moyes

A NOVEL

After
YOU

DEAR READER,

It has been such a pleasure revisiting Lou and her family, and the Traynors, and confronting them with a whole new set of issues. As ever, they have made me laugh, and cry. I hope readers feel the same way at meeting them—especially Lou—again.

—JOJO MOYES

1

The big man at the end of the bar is sweating. He holds his head low over his double scotch and every few minutes he glances up and out behind him toward the door, and a fine sheen of perspiration glistens under the strip lights. He lets out a long, shaky breath disguised as a sigh and turns back to his drink.

"Hey. Excuse me?"

I look up from polishing glasses.

"Can I get another one here?"

I want to tell him that it's really not a good idea, that it won't help. That it might even put him over the limit. But he's a big guy and it's fifteen minutes till closing time and according to company guidelines, I have no reason to tell him no. So I walk over and take his glass and hold it up to the optic. He nods at the bottle.

"Double," he says, and slides a fat hand down his damp face.

"That'll be seven pounds twenty, please."

It is a quarter to eleven on a Tuesday night, and the Shamrock and Clover, East City Airport's Irish-themed pub that is as Irish as Mahatma Gandhi, is winding down for the night. The bar closes ten minutes after the last plane takes off, and right now it is just me, the intense young man with the laptop, the two cackling women at table 2, and the man nursing a double Jameson's waiting on SC107 to Stockholm and DB224 to Munich, the latter of which has been delayed for forty minutes.

I have been on since midday, as Carly had a stomach-ache and went home. I didn't mind. I never mind staying late. Humming softly to the sounds of *Celtic Pipes of the Emerald Isle Vol. III*, I walk over and collect the glasses from the two women, who are peering intently at some video footage on a phone. They laugh the easy laughs of the well lubricated.

"My granddaughter. Five days old," says the blond woman, as I reach over the table for her glass.

"Lovely." I smile. All babies look like currant buns to me.

"She lives in Sweden. I've never been. But I have to go see my first grandchild, don't I?"

"We're wetting the baby's head." They burst out laughing again. "Join us in a toast? Go on, take a load off for five minutes. We'll never finish this bottle in time."

"Oops! Here we go. Come on, Dor." Alerted by a screen, they gather up their belongings, and perhaps it's only me who notices a slight stagger as they brace them-selves for the walk toward security. I place their glasses on the bar, scan the room for anything else that needs washing.

"You never tempted then?" The smaller woman has turned back for her scarf.

"I'm sorry?"

"To just walk down there, at the end of a shift. Hop on a plane. I would." She laughs again. "Every bloody day."

I smile, the kind of professional smile that might con-vey anything at all, and turn back toward the bar.

———

Around me the concession stores are closing up for the night, steel shutters clattering down over the overpriced handbags and emergency-gift Toblerones. The lights flicker off at gates 3, 5, and 11, the last of the day's travel-ers winking their way into the night sky. Violet, the Con-golese cleaner, pushes her trolley toward me, her walk a slow sway, her rubber-soled shoes squeaking on the shiny Marmoleum.

"Evening, darling."

"Evening, Violet."

"You shouldn't be here this late, sweetheart. You should be home with your loved ones."

She says exactly the same thing to me every night.

"Not long now." I respond with these exact words every night. Satisfied, she nods and continues on her way.

Intense Young Laptop Man and Sweaty Scotch Drinker have gone. I finish stacking the glasses and cash up, checking twice to make sure the till roll matches what is in the till. I note everything in the ledger, check the pumps, jot down what we need to reorder. It is then that I notice the big man's coat is still over his bar stool. I walk over and glance up at the monitor. The flight to Munich would be just boarding if I felt inclined to run his coat down to him. I look again and then walk slowly over to the Gents.

"Hello? Anyone in here?"

The voice that emerges is strangled and bears a faint edge of hysteria. I push open the door. The Scotch Drinker is bent low over the sinks, splashing his face. His skin is chalk-white.

"Are they calling my flight?"

"It's only just gone up. You've probably got a few minutes."

I make to leave, but something stops me. The man is staring at me, his eyes two tight little buttons of anxiety. He shakes his head. "I can't do it." He grabs a paper towel and pats at his face. "I can't get on the plane."

I wait.

"I'm meant to be traveling over to meet my new boss, and I can't. And I haven't had the guts to tell him I'm scared of flying." He shakes his head. "Not scared. Terrified."

I let the door close behind me.

"What's your new job?"

He blinks. "Uh . . . car parts. I'm the new Senior Regional Manager bracket Spares close bracket for Hunt Motors."

"Sounds like a big job," I say. "You have . . . brackets."

"I've been working for it a long time." He swallows hard. "Which is why I don't want to die in a ball of flame. I really don't want to die in an airborne ball of flame."

I am tempted to point out that it wouldn't actually be an airborne ball of flame, more a rapidly descending one, but suspect it wouldn't really help. He splashes his face again and I hand him another paper towel.

"Thank you." He lets out another shaky breath and straightens up, attempting to pull himself together. "I bet you never saw a grown man behave like an idiot before, huh?"

"About four times a day."

His tiny eyes widen.

"About four times a day I have to fish someone out of the men's loos. And it's usually down to fear of flying."

He blinks at me.

"But you know, like I say to everyone else, no planes have ever gone down from this airport."

His neck shoots back in his collar. "Really?"

"Not one."

"Not even . . . a little crash on the runway?"

I shake my head.

"It's actually pretty boring here. People fly off, go to where they're going, come back again a few days later." I lean against the door to prop it open. These lavatories never smell any better by the evening. "And anyway, personally, I think there are worse things that can happen to you."

"Well, I suppose that's true."

He considers this, looks sideways at me. "Four a day, huh?"

"Sometimes more. Now if you wouldn't mind, I really have to get back. It's not good for me to be seen coming out of the men's loos too often."

He smiles, and for a minute I can see how he might be in other circumstances. A naturally ebullient man. A cheerful man. A man at the top of his game of continentally manufactured car parts.

"You know, I think I hear them calling your flight."

"You reckon I'll be okay."

"You'll be okay. It's a very safe airline. And it's just a couple of hours out of your life. Look, SK491 landed five minutes ago. As you walk to your departure gate, you'll see the air stewards and stewardesses coming through on their way home and you'll see them all chatting and laughing. For them, getting on these flights is pretty much like getting on a bus. Some of them do it two, three, four times a day. And they're not stupid. If it wasn't safe, they wouldn't get on, would they?"

"Like getting on a bus," he repeats.

"Probably an awful lot safer."

"Well, that's for sure." He raises his eyebrows. "Lot of idiots on the road."

I nod.

He straightens his tie. "And it's a big job."

"Shame to miss out on it, for such a small thing. You'll be fine once you get used to being up there."

"Maybe I will. Thank you . . ."

"Louisa," I say.

"Thank you, Louisa. You're a very kind girl." He looks at me speculatively. "I don't suppose . . . you'd . . . like to go for a drink sometime?"

"I think I hear them calling your flight, sir," I say, and I open the door to allow him to pass through.

He nods, to cover his embarrassment, makes a fuss of patting his pockets. "Right. Sure. Well . . . off I go then."

"Enjoy those brackets."

It takes two minutes after he has left for me to discover he has been sick all over cubicle 3.

———

I arrive home at a quarter past one and let myself into the silent flat. I change out of my clothes and into my pajama bottoms and a hooded sweatshirt, then open the fridge, pulling out a bottle of white, and pouring a glass. It is lip-pursingly sour. I study the label and realize I must have opened it the previous night then forgotten to stopper the bottle, and then decide it's never a good idea to think about these things too hard and I slump down in the chair with it.

On the mantelpiece are two cards. One is from my parents, wishing me a happy birthday. That "best wishes" from Mum is as piercing as any stab wound. The other is from my sister, suggesting she and Thom come down for the weekend. It is six months old. Two voice mails are on my phone, one from the dentist. One not.

> Hi Louisa. It's Jared here. We met in the Dirty Duck? Well, we hooked up [muffled, awkward laugh]. It was just . . . you know . . . I enjoyed it. Thought maybe we could do it again? You've got my digits . . .

When there is nothing left in the bottle, I consider buying another one, but I don't want to go out again. I don't want Samir at the Mini Mart grocers to make one of his jokes about my endless bottles of pinot grigio. I don't want to have to talk to anyone. I am suddenly bone-weary, but it is the kind of head-buzzing exhaustion that tells me that if I go to bed I won't sleep. I think briefly about Jared and the fact that he had oddly shaped fingernails. Am I bothered about oddly shaped fingernails? I stare at the bare walls of the living room and realize suddenly that what I actually need is air. I really need air. I open the hall window and climb unsteadily up the fire escape until I am on the roof.

The first time I'd come up, nine months earlier, the estate agent showed me how the previous tenants had made a small terrace garden, dotting around a few lead planters and a small bench. "It's not officially yours, obviously," he'd said. "But yours is the only flat with direct access to it. I think it's pretty nice. You could even have a party up here!" I had gazed at him, wondering if I really looked like the kind of person who held parties.

The plants have long since withered and died. I am apparently not very good at looking after things. Now I stand on the roof, staring out at London's winking darkness below. Around me a million people are living, breathing, eating, arguing. A million lives completely divorced from mine. It is a strange sort of peace.

The sodium lights glitter as the sounds of the city filter up into the night air, engines rev, doors slam. From several miles south comes the distant brutalist thump of a police helicopter, its beam scanning the dark for some vanished miscreant in a local park. Somewhere in the distance a siren wails. Always a siren. "Won't take much to make this feel like home," the real estate agent had said. I had almost laughed. The city feels as alien to me as it always has. But then everywhere does these days.

I hesitate, then take a step out onto the parapet, my arms lifted out to the side, a slightly drunken tightrope walker. One foot in front of the other, edging along the concrete, the breeze making the hairs on my outstretched arms prickle. When I first moved down here, when it all first hit me hardest, I would sometimes dare myself to walk from one end of my block to the other. When I reached the other end I would laugh into the night air. *You see? I am here—staying alive—right out on the edge. I am doing what you told me!*

It has become a secret habit: me, the city skyline, the

comfort of the dark, and the anonymity and the knowledge that up here nobody knows who I am.

I lift my head, feel the night breezes, hear the sound of laughter below and the muffled smash of a bottle breaking, see the traffic snaking up toward the city, the endless red stream of taillights, an automotive blood supply. It is always busy here, above the noise and chaos. Only the hours between 3 to 5 a.m. are relatively peaceful, the drunks having collapsed into bed, the restaurant chefs having peeled off their whites, the pubs having barred their doors. The silence of those hours is interrupted only sporadically, by the night tankers, the opening up of the Jewish bakery along the street, the soft thump of the newspaper delivery vans dropping their paper bales. I know the subtlest movements of the city because I no longer sleep.

Somewhere down there a lock-in is taking place in the White Horse, full of hipsters and East Enders, and a couple are arguing outside, and across the city the general hospital is picking up the pieces of the sick and the injured and those who have just barely scraped through another day. Up here is just the air and the dark and somewhere the FedEx freight flight from LHR to Beijing, and countless travelers, like Mr. Scotch Drinker, on their way to somewhere new.

"Eighteen months. Eighteen whole months. So when is it going to be enough?" I say into the darkness. And there it is, I can feel it boiling up again, this unexpected anger. I take two steps along, glancing down at my feet. "Because this doesn't feel like living. It doesn't feel like anything."

Two steps. Two more. I will go as far as the corner tonight.

"You didn't give me a bloody life, did you? Not really. You just smashed up my old one. Smashed it into little pieces. What am I meant to do with what's left? When is it going to feel—"

I stretch out my arms, feeling the cool night air against my skin, and realize I am crying again.

"Fuck you, Will," I whisper. "Fuck you for leaving me."

Grief wells up again like a sudden tide, intense, overwhelming. And just as I feel myself sinking into it, a voice says, from the shadows: "I don't think you should stand there."

I half turn, and catch a flash of a small, pale face on the fire escape, dark eyes wide open. In shock, my foot slips on the parapet, my weight suddenly on the wrong side of the drop. My heart lurches a split second before my body follows. And then, like a nightmare, I am weightless, in the abyss of the night air, my legs flailing above my head as I hear the shriek that may be my own—

Crunch

And then all is black.

ME BEFORE YOU

Jojo Moyes

An Introduction to *Me Before You*

"The thing about being catapulted into a whole new life—or at least, shoved up so hard against someone else's life that you might as well have your face pressed against their window—is that it forces you to rethink your idea of who you are" (p. 66).

Louisa Clark never wanted to leave her job at the Buttered Bun. After six years, she felt secure in the routine of making tea and chatting with the café's regulars. But when her boss closes the business, the unskilled twenty-six-year-old must take a new job as a paid companion to a wealthy ex–Master of the Universe, who is wheelchair bound after an accident. Prickly and embittered, Will Traynor nonetheless opens Louisa's eyes to the limitations she has imposed upon her life—and the infinite possibilities that only love can awaken.

A few short years earlier, Will was a major corporate player who bought and sold companies for obscene profits. He climbed mountains and dated cover girls. All that changed after a speeding motorcycle crushed his spine. Paralyzed from the neck down and unable even to feed himself, Will believes that life as he knows it is over—and he is not interested in exploring a new one.

Louisa feels intimidated by Will; his commanding mother, Camilla; and the Traynors' grand home, but the position pays a lot more than her waitressing job did and her family doesn't hesitate to remind Lou that she has few options otherwise.

At first, Will resents Louisa's very presence. When he destroys a shelf full of pictures, Louisa tries to repair the damage. Furious, he lashes out, "It would be nice—just for once—if someone paid attention to what I wanted. Me smashing those photographs was not an accident" (p. 63). Yet, the blowout is a turning point. Louisa stops trying to second-guess Will's decisions, but also refuses to bear the brunt of his frustration.

Louisa is accustomed to putting herself last. Her parents never hid the fact that they considered Louisa's younger sister, Treena, to be the more intelligent sibling. Patrick—Louisa's boyfriend of six years—is a self-absorbed personal trainer concerned only with his performance in the next triathlon. As she and Will grow closer, he convinces her that she deserves more respect from everyone in her life, including herself. Still, Lou has her reasons for wanting things to stay the same as they have always been.

When Lou learns that Will has shocking plans of his own, she sets out to show him that life is still worth living. She begins researching technologies that can give him more autonomy and looking for outings that he might find appealing. Each for the other's sake, Louisa and Will push beyond their comfort zones and, in turn, change each other in ways that neither could ever have anticipated.

As inspiring as it is heartbreaking, *Me Before You* is Jojo Moyes's international bestselling breakout novel—and the captivating tale of two people whose improbable romance sets them both free.

ABOUT THE AUTHOR

Jojo Moyes was raised in London. She writes for the *Daily Telegraph*, *Daily Mail*, *Red*, and *Woman & Home*. She's married to Charles Arthur, technology editor of *The Guardian*. They live with their three children on a farm in Essex, England.

A CONVERSATION WITH JOJO MOYES

What was the inspiration behind Me Before You?

It was a number of things. I had two close relatives who were dependent on twenty-four-hour care, and the issue of quality of life and how we behave around the severely disabled was high in my mind. But the novel was really spurred by a news story I heard, about a young rugby player who was left quadriplegic after an accident and who persuaded his parents to take him to Dignitas, the Swiss clinic, to allow him to go through with an assisted suicide. I couldn't believe any parent would agree to do that—and yet the more I read up on his story, the more I realized the issue was not as clear-cut as I would have liked to believe.

With Louisa and Treena, you perfectly captured the love-hate relationship that sisters often share. Do you have sisters yourself?

I have half sisters, who are much younger than I am. I've always been fascinated by their relationship and the relationships some of my friends have with their sisters. What I'm most captivated by is that ability to be at each other's throats one moment and yet totally bonded and presenting a united front in the next. If you are an only child, as I was for nineteen years, that kind of relationship is pretty mesmerizing.

The novel reflects an in-depth knowledge of the issues related to quadriplegia. What kind of research did you do? Were some of the characters in the quadriplegic chat rooms based on real people?

The chat room characters are an amalgam of attitudes that I heard online. And I had a lot of personal experience from within my own family and friends as to how people treat the disabled, and of some of the issues they face.

As far as other research goes, there are quads who upload footage of their daily routines to the Internet, and this was a great help in making sure I could accurately represent some of the procedures. I've had a lot of carers and families of quadriplegics get in touch with me since the book was published, and I have been relieved that they thought I had represented their lives accurately.

Louisa narrates the first third of the novel, but the remainder is divided between various other characters, including Treena and Mr. Traynor. Why did you choose to organize it this way?

In the early part of the novel I wanted readers to go through a journey of almost blind discovery with Lou, and to feel as out of their depth as she does. Later, I thought it was important for the other characters' dilemmas to become a bit more three-dimensional. The only person whose mind I couldn't enter was Will's, because I wanted his intentions to be one of the central tensions of the book.

Whose voice did you find easiest to write? Whose was the most difficult?

Unusually (for me), I found them all easy, possibly because they were so different, and because they were each so clear in my head. The hardest was actually Treena, because she was the closest to Lou, and I needed them to be distinct from each other.

Treena can't relate to the way Louisa feels about Will because she's never really been in love before. She can only do so by imagining the way she would feel if her son, Thomas, were in Will's situation. Maeve Binchy's death revived the ongoing debate about whether a woman writer needs to have children in order to really understand the human condition. Where do you weigh in?

Oh gosh. That's a toughie. I have writer friends who would kill me if I dared to suggest they couldn't imagine their way into some aspect of the human condition because they'd never given birth. But all major life experiences will change you as a writer—they have to. I acknowledge that when I had children I personally felt like I'd lost a layer of skin, and I do wonder whether that visceral level of love and fear does somehow feed its way into your writing. I know it does into other aspects of my life.

You're a two-time winner of the Romance Novelists Association Book of the Year Award. What do you think distinguishes a really great romance novel from a merely good one?

For me, it's steering away from the obvious; also, perhaps, taking the reader into settings where she might not normally go, whether that be into the past or some extreme situation.

Do you like reading romances as well as writing them? Who are some of your favorite writers?

I don't tend to read romances per se, but I read across all sorts of genres and most of what I read has a love story at the heart of it (don't most books?). Some of my favorite writers include Kate Atkinson, Nora Ephron, and Barbara Kingsolver. More recently I loved the Hunger Games trilogy and Gillian Flynn's *Gone Girl*.

You've been writing fiction for more than a decade, but your previous book, The Last Letter from Your Lover, *won you the attention of a much wider audience. Has your suddenly higher profile changed the way you write?*

It's made it harder! I find I'm questioning what I'm doing from a much earlier stage: Is this plotline going to tie me in knots later? Is this character relatable? Is this story too slow getting going? I feel as though, ten books in, I'm only just learning my craft.

What are you working on now?

Several things—as seems to be the case these days. I'm writing the screenplay for the film version of *Me Before You*, and I'm starting work on a new novel. It's very much in the cooking stage right now, but I quite like this bit, where you haven't yet written yourself into any corners.

QUESTIONS FOR DISCUSSION

1. If you were Louisa, would you have quit working for the Traynors? If yes, at what point?

2. Were you able to relate to the way Will felt after his accident? What about his outlook on life did you find most difficult to understand or accept?

3. Discuss the meaning of the novel's title. To whom do the "me" and "you" refer?

4. Louisa often finds Mrs. Traynor cold and judgmental. Is there an appropriate way to behave in Mrs. Traynor's situation?

5. What is your opinion of Mr. Traynor? Did it change after you read his side of the story?

6. Why is Louisa able to reach Will when so many others could not?

7. Were you as surprised as Lou to learn of Will's plans?

8. Compare Louisa's relationship with Treena to Will's relationship with Georgina. Do siblings know one another any better simply because they are related?

9. Would Patrick have asked Louisa to move in with him if he hadn't felt threatened by Will? If Louisa had never accepted her job with the Traynors, where would her relationship with Patrick have gone?

10. Discuss Louisa's own secret ties to the castle.

Would most girls in her situation have blamed themselves? Should Treena have behaved differently in the aftermath?

11. What did you make of the way Lou's mother, Josie, judges Lou's decisions regarding Will. Is Josie's reaction fair?

12. Before his accident, Will was a philanderer and a corporate raider who would probably never have given Louisa a second look. Why is it that people are so often unable to see what's truly important until they've experienced loss?

To access Penguin Readers Guides online, visit the Penguin Group (USA) Web site at www.penguin.com.

READ THEM ALL

After You

The *New York Times* bestselling sequel to *Me Before You*

After the transformative six months spent with Will Traynor, Louisa Clark is struggling without him. She is no longer the girl she was; her body heals, but Lou knows that she needs to be kick-started back to life. For her, that will mean learning to fall in love again, with all the risks that brings. Here, Jojo Moyes gives us two families, as real as our own, whose joys and sorrows will touch you deeply, and where both changes and surprises await.

Me Before You

A #1 *New York Times* bestseller

Louisa Clark is an ordinary girl living an exceedingly ordinary life when she takes a job working for the acerbic Will Traynor, now confined to a wheelchair after an accident. With more than six million copies sold, *Me Before You* brings to life two people who couldn't have less in common, and asks, "What do you do when making the person you love happy also means breaking your own heart?" *Now a major motion picture.*

One Plus One

A *New York Times* bestseller

Your husband has vanished, your teenage stepson is being bullied, and your math whiz daughter has a once-in-a-lifetime opportunity that you can't afford to pay for. That's Jess's life in a nutshell—until an unlikely knight offers a rescue. Only Jess's knight turns out to be Ed, the obnoxious tech millionaire whose vacation home she happens to clean. But Ed has big problems of his own, and driving the dysfunctional family to the Math Olympiad feels like his first unselfish act in ages . . . maybe ever.

PAMELA DORMAN BOOKS VIKING

PENGUIN BOOKS

READ THEM ALL

The Girl You Left Behind
A *New York Times* bestseller

Paris, 1916, Sophie Lefèvre must keep her family safe while her husband fights at the front. When their town falls to the Germans, Sophie is forced to serve them at her hotel. The moment the Kommandant spots Sophie's portrait, a dangerous obsession is born. Almost a century later, Sophie's portrait hangs in the home of Liv Halston. After a chance encounter reveals the portrait's true worth, a battle begins over its troubled history in this breathtaking love story.

The Last Letter from Your Lover

In 1960, Jennifer Stirling wakes up in a hospital with no memory of who she is or how she got there. She finds an impassioned letter from a man for whom she seemed willing to risk everything. In 2003, journalist Ellie Haworth discovers an old letter containing a man's ardent plea to his married lover, and she is determined to learn their fate in this remarkable and moving novel.

Silver Bay

Liza McCullen will never fully escape her past, but the tight-knit community of Silver Bay offers the safety she needs. That is, until Mike Dormer, a mild-mannered Englishman with too-smart clothes and distracting eyes, shows up at her aunt's hotel. Written with Jojo Moyes's trademark combination of humor and heart, *Silver Bay* is a hugely affecting and irresistibly compelling tale.

The Ship of Brides

1946. World War II has ended and all over the world, young women are fulfilling the promises made to the men they wed in wartime. For Frances Mackenzie, the complicated young woman whose past comes back to haunt her, the journey aboard HMS *Victoria*—which carries not just arms, but a thousand naval officers—will change her life forever, in this captivating and romantic novel.

PAMELA
DORMAN
BOOKS
VIKING

PENGUIN
BOOKS

"Jojo Moyes has written the perfect modern love story. You will be astonished at what you feel, and what you hope for when you are forced to face the possibility of your own dreams. It's that good. Read it now."
—Adriana Trigiani, *New York Times* bestselling author of *The Shoemaker's Wife*

"Some books make you stop and think, compel you to examine your own take on life or your position or stand on an issue. Jojo Moyes's *Me Before You* will surprise you—it is impossible not to put yourself in the characters' shoes, and you will find yourself thinking about the choices you might make if life changed in an instant. I loved it."
—Lee Woodruff, *New York Times* bestselling author of *Those We Love Most*

"A lovely novel, both nontraditional and enthralling."
—*Publishers Weekly* (starred review)

"*Me Before You* has every quality a page-turner should have, in spades. . . . This is an unusual and emotional love story melded with a satisfying coming-of-age tale that is utterly irresistible." —Bookreporter.com

"Moyes's latest is made heartwarming, thanks to the vibrancy of its main characters, both of whom will keep readers on their toes with their chemistry and witty repartee. . . . Humorous and romantic through and through."
—*Romantic Times*

"Moyes's twisting, turning, heartbreaking novel raises provocative moral questions. . . . With shades of David Nicholls's beloved *One Day*, *Me Before You* is the kind of book you simply can't put down—even when you realize you don't want to see it end. . . . A bighearted, beautifully written story that teaches us it is never too late to truly start living."
—*BookPage*

Praise for *Me Before You*

"When I finished this novel, I didn't want to review it: I wanted to reread it. . . . Moyes's story provokes tears that are redemptive, the opposite of gratuitous. Some situations, she forces the reader to recognize, really are worth crying over. . . . With Lou and Will she has created an affair to remember."
—Liesl Schillinger, *The New York Times Book Review*

"Read it and weep."   —*Good Housekeeping*

"Heartbreakingly truthful."   —*Booklist*

"Masterful . . . A heartbreaker in the best sense . . . *Me Before You* is achingly hard to read at moments, and yet such a joy."   —*New York Daily News*

"Funny, surprising, and heartbreaking, populated with characters who are affecting and amusing . . . a thought-provoking, thoroughly entertaining novel that captures the complexity of love."   —*People*

"There are books that you cannot put down. There are also books where you become so invested in the characters, you force yourself to stop reading to prolong the experience because you don't want the story to end, and that's what can happen when you read Jojo Moyes's latest book, *Me Before You*. . . . You'll find yourself laughing, smiling, feeling angry, and, yes, crying. My only suggestion: *Me Before You* should be sold with a pack of tissues."
—Associated Press

"A delicious surprise—funny and hopeful and heartbreaking, the kind of story that will keep you turning pages into the night."
—Eleanor Brown, *New York Times* bestselling author of *The Weird Sisters*